A Tale of Two Sisters

Tale *of* Two Sisters

MERRYN ALLINGHAM

CANELO

First published in the United Kingdom in 2019 by Canelo

This edition published in the United Kingdom in 2019 by

Canelo Digital Publishing Limited
57 Shepherds Lane
Beaconsfield, Bucks HP9 2DU
United Kingdom

Print ISBN 978 1 78863 580 6
Ebook ISBN 978 1 78863 270 6

Look for more great books at www.canelo.co

Printed and bound in Great Britain by Clays Ltd, Elcograf S.p.A.

To Alan and the trip we shared on the Orient Express.

Fingers of pink-tinged cloud drift through a sky of blue and mauve and deep violet. The sun is rising, breaking through the dark horizon, spooling the surface of the Bosphorus with gold. Its waters are satin, washing gently against fishing boats already out to sea. In the Eyoub Cemetery beside the city walls, an army of turban-topped headstones look drunkenly across the bay, and within the walls, the spires of Hagia Sophia thrust upwards amid the crumbling beauty of narrow streets and winding alleys. A city at peace. Then the muezzin's call to the faithful, echoed in a thousand mosques. The miracle of another dawn. Another day.

Chapter One

Another day and no letter. Alice snatched up the pile of envelopes from the console table and shuffled through them, one by one. She had been so certain that today she would hear, but there was nothing. Still not a word from Lydia. What was happening to her sister that she could find no time to write? A note only, that's all she asked, some reassuring lines to say all was well, all was happy in a palace several thousand miles away. It surely wasn't too much to expect, after all the trouble her sister had caused, unless... but Lydia *should* be safe. As governess to two small girls, there could be nothing that would stop her writing.

For minutes, Alice stood motionless. Her eyes were fixed on the dark oak of the front door, but it was not its fine mouldings she saw, nor the decorative glass splashing colour across an otherwise gloomy space. It was Lydia's face. She had dreamt of her sister last night, but didn't she always? This had been different, though. Last night she had been with Lydia again; she had searched and she had found her. Old resentments had dissolved to nothing and instead she had thrown her arms around the girl and hugged her slight frame, never to let go. Lydia's stubbornness, her irresponsibility, were forgotten. She had found her dear sister and that was all that mattered. The

2

waking disappointment had been almost too much to bear. And now these letters. Or rather, no letter. Another day of pretending that nothing was amiss, of putting on a reassuring smile. She would need time before she faced her parents again.

She was at the bottom of the stairs on her way to her bedroom when she heard her name called.

'Alice.' Her mother's voice held the suggestion of a quaver, but fretfulness was uppermost.

She felt a tremor of impatience, instantly suppressed. She must not blame her mother for the constant need of attention. Edith Verinder had never coped well with life and, since Charlie's death, what little fortitude she'd possessed had faded without a fight.

'Alice!' The fretfulness had become peremptory. 'When will your aunt be here?'

'I'm not sure,' she answered, retracing her steps into the sitting room. 'Very soon, I would think.'

Her mother was sitting by the window wearily resplendent in a wing chair, a thick wool shawl around her shoulders, a blanket at her feet. Alice automatically retrieved the blanket and laid it across the bony knees.

'You will bring Cicely to me, won't you, when she arrives?'

'Of course, Mama, I'll bring her immediately. I'm not certain when the York train gets in but there's always such a crush at King's Cross. I expect Aunt Cissie has had to queue for a hansom.'

Her mother gave a long sigh as though she, too, were queuing for the hansom. 'Make sure that Dora has the tea things ready – and the best china, mind.'

'And don't put out too many madeleines.' She hadn't noticed her father hunched into a matching chair at the other side of the

3

room. He spoke without taking his eyes from his newspaper. 'Your aunt has rather too healthy an appetite.'

'I'll tell Cook,' she said a trifle distractedly, halfway back to the door.

There were a hundred jobs waiting to be done and Cicely's room had still to be made up. Her aunt enjoyed the freedom of wealthy widowhood, travelling when and where she chose from her home in the shadow of the Minster, but why she had decided to visit London at such short notice, Alice had no idea. It was another burden on a household already besieged.

'And Alice,' her mother called after her. 'Fetch Lydia's letters from your room. Cissie will want to read news of her niece.'

She felt her chest tighten. She had letters, certainly, a tidy sheaf of them, but if she were to show them to her aunt, Cicely was quick-witted enough to notice that the last message from Lydia was dated months ago. So far Alice had managed to keep this knowledge from her parents by dint of reading the letters aloud, selecting passages from here and there, and pretending the news had arrived only that morning. Before the letters stopped entirely, they had become less frequent and less informative, but she had still kept up the pretence. She couldn't allow them to know that Lydia had seemingly vanished without a clue to her whereabouts. Not in their weakened state.

She gave swift instructions to Cook to fetch down the bone china from a top shelf and made a strict count of the number of madeleines to appear on the tea trolley before she climbed the stairs to the guest bedroom. Dora was already there and giving the satin counterpane a final smooth when Alice put her head around the door.

'What else needs doing?' she asked the maid.

4

'Just the flowers, miss. Dibbens delivered the narcissi an hour ago and they're soaking in the kitchen, but they need a bit of arranging. I'll run down and get them.'

'Bless you. My legs have turned to jelly.'

'And no wonder. You've been up and down these stairs all morning, fetching and carrying.'

Dora sniffed loudly, but she allowed the moment to pass. Alice knew the maid's opinion of her mother's illness. Domestic servants did not have the luxury of nerves. But Dora was wrong. Her mother had always been fragile. It was her husband who had given Edith stability and, when he'd fallen ill so shortly after Charlie's death, the spirit had gone from her completely.

She arranged the narcissi as best she could in a favourite Murano vase and was making her way downstairs again when the thud of the door knocker echoed through the empty hall. Aunt Cissie. King's Cross could not have been that busy. Her aunt's arrival would at least bring cheer to the house. When the telegram had first arrived, Alice had thought of confiding her worries, but realised almost immediately that Cissie was likely to go straight to her sister with Lydia's tale. The two women were closer than twins. And if her father learned that his younger daughter was missing, possibly in danger, it could prove fatal. His heart attack had left him vulnerable to a final blow, which would be enough to seal her mother's fate, too. No, she couldn't tell. She must keep up the pretence that Lydia was alive and well and enjoying teaching in a foreign land. And believe, believe, that her sister would write soon – from wherever she was.

Alice had written to Topkapi – the Sultan seemed to own a bewildering array of palaces – but Topkapi was the address Lydia had written on each of her letters. The official who responded had been adamant that her sister was no longer with them. There remained at the palace only a few of Lydia's personal possessions that he would be happy to send: two pens, several photographs, a few watercolours and a book. His letter had been brief and its curt disapproval had shone through the uneven English. Sultan Selim was most displeased. His daughters' governess had left without warning and no one had an idea where she was. Alice could not quite believe that. If it were true, it would be completely out of character. Lydia might be impulsive, thoughtless even, but Alice was certain she would never simply disappear without telling her family.

'Darling, how are you?'

Cicely's substantial figure filled the hall. The cabbie bundled in behind her, puffing heavily from dragging several large pieces of luggage up the front steps. Alice wondered just how long her aunt was intending to stay. The older woman held her at arms' length and gave her a prolonged stare.

'Not too well, by the look of it,' she said, answering her own question. 'You're not just pale, my dear. You look positively sickly. What ails you?'

'Really nothing, Aunt,' she protested. 'I have two invalids to look after. I'm not able to leave the house for long and this winter seems to have gone on forever.'

'Well, now I'm here, I shall make sure you do get out. Put some pink back into those cheeks. I'll sit with Edie and keep her amused. It won't be difficult.'

Cicely was right. She knew just how to handle her sister. Her brother-in-law, too, if it came to that. It might give Alice more time to think, space in which to decide just what to do, or even if there was anything she *could* do. In the meantime, she must find a way to keep her aunt occupied this evening and as far from Lydia's letters as possible.

'And how is Theo?' Her aunt had divested herself of a voluminous coat, several bright scarves and a large felt hat.

'Papa is doing well, I think.'

'That's good to hear. It was a bad business about Charlie. A foolish young man, I'm afraid, but still a very bad business.'

Alice stiffened. A sharp sense of loss battled against her aunt's seeming indifference. She wanted to leap to her young brother's defence, but she knew Cissie was right – Charlie had been foolish. Attempting to scale Balliol's medieval walls in the dead of night, after drinking heavily, was foolhardy in the extreme. He had paid a dreadful price for it, and so had they all. Even Lydia. But foolish or not, Charlie had been a loved brother. A sunny, carefree individual who had breezed noisily through every day of his short life with a smile on his face. He had brought joy to the staid house in Pimlico. So she said nothing and instead led her aunt into the sitting room.

'Aunt Cissie is here, Mama,' she announced as cheerfully as she could.

–

Later that evening when her sister was safely tucked into bed and Theo snoring gently by the fire, Cicely ordered a tray of tea to be brought to the sitting room. She took an armchair by the window and signalled for Alice to join her.

'None of your chairs are at all comfortable,' she complained, trying to make a nest for herself on the lumpy seat. 'I remember them when they were new – very different then – and those curtains. Chenille, I think. They were the most beautiful colour.' She pointed to the faded loops of duck egg blue encasing the long windows that overlooked a rear garden. 'Edie always had exquisite taste. Such a shame there's no money to refurbish.'

7

Alice was saved from answering by Dora's knock and jumped up to help the girl manoeuvre the heavy tray onto the rosewood table. 'We won't need you again this evening, Dora. I'll take the tray back to the kitchen myself.' The maid gave her a grateful smile and whisked out of the room.

Alice poured for them both and waited while her aunt stirred her tea. Cissie had been making small talk, she was sure, and at any moment would begin on what she really wished to say.

'You don't look well, my dear.' She had returned to Alice's wraith-like appearance. 'You must not allow yourself to be worn down. What has happened is a tragedy, but it's a tragedy that everyone must deal with, and not just you. I was quite shocked, I have to admit, when I heard that Lydia had left – and for Turkey of all places. I know Edie is bursting with pride. She's full of Lydia's doings, but I doubt she knows the half of it. It has always seemed to me that she feels the girl is special in some way.'

'She is special,' Alice interrupted. The image of her sister, dark curls flying, eyes bright blue and sparkling, filled her mind, and for an instant she felt the most tremendous pain.

'That's as may be,' her aunt continued. 'Lydia is a free spirit, we've known that since she was a child. And no doubt she's off having marvellous adventures. But she is also selfish, my dear. She's left you shouldering the burden of your parents in this sad house.'

'I don't mind,' she said quickly. 'Really, I don't. Lydia is young – she deserves to be selfish.' She hadn't always believed that, but in the last few months irritation with her sister's wayward behaviour had been superseded by fear for her well-being.

'No one deserves to be selfish,' her aunt said firmly. 'And as for being young, what are you?'

'I'm twenty-six. My star has waned.'

And it was true. She had never thought herself attractive, but she'd had the chance to escape several years ago. A young man, a trainee lawyer working for the same practice as her father. He had visited them in Pimlico once or twice and her mother had jumped at the possibility of an engagement, urging her to consider the benefits of marriage to an up-and-coming solicitor. He had been perfectly nice, with a pleasant face and pleasant manners. But dull, too, and she had dragged her feet. She didn't know why; the feeling perhaps that there had to be more than this, good man that he was. The affair had fizzled out and here she was, twenty-six and unwed, the spinster daughter. Her life was one of service to others. She had even begun to dress the part: the plain grey skirt, the stiff white blouse. All that remained of an earlier Alice was the lace-bedecked silk petticoat she wore beneath.

'Your star has waned! What nonsense! You are melancholy, that's what it is. I'd be surprised if you were not, living in this house. You need a holiday and I've decided you shall have one. A week away, two weeks perhaps, and you'll return a new woman. I can look after Edie – and Theo. What do you say? I would like to be useful.'

She reached out and clasped her aunt's hands. 'You are very kind, but you are here as our guest. I couldn't impose on you in that way.'

'More nonsense. How is spending time with a sister I love imposing on me? Edie needs bolstering and I'm the one to do it. And by the look of it, you need bolstering, too. A holiday will be just the thing. Devon, maybe, though it might be a trifle chilly.'

'Venice,' Alice blurted out. She was startled to hear herself say the word. She had never once ventured out of England. Her father's attitude had always been that nothing of value lay beyond the cliffs of Dover, and their holidays had been spent in Southwold or Bournemouth or somewhere equally genteel. So why on earth had she said Venice?

'Venice will be chilly as well this time of the year. But a wonderful place. Think of those buildings. That art. Yes, definitely a place to replenish the soul. You must go.'

'I couldn't. I couldn't go there alone. I don't know why I said that.'

'You said it because it's right for you. And you won't be alone. I have a good friend, who has lived in Venice for many years – an unfortunate marriage to an Italian, I'm afraid – but I know Julia would be delighted to take you under her wing. And as for travelling… there's a train. I've been reading about it. It leaves from Victoria station and goes directly there.'

Alice had read about it, too. Only a few weeks ago, her father's *Daily Telegraph* had devoted a half page article to the subject. It was the train on which Lydia had travelled. A different route but the same train. The Orient Express.

'Tomorrow after breakfast you're to put on your hat and coat and visit the travel agent. Dean and Dawson, they're the chaps – they're in Trafalgar Square. They can reserve you a seat and ask the train conductor to look after you during the journey. And they will book a hotel, too – Julia has only a very small apartment and you will need your privacy.' She bent down and burrowed into her handbag, bringing out a small packet which she pressed into her niece's hand. 'You will need this as well.'

Alice glimpsed a bundle of notes filling the manila envelope. 'I couldn't possibly take this, Aunt Cicely.'

'You can and you will. I can't have you worrying about money at this time. And no fretting about a passport either – it's still possible to travel abroad without one. I've done it myself.'

'This is so generous of you.' She shook her head. 'I can't…' she began, and then finished lamely, 'I'll think about it.'

–

Once the household was settled for the night, she made her way up the stairs for the last weary time that day. Outside her sister's bedroom, she paused. Every week she made sure that Mrs Ferris cleaned thoroughly, though what dust the room could have attracted in seven days was questionable. But she had not entered it herself since the moment she became convinced something was amiss. She had a foolish notion that if she kept away, somehow Lydia would be sleeping there, safe and untroubled, life as it had once been. And in the morning, she would hear her sister's voice, happily off-key, singing the chorus of one of the music hall songs she loved.

Alice's hand grazed the door, then she crossed the landing to what had been her brother's room. Nothing was changed there since the morning he'd left for Oxford. A pile of vacation reading still sat on the square mahogany desk – Aristotle's *Poetics*, Walter Pater, a copy of *Paradise Lost*. The leather-backed brush set Cissie had given him for his twenty-first birthday, and that Charlie had deemed too precious for his college room, remained on the dressing table. The silver cups he'd won for cross-country running shone from the mantelshelf. Dora refused to allow Mrs Ferris to touch them and every week polished them herself. She had adored Charlie. They all had.

Alice strolled to the window and looked out onto the street below. The grass square opposite glimmered dimly in the lamplight. A cat was twining his way through its railings, off on his nightly prowl. From somewhere in the distance, a horse's hooves rattled through the city. An overwhelming loneliness wrapped her in its shroud.

She had been three when her brother was born and she could still remember the way she had hung over his cradle, fascinated, shaking rattles or tickling him with her favourite pink rabbit or counting his fingers and then his toes over and over again, entranced by their small perfection. And he had stayed perfect. Over the years, he had become her one support: when their father's practice had taken a downturn and begun to lose clients, when Mama's nerves reached breaking point, when Lydia was at her most impetuous. Despite his youth, he had been a wise counsel, a sane voice. Except for that one moment of insanity on a night in Oxford. If only he were still here with her. 'What do I do?' she asked aloud. 'How can I help Lydia?'

Her aunt had said that Alice should think about her offer and, for hours on end, she did just that. After a sleepless night, she walked out into the cold, crisp morning and made her way to Dean and Dawson in Trafalgar Square where she bought a train ticket as her aunt had ordered. But she made no mention of a hotel reservation. Instead she sent a telegram. Then in a daze she walked home through the London streets, as though sleepwalking her way back into that vivid dream. Her hand clasped tight to the slip of card in her pocket. A ticket not to Venice – but to Constantinople. She would go to find her sister.

Chapter Two

The crossing had been rough. Alice had only ever seen the sea from the safety of a promenade, and the mountainous white foam, swelling, curling, crashing all around her, was terrifying. The ship wallowed left to right then back again, cutting a tortuous path to the French coast while her stomach heaved and her hands clutched tightly to the arms of her chair. She had found sanctuary in one of the luxurious saloons for which *The Queen* was famous and remained there for the entire crossing, her form rigid and her eyes resolutely closed. It was the tide of fur-swathed passengers bound for the Orient Express that swept her down the ferry gangway at Calais and eventually deposited her on a platform running alongside the dock. She hardly knew where she was headed, though vaguely aware that her suitcase had been loaded onto the *fourgon* at the rear of the waiting train. Somewhere in the distance she could hear the noise of trolleys, of porters yelling, and the shouts of the train crew in their blue and gold uniforms issuing directions in French, in English, in every language on the planet, or so it seemed.

One of the porters hurried towards her, urging her to take her seat.

'My compartment—' she began.

He glanced quickly at the ticket she held between gloved hands. 'The middle of the train, mademoiselle. For Constantinople,' he called over his shoulder, continuing his swift passage up the platform.

She was still unwell from the sea journey and badly confused by the rush and bustle. In the distance she glimpsed people gathered outside the carriages the porter had indicated, and knew she must move towards them. But her body felt strangely limp and she had to force herself into a slow walk. Clouds of steam engulfed her and the words *Compagnie Internationale* on the side of the golden wood carriages hazed and disappeared. She was almost at the door of the first carriage when she sensed her legs buckle and feared she would fall. She had eaten nothing since last night's dinner and had slept no more than an hour.

'May I help you?' The voice was unassuming, a quiet English voice.

She half turned and through blurred vision saw a young man, a concerned expression on his face. 'May I fetch you a drink?'

'Thank you,' she managed. 'A glass of water, perhaps.'

She thought he had disappeared, but in a few moments he was back bearing a small glass. 'I'm afraid the sea crossing did not agree with me,' she said awkwardly.

'I can understand that. It wasn't the smoothest, though I've known worse.'

'You are a regular traveller?' She felt obliged to say something, though she found the situation uncomfortable. Her mother would be shocked that she was making conversation with a man of whom she knew nothing.

'I've done the trip a number of times. I must be used to being tossed around. My name is Harry Frome, by the way. How do you do?'

It was all most unconventional, but then travelling so far and alone was hardly conventional. Her aunt had accompanied her to Victoria and seen her safely into the hands of the train conductor. It was fortunate, Alice thought guiltily, that there had been only a few minutes for Cicely to say goodbye before she'd had to return to Pimlico. She'd had no time to realise her niece was bound for a quite different destination to Venice, and for most of the journey would be travelling alone.

'I am Alice Verinder,' she said as boldly as she could, uneasily aware she lacked an escort.

He frowned and she wondered if he were judging her for it. 'May I ask where you are travelling, Miss Verinder?'

'I'm on my way to Constantinople.' It sounded ridiculous when she said it aloud. That she, Alice Verinder, should have reached Calais was extraordinary in itself, but Turkey was a universe away.

'I thought you might be,' he said slowly. 'Your face is a little familiar. I'm employed at the Topkapi Palace.'

She gave a small gasp. 'Then you must know my sister, Lydia.'

'I've met her, certainly. But what a coincidence! Turkey must have a strong attraction for your family.'

She brushed the remark aside. It was his acquaintance with Lydia that was important. 'Where did you say you met her?'

'I didn't, but it was in the library. I saw her there quite often. It's where I work. She often brought her pupils with her – she was eager for them to know how a library worked. They would stay an hour or so, wandering the shelves, finding new treasures. She seemed a person who delighted in books.'

'A library – at the palace?'

'There has been one at Topkapi since early in the last century. The Ottomans inherited the customs of ancient Persia, you know, and the Turks are a most cultured people.'

'I was not suggesting otherwise,' she was quick to say. 'But an Englishman in a Turkish library? That must be unusual.'

'I work in the new library. There are two at Topkapi, one very old and much smaller, but the most recent was founded by a Frenchman, in fact. A Monsieur Valentin Boucher, a great philanthropist. Monsieur Boucher is still involved in its development, but I am responsible for the library's day-to-day running. We own a wide range of literature and some very beautiful volumes. A few are extremely rare.'

'It sounds most interesting.'

She could imagine Lydia loving the library. Her sister had always been a great reader, so often fired by the ideas and philosophies she consumed. It was only when theory took a practical turn that trouble surfaced.

'I would enjoy telling you more.' He looked across the heads of the people still crowding the platform and fidgeted with the small valise he carried. 'I wonder – would you have dinner with me tonight, once we leave Paris?' He sounded slightly diffident.

In the last few minutes she had begun to feel a good deal better, able to contemplate the long journey ahead with some equanimity, but his invitation shocked her. It was presumptuous. That was what her mother would say, and Cissie, too. But... Harry Frome appeared unexceptional, and he had known Lydia or at least met her sister several times. He could be the person with whom to begin her search.

She had hesitated a fraction too long, and when he spoke again his voice was clipped. 'Naturally, I understand if you prefer to eat privately.'

She could see that she had offended him and made haste to mend her fences. 'No, no, not at all. I would enjoy dining with you, Mr Frome.'

The serious expression he seemed habitually to wear broke into a smile, and his grey eyes warmed. For the first time she thought him an attractive man. 'That's settled then. I shall be in the dining carriage around seven this evening.' He gave her a brief nod and walked away.

The compartment she was shown into was astonishingly small. A long sofa, a tiny table and an even tinier wash basin that hid behind lacquered sliding doors. An array of cupboards and drawers had been artfully fitted into the nooks and crannies of the gloriously decorated woodwork, and she soon found space for the few belongings she had with her. Compact the space certainly was with barely room to turn and, since her aunt's gift had not stretched to a private compartment, she wondered how on earth she would manage to share it with another woman. She did not have to wonder long. A whistle sounded, the uniformed guard waved his flag and touched his cap, and they were off. Her unknown companion had not boarded at Calais.

She sank back onto the sofa and watched the countryside flow past. The sky was wide and the landscape flat, barely broken by the occasional poplar-fringed road or small village, its church steeple stark against a leaden sky. Her mind strayed to the evening ahead. The young man – Harry Frome – had been very kind. A little too forward maybe in approaching her, but good enough to find water when she needed it. And he had evidently not thought a dinner invitation was in any way questionable. Indeed, he had prickled when she'd hesitated to accept.

But now in the quiet of the compartment, her mother's warnings sounded in her ears, insisting on how necessary it was to have a male travelling companion. How important for a man to organise one's journey, to supervise the luggage, to fend off unwelcome attentions. Edith had been unhappy with the idea of the holiday to Venice, at the idea of a holiday anywhere, until Aunt Cissie had smoothed things over, assuring her sister that Alice would be well looked after on the train and would have Cissie's friend, Julia, as chaperone once she reached Venice.

Alice needed a break, her aunt had said, and once she'd had her fill of art, she would be more than eager to return to the domestic fold. Her mother had agreed eventually that perhaps it wasn't such a silly idea. Her father had merely snorted and said she was quite mad. If she wanted a holiday – though he couldn't for the life of him see why she should – then Bournemouth was the ticket.

She closed her eyes against the low winter sun slanting through the window. The empty fields stretched before her, mesmerising in their monotony. Gradually her head drooped and she fell into an uncertain sleep.

A sharp jolt of the carriage woke her; the fields had disappeared and in their place grimy buildings and tattered hoardings. Paris – and they were pulling into the Gare du Nord. She had been told that once she boarded at Calais, she would stay on the same train until she reached Constantinople. She hoped that was so, but after several stationary minutes they seemed to be going backwards. And then they were drawing into another terminus, the Gare de Strasbourg, and she could relax. She knew this was where trains for the East departed. It was also where she might gain an additional travelling companion. But once again, no one appeared. It was a Sunday evening and perhaps the pious refused to travel. The conductor, checking on her wellbeing, worried that mademoiselle might feel this uncomfortable and suggested finding another young lady with whom to share if it was a problem.

'It's no problem,' she assured him, grateful to be left alone.

For a moment, while he hovered in the doorway, she toyed with the idea of asking him to take a message to the dining room to cancel the arrangement she had made, but then scolded herself for her cowardice, remembering that she was on this journey for one reason alone, and that was to find Lydia. She must grab whatever help came her way and it had been a stroke of luck meeting Mr Frome. At the moment he did not appear too promising – he'd had little to say of her sister – but she must start somewhere. She could not let good fortune pass her by.

Chapter Three

He was already in the dining room when she walked into the beautifully appointed salon. Panels of gleaming mahogany lined the walls, inlaid with the most intricate marquetry. On the floor were brightly coloured oriental rugs and at the windows velvet curtains of deep ruby. A dozen tables sported dazzling white cloths and napkins, artistically folded by the sommeliers. Crystal glasses glittered, some filled with wine the colour of the curtains. A few silver champagne buckets were already in prominent positions. Along with every man there, her companion wore a dark suit and plain white shirt, not the full evening regalia she had feared, but she was glad she had chosen the one truly elegant winter dress she possessed, a wide-sleeved wool chiffon. Its subtle grey-blue enhanced the colour of her eyes, or so she had been told. She hoped it would give her courage.

He came towards her as soon as she appeared on the threshold.

'Miss Verinder, good evening. How are you feeling now?'

'A good deal better, thank you. I'm sorry I was so distracted earlier.'

'No apology needed. You had every reason,' he said gallantly.

Forestalling the waiter, he pulled out the velvet covered chair for her, then walked around to the other side of the table, gathering up a starched napkin on his way. He seemed perfectly at ease, but then he would have sat in this carriage many times. The waiter in the familiar blue and gold reappeared at his shoulder and murmured in his ear.

Harry Frome leant across the table. 'Would you care for some wine?'

'Thank you, but no.'

She wondered if she had appeared shocked because he said defensively, 'The wine is very good. You might find a small glass beneficial.'

She shook her head and looked down at her lap. 'I have never drunk wine,' she confessed. Then added somewhat unnecessarily, 'I am not a traveller.'

'You don't have to travel to enjoy wine.'

There was something brusque in his manner that flustered her. He had invited her to eat with him for no other reason, it seemed, than wanting her company. Yet she had the distinct feeling that in some way she was on trial. She felt like making her excuses right there and then, but Lydia was a constant in her mind and she knew she must stay.

'I have never even been out of England before,' she said quietly.

His eyebrows rose. 'Then you are very brave – tackling Constantinople for your first journey. What takes you there?'

She thought it an odd question since he knew Lydia was in the city, indeed had worked for many months under the same roof. 'I am travelling to see my sister.'

He gave a polite smile. 'And where is she living now?'

That sent her spirits tumbling. 'I had hoped I would find her still at the palace.'

He looked puzzled. 'I am afraid you will be disappointed. I have been in England only a short while, but I'd not seen her for many weeks before I left.' He paused for a moment, as though wondering whether to go on. But then he said, 'I did hear – and I have no idea how true it is – that she left the palace suddenly and without a word to anyone.'

'That is what I've been told.'

'So why make such an arduous journey?'

This was her chance to open the topic uppermost in her mind, but before she could, the waiter arrived at their table bearing bowls of soup.

'Consommé Xavier. The soup,' Harry explained, gesturing with his spoon. 'An old favourite. Although who Xavier is or was, I have no idea.'

She acknowledged the pleasantry with a brief smile and took an exploratory sip before she returned to his question.

'I thought I should come. My sister left behind a few personal possessions which I am to collect. And' – she paused, wondering whether she dared say what was in her mind, but then plunged onwards, – 'and I don't think I believed what I was told.'

She saw the stunned expression on his face. 'Lydia would never leave in such a fashion,' she said emphatically.

'Are you sure your natural partiality is not blinding you? If a palace official has confirmed your sister is no longer with us, I think you can assume it is the truth.'

'My sister is young and sometimes naïve. Her nature is spontaneous, too impulsive at times, but she would never disappear without a word. She would never leave her family in ignorance of where she is or how she is.'

Her voice had grown stronger as she defended her sibling. Harry put down his spoon and looked hard at her. 'You have heard nothing from her?'

'Nothing.'

'I imagined she had travelled back to England.'

It was Alice's turn to lay down her spoon. 'Well, she hasn't.'

'If she is not at the palace and has not returned to England, where is she?'

'That is what I intend to find out.'

'Have you thought of contacting the Foreign Office? I'm sure the British ambassador would help if he knew of the problem.'

'There are reasons I wish to find her myself.' She was being deliberately vague. The Foreign Office was a last resort. Alerting them would mean alerting her parents to Lydia's disappearance, and that was the last thing she wanted. 'May I ask when you saw her last?' she hurried on to say.

He frowned, evidently thinking back over the previous months. 'She came into the library... I think it was a day or so before I heard the first rumours she had left. Sultan Selim's young daughters had spent the summer months at Dolmabahçe Palace – that's the family's home on the shore of the Bosphorus,' he explained. 'And your sister came for a book the girls wanted to read when they returned. On Arabian mythology – a Turkish translation, if I remember rightly.'

'And at the time she said nothing to you about leaving?'

'I was not a close companion of hers, you understand. But no, she said nothing.'

'Do you think she would have mentioned it, if she were expecting to go?'

'I suppose she might. She would have had to arrange a time for the girls to come to the library to collect the book.'

The soup bowls had been replaced by plates of roast chicken and two silver tureens of potatoes and carrots and peas. They were spicy to the taste, certainly nothing like Cook's overwrought vegetables, but Alice found them tasty and surprised herself by enjoying them. They were halfway through the meal before she ventured the question that was burning through her mind.

'Your acquaintance with my sister was slight, Mr Frome, I understand that, but when you saw her on that last occasion did she appear any different to you?'

'In what way "different"?'

'Worried, anxious maybe.'

'No, I'm sure not. In fact, I would say happier, if anything. I believe her work was highly valued by the palace – the princesses seemed to like her more modern way of teaching. She told me they had written to her recently to say how much they were looking forward to seeing her.'

Alice stopped eating. Nothing Harry Frome had said made sense. If her sister had been happy, delighted her pupils would soon be with her again, what was she doing packing her bags without a word to anyone?

She felt him watching her closely.

'I must admit I was surprised when I heard she had left,' he said, 'but I'm sure you will find there's a rational explanation. I am not the right person to ask. You should talk to the women she lived with. They will know her far better than I.'

It was sound advice and she thought it best to change the subject. 'Tell me about the library. It sounds a fascinating project.'

He needed little prompting. 'It is. A wonderful enterprise. My employer set up a charitable foundation in the city some years ago. It does amazing work in the poorer areas – funding a hospital, building a new school, that sort of thing. But he wanted to do something for the palace. Sultan Abdülhamid is a good friend. The palace had everything, as you can imagine, or so it seemed. But then Monsieur Boucher hit on the idea of a new, more comprehensive library that would house the precious Islamic texts that were kept in the Sultan's private apartments. But not just them. There are ancient works by Greek and Arabic scholars, too: on astronomy, mathematics, physics, many translated into Turkish, and of course, literature from across the world. We have built an impressive collection and it is growing all the time.'

'And how did you come to be working there? Does your family know Monsieur Boucher?'

She could feel the chill even before he spoke.

'I had never met him before I took the job. My family does not move in exalted circles. I won my position on merit. That and hard work. I have a first-class degree from Oxford.'

She was about to apologise, to smooth feathers, but decided she had not the energy. Mr Frome was a prickly character and she had learned virtually nothing about her sister. If he was determined to be difficult, she would keep her own counsel. When the waiter offered them the dessert menu – a Souffle Alaska or a Corbeille de Fruits – she shook her head and got up to leave.

He seemed to be regretting his earlier sharpness and said in a conciliatory voice, 'We will be travelling for another two nights and if there's anything more I can tell you about Topkapi, I shall be in the dining room every evening. Do come and find me.'

'You are most kind, thank you.' Her sentiment lacked any sincerity.

But then he said, 'I'm sorry I could not be more help. If I think of anything, I will let you know. Where are you staying in the city?'

'I have been given a room at the palace. I telegrammed a few days ago and they were kind enough to invite me to stay.' It had taken a morning of hovering by the front door, on constant watch for the telegram boy, to ensure only she was privy to their response. 'Mr Frome—'

'Harry. You must call me Harry. We are to be fellow inmates as well as fellow travellers, it seems.'

'Mr Frome, Harry, perhaps you could advise me on this? I feel some awkwardness that in truth I have invited myself. I would like to offer some recompense but have no idea what that should be.'

He smiled and she thought again what a difference that made. He was a pleasant enough looking young man, but nothing more – Lydia would have called him 'ordinary' – but the smile was transformative. She found herself staring at him for far too long, and, embarrassed, bent her head and picked an imaginary loose thread from her dress.

'The Turks are a most hospitable people and would be insulted if you were to attempt to pay for your accommodation,' he replied. 'Very few foreigners are invited to stay, and you have been honoured. But in any case, there are so many rooms in the harem that one more occupied is neither here nor there.'

'The harem?' She looked aghast and he gave a small laugh.

'It is not quite what you imagine. The harem houses the women's quarters. Of course, the Sultan's favourites live there, too, but so do a good many other women who have no personal connection to him. The Valide Sultan, the Sultan's mother, is in overall authority and she runs a strict regime.'

'And it is the Sultan who employed my sister?' As she spoke, she wondered if she might gain an audience with this great man.

'Not Sultan Abdülhamid, no, but one of his many brothers, Sultan Selim.'

'I see.'

She wasn't sure that she did, but once at the palace she hoped the situation would become clearer. When she had asked Lydia

26

who was actually employing her, her sister had seemed hazy and too grateful for the job to request much in the way of detail from the previous governess. It was enough that Miss Lister had facilitated her escape abroad. *It's quite common for wealthy families in Turkey to hire English or French governesses*, Lydia had said airily. *We add cachet, you know!* That was typical of her sister's impulsiveness, plunging into a new life without thought and without any true idea of what it involved.

'I will bid you goodnight then, Miss Verinder.'

'Please, Alice.' She blushed again, thinking how shocked her mother would be at such informality.

'Goodnight, Alice. I hope you sleep well.'

She couldn't imagine she would sleep well. The train was rocking in an unnerving fashion and she was bounced along the narrow corridor to her compartment. But when she slid back the door, she saw that in her absence the steward had been busy. A comfortable bed had appeared in place of the sofa and its crisp white linen looked inviting.

She put on her nightgown and brushed her hair in front of the small oval mirror. A year ago Lydia must have done the exact same thing, tugging a brush through luxuriant curls that by bedtime would have been a wild tangle. How many hours every night had she spent trying to tame her sister's hair, unknotting knots and rolling curls into rags, with Lydia squeaking when she tugged too hard and squirming this way and that until the rags hung lopsided. Not that it ever mattered. The morning would see Lydia's hair once more a glorious, rippling mane.

She wondered if her sister had found the journey equally unsettling. She thought not. Lydia was bold, she would have taken it in her stride. And taken it in her stride if she had met Harry Frome. Alice remembered now that somewhere in the letters there had been a mention of a library and of encountering someone on the train. In that first letter, she thought. Who was it that Lydia had written about?

She delved into the cloak bag stowed in one of the small cupboards and brought out the precious letters, pulling one from the bottom of the stack and beginning to read. Lydia had found the Channel ferry exciting and here she was at Calais. There was a long description of the noise and bustle of the station, several sentences rhapsodising over the ingenious arrangements on the train, and then… she skimmed down a paragraph. Yes, here it was. Lydia's first meal on board.

I shared a table at dinner tonight with a delightful couple. They are also travelling to Constantinople and as it turned out they have a connection to Topkapi. What chance of that, I wonder? Quite a large chance, Alice thought. I met Mr Frome, after all. The journey to Constantinople on the Orient Express was expensive and more than likely to attract people who had connections to the palace. *Their name is Boucher – they are French, how delightful. Paul's father – and I was invited to call him Paul, everything is so informal beyond Dover – is a very important person at the palace. A philanthropist. Have I spelt that right? Never mind, dear Alice, you will correct me as I go along…*

Chapter Four

Lydia
The Orient Express, August 1905

Lydia enjoyed travelling alone. It hadn't been difficult to invent a suitable story to allay her family's fears: she had found a female companion for the journey, she'd said, a nursemaid travelling to an English family in Constantinople. They had been too immersed in their grief for Charlie to raise doubts – even Alice – and she had gained this wonderful, unfamiliar freedom. No tiresome chaperone preaching rules, no irritating demands from sick parents, no elder sibling fussing over her. The thought made her feel guilty. As well as loving Alice, she had huge respect for her caring, dutiful sister.

At times, though, that sense of duty was almost too strong. It could become a conviction that no one else was right but Alice. Their father's new office manager, for instance. He had come to dinner in Pimlico and Lydia had mistrusted him immediately. He was too smooth, flattered too much, and he seemed to Lydia to hesitate whenever matters of finance were raised. When she had said as much to her sister, Alice had told her to keep silent. The man their father had chosen was perfectly competent and it was their duty not to worry Theo with silly doubts. Three months later the man had absconded with a large amount of clients' money and, once the news spread, their father's practice began its long decline.

But it was her sister who had held the family together these past few months. And her sister who had negotiated with the Honourable Member for Islington, though the necessity for doing so still made Lydia furious. Surely it had to be right that women took action to defend their interests. And what, in fact, had she actually done? Broken a window, that was the full extent of her felony, and no matter what Alice said, there had been little danger to anyone. She had heaved the brick into his downstairs scullery, but not before the kitchen staff were safely out of the room. And then she'd offered to pay for the window, though if there were any justice in the world he should be the one paying. And for more than a window. But there wasn't any justice. The man was implacably opposed to women's votes and continued to make incendiary speeches on the topic. He deserved more than a brick, but if hers had worked to remind him that women possessed the power to disrupt, that was to the good. And there was poor Alice having to humble herself, to beg forgiveness for her sister's outrageous crime. It made Lydia sick to think of it.

But that was all behind her now. She was here on a train bound for Constantinople and a new life, and it was Alice who had won her that freedom. Freedom from the relentless gloom of home, from the memory of Charlie, the golden son and heir. No, not freedom from Charlie. He lived in her heart and always would. But the exhilaration of travelling to a foreign land, a very foreign land, could not be suppressed. Nor her sheer amazement that for the first time in her life she had a job. Two darling little girls to whom she was to teach English. How difficult could that be? And how magnificent the palace looked. She had taken a cab to the London Library – Theo Verinder still paid a subscription – and found photographs of Topkapi in an old edition of *Picture Politics*. She had gazed at the palace in awe, hardly able to believe its splendour, and in two days' time she, Lydia Verinder, would be a part of it.

Independence was delightful, but she was glad she would have dinner companions this evening. She had been feeling unaccustomedly nervous about eating alone in a public place. Would people think badly of her, think she had no friends, no family, that, heaven forbid, she was no better than she should be? But she had been rescued by a delightful couple: the Bouchers. She had literally bumped into the husband at the Gare de Strasbourg. The train had waited there a good thirty minutes and she had decided to stretch her legs on the platform while she could. Paul Boucher had been supervising the loading of what looked an incredible amount of baggage and somehow she had become entangled, turning quickly and running straight into him. He had been the one to apologise. He'd gazed at her rather too interestedly while he apologised, but she was used to that. It was how most men reacted when they met her. Fortunately, his wife appeared at his side at that moment and after general introductions, they had invited her to dine with them.

She had been delighted to discover they were bound for the same destination: they made an elegant couple, seeming to possess the French flair she had read so much about. She had been looking forward to sharing a table with them, but half an hour into the meal had begun to wonder if she'd been mistaken. Madame Boucher might be beautifully dressed, but she said little. And as for Paul, he was simply dull. Dull, but amiable.

'The Court is only temporarily at Topkapi while refurbishments are taking place at the Yıldız Palace, but I'm sure you will enjoy life there,' he was saying.

'There is more than one palace?'

Paul Boucher smiled sympathetically. 'There are many. But you will be at Topkapi for some time – the work at Yıldız goes slowly – and the young princesses are very much looking forward to welcoming you there.'

Lydia was relieved he spoke in English. Her schoolgirl French would have made the conversation a struggle.

'They know I am coming?'

'Most definitely. As soon as Sultan Selim received the recommendation from Miss Lister, he called the girls to him and told them they would very soon have a new governess. Arrangements for your arrival were already in place before we left for Paris.'

Lydia sent a silent thanks to Florence Lister. It had been central to Alice's difficult conversation with that vile man, the dishonourable member for Islington, that her sister left the country immediately. If Lydia went abroad, he'd said, he would not press charges. And where else could she have gone? A ghastly spa town in Bavaria or some mean *pension* in the French countryside. It had been Florence who had paved the way to a wonderful job in a wonderful country.

'The princesses have already reorganised the schoolroom,' Paul said between mouthfuls of baked salmon and asparagus. 'They have collected together all the work they did for Miss Lister so that you can see how they have progressed. Then ordered new pencils and pens, and had the furniture moved – your desk now has the most beautiful view of the Bosphorus. They invited Elise to see their schoolroom when it was finished. I know they are hoping very much that you will like it.'

'I will like everything,' she said, and meant it. Her face broke into a wide smile and her deep blue eyes danced. He smiled back and she knew he was drawn to her. What kind of marriage did these two have? she wondered. It was probably best not to enquire too closely. But if everyone at Topkapi were as good-natured as this man, she would be fortunate.

'And where do you work in the palace, Monsieur Boucher?'

'Paul, please. And this is Elise. There are very few Europeans at the Ottoman court and we don't stand on ceremony. I work with my father, Monsieur Valentin Boucher. He is a great man, is he not, Elise?'

Elise nodded, but Lydia saw her eyes close slightly. Paul might be amiable, but she was not so certain of his wife, suspecting her silence hid a sharp and possibly hostile intelligence.

'What kind of work do you do there?' She wanted him to talk, to tell her everything there was to know.

'My father set up a charity some years ago. We call it The Foundation. It has done great work in the city and provided several schools for the poor and a splendid new hospital. His last project was the Abdülhamid Library. It is a magnificent structure and quite, quite beautiful.'

'And you assist him in the library?'

'Oh, no. We employ a librarian, a young man from Oxford. I work in the office, snowed under with paperwork. There are so many projects to administer – you can imagine how many letters arrive, how many requests we receive.'

She wondered how hard his days really were. Somehow, he did not seem made for work. His clothes were worryingly stylish and there was a flimsiness about him, as though if you pushed your finger into his chest, it would meet no resistance. It was an uncomfortable image and Lydia gave herself a mental shake. She was determined to like everything and everybody at Topkapi.

'Have you been a governess for long?' It was Elise who asked and hearing her voice came as a shock.

Lydia flushed. She had been hoping no one would enquire too deeply into her credentials. Florence Lister had trained at Homerton, but her own education had been basic, to say the least. Florence would never have recommended her if it had not been for the camaraderie they'd established during several suffragette marches. But a basic education meant she could read and write English and that, after all, was the main requirement. She hoped so, or the young princesses would see her floundering.

'I have been teaching only a short time,' she lied. 'But I am determined to find ways of interesting the girls to help them learn. What are their names? Miss Lister made no mention, but perhaps I must call them by their titles.'

Paul laughed. 'They are precisely eight and six years old. It will be quite in order for you to call them by their given names. They are Esma – she is the elder – and Rabia. Their father, Sultan Selim, is the fifth brother of Sultan Abdülhamid.'

'And that is significant?'

'It means only that he is a little removed from the centre of power.'

'And you? As a European, are you similarly removed?' She could feel her interest quickening. Centres of power were intriguing. She had dared to challenge a centre of power; that was the very reason she was sitting in this carriage.

He brushed the query aside. 'I am an office man, pure and simple. It is my father who enjoys friendship with Sultan Abdülhamid.'

She had her answer. The man sitting opposite her had no importance within the Court, but his father had. She wondered about his wife – where did she fit in?

'Are your parents living in France, madame?' she asked politely. She couldn't quite bring herself to call her Elise.

'They are, Miss Verinder. They live in Paris and we have been visiting them these last few weeks.' For the first time the woman's face came alive.

'But I imagine you see them in Constantinople, too?'

'That would not be advisable.'

Lydia's surprise must have been evident because Paul intervened. 'Elise and I are cousins – her mother is my father's sister. We would not wish the court to feel overwhelmed by Bouchers. Two families are sufficient, I think.'

'You have children then? Do they live with you in Turkey?'

Two blank faces stared back at her and she knew she had asked the wrong question.

'No children, not at the moment, but one day perhaps.'

His voice was so quiet that she could hardly hear him and she felt herself redden. Unwittingly she had touched on a raw subject. And after he had been so hospitable, inviting her to eat with them so that she would not dine alone, answering her inane questions about life at the palace. It was perhaps the moment to leave and when the waiter appeared with a coffee pot, she was quick to rise from her chair.

'Thank you so much for a delightful evening.' She managed to conjure a smile.

'Delightful,' Elise murmured, her accent more noticeable now.

Her husband got to his feet. 'It has been most enjoyable meeting you, Lydia. No doubt we will see a good deal of you at the palace. You can find me most days in my small office – do visit at any time. I shall be happy to help if I can.'

Elise Boucher straightened her shoulders and gave a tremulous smile. 'And eat with us again tomorrow evening, if it suits you. We will be here at seven o'clock.'

Lydia was too surprised at the unlikely invitation to say anything. Instead she gave what she hoped was a friendly nod and left for her compartment. The evening had given her much to think about. There was something disturbing about the Bouchers' relationship, but she couldn't put her finger on it. Elise was certainly a mystery. She sensed there was a woman there, within that rigid carapace, a woman who could one day become a friend, but whether that would ever happen she doubted. And as for Paul Boucher, he was pleasant enough, but evidently of small consequence within the palace. It might be helpful, though, to recognise a familiar face if ever she needed one.

–

In her absence, the compartment had become a bedroom and she looked forward to the night ahead. There was an excitement in travelling through darkness, anonymous and untethered. It was another kind of freedom. She remembered to hang her frock on one of the many hooks that dotted the carriage. Tidiness did not come naturally to her, but in such a confined space it was essential. It was fortunate she had the compartment to herself – the palace had paid for a single berth. She slipped on her nightgown, feeling the swift chill of nakedness, and unhooked the pendant she was rarely without. Looking for a safe resting place, she decided on a small shelf above the bed. Charlie had given her the sapphire necklace on the last birthday she had spent with him. *It matches your eyes*, was all he'd said. A rough, brotherly compliment, but it had been precious.

She clambered into the bed and took up her notebook. She had decided before she left London to keep a diary and tonight she would write about the dinner she had just shared. From

Paul Boucher she had learned a little of the place she was to call home, but she was keen to discover more. In particular, to know something of his father since it was evident the older man held sway in the Court. If she took up Elise's invitation, she would have the opportunity. For a while she chewed on her pencil, staring ahead at the wall of shining wood. The next two evenings could prove interesting – as long as there was no more mention of the qualifications she lacked.

That prompted a smile. Alice would have made a far more convincing governess than she would ever be. But imagining her sister travelling to Constantinople had her laugh out loud. The sky would need to fall before that was ever likely. She must write and tell her all that had happened since the moment they'd kissed their goodbyes at Victoria station. She would make sure to send Alice every piece of news she could. Her sister deserved that at least.

Chapter Five

Alice kept to her compartment for the remainder of the journey, the steward bringing her what food she needed. Not that she needed much, since the lack of activity had affected her appetite badly. She felt unsettled, her mind skittering and her hands longing for something to do. After a day of gazing through the window at the changing landscape, she reached for her book, but managed to read scarcely a chapter. Even the short stops the train made – at Munich, Vienna, Budapest, Bucharest – failed to interest her for long. At home, she had yearned for solitude and to be free of the constant demands on her time, but now she found herself desperate to hear the familiar call of 'Alice'.

The situation was entirely her fault. She might have passed at least some of the wearisome hours with her fellow passengers – the steward had told her of a ladies' drawing room aboard – but she had made the decision to remain in her compartment, to hide away, in fact. After the difficult meal with Harry Frome, she'd felt unable to face another and had wanted to keep her distance from him and from everyone else on the train. She was unsure what to make of him, whether he could prove a friend or quite the opposite. At times he had relaxed and been a charming companion, but at others he'd taken offence at comments she had thought innocuous. *A touchy cove*, Charlie would have said, *steer well clear.*

And so she had, but at a price. Over the last three days, her solitude had forced on her the realisation of how foolhardy this journey was. If she could have turned tail, she would have. Why would the palace say Lydia had left them if she hadn't? There was no sensible reason, and it had been instinct alone that suggested otherwise. And if the palace were speaking truly and her sister had gone without a word, how was she to find her? She was a woman travelling alone and unprotected, a stranger in a country of which she knew nothing. She had no idea even what would happen when she reached Constantinople. Would she be expected to share a conveyance with Harry? She imagined someone from the palace would meet them both – if not, she had no clue how she would go on.

In the event, she need not have worried. When the train pulled into Sirkeci station, a line of carriages were drawn up for hire and before she'd had time to enquire how much it would cost to take her to Topkapi, a splendidly uniformed man came forward, whip in hand.

'Mees Werinder?'

'Yes.' She was uncertain.

'Come.'

'But—' she began nervously.

'Come,' he ordered.

There was no doubting his meaning. And he had to have come from the palace, hadn't he? How else would he have known her name? She allowed him to hand her up into one of the waiting vehicles, seeing with relief that her suitcase had already been loaded. Looking across at the queue of horses, she glimpsed Harry Frome climbing into a second carriage. He gave a brief wave of his hand before both vehicles trundled from the station.

The journey to Topkapi proved full of interest and though she was tired and her eyelids drooping – sleep had not been easy on the train – she was riveted, glancing from right to left and then back again. Despite a smattering of rain, the streets were filled with movement. Stalls lined each alleyway, some piled high with spices, others with fruit and vegetables of every shape and colour. A gaggle of geese pecked its way from street to street, while a cobbler mended shoes on what looked to be a blanket. And passing him, a potter carrying a huge basket of bowls on his back. The driver had to slow abruptly when a coffee seller, wooden bar strung across his shoulders, a wonderful aroma following his every step, darted in front of them.

But they had travelled only a short while when the bells on the horse's reins began to jingle less loudly and she realised they were slowing down. She lifted her eyes and looked ahead. Then took a very deep breath. She had read of the palace's immensity, but nothing had prepared her for what she saw.

Two enormous towers, their conical roofs almost reaching the sky, stood on either side of a magnificent white and grey marble archway. Sentries stood in niches carved into the marble, dwarfed by their surroundings, but dressed from head to toe in scarlet and bearing rifles that looked ready for use. Above them and either side of the arch, plaques of spun gold spelt out what Alice took to be Turkish lettering. Without a sound, the tall gates swung open, allowing her a view of distant trees and, towering above them, a gold-topped dome. The driver flicked his whip and they passed into a large gravelled square bounded by a cluster of buildings.

But they were not to stop here. Through yet another guarded entrance and into a second courtyard, even larger if that were possible, this time ringed on three of the four sides by colonnaded buildings, its central space dotted with small kiosks and decorated pavilions. It was here the driver finally pulled the horse to a halt. Alice was relieved. The further they had travelled from the main gate, the greater the sense of enclosure she had felt. The driver helped her down and swung her luggage to the floor. He led the way to a door in the middle of one of the colonnades.

In a few seconds, a young woman appeared at the doorway and came towards her. Large black eyes beneath well-shaped brows looked out from a head covering of finest silk. Those eyes seemed appraising.

'I am Sevda,' the young woman said. 'I am guide, Miss Werinder.' She waved her hand at the driver, dismissing him.

Stunned by her surroundings, Alice somehow found her voice. 'Thank you, Sevda. I think I may need a guide.' She gave the girl a cautious smile, taking in the young woman's beauty and feeling herself decidedly travel-stained.

Sevda seemed not to be dressed in any kind of uniform, but in trousers that fell loosely to the ankles, ending in a cuff. They were made from a rich satin and brocaded with silver flowers so that as the girl moved, she gave the appearance of walking through a garden. Over the trousers she wore a long-sleeved robe of figured damask, held fast by a girdle at least three fingers broad and fastened by a brooch of pearls.

'This *haremlik*,' Sevda announced, gesturing to the rooms that lay ahead. 'This where women of palace live – and Sultan and sons. No other men. I show you room.'

Seemingly out of nowhere, a man dressed in palace uniform appeared at Sevda's shoulder. The girl issued a sharp command

and he took Alice's suitcase in one hand and her cloak bag in the other.

She was puzzled. Hadn't her guide just said there were no men in the harem other than the Sultan and his sons? Her face must have shown her confusion because Sevda said, 'Not man.'

For a moment, Alice did not understand, then when the significance of the girl's words became clear, her face flushed scarlet. Sevda looked delicately away until her guest had regained her composure. She said something to the servant sagging beneath the weight of luggage and the little trio set off.

They were soon passing what seemed to be a guard room, then walking the length of a wide corridor until eventually it opened out into a space so large it was almost a courtyard in itself. The room was marble-floored and its walls bore a dazzling scheme of patterned Iznik tiles. A fountain played at its centre and the splash of water echoed around the tiled walls. In an odd contradiction, braziers of hot ashes stood in each corner.

They were not alone there. A number of women were seated on scarlet and gold covered divans which ran along each side of the room, while others occupied silk cushions placed at a distance. A social distinction, Alice wondered? Some of the women sewed, some were reading, many simply talked in low voices.

Sevda pointed towards them. 'This ladies' room. You come here.'

Several of the women looked up and smiled. 'You meet later,' Sevda said, and on they went, winding through a labyrinth of narrow spaces and interlinking rooms. 'And this schoolroom.' They were passing a huge cedar wood door set off with silver nails. 'Your room just behind.'

Just behind proved a lengthy trudge through a network of green and blue tiled corridors. Occasionally Alice caught a glimpse through a window of distant minarets, or the glint of the sea, that told her the outside world still existed, but the sense of the hidden was strong and for the first time in her life she began to feel claustrophobic. If Alice had felt bolder, she would have asked how on earth she was ever to find her way in this maze of rooms and passages. But she wasn't feeling bold. Just the contrary. She was feeling almost a prisoner, irreparably cut off from a world she understood.

At the end of yet another narrow passage, they stopped at a cedar wood door, indistinguishable from all the others except for the mother-of-pearl that ornamented its carving. The servant dropped the luggage with a grateful puff while Sevda produced a large iron key that had Alice's heart dropping further. Until, that is, the door opened and she walked into a bright, square room, wainscoted in cedar and painted with flowers. The wooden ceiling, inlaid with more flowers, was a riot of blue and gold and red. A large divan, covered in deep blue silk, sat against one wall, its entire surface filled with a profusion of cushions, some of brocade, some of white satin embroidered in gold wire. White linen curtains were at the window and moved slightly in the breeze and, beneath the window, silver bowls of sweet-smelling herbs sat in little arches.

Alice was immediately drawn to the window. It overlooked a wilderness of trees, a green cavern full of shadow, with scattered pools of water amid the sound of small streams. A grape hyacinth grew close to the window, along with a group of tiny sea green iris already in bud.

'It is beautiful.'

Sevda's smile was genuine. 'This room your sister's. You like to stay here.'

Lydia's room. Lydia had been here, sleeping in that divan, sitting in that chair in the corner, looking out at this very view. Alice's heart did a little jump. Could she feel her presence? But no, there was nothing. The wooden walls looked back at her, the chair stayed untouched and the bed was newly made. There was nothing of her sister here. Not even a whisper of Lydia. The heaviness in her heart returned, but she was given no time to dwell on the harrowing sense of loss.

'And this Naz.' A younger girl had slipped through the open doorway. 'She your slave,' Sevda said. 'She look after sister.'

Your slave. The words were ugly.

'Everyone has slave – even slaves,' Sevda said indifferently, reading aright Alice's expression.

Naz bowed her head, her eyes downcast. Why was it then that Alice could feel her scrutiny? A scrutiny that was in no way friendly.

'I take you to Valide Sultan's rooms,' Sevda was saying. 'She commands. Her rooms near – between Sultan's and slave women's.'

Alice felt her breath catch and the palms of her hands grow clammy. A nervousness had been gathering strength as they'd journeyed through the harem and now reached such a pitch that she felt physically sick. She had known that at some point she must face the Valide Sultan – according to Harry Frome, the first female of the Court – and so of crucial importance to her mission. But she had expected she would have time to prepare herself, time to ensure she looked her very best for a meeting she prayed would throw light on her sister's disappearance. It was evident she was not to be given that time; the Sultan's mother had issued her command and clearly it must be obeyed.

Chapter Six

Within minutes Sevda had delivered her to a suite of rooms lying, it seemed, directly beyond the schoolroom. They had retraced their steps along several narrow passages and reached a corridor as wide as a small river. The Golden Road, as Alice learned later, was the shortcut between the Sultan's apartments and those of his mother that led to the very heart of the palace. She was standing now in what she thought must be the Audience Chamber. Several of the connecting doors were open and she glimpsed the rooms beyond – a drawing room, a bedroom, a bathroom – each space elegantly decorated and filled with costly furnishings. The Valide Sultan's quarters were magnificent.

Persian carpets covered the floor, crystal chandeliers dripped from the ceiling, and gold and silver candle holders lined the walls. There were several divans in the room, covered in heavily embroidered silk. And velvet curtains of the deepest blue hung at a wall of windows that framed a view of the gleaming Bosphorus. Opulence was this room's *leitmotif*.

A woman, clothed from head to toe in black, appeared through an open doorway and walked towards Alice, her hand outstretched. 'Rahîme Perestû sends her apologies, Miss Verinder. She is unable to see you but asks that I welcome you to our home. My name is Fatma Hanim. I am sister to the Valide Sultan.'

'I am delighted to meet you,' Alice stammered. She felt relief and disappointment; it appeared she was not to meet the great woman after all.

'Please, sit.'

Her companion clapped her hands and immediately a servant came forward with a tray of drinks and an array of small gold and crystal bowls brimming with sweetmeats. Alice accepted the glass that was offered and gladly took a sip of grape juice.

For a moment the face opposite softened. 'You must be thirsty. And very tired. It is a long, long journey, is it not?' Her English was excellent, Alice noted, and felt ashamed that she knew not one word of Turkish.

'It is, but I am very glad to be here.'

'And we are pleased to have you.' So far, so polite. 'Your sister, Miss Lydia, was well liked in the palace. We were very sorry to lose her. Particularly the princesses.'

'I am glad to hear she was so well thought of. But…' Fatma Hanim's eyebrows rose and Alice was not brave enough to continue.

'Miss Lydia left a few belongings with us, I believe, and you have come to collect them. Is that so?'

'Yes. I had already planned a trip to this part of the world, and I thought it a good opportunity to visit. I wanted to thank you for your care of Lydia.' It was a sentiment verging on the hypocritical, but gratitude, even false gratitude, might allow her to pose the questions she was desperate to ask.

The woman allowed her mouth the hint of a smile. 'How very kind of you, Miss Verinder. I will convey your good wishes to Sultan Rahîme. Sevda will bring you your sister's possessions, such as they are, before you leave.'

46

It was a clear hint that her stay would not be long. 'It will be a comfort to have them,' she said. 'Then I will be on my way. In a day or two – as soon as I have rested.'

She hoped this might reassure the Valide Sultan when she was told her unwanted guest could soon be forgotten. Perhaps, though, she would not need to be told. Alice had the uneasy feeling that the woman was listening to their conversation behind one of the open doors.

'You must stay a little longer than a few days. My sister would wish it. Constantinople is a city of great variety. It would be a shame if you were not able to discover its beauty.'

This was her chance and she grabbed it. 'The Valide Sultan is most generous. I would love to see more of your wonderful city.'

'That is agreed then. And where do you travel to from Turkey?'

She was welcome, but only up to a point. Fatma Hanim no doubt had instructions to speak plainly. 'I have friends in Syria and have arranged to visit them.' She excused herself the lie.

'That is a beautiful country, too.' Now that she knew Alice's visit to be of short duration, her companion appeared to relax and become more expansive. 'I am sure you will take back to England many happy memories.'

'Have you been to England yourself? And the Valide Sultan?' Alice found the courage to ask.

If she were to discover anything of her sister's disappearance, she had somehow to persuade this woman to speak personally of Sultan Rahîme, though how much contact there had been between her and Lydia she could only guess. It was feasible the Valide Sultan had interested herself in the upbringing of her grandchildren, but had Lydia even met the Sultan's mother?

Or had the woman stayed shrouded in mystery, a silent hand orchestrating events, as she was doing today?

'We are both often in England,' Fatma announced. 'We find the shopping very good. We stay at Claridge's. Do you know it?'

The mention of Claridge's effectively brought the conversation to an end. 'I know it,' Alice tried to sound suitably casual, 'though I have never stayed there myself.' And never would since such luxury was unknown to her family.

'It is a good hotel. And we have friends in Surrey.' She pronounced Surrey with a violent rolling of the *rrs*. 'When we are in England, we spend a weekend with them – they have an estate in the country somewhere. I cannot recall the name…' Country estates were evidently too numerous to remember.

'But you will wish to wash and change,' she said suddenly, and Alice realised she was being dismissed.

There had been no opportunity to ask Rahîme Perestû the questions that troubled her and now she had lost the chance of asking them of the woman's sister. Fatma Hanim clapped her hands and in a blink of an eye a servant had whisked away the tray, and Sevda had appeared at Alice's side ready to usher her from the apartment.

'I am to escort you to your room,' Sevda said. 'But first I must show you where you may walk in the palace.'

There it was again, that sense of enclosure. She was not free to wander at will but must be carefully contained. How had Lydia managed, she wondered? Her sister was not a girl for whom containment would come easily. If she had refused, if she had transgressed the palace's rules… what would have been the consequences?

Deep in thought, she followed Sevda along the wide corridor and back into the maze of narrow passages until they once more stood outside Lydia's bedroom. That was how Alice thought of it; the room would always be her sister's.

Sevda turned to her. 'It is important you know when we pray – five times a day. This is when you will find the palace quiet.'

'I understand.'

'It is also important that you know where you may go. We will visit now the place where you arrived. Please follow me.'

An echo of Lydia's spirit emboldened her to ask, 'Why must I know where to go?'

'Some of the palace is not for women, some is not for men,' the girl answered reasonably.

'I see. But do the two never meet?'

'For Turkish women, no. But for you it is different. I will show you.'

Sevda's speech had subtly changed. Her English now appeared more fluent. Had the girl deliberately hidden her facility with the language? But why on earth would she do that?

They retraced a path to the large chamber where now even more women were gathered, then along several more corridors until they passed the guard room and reached the courtyard where Sevda had first met her.

'Here you may walk. It is called the Square of Justice.' The girl waved an arm across the immense space, dotted with the pavilions and kiosks that Alice had glimpsed earlier.

'The courtyard is so large, I doubt I'd get halfway round. Tell me, did Lydia walk here?'

'Perhaps.'

'You don't know? I thought you were her friend.' Sevda looked down at her feet but said nothing.

'You didn't know her well then?' In the face of the girl's obvious discomfort, Alice was persistent.

'I know her a little.'

'So, you might know where she is?'

'No, Miss Verinder,' she said firmly, and looked away towards the archway that loomed ahead. 'You—'

'Do you know why she left the palace?' Alice interrupted.

The girl's eyes flickered, but she gave a swift shake of the head. 'No,' she said even more firmly. 'You may walk also beyond the Gate of Felicity.' Sevda pointed to an opening in the adjacent wall. It was as though Alice's questions had been rubbed from the slate. 'The archway leads to a third courtyard. You will find the library there – it is the second building you come to. You must not enter the first building. That is the Sultan's Audience Chamber. The Sultan hears petitions there – from Constantinople and from all over the empire. People travel far to speak to him. The empire stretches thousands of miles, you know.' There was pride in her voice.

Alice nodded, thinking that for now she must relinquish her probing, but later she would press Sevda again. She had read a good deal about the empire before her sister left for Turkey. It was why she had chosen to name Syria, an integral part of Ottoman lands, as a place to which she intended to travel.

'I would like to see the Audience Chamber for myself,' she said half mischievously. 'Perhaps one day I might explore there.'

Sevda looked horrified, but then pointed to a smaller opening at one corner of the colonnade. 'Through there is a beautiful garden. You may walk there if you wish, although our garden in the *haremlik* is nicer, I think. It has also a bathing pool.' The girl grinned, looking suddenly much younger. 'Maybe I show you later.'

'That would be kind.'

Alice felt unaccountably cheered by the grin. It suggested that Sevda might after all be a friendly presence. Until now, she had been too confused by the immensity of the palace, the strangeness of its furnishings, the unfamiliarity of its inhabitants, to think much of how she would cope for the rest of her stay. But now she thought of the days ahead and was glad to have Sevda by her side. Friendly presences had so far been thin on the ground.

'Now we must return,' her companion said. 'Naz has unpacked your suitcase and you will wish to change.'

They had moved a little way into the courtyard so that Alice might see the narrow opening that led to the garden, but as they turned to walk back into the harem, a man erupted through the Gate of Felicity and began to march across the open courtyard. He appeared to be making for the main gates of the palace, but was walking so fast, looking down at the ground and muttering to himself, that he almost bumped into them. Sevda clutched Alice's arm and edged her to one side. She noticed the girl was swift to draw her veil tightly across her face.

The man became aware of them then, pulling up sharply and beginning to apologise for his clumsiness, or so Alice imagined, since she could not understand one word of the Turkish. He was mid-sentence when he stopped speaking and stood stone-like, staring at her.

Sevda plucked at Alice's sleeve. 'We must go, Miss Verinder.'

'Verinder?' The man pounced on the name. 'You are Miss Verinder?'

'Yes,' she said uneasily. His whole attitude was too intense and it was scaring her.

'You are family to Lydia?'

She stared back at him, for a moment too shocked to speak. How could this man know Lydia? 'You are acquainted with my sister?'

'Sister? That is right. I saw it immediately.' He peered at her closely and nodded his head. She had long considered the resemblance between herself and her beautiful young sister to be minimal, but it was evident this young man thought differently. 'Lydia spoke of you.'

Sevda had given up tugging at her sleeve and when Alice turned to speak to her, she saw the girl had disappeared back into the *haremlik*.

'I am Ismet Kaya,' he said. 'I am a friend of your sister's.'

Brown eyes held her in a warm gaze. He was a very attractive man, she decided, in his own way as beautiful as Lydia. It was unsurprising they had become friends. His appearance in the palace was another piece of luck, or maybe it was simply that this world was such a small one, she was bound to meet people her sister had known. He had spoken in the present, which surely meant he would have Lydia's direction.

'Do you know her well?' she asked eagerly.

'Once maybe.'

It was an odd response, but Alice was too excited to question it. 'Do you know where she is?'

His face clouded. 'I am sorry, no. I've not seen her for many months. I have not myself been to the palace for a long time. I was dismissed from my work in the library – that is where I first met your sister.'

'I have been told she went away – suddenly.'

'I heard this, too, from gossip in the city. I thought it strange. Do you believe the story?'

She knew nothing of this man, other than his name, and it was possible he was a palace official ready to report her every word. 'It is strange,' she said cautiously. 'It would be quite unlike Lydia to disappear, not without telling her family where she was going.'

There was a long silence and then she decided to take a chance. 'Did she ever mention her plans to you, Mr Kaya?'

'Ismet, please. No, she said nothing. I imagined she would make her life here, at least for a while. But as I say, we have not spoken for over a year.' He fixed her with a clear gaze. 'When I heard she had left so suddenly, I tried to find out what had happened, but there is a very big wall, Miss Verinder.'

'In what way, a wall?'

'Silence. Secrets. Things not spoken of. And I am in no position to find out. Since my dismissal, I have not been welcome at the palace.'

'But you are here today – why is that?' Her question verged on the impolite and she surprised herself in asking it.

Ismet looked around him. A servant passed by and vanished into a far doorway, but otherwise the courtyard was empty. He seemed satisfied. 'I know I can trust you. I remember what Lydia said – that her sister was the most honourable person she knew.'

She felt a sudden emptiness in the pit of her stomach. Did she really want to be party to this man's secrets? She had barely met him.

'I am here on behalf of a friend, but also to talk to whoever is willing, to discover the information I need. We need.'

Who were the mysterious 'we'? Despite her fear of being embroiled in the young man's plans, she needed to know more. 'What information?' she asked aloud.

'There is corruption. Everywhere. And I must help the CUP to root it out.'

She looked at him blankly and he shook his head, as though chastising himself. 'Of course, you will not know this group. It is the Committee of Union and Progress. Here we are known as the Young Turks.'

'I see,' she said, though she remained as much in the dark as ever.

'The group I belong to is outlawed,' he said flatly. 'But not outwitted. There are many small cells in Constantinople, all of them active. We work to gain democracy for the empire. That is not popular.'

'I imagine not. But your being in the palace – is that wise?'

'Not at all wise, but if I am stopped, I have good reason to be here. I have brought clothes for my friend. Yesterday he was detained by the Sultan's secret police, accused of holding street rallies and of being a member of the CUP.'

'But you are a member, too, yet you walk freely.'

'I am suspected, but nothing so far is proved. Only you and my friend in this whole building know of my allegiance.'

It was a sudden and disturbing responsibility. 'I will say nothing,' she was quick to say.

'That is what I believed. You are Lydia's sister.'

Somewhere, deep within Alice, an alarm sounded. Lydia and politics. Surely not again. Not after all the letters, the deplorable interviews, the humiliation of begging for her sister's pardon.

'Did Lydia know that you belong to such a group?' She knew the answer already but clung to the hope that she was wrong.

'But naturally. She was most enthusiastic. For a woman, she had much political knowledge.'

What mess had her sister landed herself in now? 'Out of the frying pan, into the fire' was an overused proverb, but it fitted perfectly. From the corner of her eye, she became aware of two large men in palace uniforms emerging from the archway that Ismet had passed through earlier and beginning to walk towards them.

Ismet had seen them, too. His expression changed and he sounded agitated. 'We cannot speak now. I will contact you. We must talk more.'

She was unsure she wanted to talk more. At this moment she felt angry and resentful. She had worked hard, abased herself, to give Lydia a new start and what had she done but fallen into the exact same trap? It was a script familiar to Alice – her sister seemed destined to repeat her mistakes. There had been a boy in Bournemouth, she remembered, a boy so unsuitable it was hard to imagine Lydia could have befriended anyone worse. The family had been holidaying in the town and Lydia had fallen madly in love and written him compromising letters, whereupon he'd demanded payment for them – or he would take them to her appalled parents. It had been Alice who had confronted him, not to pay him off but to threaten him with the police in a clear case of blackmail. And what had Lydia done? A few days later, she had sought him out again. Not only that but taken with her the few pounds she had saved from her small quarterly allowance. She had felt sorry for him, she said.

Had she felt sorry for Ismet, too? Alice stopped herself mid-thought. She was going too fast, assuming too much. Lydia might not have met with trouble of a political kind. It might simply be that in Ismet Kaya she had recognised a kindred spirit and shared with him her interest.

She turned her back on the two guards, who by now were standing only paces away, and walked back through the harem door. She would retrace the journey she had made with Sevda, fairly certain the men would not follow. Whether she would find her way back to the room, to Lydia's room, was another matter.

'Mees Werinder.'

It was Naz, the slave girl. Naz, at her elbow. From where had she materialised? Had the girl been watching her? She must have been, and a small shiver passed along Alice's spine. But she said nothing and allowed herself to be steered along the narrow passageways to her bedroom. When she turned to thank her guide, the slave lowered her gaze, but not before Alice had seen the greediness in her eyes. Greedy for what, though? She had no idea, but she knew she did not like her.

Chapter Seven

Lydia
Constantinople, August, 1905

After three days in the *haremlik*, Lydia felt bemused. Both by the vastness of the place and by the huge number of women who lived beneath its roof. She had already met a number of them in the space that functioned as a communal living room, and they had been charming and courteous to the stranger in their midst. One, Sevda, had been especially kind. She was a young woman, around Lydia's own age, and fabulously beautiful if you dared look long enough. But like all the harem's female inhabitants, she was covered from head to toe in a way that made discovery difficult. But Lydia could see enough to be fascinated – a graceful bearing, beautiful skin, kohl- edged eyes and fingernails half painted with henna.

She was very different from Naz, the girl appointed to wait on her. Lydia had disliked Naz on sight and nothing since had made her change her mind.

'Do I have to have a servant?' she had asked Sevda after her first day.

'Naz is a slave. She must serve,' Sevda had replied.

'But I hate the whole idea of having a slave, particularly one who doesn't like me.'

'You are wrong, Miss Lydia. Naz does not dislike you. You are her mistress and she must do her job. Her family is very poor and have sold her so she can have a better future.'

'A better future as a slave!' Lydia could not help raising her voice. It was an extraordinary claim.

'She is a slave for nine years only, then she is freed. Her colour is white, so she works for guests and important ladies. And while she is a slave, she has good food, good clothes, and she learns the Koran and to read and write. Also to sew and embroider and, if she has talent, to play a musical instrument or to sing or dance. These are very good skills. When she is freed, she will be found a husband if she wishes. And maybe he will be an important man in the Court. But if she does not marry, she has a pension and will be looked after.'

It was a novel idea: slavery as a means of social advancement rather than a badge of disdain. But it did not mean she liked Naz any more and she certainly didn't trust her. Still, Sevda's words had hit home and she understood she must tolerate the girl. She could not be responsible for destroying another woman's future.

'And what of you, Sevda? Did your parents send you here?'

'I come to the Valide Sultan to train when I am very young. My father was a most brave soldier. He won many medals, so then he became part of the *askeri*. They are the rulers. Now my father is an important man – he is deputy to the Grand Vizier.'

'So, you were born with a silver spoon in your mouth?'

She looked puzzled, but said simply, 'I am most fortunate.'

Every morning, Sevda called at her room, bringing dishes of scented sherbet that she had prepared herself or a small gift of fruit. Lydia was waiting for her now, since today she would be meeting her pupils for the first time and Sevda was to escort her to the schoolroom. She had been there once already under the girl's guidance and taken time to set out her desk in what she hoped looked a professional manner. It hadn't made her feel any less anxious. She was no teacher and she feared that Esma and Rabia would soon discover the fact.

But time was getting on this morning, and she worried she would be late for this very important meeting. Sevda must have been delayed and, unwilling to wait any longer, she set off on her own. She was still confused by the warren of narrow corridors that often led nowhere, but the journey to the schoolroom had seemed a relatively simple one and she was sure she could reach it without guidance.

In this she was wrong. It needed only one false turn and she was in a passageway she did not recognise. Another turning and the narrow corridor was even less recognisable. There was a flight of stairs in front of her. Had Sevda and she walked up a staircase to the schoolroom? She could not recall doing so, but now she wondered if she was mistaken. At the top of the stairs, she found herself in yet another passage. There was some kind of construction halfway along, hanging from the ceiling. She walked up to it to take a look. A cage, it seemed, an iron cage. What on earth was it for? Something told her it was for nothing good.

'Miss Lydia, what are you doing here?' Sevda hurried up to her, slightly out of breath, an anxious expression just discernible beneath the thin silk veil.

Lydia pointed to the cage. 'Whatever is that?'

'Nothing that need worry you.'

'But I want to know.'

'You should not be here, Miss Lydia. These are the concubines' quarters. Allow me to escort you to the schoolroom. I am sorry I arrive late, but the Valide Sultan called me to her. She wishes to see you. But later.'

She took a firm grip of Lydia's arm. 'Come, please.'

'I'll come when you tell me what I am looking at.' All Lydia's stubbornness came into play.

Sevda gave a long sigh, as though she were beginning to recognise the determination of the young woman she must guide.

'It is a punishment cage.'

'For what? For whom?'

'For concubines who do not behave,' Sevda said curtly. 'Now you come with me.'

Lydia stood, her mouth slightly open, unable to move. She was aghast. But Sevda tugged at her arm and eventually she allowed herself to be pulled back along the passage, down the staircase, and along a winding route that led to the schoolroom.

A cage for women who did not behave. It was an image she feared she would never banish from her mind. But as she entered the schoolroom, two bright young faces beamed at her from identical desks and she began to feel a little more cheerful.

'Good morning, Miss Lydia,' they chanted together.

'Good morning, girls.' She was delighted by their welcome and determined to blank from her vision the dreadful sight she had just encountered.

'I will leave you now,' Sevda said, and slipped quietly out of the room.

Lydia had not prepared formal lessons for this first day, unaware of how much English the young girls understood. Her own attempt at mastering even a little Turkish had not been a great success and she feared that communication would be their biggest problem. She had brought with her several children's games which both girls, even the younger, understood surprisingly quickly. All the time the games were in play, she encouraged them to speak whatever English they could and was relieved to find that if she kept her vocabulary simple, she was able to make herself understood. But when she asked them to find a book they could all read together, the one Esma produced was far too difficult, and when the child said she hated the book and did not want to study it, Lydia could only agree.

'Have you no other?' She was cross with herself for not having thought to bring at least a few reading books along with the games.

'Not here,' Rabia said. 'But we go to library.'

She doubted the library would hold any children's books, but at the same time she was curious to view the place Paul Boucher had praised so highly. She had seen nothing of him since she arrived, had not even discovered the whereabouts of his office.

'Our brother had English books,' Esma put in. 'He was in palace school – for boys.'

Somewhere, then, there might be books that were suitable. 'Why don't we take a look?' she suggested. It would at least be a way of introducing the girls to using a library. 'You must show me the way because I have no idea where I am going, and I may end up in the Bosphorus.'

The girls stared at her for a moment. Then when they understood, they fell into a fit of giggles. A joke would go a long way, Lydia could see.

Rabia tucked her hand into Lydia's and Esma led the way. Left, right, along, until they arrived at the doorway to the *haremlik*. Then into the immense courtyard Lydia was beginning to know, but this time continuing a straight path past several of the pavilions to the colonnade that lay directly ahead. Another ornamental gateway to pass through and then they were walking into a large domed room.

'This is Audience Hall,' Esma turned to say.

The room blazed colour, tiled from ceiling to floor in beautifully vivid patterns. Blues, gold, pinks, a rainbow of colour. Lydia almost stopped breathing for a moment. It was as though she had strayed into a tale from the *Arabian Nights*. At one end and raised onto a dais was a velvet upholstered divan.

'Imperial throne,' Esma said, bobbing her head.

For a moment, Lydia wondered if she should be here, if the children should be here, but then shrugged her shoulders and allowed herself to be led out of a doorway and into a third courtyard. How many were there, she wondered, dazed by the splendour of the room they had just left. Another building, a good deal smaller, stood in their path.

'Is this the library, Esma?'

'This is old library, Miss Lydia. New one is behind.'

And so it was. It had been clearly designed to complement the older structure, the buildings being of a similar size and faced with the same pink marble. The new library blended into the existing landscape without in any way challenging it. Clever, Lydia thought. The older Monsieur Boucher was no doubt a man skilled at dealing with imperial pride.

The building was set on a raised base in order, she imagined, to protect its contents from moisture and a flight of steps led to a columned portico. Esma ran ahead and into the library. She followed more slowly with Rabia by her side, but the instant they walked through the door, a young man came forward. Despite the heat, he was formally dressed in a dark three-piece suit with a tight-fitting jacket and waistcoat.

He inclined his head to the two princesses and held his hand out to Lydia. 'You must be Miss Verinder.'

She smiled warmly at him and in response he allowed himself the merest glimmer of a smile. He was not going to be susceptible to her charms, she decided.

'I am Harry Frome, the librarian. I hope you will allow me to show you around.'

'How nice to meet you, Mr Frome,' she said in her most gracious voice. She had not entirely relinquished the idea of beguiling him. 'I would love to take up your offer, though I already know a little about your library. I met Monsieur Boucher on the journey here and he was full of praise. He told me the library was wonderful – and it is.'

She looked around her. The room was built in a series of arches, the walls tiled in blue and green, the colours of the ocean in all its moods. Above the beautifully patterned walls, a three-foot frieze displayed flowers of every type and colour, and on the tiled floor rugs and large cushions gave warmth to the space.

'Monsieur Boucher?' The name appeared to concern him.

'Monsieur Paul Boucher. He has an office in the palace, I believe.'

'Yes, yes, of course.' His shoulders lost their tension. 'You will find our collection of books on the two walls opposite. The bookshelves are built from Anatolian wood – the very best. The third wall contains precious manuscripts. As you see, they are leather-bound to protect them, but for safety we keep them behind wire mesh.'

'Very impressive,' she murmured.

Gratified, he waved a hand towards a niche at the far end of the building. 'Over there you will see the private reading corner of the Sultan.'

Lydia followed his gesture and saw through an arch of pink and grey marble an alcove, each of its sides lined by a velvet covered low divan. It did not look that well used, and she wondered how often the Sultan visited the library. If she were ever to meet him here, would she dare speak? She thought she probably would. She would be keen to talk of the wire cage she had seen in the concubines' quarter this morning.

'If you are looking for anything in particular, I should be able to help you.' Mr Frome had begun to look anxious again.

'We come for books,' the younger child chirped up.

'Well, there are plenty here.' He made an attempt at a smile.

'But not quite what we are seeking,' Lydia was quick to say. 'The girls believe there are children's books that may have found a home here.'

'Not here, surely.' He looked almost scandalised.

'There *is* a large box at the bottom of your cupboard.' Another voice had joined them.

Harry looked surprised. 'The cupboard?'

'The one in your office.'

It was a young man who strode forward. His smooth brown skin and shining brown eyes presented an attractive picture and Lydia instinctively smiled at him.

Harry seemed flustered, but remembering his role as host, made haste to introduce the stranger. 'Miss Verinder, this is Ismet Kaya. Ismet helps from time to time in the library.'

'I am a demon translator, Miss Verinder. I tackle the manuscripts that my friend, Harry, cannot decode, despite his Oxford education.'

She could see that Ismet was completely at ease, but that he made Harry Frome irritable. 'Ismet also attended Oxford, which is something he is prone to forget. But perhaps you could unearth the box you mentioned, Ismet?'

'In two seconds. Come with me, Miss Verinder, children.'

And he led the way through a small door that she had not noticed before and into a tiny cubicle barely large enough to take a desk and the famous cupboard. Like everything in the palace, the cupboard was not just an assemblage of wood, but a work of art, intricately carved and inlaid with tortoiseshell and mother-of-pearl.

Ismet bent down and pulled from the depths of the bottom shelf a large and extremely dusty wooden box. 'Here. Be careful as you open it. It is roughly made and you may catch a splinter.'

The girls seemed not to hear his warning but threw back the lid and were into the contents in a flash. One book after another was hooked out and thrown onto the small rug on which they knelt.

'Wait, wait.' Lydia was laughing at their enthusiasm and Ismet joined in. 'You must choose carefully.'

Harry appeared in the doorway. 'Why not take the box to the schoolroom?' It was a sensible suggestion. 'You can take time then to make your choices. Ismet will carry it to the *haremlik* and Miss Verinder can summon a slave to carry the box from there.'

'An excellent idea,' Lydia said. She was not averse to the chance of speaking to Ismet alone.

Once they were outside, the girls skipped across the court-yard towards the harem and Lydia was able to ask one of the many questions bubbling in her mind. 'Mr Frome said you help in the library. Do you actually work there?'

He looked surprised and she wondered if he was unused to women speaking so directly.

'I receive no money, if that is your meaning.'

'You are doing skilled work. Perhaps you should.' When his eyebrows rose further, she said, 'A labourer is worthy of his hire, is he not?'

'It is possible I receive my reward in other ways.'

She wrinkled her nose. 'That sounds intriguing. Tell me.' She was enjoying this encounter.

'I think I had better not. You would not approve.' His smiling eyes destroyed any severity in the words.

'How do you know that?'

'I don't. Not for sure.' He looked at her for what seemed a long time, trying, she thought, to measure her in some way.

'Miss Verinder. Come quick.' It was Rabia, waving to her in the distance.

She turned to follow her pupils and the action seemed to make up his mind. 'I think perhaps I will tell you,' he said impetuously. 'But only if you are interested in Turkey's future – in democracy. I have a feeling you might be.'

'I am a great advocate for democracy – wherever in the world.' There was an edge of passion to her voice.

'Then you must come to a meeting and learn why I work for nothing.' He put the box down on the gravelled earth and took from his pocket a small notebook and pen. 'Here. This is the address and the date when my comrades and I next meet. Come and discover what my reward might be.'

She wanted very much to go – Ismet's meeting was bound to be interesting – but she felt uncharacteristically wary. Life in the palace, she had already learned, was so hedged with restrictions she was unsure she could escape its clutches. And she lacked any knowledge of the city. To go alone would be difficult.

'If I did come… how might I get there?'

'It will not be a problem for you. You must go through the main gates, then walk to where the carriages wait for hire. As a European visitor, you will not be stopped by the guards. But say nothing to anyone in the palace of where you are going or why.'

She stared at him.

'As a group of friends, we may meet, but if it is known we have a political agenda… it is very important you keep silent, you understand?'

'Yes,' she stammered. It appeared she had fallen into an intrigue. It was a little alarming but very exciting. Of late, her rebelliousness had been tamed, battered by law and family loyalty, but now she need worry about neither. It was sufficient to make up her mind.

'I *will* come, Ismet,' she said. 'You can depend on me.'

Once back in the schoolroom, she helped the children go through the box, book by book, another hour passing before she realised how late it was. By then, the girls had decided on half a dozen volumes they thought they might want to read. It would be a start at least, and depending on how they progressed, she might persuade them to look at others. When their nursemaid came to collect them for lunch, she felt tired enough to decline an escort to the communal meeting room where the women took their meals. Sevda would be there and she had begun to look forward to their talks over the dolmas, börek and pilaf, but today she was too fatigued to eat and preferred to return to her room.

This time she made the journey between schoolroom and bedroom without mishap. The moment she opened the door, she knew something was wrong. The curtains had been drawn against the sun and the room was dim, but she sensed a movement in the shadows. She clutched at the door handle, wondering whether to yell for the harem guards or to flee. She did neither. Instead, she allowed her eyes to grow accustomed to the muted light and could just discern a female figure standing beside her dressing chest. The woman had her head bent and something bright was in her hand.

'Naz?'

The girl spun round and dropped the necklace she had been holding on to the chest top. It landed with a thump that sounded unnaturally loud in the silence.

'What are you doing?'

'Clean, mistress.'

'Cleaning?'

Naz nodded, her eyes never meeting Lydia's.

'I see.' She made a swift decision to accept the puny excuse. 'Thank you for looking after me, Naz, but you have done enough today and you may go now.'

The girl nodded again and Lydia stood back, waiting for her to shuffle out of the door. Cleaning! As though she would believe that from a woman with her hands in a jewellery box that was not hers. But in that instant, she had decided to pretend belief, judging that in this strange world, it was probably best to pick her quarrels. Particularly now, when if she went to the meeting Ismet had spoken of, she might well be walking into trouble.

She crossed to the dressing chest and picked up the pendant Naz had dropped. The girl was definitely a thief as well as untrustworthy. What was the penalty for theft, she wondered, and remembering the iron cage, shuddered. She lay the necklace face up on her palm and stroked the beautiful sapphire, tears pricking at her eyes. It would break her heart to lose her one remembrance of Charlie. Perhaps now that Naz had been discovered in wrongdoing, she would be prudent, but Lydia could not be sure. The pendant obviously had an attraction for the girl. So, what was the answer? She could keep it on her person at all times, but it would be difficult. When she bathed, or even when she slept, where could she leave it for safety? She looked around the room. She must find a place where Naz would not think to look. But where?

Chapter Eight

Alice
Constantinople, February 1907

Alice slept surprisingly well and was amazed when she woke to find that the hands on her silver travelling clock pointed to eight o'clock. She had slept almost twelve hours. Last evening, she had followed Sevda to the huge chamber with the fountain at its centre. The women of the harem ate in this room as well as using it as a place to meet, and for the female slaves it was a place to sleep, too, their bedding stored in the large cupboards that made up a fourth wall. There had been several musical entertainments after the meal and a trio of young women had given a display of folk dancing, but in the main it had been chatter that filled the air.

The younger girls had seemed fascinated with their visitor, uncovering her shoes, marvelling at the hair that she'd swirled into pin rolls, stroking her *crêpe de chine* dress. Its pinched waist and heavily frilled bodice drew prolonged giggles from them. Surely, though, they would have seen a similar dress on Lydia? The sense that her sister had somehow been blanked from the life of the palace overwhelmed her and she had to swallow hard. But perhaps, she comforted herself, Lydia had adopted the baggy trousers and loose-fitting overdress that these girls wore. It would make sense when the weather was hot, as it would have been when her sister first arrived.

Alice had found herself besieged with enquiries about life in England from those women who spoke English, and her life in particular. The questions came thick and fast: are you married? have you children? who is your father? where do you live? But as soon as she mentioned Lydia's name to them, there was again that strange silence she had experienced yesterday in the courtyard with Sevda. Either her sister had offended badly by leaving so suddenly, or there was something else to it – and that was more worrying.

She had withstood the women's attentions for an hour and then apologised profusely, explaining to Sevda, who sat close by, that she was very tired and needed to rest. The women had immediately clustered around her, taking her hand, nodding their heads in perfect understanding. She'd had the impression of sincere good nature and been reassured, thinking she must have misread their silence. But this morning, looking back, she still found it odd that no one had mentioned Lydia, though the girl had lived and worked in the *haremlik* for over a year.

There was a gentle knock on the door, just as she had roused herself sufficiently to swing her legs from the bed. It was Naz, bearing breakfast. A basket of bread with butter and honey sat on one side of the tray, a plate of cheese and a bowl of tomatoes on the other. A tiny vase containing a single winter aconite stood next to the coffee pot.

Alice struggled to her feet. 'Thank you. It looks delicious.'

Naz merely bowed and slipped out of the door. The bright yellow flower was a lovely touch and Alice thought that maybe she had misjudged the girl. She must try to be more generous in the future.

She surprised herself again by eating her way through most of the food and drinking two cups of very hot, strong coffee. But really she shouldn't have been surprised. She had barely eaten on the journey, and last night she had been too fatigued to do more than pick at the meze that had been served. She laid aside the tray and then thought to keep the flower. The aconite would make a bright room even brighter. She would find a place for it on one of the shelves above the carved wooden desk that faced the window.

A couple of small bowls were already there, pretty trinkets made from crystal, and she moved them to one side to make space. But when she tried to position the vase, it refused to sit straight. She wriggled it around, first to the left, then to the right, but it continued to tilt to one side. The shelf seemed to be uneven and she squinted at the wood. Yes, there was a definite bump. A rough square had been cut and the wood replaced, leaving the surface very slightly raised. No wonder the vase had wobbled. She went to replace the bowls – they appeared unaffected by the bump – but then it suddenly became important to arrange the flower where they had been. She would push the offending piece of wood back into place, or at least try, but when she pressed hard, the small cut section came away in her hand, leaving behind a shallow dip. And there was something in the dip. Her fingers wrapped themselves around a small oval object and drew it out. Something blue, deep blue. Sapphire. A pendant. Lydia's pendant!

The shock sent her tottering backwards, the necklace still in her hand. She almost crawled to the nearest chair and then sat for a very long time, staring out of the window at the greenery beyond but seeing nothing. Gradually, she felt her breathing return to normal and gave herself a good scolding. She was behaving like the kind of woman for whom she had no time, a woman who put on die-away airs at the very smallest upset. But this wasn't small, and seeing her sister's pendant had almost robbed her of breath.

She opened her hand and cradled the jewel in her palm. It was beautiful, as beautiful as Lydia herself. But what was it doing hidden in a shelf in the harem of the Topkapi Palace? Had Lydia hidden it, and if so, why? The roughness of the cut wood testified to it being an amateur attempt, the carving done by a kitchen knife, say, rather than any proper tool. It had to have been Lydia. Her sister had secretly hidden the pendant and then walked away.

She would not have left it, Alice was absolutely sure. At least, not willingly. The pendant had been Charlie's last present to her and her sister would never have abandoned it. Unless she had been made to. Alice jumped to her feet and began an agitated walk back and forth across the room. A thought never far from the surface rose now and hit her full strength. The pendant was still in its hiding place because Lydia had had no opportunity to retrieve it before she had been forced to leave – suddenly. And since she had not reappeared either in Turkey or England, or anywhere else as far as Alice knew, what could have happened to her? What could have happened to a girl who had disappeared without a trace? She bit down hard on her lip and drew blood. The appalling prospect she had resolutely pushed from her mind had become more certain: her sister had been kidnapped.

If that was so, who could she tell? Sevda? The other women? But they would not speak of Lydia. Was that why? Her heart did an unpleasant jump. They knew what had happened to her sister but had been sworn to silence. Or they themselves were complicit in her abduction. She could not bear to think it. Who else could she go to? The Valide Sultan, who had refused to meet her? Hardly. If anyone had ordered the kidnap, it would have come from on high and who higher in the harem than

Sultan Rahîme. But why would her sister have suffered such a fate? It made no sense.

Then she remembered Ismet Kaya and Lydia's friendship with him. Was that the answer? Her heart did several more jumps. It was what she had feared since meeting him yesterday. *Please don't let it be*, she pleaded silently. She had to find out, and there was only one person she knew to whom she could talk. She would go to Harry Frome. It was unlikely he could tell her anything substantial, but she had to try. He must know Ismet well since he had worked with him until quite recently. She would go to the library on the pretext of wanting to view the beautiful building of which he had talked, and try as subtly as possible to discover what he knew of his former colleague's political activities and what rumours, if any, he had heard concerning Lydia's support for them.

–

She found the library easily, remembering the directions Sevda had given her, and was soon walking through its green and blue magnificence – or swimming, rather, she thought – it was like being immersed in the waters of an ocean. There was an open door in one of the far arches of the room and she made for it immediately. It was lucky for her that Harry was alone in the little cubicle of an office, head bent and writing industriously.

'Mr Frome?'

He sprung up and tried not to look surprised. 'Miss Verinder, Alice. How good to see you! I hope you are recovered from your journey.'

'Thank you, yes. I slept well.'

'I am told the *haremlik* is a most peaceful place. It has a remarkable quality of silence. But on your first full day in the

73

city, you have come to the library! I am honoured – and very happy to welcome you.'

'I can see the building is as wonderful as you described.' She could be honest about that at least.

He looked genuinely pleased. 'Do feel free to wander. And then perhaps I might show you some of our most precious volumes?'

'I would find that interesting and I will certainly come again, but for the moment I wonder if I might talk to you on another matter?'

He looked disappointed but pulled out a chair for her and sat down opposite, waiting for her to begin. With some hesitation, she told him how she had come to find the pendant. It was still difficult for her to believe she held in her hand a jewel that a short while ago Lydia had held herself.

'May I see what you have found?' he said, as she ended her recital.

She opened her hand and showed him the sapphire. 'It is certainly very beautiful. And valuable, I imagine. Your sister must have hidden it because she feared theft, though she should not have done. Theft is brutally punished, as I'm sure you are aware.'

'That may have been her reason,' Alice agreed, unwilling to discount his theory immediately. 'But why would she leave the pendant behind?'

'Could she have forgotten it, in the rush to be off?'

Alice shook her head. 'No matter how rushed she was, she would not have left it. It was a present from our brother.' She paused for a second. 'The necklace was quite possibly the most precious thing she owned.'

'We can sometimes forget even precious things in the heat of the moment,' he remarked mildly.

'Or if we have no choice.'

His brow wrinkled. 'What do you mean?'

'If she were forced to leave, she would not have had the chance to retrieve it.'

'Forced? How can that be?'

'I don't know, but… I'm coming to believe that she did not go willingly… that she was abducted.' The words exploded into the air between them like small bullets and he leant back sharply, as though pinned to his chair by a physical force.

'Abducted?' He stared at her as though she were a madwoman. She probably was, Alice reflected. But she knew her sister and her sister's love for Charlie.

'Lydia would not have abandoned this pendant, unless she were under duress.' Her voice rang with certainty.

'You know your sister, naturally. But still…' A crisis had appeared on his horizon out of the blue and he was struggling.

'I do know her, and our brother, too. Charlie was the nicest man you could ever meet. He was deeply loved and the pendant was all she had left of him.'

'He has passed away? I am sorry.'

'He fell to his death in a stupid accident. From an Oxford tower. Balliol.'

Her companion grimaced. 'I know the tower. How high it is and how dangerous. In my salad days—'

'But you survived whatever pranks you engaged in,' she interrupted. 'You are alive and you are here, so please aid me.'

'How can I?' He sounded bewildered.

'Lydia met a man here called Ismet Kaya. I believe he worked with you. How well did you know him?'

He was cautious in his reply. 'I was at Oxford at the same time as Ismet, though we were not close acquaintances. Then he worked here in the library with me for a year or so.'

'So, you must know him reasonably well?'

He nodded, but then said in a tight voice, 'It would be best if you forgot Ismet and best that you don't mention his name in the palace.'

'Your warning comes too late. I have already met him.' Harry frowned. 'Yesterday, when Sevda was showing me the layout of the courtyard, he bumped into us. He said he had been to see a friend who is imprisoned here.'

Harry's expression was grim. 'That will be one of his comrades, no doubt. Ismet is suspected of belonging to a group that is banned. That's why he had to leave his work here. A great nuisance to me – his skill at translating ancient manuscripts was invaluable.'

She looked at him hard and he had the grace to apologise.

'I'm sorry, that's neither here nor there. But the group is dangerous and anyone suspected of associating with them is a danger, too.'

'Lydia seems to have known him well,' she insisted. 'They were friends and Ismet wants to speak to me. I believe he may know something of what happened to her. He says not, but it is possible he holds a clue without realising it.'

Harry reached out and took her hand in a strong grip. The surprisingly intimate gesture seemed to testify to the depth of his concern and she softened towards him. 'You should not speak to him, Alice. Anyone who works against the Sultan is in danger and it is best not to know them. It has always been so, but now it is a good deal worse.'

'In what way?'

'There has been dissent of some kind or other in the empire for centuries. There always will be when one country imposes its authority on another, but the political system here has always managed revolution and kept the country stable. That's no longer so. The Ottoman dynasty might have lasted seven centuries, but it's facing its gravest danger.'

'Why have things changed so dramatically?'

'Discord has become more widespread since the Crimean War and far more vocal. The war was sixty years ago, but there was much anger at the time and it is still remembered – the Turkish troops were badly led and many died of disease. The last sultan was worried enough to move from Dolmabahçe palace to Yıldız because Dolmabahçe is located on the shore of the Bosphorus and he feared an attack from the sea. Sultans have always been ready for likely treason, but Abdülhamid is even more ready than his ancestors.'

'I imagine he might have good reason.'

'The situation has become more volatile of late, certainly. There is a group calling themselves the Young Turks. They are Ottoman exiles – students, civil servants, army officers – who wish to replace an absolute monarchy with constitutional government. The group is based in Paris, but there must be small cells all over Turkey, and in Constantinople in particular. Ismet is thought to belong to such a cell. That is why he is dangerous to know.'

His words brought with them nothing but dismay. Lydia was a political creature, a rebel too, and if she had not just known Ismet Kaya but involved herself directly in his activities, the motive for her disappearance was all too obvious.

'Ismet may be dangerous to know, but I must talk to him,' she insisted. 'He is my only chance of discovering Lydia's fate. If he sends me word, I will go to him.'

He leant forward again and recovered her hands. 'I beg you not to. Ismet cannot know any more than we do and by meeting him, you put yourself under suspicion.' He lowered his voice.

'There will be people watching, people who will report your actions to the Valide Sultan and she to the Sultan.'

'And if they know I have met Ismet, what can they do to me?' She had grown a whole tree of courage but had no idea when it had taken root. 'They can expel me from the palace and that would be sad, but they cannot expel me from Turkey.'

'Don't be too sure. You could find yourself shipped out of the country on an early morning train bound for wherever, without any say in the matter.'

'Then so be it. I have to try. I have to talk to him.'

Harry sat back in his chair, his expression unreadable. Then he nodded, the slightest sigh escaping his lips. 'If you must, then I will go with you. You cannot go alone.'

Chapter Nine

Once more back in her room, she sank onto the bed with a small whoosh of gladness. She had not persuaded Harry Frome that her sister had been kidnapped, but she had persuaded him to accompany her to meet Ismet. He was playing the gentleman, of course. He thought her mission foolhardy, but he would not let her go alone. He was probably right. By all accounts, Ismet Kaya was engaged in a perilous game and she had already seen enough of the palace to know that Harry's contention she would be watched was likely to be true. But he would be watched, too, if he came with her, and she felt an immediate misgiving.

Had Harry considered what his offer would mean? His promise had been made when he saw how deeply upset she was, but when he'd had time to think, he might change his mind. By accompanying her to the meeting, he could endanger his job, endanger the work of which he was rightly proud. Her shoulders slumped against the pillow. If he chose to forget his promise, to avoid her, she could hardly blame him, but she would be left then to meet the young man alone at whatever location he chose. And how on earth would she find her way, with not a word of Turkish and no understanding of the city? She gave herself a small shake. She had to believe Harry Frome would help. If he were interrogated, he could plead courtesy to a guest of the palace – Miss Verinder had insisted on the meeting, he could say, and he had merely volunteered to see her safely there and back.

Her earlier joy had disappeared and tension taken its place. Was she courting danger unnecessarily, as Harry claimed? Perhaps, but she had to believe that Ismet could tell her something, even the smallest clue, that would help her find Lydia. Her sister had been kidnapped, she was certain, and while friction could sometimes rub the two of them sore, she knew the fierceness of Lydia's loyalty. Her sister would not have left her family in distress, would not have abandoned a loved necklace, unless taken away by force. Lydia possessed courage and passion, qualities she admired – she was so lacking in them herself – but no matter how strong her courage and passion, her sister would have floundered against the power that resided within these stone walls. Alice had felt it from the moment she had passed through the immense gates. The feeling that she was encircled, that she had been made small and helpless.

She turned herself onto her back, bunching the soft pillows behind her head, and looked up at the bright flowers sprinkled across the ceiling. Out of the corner of her eye, she caught sight of the damaged shelf and clutched the pendant more tightly still. From now on, she would not let it out of her sight. But something about the shelf bothered her and she got up to look. Sure enough, the small square she had replaced in its niche had gone and the shallow dip lay exposed. Someone had taken the chip of wood. Had they known to look for something when they disturbed the shelf? Or was it simply its unsightliness that had drawn their attention? Now the crystal bowls had a new home, the damaged wood was evident.

But suspicion made her go to the dressing chest and open the drawers. One by one, she looked into them and knew without a doubt they had been searched. For what? For the pendant? Was it Naz who fancied this expensive piece of jewellery? The girl had been in the room this morning, clearing the breakfast tray and making the bed. But how would she have known about the necklace?

Alice sat down at the desk to think, then noticed the linen wrapped package. She took it up and peeled back the cloth. Nestled inside were pens and paper, a book, several handkerchiefs and one or two watercolours. They were the items she was to collect – they were Lydia's – but there was too much missing. It was completely out of character that her sister had not left a stitch of clothing. Lydia's mode of travel was amazing to behold, careless and idiosyncratic, and Alice had always been sure to pack for them both since they were children. And after she had finished and gone downstairs, she remembered, Lydia would always sneak into the bedroom and put a small treat into her sister's suitcase to say thank you – a few sweets when she was little, a new handkerchief or stockings as she grew older.

Near to tears, Alice looked at the small collection again. The palace could have sent these few possessions to London; they were hardly worth an expensive trip. Then she picked up each item and held it to her cheek, trying to feel Lydia close, but there was nothing she could hold on to. Her eyes closed at the stab of pain; it was a while before she could think rationally again.

Then an idea began to emerge, vague in form. Lydia had worn the pendant every day in the weeks before she left for Turkey and no doubt had worn it daily once she arrived. People here would be accustomed to the necklace as part of her dress, and if there *had* been foul play – she was more certain of it than ever, otherwise how had Lydia remembered every morsel of clothing and swept all into her valise? It could only be that others had swept for her, those unknown figures behind her abduction. So there *had* been foul play, and whoever had come for her sister must have expected to see the necklace on her person. Or expect to find it somewhere in her room. It was obvious she could not have been wearing the pendant when they arrived, but equally obvious they had not found it when they cleared the room of her possessions. They would realise then that the necklace was missing, and a missing necklace was dangerous.

Dangerous, because if it were found by anyone who knew Lydia well, as it had been by Alice this morning, it would raise an immediate alert. That person would know Lydia would never simply abandon her jewellery and would suspect immediately she had not left willingly. Whoever was behind her sister's disappearance had needed the necklace, had no doubt searched this room many times without success. Until today, when the damaged shelf had suggested the pendant had at last been found but must instantly be recovered for its damning evidence. So, someone had searched again. But why was she imagining a vague 'someone'? It was almost certainly Naz who had searched, on orders from above. The mystery was now a little less mysterious, but a good deal more distressing.

–

It had been four long days since she had met Ismet Kaya in the courtyard, almost a week since she had waved goodbye to Cicely, and she was no further forward. She stayed curled in bed for a long time, then stretched her limbs along the length of the divan in a vain effort to relax. The guilt at having misled those she loved was ever present and made greater by the fact that her deception so far lacked any discernible gain. In a week's time she would have to pack her suitcase for the journey home, since she dared not stay longer than her supposed holiday. She had made no formal arrangement to meet Cissie's friend in Venice, merely writing to Julia that she would contact her when she reached the city, counting on the woman forgetting she had ever been asked to entertain her friend's niece. If not, and she had raised the alarm, the Verinders might already have set in motion the kind of search that would spoil any chance of Alice getting to the truth. She could only cross her fingers that it wasn't so and breathe deeply.

But surely Ismet must contact her soon. She felt foolish to have placed all her hopes in this one man, but what other did she have? She had tried and failed to discover anything of Lydia in the *haremlik*. The women were always eager to talk, but their sociability underwent a subtle change if ever she introduced her sister into the conversation. It was not that they stopped talking, or turned away from her, but that their words no longer sounded their own. It was as though they had learned a speech and any mention of Lydia produced the same few sentences: her sister had been a most pleasant young woman, they had liked her a lot and she had worked hard with Sultan Selim's daughters, who had been very attached to her. It was sad for the girls that she had decided to leave – Sultan Selim had ruled against a new governess after losing one so prematurely, and the children were no longer progressing with their English studies.

Last night, she had made one last attempt to break the wall of silence, and deliberately found a seat next to Sevda. She had encouraged the girl to talk of the things she enjoyed doing most and Sevda had mentioned the fine sewing in which she was engaged.

'I am embroidering a new counterpane for my bed,' she said. 'See here.' And she had jumped up and gone to one of the cupboards that lined the walls of the women's meeting room. When the bedcover was unrolled, Alice stared in amazement.

Its edges were scalloped in deepest red, each embroidered arc exactly the same size and hue. Blue and green tendrils weaved their way around the perimeter and in the centre of the counterpane, half-finished, a profusion of flowers, golden-centred and with petals of deep red and even deeper blue.

'Have you done all this yourself?' The girl nodded. 'It is so very beautiful. What a fine needlewoman you are!'

Sevda smiled proudly. 'I learn for many years, that is why I do not make so many mistakes now. For Miss Lydia, it was more difficult.'

Alice's ears pricked up. At last a mention of Lydia. 'You say my sister sewed? I can hardly believe it.'

Sevda was laughing. 'But yes, I was teaching her. Very slowly. She was making a small purse for me, but all the time her fingers were pricked. She had embroidered the sides and the top, but if she was skilful enough she would embroider my name, too.'

'Why would she do that if you were not a friend?' When the girl stayed silent, Alice repeated, 'I believe you told me you were not particular friends?'

'The purse was practice for Miss Lydia, that is all.'

'Do you have it with you? I would love to see my sister's handiwork. I can't remember a time when she ever held a needle at home.'

A shadow passed across the girl's face. 'Miss Lydia took the embroidery with her. She had not finished it.'

'She could have left the purse and you could have finished it.'

'She wished to do that herself – then she will send it to me.'

'Only if she can.' Alice had decided on recklessness; she had nothing to lose.

Small creases appeared on Sevda's brow. 'But why would she not send it?'

'She might be unable to – if, for instance, she was a prisoner somewhere.'

The women's chatter quietened and the one or two who sat nearby looked at Alice in astonishment. She felt Sevda's figure beside her grow rigid.

'I do not understand,' the girl said.

'It's not difficult, Sevda. My sister disappeared without a word. No one here – apparently – knows where she is. So, it is at least worth considering that Miss Lydia has been kidnapped.'

She kept her voice quietly even, but the chatter had ceased entirely now and Sevda's hand had flown to her mouth. 'You must not think such a dreadful thing. Miss Lydia is safe.'

'Then prove it by telling me where she is.' It was a bold challenge and she hoped desperately it would be met.

The girl's beautiful eyes were suddenly expressionless. 'I do not know. We do not know.' There was the smallest pause and then she asked, 'May I bring you more tea, Miss Alice?'

–

Over days, the unchanging litany with which the women had met her questions stirred an anger in Alice that she hadn't expected. Last night had been her final attempt to break through their secrecy, but she saw now that continuing to search for the truth was pointless and she began to avoid the chamber where the women met. Instead, she walked in the garden. She knew her way to the harem entrance now and followed the route that days ago Sevda had indicated, through the small opening at the corner of the colonnade and into an oasis of green. The garden seemed almost abandoned, a tangle of briars and grey sage, and here and there a Judas tree, soon to burst into flower, its royal purple, she imagined, vivid against the dark green of its surroundings.

Every day she penetrated further into the garden, finding it sheltered, though the weather remained cool and wet. Shrubs of myrtle and boxwood protected her from the breeze that blew from the Bosphorus and two days ago she had crossed a small wooden bridge to find a tumbledown pavilion on the other side of the stream. A kind of summerhouse, she had decided. Rough wood pillars supported a latticed roof and beneath was a floor of brushed earth with a long wooden seat filling the rear. She thought the shelter must have been built many years ago, since a tree had grown its gnarled trunk around the entire length of one of the pillars. It was soothing to sit beneath the lattice and listen to the ripple of water flowing along the blue tiled channels, built by hands long dead.

But today her nerves were wound tight and she stayed only a short time. She was plagued by the thought that she would never hear from Ismet, that he had only been offering comfort when he suggested they talk. That, in fact, he had nothing to say. She had always thought it unlikely he could help, so why was she persisting in the fiction that meeting him mattered? It might be there *was* nothing to find, that she was clutching at scraps. Perhaps she had jumped to conclusions about Lydia's disappearance and her sister was happy and well, but for some unknown reason had decided not to contact her family. Perhaps, as Harry suggested, she had forgotten the pendant in a rush to leave. Lydia was impetuous – Alice knew that to her cost. Her sister could have decided on the spur of the moment to pack and go.

But in her deepest heart, she did not believe it. There was a frightening mystery here and she was the only person who would or could solve it. *I have to act*, she thought. *Now*. She could not pass one more day waiting for a message that might not come.

She had been wrapped in thought while she retraced her path through the garden and was surprised to find herself already back in the third courtyard, standing a few steps from the new library. An idea came fully formed into her mind. It was so obvious she couldn't imagine why she had not thought of it before. If Ismet would not come to her, she would go to Ismet. Harry Frome would know his address – they had been colleagues, perhaps friends at one time – and Harry was close by. She turned towards the beautiful building, its marble pediment silhouetted against the morning's vivid blue sky. A bird was drinking from the fluted bowl of the fountain that sat beneath the building's central arch. He was balanced precariously on the rim of the bowl, while the bright sun flashed a halo of red and gold around his small body, its rays bouncing and refracting off the brilliant tiles.

For a moment she stood watching the bird, thinking what she would say to Harry. He was unlikely to have heard from Ismet when she had not, but he would know where the man lived. She felt awkward, a single woman asking for a young man's address, especially from someone with whom she had little acquaintance and who clearly considered her claim of kidnapping bizarre. She had seen Harry only once since her visit to the library that first day. He had been talking with another European in the harem courtyard, a Frenchman, she thought, from the words that reached her, but he had turned without seeing her. Still, she must do it and do it now.

After the bright sunshine, the shadowed depths of the library rendered her blind for an instant. But then her eyes focused and she saw him standing by an open bookcase with a large leather-bound book in his hands, reverently turning its pages, his brow knitted in concentration. He looked up when he realised he had a visitor and smiled.

'Look at this, Alice. It's a beauty, isn't it?' He almost stroked the illustrated plates of what appeared a luxuriously produced volume. 'It has been given to the library. Paul Boucher – have you met him yet? No? He hinted the other day that we might be lucky, and here it is. Somehow he has prevailed on the owner to donate it.'

'I'm glad. It looks beautiful. Is Monsieur Boucher here?' It would be impossible for her to broach the subject if he were.

'No, no. He has an office in the administrative wing. Why do you ask?'

'I hoped to find you alone. I was wondering if you had heard from Ismet,' she said cautiously.

'I doubt that I would. He left here under a cloud and we haven't spoken since. I take it you have had no message.'

'I have heard nothing.'

She looked crestfallen and he replaced the book on its allotted shelf and came towards her. 'If he promised to contact you, he will. Whatever else Ismet may be, and we have had our differences, I have always found him a man of his word. But you shouldn't put too much hope in what he has to say.'

He was trying to prepare her for disappointment, she knew; it was only what she feared herself.

'I'm sure he is an honourable man, but I cannot wait much longer. I am here in the palace on sufferance – Fatma Hanim made that plain when I first arrived. And in a week, I will have to leave for home. I must do something.' He looked questioningly at her. 'I have decided to go to his house,' she said bluntly.

'Alice, consider! You cannot do that.'

'I think I can. I think I must. You will know where he lives. Please tell me.'

'I know where he *used* to live.' He moved closer and took hold of her shoulders, giving her a gentle shake. 'You must understand how things are. Ismet is under grave suspicion, watched from morning to night. He cannot live at home. If I am not mistaken, he is forced to sleep under a different roof most nights. It would be a bad mistake to visit his old address.'

'You think I will be watched?'

'Precisely. Ismet is an enemy of the empire, and if you go to his house, you will be seen as an enemy, too.'

'Then what can I do?'

'You must wait. Somehow, he will get word to you. He will say where and when it is safe to meet.' The words were soothing, but his expression said clearly that he thought such a dangerous encounter had little point.

'I am sure you're right, but I'm finding it very difficult to wait.'

'Then you need some distraction. A little sightseeing maybe? The city is rich in treasures.'

She sighed. 'It's true there are sights I would love to see. I have been reading my copy of Murray, and I know it's the way the Valide Sultan expects me to use my time here.'

If the woman's spies were keeping watch, a visit to the Hagia Sophia mosque might be just the thing. 'I was wondering if I should visit the Hagia Sophia,' she said aloud. 'Last night I was reading a description. The mosque sounds amazing.'

Harry nodded enthusiastically. 'It most definitely is.'

Chapter Ten

'What is amazing? Do tell me, Harry.'

A woman had appeared on the threshold, silhouetted against the winter sunshine that poured through the open door. She was dark-haired and elegantly dressed in what Alice took to be the latest Parisian fashion. A tall man hovered at her shoulder, bearded and muscular. He wore traditional Turkish clothing and Alice noticed that his right hand constantly fidgeted with the broad leather sash wrapped around his waist. She thought she caught the glint of steel.

'The Hagia Sophia,' Harry answered. 'But I don't believe you know Miss Verinder, Elise.'

The woman looked at her then and Alice thought she detected the ghost of pain in her face, though she might have imagined it. These days she was so tense her mind prompted the most foolish thoughts.

'Alice is Miss Lydia Verinder's sister,' Harry said smoothly.

'*Enchanté*, mademoiselle. How good to meet you.' This was the woman in the letter, the woman Lydia had met on the train. 'Alice, this is Madame Elise Boucher.'

The two women shook hands, but when Elise spoke again, it was only to Harry. 'I am looking for Paul. He is not at home and I cannot find him in the palace. His father wishes to speak to him.'

'I'm afraid he is not here. You have tried his office?'

'Naturally, I went there first.' There was a new agitation in her voice. 'His father wishes to speak to him,' she repeated, 'urgently.'

Harry spread his hands and began to make polite apologies for his unhelpfulness, but Alice had questions that needed an answer and politeness would have to wait. He looked surprised at her lack of grace, but she was determined to seize her chance.

'You must have known my sister well, Madame Boucher. I recall a letter she wrote, telling me how she met you and your husband on the journey here.'

'Yes. We met very briefly. We ate together one evening.' The woman's voice had grown colder.

'But I imagine you met again in the palace. As fellow Europeans?'

'No, no. Our acquaintance was of the slightest.'

'So, you did not know my sister?'

'Only a little, I'm afraid, Miss Verinder.' Everyone, it seemed, knew Lydia only a little – the women in the harem, Harry, now Elise. Only Ismet admitted to knowing her well and he had vanished.

'There was a party, wasn't there?' Alice pursued. She would not let this woman go without a fight. 'I seem to remember Lydia writing of a party.'

Elise threw her hands in the air in a theatrical gesture. 'Yes, of course. How stupid I am! I met Miss Lydia at the Sultan's party a few weeks after we arrived back from Paris. But there were so many people – always, this is so – that we spoke only a few words together.'

She looked into the woman's eyes and was certain she saw falsehood there. Sadness, too; a strange combination. Elise Boucher had met Lydia on more than two occasions, Alice would stake her life on it. The woman had known her sister

91

a great deal better than she admitted, so why was she refusing to speak of her? It was the same refusal Alice had encountered in the *haremlik*. Everyone, this woman included, knew more than they would say.

An awkward silence developed and it was Harry Frome who stepped into the breach. 'We were about to set off for the mosque, Elise. So far Miss Verinder has not had the opportunity to see much of Constantinople. Would you care to join us?'

'Oh no!' She turned her head slightly, glancing at the man who stood silently at her shoulder. 'I must go home. Monsieur Boucher is waiting and I have to find my husband.'

Something worries her, Alice thought, *and worries her badly*.

'We can walk there,' Harry said. 'The mosque isn't far. But if you would rather, I can find a carriage.'

'No, let's walk. I need the exercise and it's a beautiful day.'

It was still winter, but today the sky was an extraordinary blue and the sun, though low, shone bravely. The buildings, the alleys, the stalls selling food and clothes and household goods, had acquired a new brightness. Alice felt her spirits lift as she began a walk through the city streets with Harry by her side. For some reason she had donned the blue-grey dress this morning and was glad she had. It was her most flattering outfit and she wanted to look her best – she felt quite shocked at how much she wanted it. Her search for Lydia was going nowhere, yet she felt happier at this moment than at any time since arriving. She was glad of Harry's company, that was it. Very glad.

He was her countryman, but it was more than that. She felt drawn to him as a friend, someone on whom she thought she might depend. That was a comfort. From the beginning she had not been at ease in the harem and with each day that passed felt increasingly insecure. It was an enclosed and secret world of which she had no part, a world where lips were closed and eyes watched. It had not needed Harry to tell her that her every movement would be noted and reported on. She had felt it in the curious glances of the women, in the lowered eyes of the servants, in the way Naz was everywhere she was not expected.

'You find the city interesting?' he asked.

She had been looking around her while they walked, drinking in the sights and sounds that earlier had fascinated her on the short drive from Sirkeci station.

'More than interesting. It's like nowhere I could have imagined.'

'Very true. And no matter how long you live here, it never fails to interest. There is always something to intrigue you. Let's cross the road. There's a shop I think you might like.'

He led the way across the street to a narrow window. 'They sell illuminations – in sheet form or as book covers. It's an old Ottoman art. Past Sultans would commission manuscripts or painted miniatures from illumination artists. Always non-figurative, of course. See here.' He took her by the hand and pointed to one side of the window. 'Those are sheets for albums.'

'The colours are astonishing. And the calligraphy, too.'

'It's hugely skilful.' Then, realising he still held her hand, he quickly let it drop.

'Are they religious texts?' she asked, to cover their moment of embarrassment.

'Some are, but there are also verses from poems or proverbs. Sometimes the drawings can be purely decorative. The sheets are gathered into albums which in themselves are works of art. We have some prize examples in the library.'

'I must see them when I visit you next.' *When I'm not so preoccupied*, she thought, *if that time ever comes.*

'I sent my father an album for his last birthday. Nothing as grand as these – they are far too expensive – but I knew he would love it, and he did.'

The mention of his father emboldened her to ask, 'Is he a librarian, too?'

His smile did not quite reach his eyes. 'He is a very well-read man, but not a librarian. *His* father owned a bookshop, though.'

There was a slight edge to his voice, but he said nothing more until they had recrossed the street. 'My father should have taken over the business when my grandfather died, but it turned out the shop was mired in debt and had to be sold. My father thought it his duty to pay the money owed and has spent his life doing so.'

She was genuinely upset. She had thought her own story an unhappy one: the Verinders had seen their income decimated when Theo's practice began to fail, and she had been forced into all kinds of unpleasant household economies to allow the family to continue in the Pimlico house. But this was far worse.

She wasn't sure if she should say more, aware that his voice had taken on the prickliness she'd heard on the train. 'He has managed to meet those debts, I hope?' she said eventually.

'Just about. Since he became bailiff, things have been a little easier, but for years he was forced to work as a labourer. It was all that was open to him. My family is from the country – Wiltshire – and there's little employment other than farm work.'

When she said nothing, he added, 'The pay is low and the conditions very harsh. Over the years my father's health has been badly affected, my mother's, too, but there has been no money to pay for the medical treatment she needs.'

'I'm so sorry.'

'I am sorry, too. Year after year, my parents went without, to pay off the debt and to scrimp and save to send me to Oxford.'

She felt the anger in the words, the deep hurt they contained, and walked on in silence until he said rousingly, 'Still, we must forget the past. This is far too lovely a day to be gloomy. How would you like a sunshade?'

They were passing a stall crammed with line after line of gaily patterned sunshades. She laughed but refused his offer. 'The sun is gentle enough and my complexion shouldn't suffer. I imagine, though, it's different in summer. It must get very hot.'

'Stifling,' he agreed. 'This is by far the most pleasant season for a visit. Was it your family who suggested you come now?'

She said nothing and felt him looking hard at her. Her face coloured a guilty pink. 'They don't know you are here, do they?' he said quietly.

She shook her head. 'How did you guess?'

'I had my suspicions when we first met. You told me this was your first trip abroad – do you remember? I thought it an odd choice. And even odder that you were travelling alone.'

'You didn't say anything.'

'It would have been discourteous if I had. We had only just met and I couldn't pry. But I know you a little better now, and I think your family would be horrified to learn their daughter was alone in a country as far distant as Turkey.' His tone was mild, but she nevertheless felt his reproach and looked away, studying the rough earth pavement intently.

'They would, I'm afraid. It's why I must leave very soon – before they send out a search party.'

'Are they likely to? Where do they think you are?'

'They believe I am on holiday. In Venice.'

It sounded ridiculous to her ears, and evidently to Harry's, too. He suddenly laughed out loud, causing some of the stall holders to turn their heads. 'At least both cities have art in common. San Marco was inspired by Hagia Sophia, in fact, so not a million miles from each other. Before you get home, you will have to read up on Venice, then you can talk vaguely about its wonders. Hopefully, neither of your parents know it well.'

'They don't. I never thought it before, but it's a blessing that Southwold is as far as they've ever travelled.'

She felt Harry's hand beneath her elbow as they reached the end of the street. He steered her around the corner and into another long, narrow thoroughfare. 'Down here and then to the right. We're almost there.'

There were few stalls lining this new street and with no temptation to dawdle, they picked up their pace. 'You know, you're a brave woman,' he said suddenly.

She looked up at him, perplexed. 'I've never been brave.' She found the idea laughable. It was her sister who was brave, Lydia who challenged the world to live as she wanted.

'You *are* brave, Alice.' He was insistent. 'I think it must have cost you much to board that train and travel thousands of miles alone. Let alone coping with life at Topkapi once you arrived.'

'I haven't found it easy,' she confessed. 'But whenever my spirits flag, I think of Lydia. She would be bold and I have to be bold for her.'

He kept a silence and she knew he was thinking her efforts misplaced. But it made no difference. She would keep on digging until the moment she was forced to board the Orient Express for home.

A man with a heavy tray looped around his shoulders came out of nowhere and barred their passage. She had been thinking of Lydia and was startled, but Harry calmly waved him away.

'He is a souvenir seller, that's all. We are close to the mosque, so beware. From now on they will multiply.'

She took a firm hold of her handbag and he noticed her gesture. 'Don't worry. Your bag will be safe. Thieving hardly exists here. I meant only that the sellers will bother you to buy until you are driven near to madness.'

'Then I had better buy something.'

'It's best not. If you do, you will be besieged even further.'

At the crossroads, they took the left turn Harry had mentioned, and there was the mosque spread out before them. They stood for a moment taking in its fabulous size and beauty. Four tall minarets, one at each corner of the building, reached heavenwards, nurturing and protecting what seemed an exuberance of domes. An enormous central dome sat above everything, its magnificent sphere made of pure gold.

Alice was transfixed. 'The Ottomans must be astonishingly rich – all that gold.'

'They should be. They've been at the centre of trade between East and West for six centuries. The empire controlled the spice route that Marco Polo used and it's given them unbelievable wealth.'

Chapter Eleven

Together they walked into the echoing silence of the mosque. She turned in a slow circle, craning her neck to see the two floors of marbled columns supporting tiers of gloriously tiled arches, and above them, rows of arched windows higher still. The stupendous central dome towered above all. Myriad pendants hung low from the ceiling, a thousand candles bringing splashes of light to the dark interior.

'I've read there are mosaics here. Byzantine, I think Murray said.'

'There are, but most of them have been whitewashed, I'm afraid. A restoration was done last century and only a few were left uncovered.'

'Whitewashed because they are Christian images?'

'Just that. This was Emperor Justinian's first Christian cathedral, but after the Ottomans conquered Constantinople, it became a mosque. The bells, the altar – many other relics – were destroyed. There's little of the original church left.'

'How sad. But this is truly beautiful.'

She had walked towards a point where two of the mosque walls met and was standing in front of a series of figured gold arches, one within another. The semicircular niche was guarded by two colossal candlesticks and radiated gold.

'This is the *mihrab*,' Harry said, catching her up. 'It stands where the altar used to be, and points towards Mecca, the direction Muslims must face when praying.'

'With you as my guide, I have no need of Murray. I should have left him in my room!'

He took her teasing in good part. 'Then let me bore you even more. The mosaics you mentioned are in the upper gallery. As I said, most have been cleaned and re-covered, but it might be interesting for you to see what's still exposed.'

They climbed the stairs together and were halfway to the next floor before she realised she was holding his hand. Somehow, she hadn't noticed. It had seemed a perfectly natural thing to do. She gazed across at him and he gazed back, his grey eyes warm. His lips curved into a smile and she found herself tracing their shape in her mind, wondering what they must feel like to touch. She pulled herself back with a jerk. What on earth was she thinking? And what would her mother, her aunt, even her sister, think?

No, not her sister. Lydia had chided her so often for her lack of spontaneity, for the drab dutifulness she wore along with the spinster garb. *Any day something magical could happen*, she had said. *You must be ready to grab it when it comes. And dress for it, too. That horrible grey skirt you keep wearing – give it to Dora. No, don't give it to Dora. She deserves to be happy. Just put in the dustbin and buy something new. Something red and velvet. That would be perfect.* Lydia had been the one to give her the fine lace petticoat she still wore. *At least the grey skirt won't have it all its own way*, she'd said.

They stood together now in front of a wall of white.

'Beneath the whitewash there's an image of Christ and John the Baptist.' Harry let go of her hand and moved towards the painting. 'If you look closely, you can just make out the deep blue of Christ's cloak beneath the wash. There.' His finger traced the shape of a cloak. 'And on His right, John's wild hair, though that's very difficult to see.'

99

She moved to stand beside him, peering closely. 'I can see enough to know the mosaic is beautiful. How sad it should be covered. Are there no Christians left in Turkey?'

'There's still a small population, mostly Greek or Armenian, but a good many fewer than for many centuries.'

'I imagine they have been persecuted?'

He shook his head. 'Not so. Migration is mainly to blame. But numbers have also dwindled because countries who were once part of the empire have managed to secede and taken their citizens back. But persecution, no. Christians have been treated as second class citizens, it's true – they pay more tax for instance – but they have always had the freedom to practise their religion and set up their own schools. They're subjects, but not subject to the Muslim faith or Muslim law. Other faiths are tolerated, too. The Jews, for instance, have been allowed to worship as they wish. Interestingly, the worst treated are members of Muslim sects like the Druze and the Alawites.'

She had lost the last part of his speech in her elation at what she had found.

'Look, Harry. This one has been left exposed,' she said excitedly.

She had stopped in front of a mosaic of the Virgin Mary. A good deal of the mosaic had been lost but the lovely Byzantine image of the Virgin was intact. Half a gold halo hovered above the calm face, its long straight nose and shadowed eyes reaching out to Alice and tugging at her heart.

She stood looking at the image for a long time. Something in the expression bothered her. She had seen that look elsewhere and very recently.

'She was sad,' she said suddenly. 'Elise Boucher. She was sad, but worried, too. Worried at meeting me.'

'You must be mistaken.' He sounded uncomfortable.

'I don't think so. It had to do with her father-in-law, I'm sure – or her husband.'

'Not her husband,' Harry said quickly. 'Paul Boucher is the mildest of men.'

'And his father isn't?'

'Valentin Boucher has... definite ideas.'

'Such as?

'I think it was Monsieur Boucher who arranged the marriage. Paul married his cousin. I have the impression it was required of him.'

'You are saying it was not a love match?' It was a revelation that she could speak so directly to a man about marriage and love.

'I think the marriage is happy enough,' he was swift to say, 'but there have been no children and Monsieur Valentin clearly expected them.'

'He wants to be a grandfather?' This did not accord with her image of him, but it might explain Elise Boucher's unhappy eyes.

'I think it more that he wants an heir.'

'I see,' she said thoughtfully. 'I can understand that. He has built a wonderful legacy and of course he will want his family to inherit.'

'Hmm.' Harry's lack of enthusiasm surprised her.

When they were making their way back down the stairs to the floor of the mosque, she asked, 'How do you find working for the older Monsieur Boucher?'

'I see very little of him. He has allowed me to get on with my job and I have never personally experienced any trouble.' Again, Harry's response was cool and it troubled her. What kind of man was this Valentin Boucher?

'There's a "but" in there somewhere,' she prompted.

He stopped walking and stood looking down at her. His grey eyes had lost some of their warmth. 'Let's just say, there have been rumours.'

'Can you tell me what?'

'There have been stories, but nothing has been proved against the man.'

'Is that because the stories are false, or because he's made sure there's no evidence of his wrongdoing?'

'I have no idea if they are false or true. A lot may emanate from Ismet and his friends. They have an interest in blackening every important member of the Court.' He judged his former colleague harshly, she thought.

'Truth to tell,' he continued, 'I don't get involved in situations I've no power to change. My focus is my work – that's what I'm paid for.'

She felt reprimanded, but when he spoke again his tone was conciliatory. 'I hope I didn't bore you back there.'

They had walked out into the street and stood blinking in the bright sunshine. 'No, Harry, you didn't. It's been a wonderful visit. And a perfect distraction, just as you said.'

She had barely finished speaking when a loud rumbling filled the air. Then a belch of steam, a triumphant whistle, and a bull-shaped engine chugged past them on the railway track running nearby. They stood and watched as the train made its way into Sirkeci station.

'The Orient Express,' he remarked. 'Which reminds me – when is it exactly you must return home?'

She was about to answer when a figure emerged from the crowd, a man running at speed and scattering people to the right and left as he scythed a path through. He missed hitting Alice by a whisker, but then she felt a sharp pain cut across her hand. She grabbed hold of her bag and clung to it tightly.

The man tugged but then must have thought better of it and sped off again, the crowd closing behind him and hiding him from view. Alice looked down and saw the handle of her bag had been severed in two and there was blood dripping through her fingers.

'Alice, are you all right?' Harry staggered to his feet. He had been pushed to the ground by the onslaught.

Her face had turned a sickly white and she swayed towards him. He grabbed her with both hands and held her in a firm grasp until a little colour had returned to her cheeks. Then he delved into his pocket and brought out a white square of handkerchief.

'No, it's all right,' she protested, as she saw what he meant to do.

'It's far from all right. Give me your hand.' Meekly she held out the bloodstained fingers and with the greatest care he bound them with the piece of linen.

'I must find you a seat and then I'll fetch a carriage.'

'Please, no. I can walk. We are not far from the palace gates.'

'Are you sure?'

She nodded. 'But, how are you?'

'I'm fine. It was a tumble, that's all.' He bent down and flicked the dust from the hem of her dress. 'I am so sorry you should have suffered such an attack.'

'I thought you said theft hardly exists here.' She was still trembling, still clutching the bag hard against her heart.

'It doesn't – usually. I've never known such a thing.'

That said it all. Usually. But this wasn't usual, wasn't a usual theft. She had been targeted quite deliberately, her handbag the object. The man had cut the handle, meaning to scoop the bag as it fell. Her injury had been accidental and her hold too tight for him to steal it. But what did she carry that was so precious he would risk draconian punishment? A guidebook, a notepad, a pen, and a little money. In other words, nothing worth such a risk. But what *might* have been there? She put her good hand to her chest and felt the pendant, invisible beneath the woollen dress, but lying securely against her skin. The certainty was dawning on her that the theft had been another attempt to regain the pendant. She wondered how many more there would be.

'You're sure you are well enough to walk?' Harry was looking concerned.

'I'll be fine. I'm just a little shaken.'

'We should get back to Topkapi immediately. Whatever else, you will be safe there.'

She was not as certain as he, but for the moment she would say nothing. She needed time to consider. Perhaps she had jumped too quickly to the conclusion that someone in authority at the palace had decided the jewel was dangerous evidence and needed to be retrieved. The Sultan's mother had been in her mind as chief suspect. But what if these attempts to regain the necklace had nothing to do with the palace, and its inhabitants had as little knowledge as she of Lydia's fate? It would explain their infuriating silence.

Today another name had come into the frame. Whatever Harry said, Alice was certain that Elise Boucher had been desperately unwilling to talk to her. Why would she have been so reluctant if there was no connection between the Bouchers and Lydia? It was clear the woman was scared of something or somebody. Valentin Boucher? Harry had hinted that Boucher senior was suspected of bad deeds, but no proof had been found. Were the attempts on the pendant another instance of his ability to make evidence disappear? The thought made her feel a great deal worse.

They passed beneath the dispassionate gaze of the soldiers stationed at the palace gates and made for the harem entrance. The walk across the two courtyards was a fair distance and, though she leaned on Harry's arm, her legs felt weak and insubstantial. The sooner she reached her room, the better.

But when he said goodbye, she found a new strength. He reached out and took both her hands in his, cradling the damaged fingers. 'I have enjoyed our afternoon. It's one I'll remember with pleasure, though I am sorry it has ended badly. But I count myself fortunate to have had such a delightful companion.'

The look in his eyes seemed to say a good deal more than his words and brought a flush to her cheeks. But that was her heart talking. Her head told her differently. She was reading too much into a single glance and it was unlikely he admired her greatly. He was an attractive man, though there was an edge to him that could make her feel uncomfortable. But she liked the way his hair curled at his nape despite all his efforts to tame it, the way his eyes could change in an instant from cool grey to smoky warmth. What had she to offer in return? Her personality was modest and in no way compensated for a mundane appearance. Harry Frome was simply being a gentleman, as he had from the moment they'd first met.

'I'll say goodbye then,' she said, a little nervously. 'Until Ismet contacts me.'

He gave a small sigh. 'Until Ismet contacts you.'

Chapter Twelve

Lydia
Constantinople, August 1905

As soon as lessons finished for the day, Lydia left for the meeting. She was pleased with the way her pupils had progressed these last two weeks – they had read an English fairy tale that morning, *Cinderella*, almost without help, and this afternoon had been busy writing their own stories. Their obvious enjoyment in creating something of their own had given her an idea; there had been a performance in the harem last night of a traditional shadow play and her pupils had sat entranced as the single puppet master had voiced all the characters, accompanied only by a tambourine. She had promised that if one of the tales they had written today showed particular flair, she would turn it into a play for them to perform in front of their elders. The announcement had caused a flurry of excitement and the girls had tumbled out of the schoolroom door chattering loudly.

Ismet had told her the meeting would start around six o'clock in the evening, but she chose to leave the palace early to allay any suspicion of where she was going. Over the last few weeks, the guards had seen her leave for the small local market and return with a handful of small parcels. Now, bag in hand, a covering of lace on her head, she passed through the gates with a smile for the bored sentries, hoping they would assume she was once more engaged in shopping.

She intended only to while away the time in wandering the market stalls; there was always something of interest to see or discover. Huge displays of spices – chilli, saffron, muskot, red pepper, green pepper – and shops filled with brightly coloured ceramic bowls, large brass cooking pots and beautifully woven cushions and carpets and kilims. And every type of fruit and vegetable, many of which Lydia had never seen before. She bought a small bag of figs – her favourite – and beneath the covering veil surreptitiously nibbled at them as she walked.

As soon as her watch showed half past five, she left the market by a side street and was lucky to find a carriage almost immediately. When she gave the driver the address Ismet had written, a doubtful expression crossed his face, but he still accepted the fare. It was well he did. The carriage wended a path through a maze of old lanes and narrow streets where houses on either side met almost overhead. For a while the sun was blotted from view and the alleyways turned into tunnels. She would never have found her way on foot and was relieved when they emerged into the light again and drew up outside a boarded building, its bright paint now a faded orange. An old man was seated outside the house opposite and the beguiling smell of sun-cured tobacco filled the air.

She was still too early, but after she paid off the driver, she walked to the door and gave it a tentative push. Ismet had arrived early, too, and rushed forward to take her hands in a warm clasp.

'Miss Lydia. You came.' She smiled at him. He really was a most handsome man. 'And you are dressed for the occasion, I see. Thank you.'

She had worn a pair of silk trousers and a long gauze over-dress which, despite its flowing nature, showed her figure to advantage. She had thought the ensemble fetching and a good deal cooler than the heavy cotton dresses she had brought to Turkey, with their yards of bunched and swagged material. She could get used to dressing in this fashion.

'I would not know you from a Turkish lady,' Ismet was saying. 'Except for those blue, blue eyes. They are quite beautiful.'

She flushed slightly, surprised at the lavish compliment, and he hastened to find her a seat. 'This will be all right?' Anxiously, he held aloft a large cushion. 'I am afraid there are no chairs.'

She plumped herself down and gave him another warm smile. She was still enjoying the compliment. 'This is perfect, thank you.'

The door opened and several other young men trooped in, none of them, she noted, as attractive as Ismet. When they caught sight of her, they came to a halt, glaring at him and waiting, Lydia presumed, for an explanation.

'This is Miss Lydia Verinder.' He spoke in English and she was sure that was deliberate. 'Miss Verinder is governess to Sultan Selim's daughters and she is here to help us.'

She wasn't sure about that. She had been interested by Ismet's talk of democracy and had come to the meeting to learn more, but she could not remember ever promising help. In any case, how could a woman aid any kind of political cause here? Female protest was fiercely punished in London and would be doubly so in Constantinople.

'This is Abdullah.' Ismet began to introduce his fellows. 'And these are Malik, Tahir and Cezmi.' The men bowed to her unsmilingly.

'And this' – the door had banged opened and a much younger man, not much older than a boy, Lydia thought, burst into the room – 'is Latif.'

Unlike his elders, Latif appeared pleased to welcome a woman to their meeting and looked at her in open admiration. Abdullah muttered something in Turkish and Ismet reluctantly translated. 'My companions are concerned that as you work for the palace...' He paused, deciding, it seemed, how best to phrase the unpalatable. 'You might not be an objective observer.'

'A spy?' she challenged. Despite Ismet's diplomacy, she was furious at the suggestion. 'You may tell your companions that I am no spy. I am well acquainted with political protest myself. I have a personal stake in wanting to see all men and women free – and equal – in whatever society they live.'

Ismet did not bother to translate. It seemed the men had understood her message, or at least its tone, and there were no further mutterings. But she had not yet finished. 'I am surprised to find that I am the only woman present.' Ismet spoke a few words in Turkish; she hoped whatever he'd said had discomfited them.

'No good for women,' Latif said.

'As I am sure you understand,' Ismet added swiftly.

'But you are fighting for a woman's right to vote, I hope, as much as a man's?'

There was an uncomfortable shuffling among the men. 'Naturally,' her friend said smoothly. 'We cannot pick and choose to whom we give freedom.'

She had to be content, though she was unsure of their commitment. She had only to think how long women in Britain had waited, were still waiting, for the right to decide their own future, to know that Latif was right in what he said.

It *was* no good for women. *Small steps*, she told herself, *small steps*.

Ismet unwound himself from his cushion and spread his arms wide. She took this as a signal that the meeting was about to begin. He looked directly at her as he spoke. 'First, I must explain to you, Lydia, what our group wishes to achieve.'

When she nodded, he launched himself into a plea that was as reasoned as it was impassioned. 'You may not know, but there have been many attempts to reform the monarchy in this country. Since Abdülhamid assumed leadership of the empire, though, he has reversed every liberal reform gained in earlier years. He is known in Europe as the "red sultan" for his brutality in Armenia, but here in Turkey his Grand Vizier controls an elaborate system of spies to ensure that power is monopolised and opposition crushed.'

He paused and drank from the small glass beside him. Lydia looked across at the seated men, their backs straight, their figures attentive. They had not moved a muscle while Ismet spoke and were waiting for him to continue.

'He claims it is to hold the empire together, but since he has been Sultan, Ottoman power has declined. The more autocratic his rule, the more the empire will shrink. Those countries he still controls believe his rule is as bad as any by a foreign power. They want to be heard; they want freedom. Yet so far, he has refused all demands for political change. We want to force him to restore the constitution and call together a parliament. A new constitution will free citizens. It will modernise the state, make it stronger, and allow it to hold its own against outside powers.'

'And how do you think to do that when the Sultan is obviously minded to refuse such a proposal?' It seemed to Lydia a hopeless case.

'Corruption – or rather proof of corruption. If we can show that his ministers and cronies are corrupt to the point of treason, he will want to be on the right side of history. He will dismiss them and call a parliament.'

She was doubtful. She knew little of how the Court functioned, but it seemed too idealistic to be true. Autocratic rulers were most often corrupt themselves, so why would they be persuaded to dismiss their underlings for the very same crime? But she said none of this and asked instead, 'How can you prove corruption?'

'Ah!' Ismet smiled. 'This is where we believe that you can help.'

She was astonished. 'You think I can help root out corruption in the Court?' The suggestion was so ridiculous she could have laughed aloud.

But Ismet was not deterred. 'The most corrupt man in Constantinople, the man with the ear of the Sultan, the one who has persuaded him against every democratic proposal, is Valentin Boucher.'

'The man who built the library?' She had almost forgotten her initial enthusiasm for this powerful person. *Scatterbrained*, she chided herself, but the journey on the Orient Express now seemed a distant memory and her new life in the *haremlik* far more important.

'Yes, the man who built the library and who has made many other charitable bequests. But all of them false.' The other men nodded in unison.

'He is nothing but a thief,' Ismet continued. 'He thieves from the people and thieves from the Sultan, too. The library is a sop, a pat on the head, to say to the ruler that all is well. But it is not.'

'How do you know such things about him?'

'It's not difficult. Talk to those with whom he has had dealings and over time a pattern emerges. He trades his influence. He demands payment in exchange for awarding contracts. Or he uses his power to allow people to bypass laws or ignore rules, and that can cause distress and sometimes danger to those it affects. He will even take money from a person who wishes to harm another and make sure that the harm is done.'

'He sounds a most unpleasant man.'

'He is more than unpleasant, Lydia. He is venal through and through. When he is given government money to spend, which happens often since the Sultan has faith in him, he allocates the grant to those who offer him most money for it, so that only part of those funds go where they should. And sometimes he takes *all* the money and no one sees a lira of it.'

'Embezzlement?' she asked faintly.

'Exactly. This is how the man has grown so rich he can almost outspend the Sultan himself.'

'And you want to expose his corruption. But does the Sultan not realise the true nature of the man? Surely he must.'

'Of course, he knows Boucher grows rich, but he chooses to close his eyes. It suits him to do so. We want the proof that will mean he can no longer do that.'

She was still doubtful. If the Court operated on a system of bribes, she could not imagine any proof, no matter how incendiary, making a difference.

'There is also the matter,' Ismet said slowly, 'of murder.'

She gasped. 'You are saying this Valentin Boucher has killed a man?'

'Many men. Not with his own hands, naturally. They must never be dirtied. But on his orders, certainly. The men who have died are those who refused to pay him bribes or threatened to take him to court. It is still possible to have your grievance aired here before a judge. Those poor men never got that far. They lie in unmarked graves, but their names are known to us. If we can find the evidence of Boucher's dealings with them and connect it to their deaths, the Sultan – even such a one as Abdülhamid – cannot remain indifferent.'

It was a lot to take in and Lydia sat silent for some time while the men talked among themselves.

'You said your group is part of a movement called the Young Turks,' she said at last, speaking directly to Ismet. 'Is this what the movement is seeking to do, to root out corruption wherever it is found?'

'Our members have greater aims even than that. Abdullah will tell you. He was part of a conspiracy against Abdülhamid twenty years ago, initiated by the students at the Imperial Medical Academy. Abdullah is a doctor and escaped. But when the plot was uncovered, many of its leaders fled abroad. They live in exile, in Paris, and have formed the CUP to prepare the groundwork for revolution. Though maybe revolution is the wrong word. I should say they are working towards orderly reform.'

'Have you thought of joining them in Paris?' It was a seemingly innocent question, but she thought it a test of how committed he and his fellows were.

'Our hearts are with them, but our lives are here. We are a small group, as you can see. One of many other groups in the city, but we are pledged to do our best to bring about a change of government. And this is one way we can help. Boucher means butcher, you know, and so he is. A dark, evil force from a foreign land that distorts the Court and all its doings. What action we can take is small when compared with the grand sweep of history. That will be for our exiled comrades when they take power. But it is our contribution – the only one we can make. So, will you help?'

Ismet's plan sounded vague and unlikely to succeed. It also sounded dangerous, but she could see their hearts were set on it. While Ismet had been talking, their faces had worn an almost ecstatic expression, though most had understood little of what he said. It was the sentiment that swayed them – they wanted this plan to succeed. Badly. But how on earth did it involve her?

Ismet, as always, had the answer. 'You have met Paul Boucher?'

'Yes.' She was mystified. 'I met him on the journey here, but I haven't seen him since.'

'Then perhaps it is time you reacquainted yourself with him.'

'And perhaps it isn't. I have been at the palace for two weeks and have not sought his company. Neither has he sought mine.' And she had been grateful for it. Paul had been a pleasant enough man, but hardly the most interesting. 'You are saying you wish me to march into his office, wherever it is, and announce that I have ignored him for weeks but now I want to know him better?'

'You can explain to him. It is very simple. Since you arrived at the palace, you have been very busy – settling into the *haremlik*, meeting your two young pupils and beginning to work with them. It has all taken time, but now you would like to say hello again.' There was a pause. 'You did not like the man?' For the first time, Ismet sounded unsure.

'I liked him well enough. But I cannot see what that has to do with anything.'

'He is his father's son. Get close to him and you will get close to Valentin Boucher.'

She shuddered inwardly. When she'd first heard Boucher's name mentioned on the train, she had been intrigued. He had been spoken of as a powerful man and she had wanted to know more. Now that she knew more, realised what his power amounted to, she had no wish to get closer. She heard Alice's voice in her head warning her not to take risks, but Alice need not worry. This was one risk she would not take. She was settled at the palace, she loved the little girls she was teaching, and though life could be dull it was all the better for being so. She had told these men she was passionate for the freedom she believed democracy could bring, and so she was. A belief in equality was the very seal of her identity. But she could not involve herself in a mission likely to be so perilous.

The men were looking at her, studying her expression closely, their faces blazing with a hope that made her feel small. These were people wholly committed to their goal, dismissing any risk to themselves, refusing to weigh the value of freedom. But it was no wonder they felt so strongly, she argued with herself, it was their country. Their country and not hers. Had she not fought the fight in her own land? And look how that had turned out.

The silence that filled the room had become stifling. Ismet was looking concerned and his comrades had begun to fidget. It seemed the despised woman was needed after all. She would be the hero of the hour – if she agreed to their proposition. Did she really want that?

'And if I meet Paul again?' she asked, not knowing where exactly those words had come from.

'You *will* meet him. In a few days there will be a big party at the palace. The Sultan and his mother are to invite the most important Europeans in the city. Paul Boucher will be there with his wife and his father. You will be invited, too. You can meet him quite naturally, speak to him, flatter him… and, well, you are a beautiful woman.'

Her shock must have registered on her face because Ismet was quick to say, 'It only needs Monsieur Paul to feel happy and wish to be friends with you. Then you can visit him in his office, and maybe there will come a time when you call on him and he is not there. But the papers are. You understand?'

'You want me to look for documents?'

'Two or three at most. They may be in the form of a ledger or a small file. They will be dated for one month in particular, and they will incriminate his father without doubt.'

'And what is in them that is so important?'

'If you agree to do this, I will tell you. Are you willing, Lydia?'

Chapter Thirteen

The invitation Ismet had spoken of arrived two days later. It was written on gold embossed card – what else, she thought – and was a summons to meet her fellow Europeans at a gathering to be held in the Audience Chamber. The Sultan would be delighted to welcome her, the card said. She should have felt excitement. The very word 'sultan' evoked an exoticism that had thrilled her when she first knew she was to live at Topkapi, but since hearing the great man traduced by Ismet, she no longer felt the same way. Yet to meet him would be an experience – so far, she had caught not a whisper of his presence – and the splendour of the Audience Chamber was an enticement. She had been astounded at its magnificence that first day she'd met the children and together snatched a few forbidden minutes there.

The evening, too, meant she would at last see the woman who ruled the harem. The promised interview with the Valide Sultan had never materialised, and she was unsure why. There might be an innocent reason: the Sultan's mother could be waiting to see how well the new addition to the harem performed her duties before deciding to meet her. But more worryingly, the woman who controlled so much, who knew the comings and goings of everyone in the palace, could have chosen deliberately to remain in the shadows. A giant spider manipulating a web in which Lydia could be caught.

Ismet's expectations still weighed heavily on her, too, certainly enough to dim her excitement. She could meet Paul Boucher happily enough, even though she was sure he would bore her. She could exchange small talk with him, trivial pleasantries, with a smile on her lips and a glass in her hand, but to set out deliberately to dazzle, to play the flirt, no doubt in front of his wife, was something at which she baulked. Ismet had been swift to quash that notion, but in essence befriending Paul Boucher would mean behaving exactly like that, if she were ever to get close enough to discover those fabled papers.

She had little idea what the documents were about, and unless she gave Ismet the promise he sought, she would remain unknowing. It was annoying and tantalising at the same time. She had not refused outright to help, assuring him she would think it over, but she knew she must not be tempted. Would she even have considered the proposal, she asked herself sternly, if the man requesting her help had been less attractive? It was a wild exploit, for even if she gained access to Paul's office when he was absent, how was she to find those few pieces of paper in what was probably a room crammed with files? On the train, she remembered, Paul had boasted of the hours he worked: writing letters, fielding requests, organising projects. How likely was it she would find the documents she needed sitting on the top of his desk, ripe for the plucking?

And if by some fluke she came across the file Ismet sought, how quickly would the trail lead back to her as the thief? If the documents were so incriminating, the Bouchers would keep silent on their disappearance, but they would be looking for them, she was sure. More to the point, they would be looking for the person who had taken them. From what she had learned so far of the older Boucher, he would show no mercy to anyone who had wronged him. Why would she walk into such a maelstrom? She was happy teaching the princesses, and if she felt hemmed in and restless, at times unbearably so, did that mean she should risk such obvious danger, even for a cause close to her heart?

Her mind was still circling aimlessly when Sevda knocked at her door. The girl's face was bright with pleasure and draped across her arm were several outfits.

'These are for you, Miss Lydia. They have given by the Sultan's favourite concubine. You have your own pretty dresses, I know, but maybe tomorrow evening you would like to be Turkish?' She spread two pairs of trousers and two long tunics across the bed. 'They are made from the finest silk – see, they weigh almost nothing – and they are decorated by the most skilful embroiderer we have in the harem.'

'What a clever idea, Sevda. In this weather Turkish clothes are far more suitable than my own. And much more beautiful! I would love to wear one of these outfits.'

She picked up a pair of baggy trousers and held them against her figure. 'These are a wonderful colour.' Shades of sapphire glistened beneath the lamplight.

Sevda was nodding her head. 'Yes, the blue is right. So lovely with your eyes and it matches your necklace, too. Here, let me dress you.'

'Shouldn't a slave be doing that?' Lydia asked naughtily.

'You joke me, Miss Lydia. But I will be your slave this evening.'

It took a minute only to don trousers and tunic, and to complete the effect Sevda fastened a pleated girdle around Lydia's narrow waist and secured it with a brooch made from aquamarines, then hung an embroidered handkerchief from the girdle.

She looked at Lydia with satisfaction. 'Beautiful… but wait, you must see.' She slipped out of the door and reappeared carrying a full-length mirror. 'See for yourself how well you look.'

She did look well, Lydia thought. She knew herself attractive to the eye, she had known that since childhood, but the person looking back at her now, dressed in whispering silk the colour of the deepest ocean, was almost ethereal.

'As an English lady,' Sevda said, 'you do not need to wear a head covering. I will braid your hair for you – you have such lovely hair – and find flowers or maybe even some precious stones to decorate the braids.'

'If I am to be Turkish for the evening, I must wear some kind of veil.' For a moment, Lydia was swept away by this vision, but then a stray thought had her looking anxious. 'I'm wondering… will not the Sultan and his mother find it peculiar that I am dressed in this fashion? I am concerned they may feel insulted.'

'Insulted? Of course not. They will be honoured you have adopted our mode of dress.'

'I have to admit I'm excited to be meeting them. Sultan Rahîme is a mystery and I've never seen even a whisker of the Sultan.'

'The Sultan does not intrude upon the women in their quarters,' Sevda said primly.

'But surely he can. Or why be a sultan?'

'Naturally he has the right to enter the apartments of his wives and concubines at all times – every Turkish husband has that right. But men rarely allow themselves to do so.'

Lydia's raised eyebrows spoke scepticism and Sevda was roused to say, 'The word "harem" means sacred or forbidden. It is a place of retreat. If a man wishes to enter, he will send a slave to announce his approach. There is respect for women, Miss Lydia. Maybe not the same respect as you know, but still…'

She wondered if she dared ask the question on the tip of her tongue. After the incident of the iron cage, she had kept clear of any mention of concubines. But the question would not be still and she blurted out, 'If men do not go to the women's quarters, then how…?'

Sevda flushed a bright pink. 'There is always one room of a harem kept for the master, and a slave will summon the consort he desires. Here the Sultan must tell the chief eunuch, who tells the chief housekeeper to inform the lady that she is wanted. He must follow custom – he must visit his concubines in strict order.'

'How very civilised.'

Sevda nodded, unaware of Lydia's irony. 'So, you have decided on the blue?'

'I have. I will be absolutely delighted to wear it. But will you be happy with the other?'

The girl looked startled. 'That is not for me. I will not be there. I do not leave the *haremlik*. The gathering is only for foreign guests.'

Lydia pulled a face. 'How miserable. I shall miss you.' And she gave the girl a big hug. 'It won't be half the fun if you're not with me, telling me what to do and what not to do, or feeding me snippets about the people I meet.'

Sevda disentangled herself from the embrace. 'The next day you will tell me all – we will speak over our sewing. Your embroidery is not going well, I think.' She looked across at the purse Lydia had left abandoned on the chest top.

'I'm sorry, Sevda. I have three thumbs and twenty fingers. I need your help.'

'And you will have it, but now I must go.'

At the open door, she looked back, seeming to hesitate.

'You are a lovely woman, Miss Lydia,' she said. 'Please to be careful.'

Then she was out of the room before Lydia had a chance to ask her what she meant.

–

The harem was always rigorously clean, not a speck of dirt or dust permitted. No one entered a room with the slippers they used outside and the floors were scrubbed every day or covered in carpets or pale straw matting that the slaves beat regularly. The women were as clean as their surroundings, with baths on every corridor and soft embroidered towels in which to wrap themselves. Lydia had a special favourite close to her bedroom and had become accustomed to a long leisurely soak every day, as all the women seemed to do. Tonight was no exception. She had finished classes early so that she could spend an hour or two enjoying her preparations for what would be the most intriguing evening of her time at Topkapi. By seven o'clock she was bathed, perfumed and wearing the stunning tunic and trousers Sevda had brought her. The girl had come earlier, wrapping and braiding her hair in gauze and jewels before disappearing back into the depths of the harem.

By now, Lydia knew that she must wait to be summoned and sure enough Naz appeared on her threshold within the hour. She had not caught the girl in any further wrongdoing and been of a mind to dismiss the earlier incident. But then she saw Naz's eyes go to the pendant she wore and thought that perhaps she should not lower her guard. And there was that remark of Sevda's which had never been explained. Why should the young woman have warned her to be careful? Did that mean someone knew of her meeting with Ismet? Naz was the one she suspected of spying. If the girl had learned of the meeting, who would she have reported to? The Valide Sultan? If so, Sevda and quite possibly the whole of the harem could have learned of her visit to the orange boarded building.

But she was getting ahead of herself. She would find some pleasure in this evening, she decided, and when Naz handed her over at the harem door to one of the palace's black servants, she forgot her fears and made ready to enjoy this unusual party. The man escorted her across the courtyard, through the huge arch to the entrance of the Audience Chamber where he ceremonially handed her over to one of the white eunuchs who guarded the door. He welcomed her with such an elaborate bow that she had to stop herself from smiling. The bow would not have gone amiss in an English royal palace. It was part of that strange mix she had found at the Court, a mix of modernity and tradition. Everywhere hints of Western influence: in the manners, the furniture, the customs. Yet the traditional survived, did more than survive in fact, blazing brightly in every corner of the palace.

Tonight, though, the West had triumphed. The room was softly lit by hanging lamps, their brass glinting a golden fire across the tiled geometry of pinks and mauves and blues. Above, the enormous dome in the shape of a gigantic flower opened anew amid trellised leaves. But chairs had been placed around each of the walls and now sat stiffly to attention. Several of the older guests, she noticed, had already taken advantage of them. Divans were magical and cushions beautiful, but they required a flexibility that could be lost. And the musicians at one end of the room, a trio of violins, played what Lydia thought might be a Debussy composition. She felt disappointed that traditional Turkish music was absent. She enjoyed hearing the women play – the harem boasted a number of gifted musicians – and had come to love the beat of the küdum and the lyricism of the tanbur.

She gave a quick glance around the room, searching the gathering for Paul Boucher. Ismet had been so certain the man would be here, but that might not be the case. If he were not, she was absolved from any duty to find him. She was not even sure she would recognise him. In the end, she had not taken up Elise's invitation on the train to join the Bouchers for dinner each evening. True, she had been eager to discover where power lay in the palace, but there had been something unsettling about the relationship of husband and wife and she had decided to eat alone, deliberately delaying her meal to avoid meeting them again.

Another quick glance, but she could see no one who resembled the man on the train and before she realised, she was being handed on to a second official, this time a giant of a man wearing a long crimson robe densely patterned in gold thread. A very superior official, she thought, and made haste to follow when he gestured to her. She imagined he was about to introduce her to one or other of the small groups of well dressed guests, immaculate in the latest Paris fashions. Instead he strode past the chattering crowd, clearing a path as though he were Moses parting the waves, and allowing Lydia a solitary passage – to the throne? A figure rose slowly from a chair that winked rubies. No Sultan, though, but a woman who stared hard at her and then extended a hand.

'Miss Lydia Verinder? I am glad to meet you at last.'

Chapter Fourteen

The woman who had stepped forward was older than she expected, which was stupid of her since the Sultan himself must be in his sixties. But the advancing years had dealt kindly with his mother. Dark hair framed a smooth complexion and the black eyes were hawkish. At her throat she wore a diamond pendant the size of a small fist and her dress was equally sumptuous: a long silk robe, olive green in colour and draped to perfection, with a figured lace ruff that acted as a collar and caressed cheeks that were only slightly lined. A headdress of gold filigree interwoven with emeralds added inches to the woman's height, though she had little need of them. Lydia thought she had never seen such a majestic and frankly terrifying woman.

'I am Rahîme Perestû.' The voice was clear and direct, used to command.

Lydia said nothing. There was something about this woman that rendered one tongue-tied. And not just her obvious wealth. It was her entire bearing. Here was a person who plainly would brook no dissent.

'I fear my son is not here to meet you,' the Valide Sultan said. 'He is a little indisposed.'

'I hope it is not a serious illness,' she murmured.

'No, no.' His mother appeared unimpressed with the Sultan's sufferings. 'You will meet him later.'

She seemed very definite, Lydia thought, but then the woman exuded certainty, radiating a forcefulness that was not to be challenged.

'Please…' The Valide Sultan waved her hand at a nearby chair. 'Sit with me a while.'

Lydia took a seat opposite the imperial throne, feeling decidedly uncomfortable. The clinking of glasses and the buzz of chatter had declined noticeably and she became aware of eyes fixed on her, at least a dozen people in the crowd showing an intense interest in this encounter. Was it that Sultan Rahîme did not normally concern herself with a new governess or was it that Lydia herself had become an object of scrutiny? An object of danger? If her visit to Ismet and his comrades were common knowledge – and it was more than possible since she had a shrewd idea how swiftly gossip must carry in the palace – someone in this crowd could be marking her out as suspicious, a person to be watched and, if necessary, dealt with. She tried to subdue the thought.

The Valide Sultan inclined her head towards her and she was jerked back to attention. 'You seem to have settled into our Turkish way of life, Miss Verinder.' The black eyes looked pointedly at Lydia's dress.

'These clothes are not mine, unfortunately. I have the loan of them for this evening. They are beautiful, are they not?'

The older woman did not answer but shifted a little irritably in her seat. 'I believe you enjoy shopping. Perhaps you should do a little more. But tell me, how are my granddaughters progressing?'

That at least she could talk about honestly. 'The princesses are doing very well. They are beginning to read English for themselves – sometimes quite difficult words – and they are most imaginative. They have composed several small stories of their own.'

Sultan Rahîme gave a gracious nod. 'Not too imaginative, I hope. But it does not surprise me they are doing well. Selim is their father. He is a clever man, but too retiring to be of use.' Another son had been dismissed. There was a pause while the woman looked at her consideringly. 'And how else, Miss Verinder, have you been filling your time?'

Lydia felt a brush of fear. The woman's earlier reference to shopping might be innocent, but she suspected not. *She knows*, Lydia thought, *and not only that I have been to the market. She knows I have met Ismet and wants to discover just what my connection with him might be.*

'I spend a good deal of time planning lessons. We are studying a simple history of Turkey at the moment.' She was thinking on her feet and was pleased with her riposte. 'And then I read and walk in the garden. And, of course, I talk – with the women in the harem. I have found them excellent companions. The whole life of the palace interests me greatly.'

'I am glad you are happy with us. It has concerned me that you might feel a trifle enclosed. You are very young and I know how Englishwomen live.'

'There are different kinds of enclosure, are there not? In many ways, women are no freer in England than they are here.'

The Valide Sultan folded her hands in her lap, her expression calm, but she had not yet relinquished her interrogation. 'So, you do not miss the world beyond the palace gates?'

'A little perhaps. But I have been to the market several times.' Lydia grasped the nettle with both hands. 'And will be going again very soon – to buy presents for my family. I would like to send each of them a small gift. And perhaps I shall buy clothes, as you suggest.'

There was a pursing of lips, then the woman actually smiled. The black eyes lightened. It was as though she had admitted defeat. For the moment.

'I will wish you luck in your purchases,' she said. Then flicked her hand very slightly.

The crimson-robed official, who all this time had been hovering to one side, stepped forward and offered his arm, leading Lydia back into the throng. A few seconds later, they had regained the centre of the crowd and stopped beside a portly middle-aged man. At the sight of a palace uniform, the man's companion melted away and Lydia found herself introduced to Herr Meyer.

'I am very pleased to meet you, Miss Verinder.' He pumped her hand several times. She was completely at sea, not understanding why she should be speaking to this man. He had small beads of perspiration on his upper lip, she noticed, although the room was not unduly warm.

'I am the principal of the Stamboul Academy.' She looked at him blankly. 'It is in the city,' he explained, 'in one of the poorest areas. We take children who are not as fortunate as those you teach.'

Now she saw the connection. They were to talk education and her heart sank. Would she be asked for the qualifications she did not possess? But Herr Meyer was not interested in qualifications, or in Lydia. He was interested in his academy.

'The Foundation built the school five years ago,' he went on. 'It has been the most brilliant project. The Sultan himself provided the funds, but it was only through Monsieur Boucher that it truly came to fruition. He is a wonderful person.'

She felt more confused than ever. Did this little round man not know the truth about Boucher? Or was it that Ismet was prejudiced and had come to believe falsehoods? Might it be that the elder Boucher really was a wonderful person?

Herr Meyer talked on and with every enthusiastic sentence, he seemed to widen another inch, so that Lydia felt quite dwarfed by his expanse. 'This year we have enrolled one hundred and fifty pupils, you know.' She raised her eyebrows, hoping this would show an interest she was far from feeling. 'The school was much needed,' he droned on. 'Christians in the empire have traditionally been better educated and in recent years have pulled far ahead of the Muslim majority. It has led to much resentment, as you can imagine. But the Stamboul Academy provides free schooling for Muslim children. They have their religious education, of course, but they also learn important subjects – English, for example. English is the key to succeeding in the modern world, I believe. If they do well, it will allow them to make a good living for themselves and to play an important role in the country's economy.' A smile of satisfaction filled his plump face.

'And do you teach Muslim girls as well as boys, Herr Meyer?'

He blinked in surprise. 'That is not possible, Miss Verinder. Girls are educated always at home.'

'Educated in English, too? Otherwise how are *they* to play a part in the economy?' She was being deliberately provoking, but the man had begun to grate on her.

'Naturally, what goes on within the home is unknown to me. I suspect not. Your young pupils are blessed in that respect. How do you find teaching them?'

She was about to answer when she felt the crowd shift to one side and a voice she recognised sounded in her ear. 'Miss Verinder, Lydia. How good to see you here. And looking every bit a Turkish lady!'

129

Herr Meyer acknowledged the newcomer with a neat Germanic bow and promptly disappeared. Paul Boucher stood smiling a few feet away. He wore a well-cut dark suit, his hair newly barbered and his shoes highly polished. He had dressed for the occasion, she thought.

'I see that you were honoured.' His tone was light, but she sensed there was concern, too.

'I was?'

'Not everyone is invited to speak to the Valide Sultan, and if they are, it is often not for some years. You have managed it in weeks.'

That tickled her and she gave a soft laugh. 'I think she was worried I might be teaching her grandchildren all the wrong things.'

'Such as?'

'Fairy tales and fantasies. Sultan Rahîme seems to prefer hard facts.'

'She would. But fairy tales have their place.'

'I think so, too.'

'Is that why you have adopted Turkish dress? Allow me to say that it suits you admirably.'

'I could say the same of you – French tailoring suits *you* admirably.'

She was flirting and did not like herself for it, but since her encounter with the Valide Sultan, Ismet's plea had been gaining strength. She was sure the woman had been threatening her, albeit very subtly, and a new resolve was beginning to form in Lydia's heart.

'I do my best,' Paul said, entering happily into the flirtation. 'But you have no drink.'

He took her by the arm and steered her towards a slave burdened by two massive silver trays of food and drink. 'This is one of the few occasions alcohol is permitted. We should make the most of it.'

She sipped at the glass of champagne he handed her. 'Are you still very busy?' she asked innocently. 'Or have you found time to walk out of your office door?'

'I have been very busy since I saw you last. But you didn't come to visit me, as you promised.'

'I am so sorry. I did mean to, but the time has flown by. It has taken a while for me to settle the girls into a routine.' She was remembering Ismet's words.

'Of course, but now you are a little freer, I hope?'

A gaggle of people making for the nearest drinks tray bumped into them. Paul put a protective arm around her and she allowed herself to sink against him. Even before the champagne, the last of her caution had seeped away, its disappearance fuelled by anger that she was being spied on and probably lied to. The urge to fight, to strike out, stirred in her once more.

Her deep blue eyes fixed Paul Boucher with a teasing glance. 'I have a few hours every day that remain unfilled.'

'Then you must let me fill them. I would love to show you the palace beyond the harem.'

'I doubt there is much I am allowed to see.' She hoped her dimples were doing their job.

'If you are with me, that won't be so.' He stood gazing at her, then seemed to give himself a shake and said, 'Come to my office as soon as you can. I promise to drop everything and take you on a magical tour.'

'Thank you—' she began to say.

'There you are!' A large man, a bear of a man, had walked up to them and clapped his hand on Paul's shoulder, ignoring her presence.

'This is my father, Miss Verinder,' Paul said awkwardly, trying to free himself of the hand.

'Verinder? The governess? Yes, I have heard your name.'

Lydia felt her breath catch in her throat. How had Valentin Boucher heard of her? As part of the news that trickled daily through the palace? Or from the Valide Sultan, who suspected her? Or from Naz, the girl who spied on her?

He thrust his hand forward and beamed. 'I am delighted to meet you, Miss Verinder.' His tone was oddly courteous and she blinked in surprise. The man had seemed uncouth, but it appeared he could charm when he needed to. 'How are you finding Topkapi, my dear? Quite a change for you, I imagine.'

'Yes, Monsieur Boucher. Quite a change, but one I am enjoying immensely.'

'So I see.' He wagged a finger towards her embroidered tunic. 'You are Turkish tonight.'

'For this evening only, though I find these clothes a good deal more comfortable than those I brought with me.'

For a minute, he seemed at a loss, but then said in a hearty voice, 'You look most taking, doesn't she, Elise?' This to the woman who had silently joined them.

'Yes, indeed.' Elise Boucher gave her father-in-law a small, anxious glance.

'Taking or not,' he said, 'it is better not to go completely Turkish. What do you say, Paul?'

His son looked uncertain. 'Miss Verinder has perfect taste. I am sure she will judge well. Allow me to fetch another glass. And one for you, too, Elise.'

Elise shook her head and her father-in-law glanced down at her, his eyes disturbingly intent. 'Elise will drink fruit juice,' he said. 'But you two ladies, you have met already, I believe.'

Yes, indeed,' Elise repeated.

She is frightened of him, Lydia thought, and remembered the way the woman had half shut her eyes at the mention of his name over the dinner table. She was as closed now as she had been on the train; what little friendship she had shown then had vanished entirely.

Lydia refused the offer of a drink and made her excuses. She was tired, she said, and she had an early start in the morning. The princesses kept her on her toes and she needed to be fully awake to be a good teacher. Murmuring her goodbyes, she made her way to the door, hoping not to be accosted by any other guest. She had arrived less than an hour ago, but the evening had been a distinct strain, testing her ability to pretend, to present an untroubled façade to a suspicious world. She thought of herself as a strong woman, but there were times when her courage failed and the vulnerability she hated showed its face. At this moment, she needed solitude.

The servant who had escorted her to the Audience Chamber was waiting patiently at the door and in silence they walked together to the *haremlik*.

Once in her room, she undressed slowly, draping the beautiful clothes, item by item, on the chair by the window. The ensemble had turned out to be the talking point of the evening. She was not completely certain of the impression the clothes had made on the Valide Sultan, but on Valentin Boucher she had no doubt. They had allowed him to warn her not to embrace Turkey too closely, and she did not think he'd had only clothes in mind. As for the Sultan's mother, Lydia imagined the baggy trousers and long tunic said more than the new governess had settled into Turkish life. It had been a similar outfit, plainer but essentially the same, that she had worn to the meeting with Ismet. She was sure now that she had been followed that evening, but somehow her final destination had remained unknown. In hiring a carriage and taking a circuitous route to the meeting place, she had shaken off whoever had been spying on her.

For both Boucher and Sultan Rahîme, the clothes had signalled a threat and in turn they had used them to threaten her back. Lydia did not respond well to threats. Her creeping sense of outrage at their attempts to intimidate her was sufficient to force a decision that had been building throughout the evening. The truth was there to discover and a brave, free-thinking woman could discover it. If finding the documents Ismet had spoken of was the key, she would try. She would contact him tomorrow and he would tell her just what she must look for.

Chapter Fifteen

Alice
Constantinople, March 1907

Her ticket for the Orient Express lay open on the desk and caught her eye every time she passed. Harry had told her to wait and Ismet's message would come, but her time in Constantinople had almost expired. She had been gone from home for nearly a fortnight but had sent no word to her family. She must do it this morning: by now Cissie would be anxious and weary of the constant reassurance her sister and brother-in-law must need. There was a British civilian post office at the Sublime Porte, in the Ottoman offices of the Grand Vizier, and Alice knew she must send a telegram to say she was well and would be home soon. It was not a task she welcomed – the telegram was clear evidence she had lied about her destination.

The visit to the post office and a hastily scribbled message took only an hour of her time, and as soon as she returned to the palace she made her way through the small opening beside the Gate of Felicity and into the garden. Lately, the sun had been gaining in warmth and she had begun to spend hours in the green oasis she had come to love. This morning she decided to ignore the summerhouse where she usually sat and take a longer walk. There was much she had yet to explore, and to her delight she discovered that by taking a smaller path to the right of the main walk, she arrived beneath her own bedroom window. She had left it open to catch the early sun and now peered over its sill, interested to see the room from a different angle. She was on tiptoe when she heard a rustle in the leaves behind her and turned, half fearful of who or what might be there. Then something small and compact sailed by her ear and arrowed its way through the open window, landing on the bedroom floor with a thump.

She turned quickly and caught the stirring of bushes and the flash of a shoe. Something had arrived in her room that was clearly secret. It would have taken too long to retrace her steps through the garden and she was anxious that someone might visit her bedroom meantime and see what was meant only for her, so without a second thought she gathered the long skirt of her dress in one hand and, holding on to the window frame, hauled herself onto the sill. Then she dropped down to the bedroom floor, scooping into her pocket what appeared to be a stone, just as the door opened.

It was Naz. Of course, it had to be Naz. 'I heard noise, mistress.'

'I knocked a book to the ground,' Alice was quick to say.

The slave looked around the room, her sharp eyes searching for the errant volume. 'Don't worry, Naz. I have packed it away. I keep all the books I brought with me in my suitcase – they are too precious to risk leaving behind. But thank you for your help.'

She hoped the girl would realise she was dismissed. Naz went, but not at all willingly. It was plain that if she'd under-stood what Alice had said, she had not believed a word.

Alice thrust her hand into her pocket. She could feel there was paper wrapped around the stone. A message at last! It was burning a hole through the stiff linen of her skirt, but she sat down in the chair by the window and counted off the minutes before she dared look at it – one minute, two. It must be safe now. Naz would not be coming back. She unravelled the sheet of paper from its anchor and threw the stone back into the garden. Then she spread out the crumpled page.

Miss Alice, it began.

Forgive me for the delay. I have had troubles since I saw you. Commissaires called the next day, and from that time I have always to move. I fear they will find me soon and I will be arrested. But tonight I am safe. You will be safe. This is my address – there followed a Turkish street name – *Come to the market tonight, to a shop called Tugra, and Latif will guide you to the house I stay in. He is the boy who delivers this message and you can trust him. Come whatever time you can.*

Your friend and your sister's friend, Ismet.

Who were the commissaires? Police, in all probability. It was as Harry Frome had predicted and Ismet was being forced from hiding place to hiding place. She hoped he was right when he promised it was safe to visit. Safe for him as well as for her, and for Harry, too. She must go to Harry as soon as possible, but Naz was on the watch and she would need a good reason to visit. Reading material, more of it, was all she could think of, and where else would she go but to a library? Once more she forced herself to wait; Naz must make no connection between the noise she'd heard and Alice's departure.

A tedious half an hour elapsed before she felt it safe to leave. Even so, Naz was loitering in the passage as she expected. She had her excuse ready.

'I have read everything I brought from England and must find something else for my last few days.' The pretence was incredibly weak, but she offered it as casually as she could, not knowing how much English the girl really understood.

'The new library has magazines, I think?'

Naz said nothing. Perhaps she had not understood after all, and Alice could only hope the smile she offered would dispel suspicion. 'I will see you later, Naz. If you wish, you may clean the room while I am gone.'

The slave maintained a blank face and she slipped past to wind her way through tiled corridors to the meeting room. Several very young girls were chasing each other, splashing water from the fountain and shrieking with laughter as they did. The clamour was unusual since in general an air of discipline and industry pervaded the harem. The girls were trained in etiquette, Alice had been told, taught to sew and embroider or trained to sing or play or dance. A kind of royal finishing school. She saw Sevda seated on a corner divan, sewing demurely. Alice waved to her but did not stop. In a matter of minutes, she had reached the courtyard, and in another was through the marbled archway and climbing the library steps.

Harry must have seen her coming and met her at the door. His gaze swept the courtyard below, then he looked back into the library making sure, it seemed, there was no one in earshot.

'You have received a message?'

'It came an hour ago.'

'Come into the office.'

She followed him across the library, this morning hardly noticing the beauty of the room. As soon as the office door was closed, she said, 'Ismet has sent an address. Will you still come with me?' Harry straightened his shoulders as if to say, *I promised, so I will.* 'If you are willing, we must go tonight.'

He nodded and took the paper from her hand. 'This is the address we must find?'

'We are not to go there directly. A boy – his name is Latif – will meet us at a shop called Tugra. It's in the local market.

138

He will take us to Ismet. I think we have the address in case we should miss Latif.'

'We shouldn't. It sounds simple enough.' He got up and strode around the small room, coming to a halt in front of her. 'Are you really sure you wish to do this, Alice?'

'I have to do it. But I will be happy to go alone if you prefer not to be involved.' She wasn't happy, but she would not force him into something from which he evidently recoiled.

He gave a brief nod. 'Then I think it best if we are both seen in the palace this evening. I will eat my supper as usual, but then slip away. It won't be remarked on – I most often return to my room after the meal. Are you able to do the same? If so, we will meet outside the palace gates.'

'It won't be quite as easy – I am sure I'm being watched. But after the evening meal, I can say I'm in need of fresh air and wish to walk in the courtyard. The slaves eat after us and I must hope that Naz takes a long time over her supper.'

'Naz?'

'She is a slave – my slave, apparently, and Lydia's before me. But she is also a spy.'

Harry made no comment, but she thought the creases in his forehead spoke loudly. What had he got himself into? those furrows said.

–

She was late meeting him. Sevda had stopped her to talk, wanting to know her opinion of Hagia Sophia, wanting to know where else Alice might be intending to visit in the few days she had left. The Valide Sultan was eager, Sevda said, that her guest should see as much of Constantinople as possible. Alice was forced to promise she would visit the Grand Bazaar tomorrow, hoping this would satisfy the woman, but since she had no intention of submitting herself to the ferment of the bazaar, she would have to pretend. In the morning, she must broadcast her intention to sightsee as widely as possible, and then find a hiding place in the garden.

Tugra turned out to be a baklava shop and, though it had closed its doors an hour before, the sweet aroma of honey-soaked filo still lingered. They stood together beneath its awning while a stream of shoppers passed and repassed, but apart from an initial greeting, they did not speak. Alice was nervous, beginning to wish she had not agreed to this clandestine visit, and she imagined that Harry, too, was thinking it a monumental mistake. She was finding him difficult to read: days ago he had offered voluntarily to accompany her to this meeting, and only yesterday on their visit to the mosque, he had seemed sincere in his wish to help. Yet beneath the surface she sensed the touchiness she had first encountered.

She was the first to break the silence. 'I want to thank you for coming. Really thank you, Harry. It worries me you could get into trouble.'

'It worries me, too.' He turned to look at her. 'Just a little.'

'If it were discovered you had visited a wanted man, could you lose your job?'

'I don't think so,' he said carefully. 'Though one never knows.'

He was making her feel more guilty than ever. It was plain that work was his entire world, since he spent little time with others and even less, it seemed, making friends. She wondered whether they would have spoken again if she had not asked for his help.

'I feel very bad about asking you to come tonight,' she said, and meant it. 'I know how important your job is to you.'

'It has to be,' he said simply.

There was silence while they watched a group of labourers in salvars pass by, their baggy trousers soiled from the day's work.

'And I'm sorry for what I said on the train.' She had an impulse to make things right between them, to clear whatever misunderstanding there might be. He looked surprised, and she added quickly, 'For suggesting you gained your job through family connections. I know I offended you, though it was not my intention.'

His smile was genuine. 'There's no need to apologise. I was being foolish. Sometimes, I'm afraid, I allow the fact that my family is poor to matter too much. It's a failing I'm trying to overcome.'

'I haven't been conscious of it mattering – except for that one time.'

'You haven't made me conscious of it. It wasn't always like that – at Oxford things were very different. I always felt a world apart from most other students. In the main, they were like Ismet, from well-to-do families, families who automatically expected their sons to attend the very best seats of learning. The boys were there to enjoy themselves, to acquire a little polish, oh, and do a little learning if they felt the need.'

'Ismet is from a wealthy family?'

'He is. He has never had to work too hard. He spent his time at Oxford smoking in his room or at parties or punting on the Cherwell, doing just enough to gain the degree his family would find acceptable. For me, it was different – to achieve a First and have any chance of a decent job, I studied day and night.'

'You sound angry,' she dared to say.

'I was, once. I could be quite antagonistic, which was stupid. I suppose I needed to prove to everyone that brains were every bit as good as money. But that's all history now.'

She wasn't so sure. His attitude to Ismet seemed complicated.

'I was never angry with you,' he said. 'You were innocent. In my heart I knew you meant no disrespect.'

'How could I? A first-class degree from Oxford? The most I could manage was a gold star for my knitting. Though I would be lucky to gain even that now.' She looked down at her bandaged fingers.

'Women do not have the same chances in life,' he said gallantly. 'I am sure you would have made a success of Oxford if you'd been given the opportunity.'

She allowed that to pass with a wry smile. 'You have certainly used your opportunity well. Your parents must be very proud of you. I know mine would be – if Charlie had done the same.' Her voice faded.

'They *are* proud, though sometimes I find it burdensome, living up to what I think they expect of me. They made great sacrifices so that I could go to Oxford, and I determined very early that I would pay them back in the only way I can. Which is succeeding at the job I do.'

'How did you hear of the post? I don't think you ever told me.'

'My tutor at Oxford drew my attention to the advertisement, though it was more a personal plea than an advertisement. I studied Classics, but the office next to my tutor's was occupied by a specialist in Oriental languages. It was he who had been sent the notice by a Turkish colleague in the university here, hoping this chap could come up with someone suitable.'

'And he did. Did you speak any Turkish at the time?'

'Not a word,' he said cheerfully. 'But I learned. At least enough to convince them at Topkapi that I could manage a conversation with the locals. And most of the books I deal with are in Latin and Ancient Greek.'

'But Ismet helped with the Turkish when he worked with you?'

'Yes, and he was good.' His face shadowed. 'I tried to warn him not to set himself against the Sultan.'

'He evidently didn't listen.'

'Ismet is transformed. He wants to change the world now. People who want to do that rarely listen.'

Chapter Sixteen

They had been talking for a long time and Alice had almost forgotten the reason they had met this evening. But then, seemingly out of nowhere, a young man arrived at their feet. His was the invisible hand that had delivered the message through her window, but she saw now that he was no more than a boy. Breaking through the mingle of people, he beckoned them to follow.

They were soon in a spider's web of narrow streets, pink and ochre washed buildings on either side, with washing that flapped from wires strung above their heads, and on nearly every corner a handsome old stone mosque. It was hard walking, often steeply uphill and on dusty cobbles, but they continued to follow the boy, keeping Latif just in sight and trusting him to reach their destination safely. At length he turned into a courtyard, hidden from the alley by a dense climbing vine, and came to a halt outside a respectable looking dwelling with several balconies showing lit rooms beyond. Latif led them to the entrance and pushed at the wooden door. It opened noiselessly and he beckoned them on, up the dark stairway to the first floor where the muted sound of family life penetrated the landing. But then on to the second floor and here all was quiet except for the creak of the oak stairway. A door at the end of the corridor was open and Ismet's figure stood illuminated in the entrance.

'Welcome, Miss Alice.' His voice was subdued. 'And Harry! My goodness, have I converted you to the cause?'

'No, you haven't,' Harry answered shortly. 'I am here to escort Miss Verinder.'

'Quite right, too.' Ismet laughed and his eyes laughed with him. If Lydia had been friends with this man, Alice could imagine how easily her sister had fallen under his spell.

'Here, I have brewed tea for you.' He pointed to the double-decker teapot sitting on a table which had seen better days. 'Latif, you must stay by the door.'

Alice glanced quickly around. The room was shuttered and bare. Boxes were piled high against one wall and what appeared to be a mattress was pushed against another. Ismet had been reduced to sleeping in a store room and she felt a degree of compassion for him. In an attempt at comfort, he arranged three cushions in a half circle and, once they were all seated, poured from the top teapot into small tulip-shaped glasses.

When they were sipping the black tea, he said, 'Have you learned any more of your sister since we last met, Miss Alice?'

'I have learned nothing.' She could not imagine why he would think she had. 'No one at the palace will speak of Lydia, unless it is to say how valued she was. The women I have talked to appear as mystified as I that she would disappear without a word.'

'*Appear* mystified?' He pounced on the word. 'So, you do not believe them?'

'I would like to, but I cannot rid myself of the sense they are hiding something. I am sure Lydia did not leave the palace willingly.' She took a breath before she added, 'Since I found the necklace, I'm convinced she was abducted.' And briefly she recounted the story of the pendant.

Ismet nodded in agreement. 'You may be right, though I cannot understand why she should be kidnapped in this way. And even if your suspicions are correct, how do they advance your search?'

She looked at him perplexed. 'I am hoping you will tell me. It is why I am here. You said you wished to talk to me, that you had something to tell me.'

'No, no.' He looked uncomfortable. 'What can I tell you that you do not already know? I hoped you would come with news that would help us both to find her. Unfortunately, things have become so bad for me that whatever help I can give now will be limited.'

'You brought me here to tell me you would help find Lydia? Is that it?'

She felt disappointment overwhelm her. For days she had been counting on this meeting, had waited with nerves twisted and raw, and it had all been in vain. She had put Harry's job at risk, compromised her own security and probably Ismet's too, to be told that after all he had nothing to offer. Her heart was crushed, the last remnants of hope flying through the open door where Latif stood guard.

For a long while there was silence in the room. Then she rallied. She must make something of this meeting. For Lydia's sake, she must.

'Ismet, there *is* something you can tell me – what exactly was your connection with my sister? If I knew that, it might help me understand what has happened to her.'

'We were friends, that is all I can tell you. I can think of nothing that would lead to such a dreadful event as a kidnapping.'

'Friends and...? Surely there was more. You said she was interested in the cause you support.'

'That is true. I am a member of the Young Turks and Lydia was interested in the political change to which we are committed, but I cannot see—'

'How interested?'

A deep and barely acknowledged fear rose to the surface. She had toyed before with the idea that Lydia's involvement in politics was at the bottom of this mystery and suddenly she knew it was so.

'She wanted to help.' Ismet shifted his position, crossing his legs, then uncrossing them.

'In what way?'

'We work towards the restoration of a constitution where the Sultan no longer has full control. Towards a country where people enjoy freedom of speech, of assembly, freedom to say and write what they wish. Lydia supported our aims.'

'She would. But how precisely did she help you?'

Harry looked across at her. So far he had said nothing, but a new stridency in her voice, a new glint of determination in her eyes, had him taking note.

Ismet was still shuffling on his cushion. 'She tried to find something, something we need.'

'Tried? Then I assume she did not succeed.'

'No, such a shame. A shame, too, that it may have alerted Boucher to our plans.' He paused, sunk in thought, but then his spirits seemed to revive. 'In the end, I suppose it was not entirely a failure. It narrowed the possibilities.' His voice had taken on a cheerfulness that jarred.

'And what does that mean?'

'It means we have a better idea now of where we should look.'

'Look for what?' Instead of the clarity she had hoped for, the situation was murkier still.

'I am sorry, but I cannot say.'

She was baffled. 'Why ever not?'

'It concerns Valentin Boucher. You have met him? He is the man in our sights, and Harry works for him. It would be dangerous to say anything.'

Harry must have seen the appeal in her eyes, but when he spoke his voice was cold. 'Whatever you are seeking, Ismet, you can be assured that I will say nothing – to anyone.'

'But you may be forced to, my friend. And I do not want to put you in that position.'

Alice was fast losing patience. Her injured hand had begun to throb and she wanted answers. 'Lydia's disappearance has something to do with the Bouchers? Is that what you're saying?'

'It is possible, but how can I be sure?'

'My sister's wellbeing, maybe her life, is at stake, Ismet. What was it she tried to do for you?'

'I asked her to look for a small file,' he disclosed reluctantly.

'Where?'

'In Paul Boucher's office. At least I imagined it would be there, but she failed to find it. It may be that I was mistaken and the file is elsewhere, though there was a drawer she could not open, so perhaps not.'

'A small file, you say. What was in it?'

Their host looked hard at Harry and Harry glared back at him. 'Several sheets of paper, a ledger for a particular month. It contains damning details of transactions that Boucher under-took when he was distributing money for a new school. A school in the Stamboul district that educates poor Moslem boys.'

'So Lydia tried and failed to find this ledger, but how did she get access to Monsieur Boucher's office? I would think it impossible,' Alice said.

Ismet had given up trying to settle and got to his feet. He strode around the room while his guests sat and watched, waiting for the truth to emerge. 'She was friendly with Paul Boucher and visited him at his office several times.'

'Friendly or not, the man would surely not have allowed her to search his room,' she said caustically.

'Lydia was to call on him when she knew he would not be there and search then.'

'How would she find one small file in an office filled with paper? She would need to visit many times to have any chance of success. The plan sounds very unlikely to work.'

'The plan sounds crazy,' Harry said bluntly.

'Your sister, Miss Alice, was a beautiful woman.'

She stared at him, trying to gauge his meaning. 'Do you mean that Lydia deliberately set out to charm this man, to befriend him in order to steal what you needed?'

'I would say – a little.'

'What is "a little"? Did you encourage her to become… close friends… with him?' She did not know how else to put such a delicate matter and could hardly believe what she was saying. But she had the bit between her teeth and she would not give up now. 'Well, did you? Encourage her into a relationship that could bring her harm?'

'I saw no harm. Paul Boucher's nature is mild.'

'But his father's isn't – or so I understand.'

Ismet stopped walking and bent down towards her, his deep brown eyes fixed on her face. 'Please believe me, Miss Alice. I never meant harm to come to her. I did not force her to do what she didn't wish. But she wanted to help us,' he repeated.

Out of nowhere, Alice was filled with a fury like no other. She burnt with an indescribable rage. This young man had toyed with her sister's life or so it seemed; at the very least, he had exposed her to danger. But Lydia was as much to blame. Her sister could not content herself with a new life in a new country. She must continue to dabble in politics and politics that were not even hers. The suffragettes had been forgotten and instead she had involved herself in another country's fight, drawn into this mad conspiracy, Alice suspected, because she could not resist an attractive face. How could Lydia do this – to herself, to her family? Charlie's death had left them bereft and now her sister's recklessness was likely to add to their sorrow.

The trouble that Lydia's impulsiveness had caused over the years! Running away from school to join a travelling group of actors, bringing back to Pimlico a lice-infected street urchin who was to be her special project, stealing their neighbour's dog and then losing him for ever while walking on Hampstead Heath. The list went on. From childhood, Alice had been the one to rescue her sister and most often been blamed for her misdemeanours. Charlie had been able to view Lydia's exploits with detachment, but that was something she had never managed. If only he were here, bringing calm to the situation, saying in his amused voice, *It's just Lydia being Lydia. You won't change her, Alice. She will learn, but she will always be a restless spirit.* Now her sister might never have the chance to learn, and she felt her heart break at the thought.

Her long silence prompted Ismet to speak again. 'This man Boucher is evil, Alice. You have no notion – those who cross him are bankrupted or they are physically attacked, or worse. There are unmarked graves in the Eyoub Cemetery and it is Valentin Boucher who is responsible for them. Lydia knew how important it was that we prove corruption against him. If we do this, we take away the power he has to hurt people.'

'But to use a girl as your tool – for that is what Lydia is – a girl so young, and new to the country.'

'It was a bad idea, I agree, but at the time I thought it would work. And even now I cannot see how it could have resulted in Lydia's disappearance. She did not find the ledger. Wherever it is, the Bouchers are not missing it. So why would they act against her? Which is what you are suggesting.'

'I have no idea.' Alice got to her feet. 'All I know is that by involving my sister, you have damaged my family, and very badly.'

'We will find her, I promise.'

She raised her eyebrows at this. '*We* will find her? Is that likely? You are threatened with arrest and I must leave Turkey in two days.'

She dusted down her skirt and pushed her hair back into place. 'Harry, if you are ready, I would like to return to the palace.' And with a brief nod in Ismet's direction, she walked through the doorway, down the two flights of stairs and out into the street.

–

'I was very severe with him,' she said, as they followed Latif back to the market.

They were negotiating the cobbled hillsides and Harry offered her his arm. 'Ismet deserved it. It was a stupid thing to have done. He is prone to act first and think later.'

'That makes two of them. No wonder this is such a dreadful mess. More than a mess, I fear.'

Once they arrived back at the baklava shop, Latif left them, and together they made their way to the palace gates, each deep in their own thoughts. Eventually she said, 'Ismet was at least right with his question to me. I don't see how looking for documents Lydia didn't find could result in her disappearance.'

'I don't know the answer to that. I wish I did. I am so sorry.'

She could see his face illumined in the light thrown by lamps that hung from the stalls on either side. His sympathy at this forlorn time was enough for tears to prick her eyes and begin a trickle down one cheek. He stopped walking then and fished in his pocket for another white handkerchief.

'I'm sorry.' She blew her nose hard. 'I shall soon have used your entire store of linen. And I am sorry, too, to have brought you on a fool's errand.'

Unexpectedly, he put his arm around her and hugged her close. She liked the feeling and had begun to relax into him when he pulled away.

'This evening may not be completely wasted.' His tone was business-like. 'We have a small clue now.' She cherished the 'we' but could not see how they were any further forward. 'If I were to speak to Paul the next time he is in the library...'

'The Bouchers are the only clue, you are right, but you may not see him for days and I cannot wait that long.' She realised then that an idea had been forming in her mind ever since she had discovered Paul Boucher's role in her sister's life. 'I must go and talk to him myself.'

'You cannot do that!' He sounded stunned and took a step back from her.

'Why not?' But then another thought hit her. 'Not Paul, perhaps, but his wife. From the moment I met her I've been convinced she is hiding something, and it will be easier for me to talk to a woman. I will go to her house tomorrow.'

He grabbed her arm and this time his hold was anything but gentle. 'Think, Alice. How can you arrive on her doorstep uninvited and then question her about her husband's relations with your sister? It is unthinkable.'

'What has happened to Lydia is unthinkable and I have very little time left.'

His hand furrowed through his hair in a despairing gesture. 'You must not let Ismet drag you into something you will regret. He may already have already harmed your sister, and you can see how he has used her. She no longer matters and he shrugs his shoulders and says he will help if he can. It's a promise he can't possibly fulfil. If you choose to follow his loose talk of the Bouchers, you may be walking into danger.'

'Danger? From a courtesy visit to Madame Boucher? I shall say I am leaving the country soon and wish to say goodbye.'

'I beg you, please do not do this.'

'Because you dislike Ismet? Because you resent him?'

'That is ridiculous.'

'Is it? It doesn't seem so to me. Or is it that you fear for your job?' She had never spoken in such a frank and angry manner to anyone, and she knew she was being unfair. But her nerves were wound tight and she longed for his support. Instead, there was only disappointment.

In silence they passed through the palace gates, with only a cursory glance from the soldiers on guard, and reached the inner courtyard. At the harem entrance, they stood facing each other.

'I ask you to reconsider,' Harry said. 'And not because I fear for my job, but because I fear for you.'

'Fine words, but it is action that is needed.' She saw his lips tighten and hated that in a matter of minutes, they had become so badly at odds. But for Lydia's sake, she knew she must speak to Elise Boucher – it was her last chance.

When he stayed silent, she said as indifferently as she could, 'I will bid you goodnight then,' and turned to walk through the harem door, aware he stood and watched her.

Chapter Seventeen

She picked at the breakfast tray Naz had delivered earlier, pushing aside the bread and honey but pouring three small cups of very strong coffee from the silver pot. She sensed she would be needing them for what lay ahead. Harry Frome was no longer her ally, that was clear, and it pained her to know she had antagonised him. The handkerchiefs he had loaned lay on her desktop, a remembrance of his kindness but a constant rebuke, too. She would put them out for the launderess who came daily, though losing them from sight would do nothing to lift her spirits. She had felt him a true friend and each time they had met, she had liked him more. Now he was unlikely to seek her out or even speak to her before she left for London.

There had been no future in their friendship, it was true. She was too sensible to think otherwise. Long ago, she had stopped believing she would meet a man she could love. Though a flicker to Lydia's flame, she was not unattractive – the trainee solicitor, after all, had seen something in her other than a future partnership with her father – but she knew herself too retiring to catch the eye of any man she would wish to marry. And really, it was for the best. She could not afford to make a life of her own when her parents had prior claim. Harry's destiny was here and hers would play itself out in that sad London house. But for a few hours these last few days she had forgotten, forgotten the duty she owed everyone, forgotten even Lydia in the enjoyment of being with him, talking to him, revelling in the admiration she thought she had glimpsed in his eyes. At least, for a while, it had felt like that. Now all it felt was wretched.

But it would not stop her from what she intended. Harry was the nicest man she had ever met, certainly the most attractive. And he understood the ties of family since he had his own. But he could not know what it felt like to lose so entirely the life you had once known: your brother dead, your parents ailing and infirm, and now your one sister gone. If only she could find Lydia… it would not return life to what it had been, nothing could do that, but it would begin the healing. Why she felt that so strongly, she didn't know. It was sufficient to feel it.

The past might be a dark cave and the future no more inviting, but she would do her utmost to change that. How much did Elise Boucher know of Paul's unconventional friendship? Somehow, she must get the woman to talk. It would be an extraordinarily difficult subject to broach and under normal circumstances she would be as aghast as Harry at the suggestion she speak to a woman about her husband's friendship with another. But these were not normal circumstances.

She carried the tray to the door and left it in the passageway. She could not bring herself to speak to Naz today. Somehow the girl's blank countenance had come to symbolise the dead end she had reached, the brick wall built to frustrate her. And this was the latest brick – how to find Elise Boucher's house. She could not ask Harry for the address, nor anyone in the *haremlik*. If she were ever to risk the question, she would be spied on even more thoroughly. So how was she to find her way to this woman?

Perhaps, after all, she should go straight to the husband. He had an office in the palace and it should not be too difficult to find him. She would have to introduce herself, but if he knew her for Lydia's sister, she hoped he would be willing to speak to her – at least initially. If she dared, she would ask him directly what had transpired between Lydia and himself. He might be so shocked that he would speak the truth. In some ways, it would be less offensive than speaking to Elise herself. Harry had protested rightly; it was unsavoury to ask a woman to detail her husband's possible liaison.

She dressed quickly and set off for the meeting chamber. At this time of the morning, it would be busy, the women engaged in fine embroidery, or practising music or dance or reading to each other. There would be small groups, too, gossiping over the coffee cups. It was the gossip she needed if she were to learn the exact whereabouts of Paul's office within this maze of a palace. But as soon as she entered the room, she realised that something untoward was afoot. The usual workaday calm had vanished and in its place was movement, noise, disquiet. It was as though an electric current ran through the assembled women, bouncing from one to the other, sending their heads nodding, their arms waving, their feet fidgeting.

She saw Sevda in the midst of one small group and went over to her. 'What—?' she began.

'No need to worry, Miss Alice. It is all over.'

'What is over?'

'The fire. You have not heard?'

'I have only just left my room. Where was the fire?'

'Not near the *haremlik*. There is nothing to worry you.'

The girl seemed intent on soothing, when what Alice wanted was information. 'But where was it exactly?'

'You will not know the place. It was in the dormitories that men use. They are at the far end of the third courtyard. But only one room was damaged and the fire is finished.'

A horrible premonition gripped hold and before Sevda could tell her again not to worry, she asked, 'Whose room was it?'

The girl looked surprised at her interest. 'It was the room that Mr Frome – he is the librarian—'

'I know,' she interrupted frantically. 'But Mr Frome – what has happened to him?'

'He is well. He escaped. You see, no need to worry.'

She turned away then, her head aching as much as her hand. Harry's room, she imagined, was one among many. Why his then? Another accident? In three days, her fingers slashed and Harry's room burnt around him. She had thought the attack outside the mosque a clear case of theft, with Lydia's pendant the prize. But what if it had been a warning, too? The man could easily have grabbed the bag without using a knife. But he had cut at it, cut at her hand, and by doing so ensured she held even faster to the bag. Not an efficient way to rob, but an efficient way to frighten.

They had been spied upon – at the mosque, and as they returned together from the meeting with Ismet. The knife attack had been a warning to her, the fire a warning to Harry. What kind of people did such things? Dangerous people. Had Lydia perhaps discovered more than Ismet knew and been unable to pass on the information before she was abducted? If that were so, her sister would have been locked away to ensure her silence, a prisoner, perhaps even bound and gagged – Alice tried unsuccessfully to quell her imagination. Or taken to a different country and left there, wandering alone without money and without the means of getting help. Wherever Lydia was, she was in danger, so how could Alice not go on? First, though, she must find Harry. No matter what their differences, she had to see him.

He was at his desk, working busily, as though nothing untoward had happened. But then she looked more closely and saw the smart suit was creased, the shoes no longer polished but white with ash and when he turned, his face was lined with tiredness. He rose when he saw her in the office doorway and the small speech she had prepared vanished. Instead, she rushed forward and clasped his hands as best she could.

'I am so sorry, Harry. This is my fault. I have brought you nothing but trouble.'

He returned the pressure of her hands and said softly, 'Don't distress yourself. I am safe.'

'But such an ordeal!'

'It was a little concerning.' It was the kind of understatement he was so good at.

'What happened?'

Still holding her hands, he led her to a chair opposite his desk. 'Simple really. I woke in the middle of the night and smelt smoke. Then I saw flames around the door – by then the wood was an oblong of fire. I started to choke and that's when I realised I had to get out of there.'

'How dreadful. You could have been killed.'

'It was fortunate I was sleeping badly, otherwise the smoke might have poisoned me before I could wake.'

She thought she might know why he'd slept poorly, since after their quarrel she had spent a wakeful night herself. 'And no other room was affected?'

'Only mine, thank goodness. I yelled for help once I was in the courtyard and the men were up and out with buckets of water in a matter of minutes, though it took some time to get the fire under control.'

'And your belongings? What happened to those?' She looked again at the creased suit and the battered shoes.

'Gone.'

'All of them?'

'Everything – except the clothes I threw on. These.' And he pointed to his shabby outfit.

'This is my fault,' she repeated. 'It's clear the fire was started deliberately. One room out of hundreds? You were targeted because of me. Because you came with me to meet Ismet.'

He smiled a little crookedly. 'I don't recall you beating me with a stick.'

'But to be punished so—'

'We don't know that for sure. But if it is a punishment, it means we were watched, and the authorities will know now where to find Ismet. *His* punishment is likely to be far more severe.'

She had given no heed to Ismet's plight. Her thoughts had been for Harry alone, but now she said, 'Perhaps he will have moved on before they get to him.'

'For his sake, let's hope he has.'

They sat for a while, saying nothing and she wondered if she dared again raise the subject of Elise Boucher. In the end, she had to. 'Harry, you begged me last night not to contact Elise. Was that because you feared something like this might happen?'

'Not that I might be smoked out of my room, no. But that you would suffer in some way. The rumours I spoke of – some of them told of reprisals against people who had displeased Monsieur Boucher. I think it's safe to say we have displeased him. Thoroughly. We went to meet Ismet, a man he knows for his enemy. If you were to seek out his daughter-in-law, too, that could bring worse trouble.'

She sprang to her feet, a decision made. 'It might, but I cannot stop now. I appreciate your concern for me and I promise I'll not involve you further. You have suffered enough and I cannot tell you how sorry I am. Whatever I do in future, I will do alone.'

He jumped up to stand beside her. 'Not so. If you must carry on, I will be with you.'

She was amazed and felt her throat tighten. 'But why?'

'The stories about Boucher were only ever stories. Nothing was proved against him and I was able to discount them. To be honest, it was better for me that I turned a deaf ear. But now I know from personal experience that most must be true, I cannot stand by and do nothing.'

'And that is enough for you to risk everything?'

'Not nearly enough, but you are, Alice. I'll not let you walk into danger alone.' There was a pause and then, as though it were dragged out of him, he said gruffly, 'I care what happens to you.'

Chapter Eighteen

She walked back along the familiar path to the harem, replaying his words in her mind. Harry cared for her – though unwillingly, it seemed. She'd heard the reluctance in his voice and sensed that if he could change or forget the way he felt, he would. No doubt he realised, as well as she, that there was no future for them. But still he cared enough to risk his job, his security, even his life, and that was something she had never imagined.

But she would keep to her word. Whatever Harry's wishes, she would not involve him any further in the perilous game she was playing. Instead, she would learn cunning. She had an enemy and she knew who he was. He had been Lydia's enemy, too – a ruthless and violent man, and her only chance of winning against him was to walk softly. She would find Paul Boucher and, once he was alone, slip unseen into his office and question him. If he was in league with his father, he would tell her nothing and she would be facing whatever else Valentin Boucher chose to visit on her. But if he weren't, if he were an honourable man, there was a chance she would learn the truth of Lydia's disappearance. And that was worth any amount of reprisals.

She did not return to her room immediately but repaired to the meeting chamber once more. The atmosphere had quietened a little, and though there was a buzz of chatter, the women had returned to their daily activities. A girl was arranging an armful of wildflowers in one of the huge antique containers that decorated the room. The red poppies were a slash of colour against the engraved silver of the vase. She had seen the girl before; she was someone who had entertained them one evening with a recitation of Persian poetry. It hadn't mattered to Alice that she had understood not a word. The music in the language had spoken for itself.

'I loved the recitation you gave the other evening,' she began.

'Thank you.'

'We may need your beautiful verse again. To calm us. I hear there has been a fire in the palace.'

'Very dreadful,' the woman agreed.

'I heard that one poor man lost his room. So sad.'

'But he is safe.'

Alice was relieved that the woman had understood her perfectly. 'Was the fire near the beautiful new library?' she asked. 'I have visited there and loved the building.'

'Not far. There are dormitories near.'

'And offices I suppose.'

Her companion looked nonplussed and Alice hastened to say, 'The size of the palace always amazes me. I get lost all the time. I think I would need a hundred years to be sure I could find my way.'

The woman smiled and nodded. It was now she needed to come to the point, but how to bring Boucher's office into the conversation? She was still trying to work it out, when there was another small flurry among the women. Several were bowing, others clustering around a half-hidden figure, and she realised that a visitor had come to the *haremlik*.

It was Elise Boucher herself. An indescribable piece of good fortune. Sevda had met her at the door and was guiding her guest through the chamber and on towards the Golden Road, a corridor that Alice knew led to the Valide Sultan's quarters. Was Elise here to discuss the mischief that had been perpetrated, or worse, to plot new mischief with the Sultan's mother? Was the whole Boucher family, the whole of the Sultan's family, part of a plot Alice could only guess? It was a terrifying thought, but she could not allow this unlooked for opportunity pass through her hands. She settled back on the divan and waited for Elise's return, all the time watching the doorway to the wide corridor beyond.

A few minutes later, Sevda walked back into the room, but without Elise. Alice rose to meet her. 'Was that Madame Boucher?' she asked, thinking that by now she must have perfected the face of innocence.

'You have met the lady?' Sevda smiled. 'She is very elegant, I think. And Sultan Rahîme considers her so.' Alice hoped the girl would go on and her hope was rewarded. 'Madame Boucher has brought journals, copies of *La Mode*, that show drawings from the fashion houses of Paris. The Valide Sultan intends to order from a *coutourier* there. The very best *coutourier*.'

It would have to be, Alice thought. 'Madame Boucher will know the best, I'm sure.'

The girl looked earnest. 'Sultan Rahîme does not want Western dress, you understand, but from the illustrations she will be able to judge – the cut, the material, the finish – and then decide who will most please her.'

'She is fortunate to have such an elegant woman to consult.'

'You, too, are very well dressed, Miss Alice.'

Sevda was lying but doing so graciously, and Alice did not mind. For the time being, her suspicions were laid to rest. Elise Boucher's visit to the harem appeared entirely virtuous.

She touched Sevda lightly on the arm, wanting to detain her. 'I fear I don't myself follow fashion. Lydia was very interested though. Do you know if my sister ever consulted Madame Boucher?'

Sevda flushed and her hands fidgeted with the wide sash she wore. 'I'm sorry but I do not understand.'

'I wondered if Lydia spoke of clothes with the lady. How well my sister knew Madame Boucher. She met her on the train, on the journey here, did you know? And she seems to have liked her.' Alice was stretching the truth, but it hardly mattered.

'I am always in the harem, Miss Alice, and do not know what happens in other places.' The girl flicked her veil a little further over her face.

'But I imagine Madame Boucher came to the harem while Lydia was here?'

'No, I don't think so. I don't know. Now if you will excuse me.'

Elise's visit had been short as well as innocent and she had reappeared in the meeting chamber within half an hour. Judging by Alice's own experience, thirty minutes appeared to be the most the Valide Sultan was prepared to offer her visitors. Sevda hurried over to the doorway to greet their guest effusively; she was delighted, Alice could see, to have evaded further questions. The girl knew something and that was sad – she had hoped the young woman would not be implicated in whatever wickedness had occurred. She had been Lydia's friend, whatever she said to the contrary, and Alice liked her.

Elise was shaking her head at Sevda's offer to escort her to the courtyard. '*Non, mon amie.* I have a carriage waiting. Please do not disturb yourself. Here – this is a journal Sultan Rahîme does not want. It is a collection of plates from Paquin. Perhaps you might like to see it?'

Sevda took the proferred volume, her face shining with anticipation, and began straight away to turn the pages. The visitor waved vaguely at the gathering of women, then drifted towards the passageway that led to the harem entrance. Alice had deliberately shifted her position so that she would not be recognised, but as soon as Elise left the room, she followed, reaching the Square of Justice a step or two behind her quarry.

'Madame Boucher,' she said. 'How delightful to meet you again.'

Elise did not look delighted. 'Mees Verinder.' She had acquired a deliberately thick accent, as if to emphasise her inability to hold any prolonged conversation with an English-woman.

'I caught sight of the volume you gave to Sevda. They are beautiful clothes.'

'I think so.'

Madame Boucher smiled faintly and moved towards the waiting carriage. As she did so, the man Alice had seen in the library appeared from behind the vehicle and took up position beside Elise, his muscular form towering over the woman's frail figure. She had assumed earlier that he was a bodyguard, but why Elise should need one had been puzzling. Now, though, she began to wonder what his true role might be. Whatever it was, he was not going to prevent her speaking.

'We talked before about my sister.'

Elise turned. 'I hardly knew your sister, Miss Verinder. This I have already said.'

'But you see, madame, I have a problem with what you have told me.' The woman's face slid beneath a sheet of ice. 'I believe you knew her better than you say. And if you did not, your husband did.'

Elise gave a small gasp. 'I must go. I have things to attend to at home.' The bearded man took a step forward as if to push Alice away, but she reached out and grasped Elise by the hand. 'Please, tell me what you know,' she pleaded.

'I know nothing.' The woman's face had frozen hard.

'But you must. Your husband, my sister, were – friends,' she finished desperately. 'He must have spoken of her to you. Perhaps she visited you at home?'

'She did not. And no, he never spoke of her.'

'Madame Boucher, Elise, I have been driven half mad by her disappearance. If there is anything you can say that will help me find my sister, I beg you to tell me.'

The woman's face changed. The sheet of ice slid away and the eyes were filled with such sadness they seemed to contain the pain of the world. 'Dear lady, I am so sorry for you.'

'Then tell me where she is.'

'I cannot. I do not know. That is the truth.'

'And your husband?'

'He does not know. You must believe me.'

'Then who does?'

The woman did not answer. This had been a last throw of the dice. There was no one else to ask, nothing more to find. Lydia was lost, and tears flowed unheeded down Alice's face.

It was Elise's turn now to clutch her arm, though the man tried to block her. 'Do not cry, Miss Verinder. She will come back.'

Alice shook her head, but Elise said again, 'She will come back, I know it.'

'How can you know that?' she asked hopelessly.

'She will come back. But for your own sake, you must stop asking questions.'

And before Alice could say more, the woman had been helped unresistingly into the carriage. The driver cracked the whip and the vehicle rolled away.

–

There was such trouble in her heart that Alice could not return to the gossip of the women's room, could not walk in the garden even though the sun shone, could not go to the library and tell Harry what had transpired. Instead, she scuttled to her room, avoiding the surprised looks of the women she encountered. There she pulled the drapes across the window and lay down on the divan, grateful for the shadows.

Once again, she wondered just how close Lydia had been to Paul Boucher. Had he suspected what she was doing at Ismet's behest? And what had Elise Boucher meant by saying her sister would come back? Three times the woman had said it, but why was she so certain? Was Lydia to come back for Paul? Surely not, yet Alice was more convinced than ever that he or someone in his family was responsible for Lydia's disappearance. She had blamed her sister's friendship with Ismet and thought her involvement in political intrigue had led to this abduction. But what if it were something more personal? Elise's manner, her words, suggested that it might be.

She sat upright. Did her sister's letters hold the answer? She had read them so many times, but if she were to look at them again with new eyes… She pulled her suitcase from under the divan and rifled through the few of Lydia's belongings returned to her. The letters were at the very bottom. Painstakingly, she read through them once more. Read and re-read to no avail. She noticed again how much shorter the letters had become, how much less open, and now that she knew what Lydia had been engaged in, she could see why. But apart from the initial mention of meeting Paul and his wife on the train, her sister had written nothing about the Bouchers. There was not even a comment on the party the Sultan had thrown for his European guests, though Alice knew for a fact that Elise Boucher had talked to Lydia at the event.

She bound up the letters once more, tying the ribbon tight, and this time packed them into the locked compartment of her case. Then gathered together the few possessions Lydia had left: pens and paper on one side of the suitcase with watercolours on the other. There was a view of Hagia Sophia, a vivid sketch of the local market, and a cemetery of some kind, water in the background and tall gravestones that stared out at her from the page, fierce and uncompromising. It was unsettling but it told her nothing. All that was left was the book her sister had been reading – *Constantine the Great* by one J. B. Firth. She picked it up, then buckled slightly under its weight. That made her smile. It was just the kind of forbidding tome Lydia would take on a journey; the serious student of history was as much part of her sister as the mad girl who launched bricks through windows or sang music hall songs at the top of her voice.

But what use was it? In a fit of impatience, Alice cast the book to one side and a bookmark fell to the ground. It was a sheet of paper, folded lengthwise in four, but when Alice unrolled it, she realised it was a page of a journal. A page that had been deliberately removed with a sharp, clean cut. And where was the journal itself? She felt her heart thump a little louder. She smoothed the page out, unable to rid it of all its creases, but well enough to read the words Lydia had written.

She scanned down the page. Nothing. At least nothing that would explain why it had been excised. There were several observations on the Court, the harem, the furnishings, the clothes and jewellery. A small pencil drawing of Hagia Sophia in the corner of the page made Alice smile. Beside it in characters so small she had to peer to decipher them, she read *PB took me here*. She was getting close, she thought, and her heart beat a little faster still. She turned the page over – and there it was. What she had been looking for. And reading it now, she understood more fully why Lydia's letters had made only the barest mention of Paul Boucher.

> *My 'romance' with Paul is going well. He is vastly attracted which is a help, but I'm also doing a little flattering here and there. He's quite a simple soul, I think, and laps it up unquestioningly. He took me to the Dolmabahçe Palace yesterday. Sevda tried to dissuade me from going. He is a married man, she said, quite shocked that I spend so much time with him. And his father will not like it. The Bouchers are powerful people – it is best not to cross them. I've no intention of crossing them, just holding on to this sweet little man long enough to get what Ismet wants.*
>
> *So far, I've been unable to stay in the office without him. I've noticed he is very particular about locking everything away and he doesn't like to entertain me there. He is always wanting to usher me out to go and look at some monument or other. I wonder sometimes why I'm doing this. I find the women in the harem so much more interesting. But Paul is beginning to trust me. He has started to talk about Elise. It seems she is unable to have children, which I'd worked out on the train, but I can see now that it's a problem between them.*
>
> *I feel quite sorry for her. She has a boring husband, a bully of a father-in-law – I reckon Valentin Boucher has already warned his son not to get involved with the*

English governess — and she has no children to keep her company. Poor Elise. I asked Paul if I could meet her, take tea with her, but he wasn't at all keen. He wants to keep me to himself, obviously. What it is to be adored!

Chapter Nineteen

Lydia
Constantinople, October 1905

Lydia dressed carefully, choosing the prettiest wrap she possessed to wear over a cashmere frock of plain grey. The weather had become chilly and she'd needed to delve into the back of her wardrobe for the several winter dresses Alice had thought to pack. Sweet, thoughtful Alice, so well-organised. And *so* in command – sometimes a little too much.

Like when she had run away from school. She would never had done it if Alice had listened to her. She was being bullied, she had told her sister, not by her fellow pupils but by some of the teachers. Alice had been shocked but certain it was Lydia's fault – her sister was imagining things or trying to be in some way special. But she hadn't made it up and she didn't feel that special. The Latin teacher in particular had been horrible, punishing her severely for the smallest of crimes, and holding her up to ridicule in the classroom if she answered wrongly. She had begged Alice to let her come home, but her sister had refused, refused even to mention it to their parents. *It's a good school, Lydia*, she'd said, *and Papa pays large fees for you to attend. The answer lies with you – you must change your attitude and things will improve.*

But they didn't, and when a group of actors came to the local town and the girls were permitted to see a performance of

Macbeth, what else was there to do but join the company when it left? She had travelled with them for several weeks before she was found, listening nightly to a different play, making the performers tea in the interval and, afterwards, tidying up props and costumes. She had found a joy in the life she hadn't expected, and that was part of the fun of living, wasn't it? Taking a chance, taking a risk, but that was something Alice would never understand.

She would certainly not understand where her sister was headed right now. Lydia was feeling the slightest bit queasy about it herself. If only she could have heard from Ismet, but she had had no contact with him since the day she had agreed to help. She needed to see his smiling eyes, needed to hear his beautiful voice telling her she was doing the right thing. Every time she met Paul Boucher, she found it more difficult to defend her actions. She could argue with herself that at least she had brought a little pleasure into the man's life – his existence, like her sister's, seemed all shade – but it was a frail defence. She tried hard to convince herself she was doing nothing wrong, writing in her journal a superficial account to justify what deep down she knew was unjustifiable. But afterwards she had thought the entry foolish and cut the page free. If it were to fall into the wrong hands, it could prove dangerous. Something had made her keep the page though, folded into the neat bookmark she used daily. It satisfied her sense of mischief.

Paul had adopted the role of guide with enthusiasm and in her hours free from the schoolroom had shuttled her from one city site to another – the Hagia Sophia, the Hippodrome, the Galata Tower, the Golden Horn – until she was dizzy with a jumble of facts and dates and scenes. Naz had watched her comings and goings with interest, almost timing her, Lydia thought, noting when her mistress left and when she returned.

No doubt the girl handed her spying on to another once Lydia travelled beyond the palace. She wished him luck – it would inevitably be a 'him'… There would be little to report other than two people viewing one historic site after another. In Lydia's case, often wearily.

Last week, it had been the turn of Dolmabahce Palace, a visit for which Paul had needed to seek special permission. The seaside palace was a good deal smaller than Topkapi, built on a more human scale, yet the Sultan's quarters were as magnificent: his study, the library, the rest rooms, a gorgeous hammam with marbles brought from Egypt. She had loved it all, loved the whole day since Rabia and Esma had been with them. When the girls discovered she intended to visit their favourite palace, they had begged to go with her, and after much to-ing and fro-ing on Sevda's part, the Valide Sultan had given her gracious permission.

Paul had not been enamoured with the arrangement, but it suited Lydia well. The girls enlivened what might have been a tedious day, and while Paul offered her the usual facts and figures and she nodded at what she hoped were the right times, she had played intermittent hide and seek with them. Their presence had saved her from boredom, but more importantly had given a veneer of respectability to the trips she and Paul made together. If the couple were happy to be accompanied by young children, their friendship must be entirely innocent. The one person most likely to object had, in any case, raised no obstacle: Lydia suspected that Elise Boucher was glad to be left alone.

Today they were off to the Grand Bazaar, but without the children. It was not a place for the young, Sevda said. Far too busy and far too noisy. They could easily get lost there.

'And you should not be going either, Miss Lydia. You have visited enough with Monsieur Boucher. I have said to you often. You will be talked about.'

'And I am not talked about already? I'm enjoying seeing so much of your beautiful city. You would not deny me that, surely?'

'Of course I would not. It is wonderful that you love Constantinople. And love the palace and your pupils. But you must show discretion. I worry for you. Stay with me today and we will finish your purse together.'

She took Sevda's hand and squeezed it tightly. 'What harm can come to me?'

'There are bad forces.' Then when she saw Lydia smile, she said, 'You are a stranger here. You cannot know. Visit these marvellous places but take with you your slave.'

'Naz, you mean. Naz as my chaperone? I really don't think so, Sevda.'

The girl sighed and disappeared, no doubt hurrying to receive her orders for the day from Sultan Rahîme. Lydia was glad. It was as well she would be alone with Paul today. She needed to step up her campaign. Six weeks of flattering and cajoling had so far got her nowhere. This morning she must try a good deal harder.

They had arranged to meet outside the harem entrance, but instead she hurried through the marbled gateway, into the third courtyard and went directly to the administration wing. She was earlier than they had agreed and was hoping to find the office empty. She was fairly sure that Paul's clerk did not work on a Saturday, and Paul himself could be elsewhere in the palace delivering his mountain of paper. It had to be worth a try.

She was in for a disappointment. He was seated behind his desk and looked up, surprised to see her. 'I thought—'

'Yes,' she said quickly. 'I woke early and thought it would be good to leave before time. I'd like to spend as long as possible in the Bazaar.'

He put away his pen, shuffled the papers he had been working on and locked them away in the top drawer of his desk. Over the weeks, she had worked out that the drawer was the only part of the office that was constantly locked. The clerk seemed to have no key for it, which meant that whatever the drawer contained was highly confidential.

He came to stand beside her, his glance appreciative. 'As always, Lydia, you look most charming.'

'Thank you, kind sir.' She bobbed a pretend curtsy. 'I have to look charming – I am to be escorted by the most attractive man in Constantinople.'

He pulled a face, but she knew he was pleased. Flattery was the easy bit. He locked the door behind him and together they walked to the palace gates where he hailed a carriage for the short drive.

They were rumbling over the cobbles when she said, 'I wasn't the only one to wake early today. You were already in the office.'

'There is always so much work to do.'

'Perhaps you should tell your father you need more help.'

'I have Ibrahim, but he is lazy and makes mistakes I have to put right.'

'Then tell him to leave – and find a clerk who is industrious and doesn't make mistakes.'

'I cannot do that.'

'Why not, if he fails to do his work properly?'

'There are reasons,' he said evasively.

They stopped talking while the carriage manoeuvred its way through carts and pedestrians and wandering animals. The streets seemed exceptionally busy this morning.

She wondered what those reasons were. Some kind of obligation to Ibrahim, some devious arrangement his father had made? When she had finally learned from Ismet the secrets she must seek, she had been shocked. Thoroughly shocked. The school that Herr Meyer had waxed so lyrical over had been built with blood money. The Sultan had donated a large sum that Boucher was to administer, but most of the donation had found its way into his pocket. The documents that Ismet needed, the sparse file from May of last year, contained details of contracts raised for the project. Each contract had been authorised by Boucher, but for far less than should have been the case. He had creamed off the remainder of the money yet gained the prestige of founding a school for poor scholars.

And it got worse. The school was built on land owned by a young man who had inherited from his grandfather. This poor man had died prematurely, falling from a ladder and breaking his neck. But apparently every contract in that ledger showed a date before the grandfather died. Had Boucher anticipated the accident – or ensured it? The anomaly might have gone unnoticed except for the fact that the young man, the new owner of the land, refused to sell to Boucher and he, too, had ended in the graveyard. Another accident? Ismet suspected murder and, when the young man's sister brought him a letter and then fled, he was convinced. The letter was from Boucher to her brother threatening him with reprisals if he continued to refuse to sell. The price named was way below the land's worth. This letter, together with the file, Ismet had said, would be indisputable proof of Valentin Boucher's criminality.

'We are here.'

Paul was offering his hand to help her from the carriage. She had been sunk in thought and hardly noticed where they were driving, only that they'd stayed within the walled city. Now she saw they had stopped at an impressive gateway, a stream of humanity passing back and forth beneath the square coat of arms that dominated an arch of marble.

'The Nuyr Osmaniye Gate. Prepare for a good deal of walking,' he said cheerfully.

'I've heard the Bazaar stretches for miles.' Climbing down from the carriage, she clung to his arm a little longer than was necessary.

'There are over sixty streets and thousands of shops. You will enjoy yourself!'

'What shops in particular?'

'Goldsmiths, jewellers, carpet shops, leather goods. Whatever you want. Until recently families could purchase their entire wardrobe here, *and* all their furnishings and household linen. Everything under this one roof.'

'Is it one roof, in fact?'

'Absolutely. Its Turkish name means a covered market. It is the oldest shopping centre in the world.'

They were through the arch and into a long narrow street. For a moment, she forgot the reason she was here and stood entranced. But Paul was eager to move on. 'This is the street of the Calligraphers – each trade or guild has its own street. Maybe this is not interesting to you.'

She crossed to look into one of the shops. 'You're wrong, I find it fascinating. Look how fine the work.' There were cards, and book covers, invitations, and what looked like framed samplers.

'The next street belongs to the Book Dealers and after that the Quilt Makers. There is an enormous amount to see so don't let's linger.'

'Why ever not?'

'Because I want to show you something special, and for that we must penetrate further into the labyrinth.'

'Then I will come back to this place. I shall buy a piece of calligraphy for my sister. It will be far easier to pack than a quilt, though they are very beautiful, too.'

He tucked her hand into the crook of his arm and marched her through the street of the Quilt Makers at a rapid pace. The smell of spice had been growing ever stronger as they moved deeper into the mass of winding streets that made up the market: cinnamon, mint, sumac, sesame. She breathed in the aroma, loving it and wanting more. If they branched leftwards, she was sure they would come upon the Spice Merchants' street, but the opportunity was lost. Paul had her in a strong grip and strode on.

The crowd was immense in these vaulted passages and he took the opportunity to keep her close, so close she could feel the heat of his body through the wool dress. She wriggled away a little. 'Is it always so busy?'

'Pretty much. The market isn't only somewhere to buy and sell. It's a meeting place, too. One of the few places ladies can be comfortable outside the home. And where, if they're lucky, they might see members of the Imperial Court. Even talk to them.'

'I can't imagine that happens often.'

He shrugged his shoulders. 'There is always the chance. It's a tradition that has grown over time. The Bazaar has been here for four hundred years or more. Not in this form, of course. It's had to be rebuilt several times – because of fires and earthquakes – and in the process, it's grown hugely.'

They were now in the street that sold carpets and rugs and were followed its entire length by calls to take a look at this or that shop, the salesmen's voices hoarse from competition. Paul appeared unmoved by the magnificent display literally hanging from the walls, but one rug in particular caught Lydia's eye. It was oblong shaped, with a geometric pattern woven in red and gold and with the slightest hint of olive. If she were staying, she would love it for her room. But was she staying? Her future was in doubt, she realised, and the man walking beside her might be the one to decide it. If she took a wrong step…

She went over to the shopkeeper and asked him for his price. Paul followed, tugging at her arm. 'That is far too expensive,' he said, when he heard what the man was demanding. The shopkeeper called after them as they moved away, 'Carpet very old,' then named a much reduced price.

'Let's not get involved, Lydia. We have several more streets to negotiate.'

Reluctantly, she allowed him to steer her away. She would have liked to possess the rug even for a few weeks, but she supposed he was right that it was too expensive. Why did he have to be so sensible, and why did she have to follow suit?

'This is the Eski,' he announced after another long walk. They seemed at last to have arrived where he wanted. 'It is where the most valuable items in the market are found. The merchandise used not to be on display – it was kept in cabinets. Then after the earthquake ten years or so ago, the market was rebuilt, and now the Eski has the same kind of shops we have in the western world.'

The street was a magnificent sight. Stall after stall of shining gold stretched into the distance, its shimmer reflected in the golden tiles of the ceiling. 'It's amazing,' Lydia murmured. 'And these are beautiful.' She stopped at a counter and picked up a thread of amber prayer beads.

'This is even more beautiful.' He almost dragged her across the narrow street, speaking to the shopkeeper with a few words of Turkish. The man bent down and lifted from a case a gold bracelet, set with sapphires.

'What do you think?' She wondered at his anxious expression. 'Try it on,' he urged. It looked far too delicate and far too expensive, but he insisted again, 'Try it on.'

'I had better not. I could not possibly afford it.'

The stall holder edged up to her then and laid the bracelet against her wrist. The sapphires were the deepest blue and huge, and in between were gold links that looked as fragile as lace. It was light on her wrist and felt as though it had always been there.

'It matches your pendant.'

'It's truly lovely, and, thank you for showing me.'

He signalled to the man and the bracelet was whipped from her wrist and disappeared behind the counter. Her arm felt strangely bare.

She smiled at him. 'Shall we go back to the calligraphy? Or would you rather explore elsewhere?'

'No, we can go back.'

'Perhaps we might find a drink on the way. There must be a cafe nearby – off to the left, perhaps. I'm sure I can smell coffee.' She sniffed appreciatively at the burnt fragrance drifting their way.

'You did, but it's no place for ladies,' he said solemnly. 'I am afraid we won't find a drink in the market.'

'But—' she began.

'The cafe is for men only – men with hookahs.'

Men with hookahs sounded exciting, but she was evidently not to drink there. She drifted to the end of the street and into the next while Paul lingered behind. He caught up with her amid a sea of fabrics.

'This is a flower garden of colour.' She twirled round. 'Just look at it! Every silk or satin or cotton you could want.'

'There used to be a lot more stalls here. I can remember them. The street still sells expensive silk, but nowhere near as much fabric as years ago. We Europeans have ruined the trade, I'm afraid, with our mass-produced textiles. But you don't wish for material, do you? Why don't we return to the first street and buy your sister's present?'

He had been eager to plunge into the middle of the bazaar and was now eager to leave. If she could, she would have stayed the whole day, the whole week. There was so much of interest, so much that was different. But her job was to keep him happy, so she left the fabrics where they were and once more linked arms with him. She noticed how much he enjoyed people looking at them. He was becoming proprietorial and she didn't much like it.

As they neared the entrance, he said, 'Maybe we should buy the calligraphy another day. When we have more time for you to choose carefully.'

'I can choose carefully now. What's the hurry?'

'I should return to my office. I have left work that must be finished.'

She wasn't sure she believed him and when he said, 'There is something I want to do first,' she was certain of it. She would have liked to have bought something for Alice. Her sister had been much on her mind lately and a small present felt right. But she hid her disappointment and went with him through the marbled archway to the forecourt beyond. Instead of hailing a carriage, though, he pulled her to one side and guided her into an adjoining tree-lined street.

'Why are we here?' She was annoyed that her visit to the bazaar had been cut short and seemingly for no reason.

'I wanted a few quiet moments with you before we return to the palace.'

Her stomach gave a little jump. He sounded serious and it worried her. Was he going to tell her that he had seen through her false friendship? That he knew what she was planning? She felt slightly sick.

His hand went into his pocket and he brought out the box she had seen in the jeweller's shop.

'This is for you. Open it.'

In a trance, she took the box and opened the lid. The gold and sapphire bracelet nestled amid folds of white silk. This was far worse than she could ever have imagined.

'I couldn't possibly accept such a gift, Paul.' She was stuttering and tried to thrust the box back into his hand.

'You must. You must wear it for me.'

'I cannot. You must see that.' She cast around for an excuse that would sound half believable. 'Women can only accept presents from close relatives.'

'I can't be close,' he said sadly. 'We can't be close – I have a wife. But it doesn't stop me from having feelings for you. The bracelet is a small token to tell you this, that is all.'

The sincerity in his voice filled her with shame. She had flattered and flirted with him and this was the result. It was one she would have done anything to avoid. Why, oh why, had she allowed herself to become involved in this tawdry plan? A little light flirtation, that was all it was supposed to be, but she was trapped now by her own success. She wanted nothing more than to walk away and never cross his path again. But she could not – Ismet had told her too much and she had given her word to him. Yet how could she accept such an expensive gift?

'I could not wear it,' she protested. 'There would be comments.'

'Then wear it only when you are with me.' He took the bracelet from its silk bed and wrapped it around her wrist. 'It looks magnificent on you.'

'Thank you.' She gave up the fight, but she knew that once she had fulfilled her promise to Ismet, she must disappear. From Paul's life, from Topkapi itself. 'It is a most beautiful present,' she told him, and for the first time she was sincere.

'*You* are the beautiful one. Do you know, the bracelet matches your eyes as well as your pendant?'

His words brought Charlie swimming into her mind, Charlie when she'd seen him last at Paddington station. He had been returning to Oxford for what would be the final time and she had been there to wave him off. Alice had been forced to stay home; the doctor was expected for Papa and she could not leave. What would Charlie say to her now? What would Alice?

Shame and grief in equal measure flooded through her, but her misery was short-lived. Suddenly Paul Boucher reached out and pulled her hard against him. Then bent his head and, before she could protest, found her lips in a suffocating kiss.

She pushed him violently away.

'What are you thinking?' She scanned the street for observers and was relieved to see it empty.

He stood, head bowed, his hands dangling by his side. 'I am truly sorry. I would not have upset you for the world. But you must understand – you are everything to me.'

'You hardly know me.'

He shook his head as though he, too, could not quite believe himself. 'That maybe true but I cannot feel other than I do. I am a lost man, Lydia.'

Chapter Twenty

Lydia was grappling with any number of bad feelings and they returned to the palace in silence. She had insisted he take his present back, at least for the moment, and nothing more had been said between them. She could only hope he would lock the bracelet away and forget he had ever made the purchase. Having to continue with Ismet's plan made the situation worse. For a few minutes she had toyed with the idea of asking Paul directly what he knew of the Stamboul Academy, what he knew of his father's business transactions, but only for a few minutes. Whenever she'd mentioned the work of The Foundation, he had been keen to extol its wonders. The hospital had saved lives, he said, the school had given hope to hundreds of children, the library was a resource for the best scholars in the land. There had been nothing but praise, not one shred of doubt in his voice. Either he was an accomplished actor or he knew nothing of the nefarious nature of his father's dealings. It would be strange if he did not, but she thought it must be the latter. She had spent hours with him of late, and not once had she sensed a calculating brain beneath the smiling exterior.

Carrying on with the search was all she could do. Paul's infatuation was unfortunate, damage she had not intended to inflict, but he was a casualty in a just war. Unhappily, so was his poor wife. There was a time when she had wondered if Elise Boucher might one day be her friend, but that was now a hollow notion. It was a sad situation and today her confidence had taken a tumble, but she must recover the conviction that she was doing right. She was fighting for freedom, for a world in which men did not live in fear of the rich and powerful and women were not handmaids, or concubines or slaves. The task to which she'd pledged herself was insignificant, a fragment of the greater crusade, but still important.

And politics was a dirty business. What seemed fresh and clean did not stay that way. At home, the suffragettes had been besmirched, traduced in the newspapers, their persons vilified, their bodies manhandled by forces of the law. It was not what she'd envisaged when she had joined the movement, but it was a lesson to heed and she would not stay to be similarly tarnished. Her contract at Topkapi had been for one year and, as yet, no one had asked her to agree to another. She was not bound to stay. She loved Esma and Rabia, delighted daily in their progress, and would feel sorrow when the moment came to say goodbye. But goodbye it would have to be. Once this horrible task was over, she would go, and she wanted it over as soon as possible.

Paul had walked her to the entrance to the *haremlik*, but instead of saying goodbye, she turned to him, seemingly flustered.

'I have been very stupid, Paul. I'm so sorry. And after such an exciting visit.' He looked perplexed. 'I think I must have left my shopping bag in your office. You see how stupid that is. Going to the Bazaar without a shopping bag.'

'But you didn't need it, did you? I was the one to shop.' He looked down at her, a tender expression on his face, and she cursed herself for not having thought of something else to mislay. But a handkerchief would have been too flimsy an object.

'It's such a useful bag,' she went on a trifle desperately. 'One of those made of linen that rolls into a ball. I use it a lot. I will need it tomorrow when I go to the local market. Would you mind awfully if we walked back to your office to look?'

'I'll go. You stay here and save your legs.'

'The trouble is I'm not sure just where I put it down. Let me walk back with you. It will only take a minute.'

He looked surprised but agreed immediately. She knew he was happy to spend a little longer in her company. When he had unlocked the office door and ushered her in, she made a great flurry of looking for the bag – delving down the sides of the chair on which she had waited for him, sweeping her hands beneath the desk, peering along the window sill, standing on tiptoe to look on a shelf of the bookcase. All the time, Paul waited patiently.

'You may not have had it with you,' he suggested, after the search had been going on for some time. 'I don't remember seeing it.'

'I am quite sure I did. But… I suppose it's possible that I left with it and then lost it later.'

'In the Bazaar?'

'No, not there. I had nothing in my hands, I remember. But perhaps on the way to the palace gates?'

'Would we not have seen it on our return?'

'Not necessarily. It's a dun colour. It would be difficult to see against the gravel, unless you were looking for it particularly.'

'You want to go back to the gates then?'

'I want to, but you were right about saving my legs. My feet are so sore from all that walking.' She sank into the one chair the office afforded. 'Would you mind very much? Would you be an absolute dear and walk back yourself, just to make sure it's not lying forlorn in one of the courtyards.'

He looked uncertain. 'I should really lock the office first.'

'There is no need, surely. I'll be here.'

He hesitated for a moment, but then smiled and said, 'I'll be back very soon – with your shopping bag, I hope.'

'I hope so, too,' she called out, as his figure disappeared through the doorway.

She allowed seconds only before she set to work. She could discount the papers on the top of his desk, though she took a brief look at them. Nothing there, but what she needed would hardly have been displayed so prominently. She turned her attention to the desk drawers. She had thought only one had a lock, but she could be wrong. Not wrong about this one, at least. The deep drawer at the bottom of the desk opened easily. She pulled out a pile of dull looking books and flicked through them, guessing they covered various aspects of Turkish commerce, but most were in such difficult French she could read only a word or two. Very carefully she replaced them in the same order. Paul must not guess what she had been at. The two shallower drawers yielded little but stationery and pens. There was an open letter in one and she pounced on it, but it turned out to be from a friend in Nantes and of little interest. The only storage left in the room was the locked drawer in the middle of the desk and the wooden filing cabinet that stood in the corner.

She went over to it and started her search from the top. Each drawer contained information on a single project that The Foundation had sponsored. In the third drawer she found the Stamboul Academy and honed in on it. There were architect's drawings for the building, an artist's impression of what various rooms would look like when finished: a classroom, the dining hall, the headmaster's study. There were lists of what must be ordered to make the building a functioning school. But nothing connected to the actual construction of the Academy. That would be in Ismet's file and the file was...

The only other place. The central drawer of the desk. The one locked drawer. Paul would have the key with him, but there must be other ways of breaking in. She tried to remember the detective books to which she had once been addicted. A hairpin, wasn't that the tool of choice? Very quickly she fished a pin from her hair and bent down so that the lock was at eye level. Now what did you do? Waggle the pin, that was it. She waggled, but nothing happened. No magic click, no smooth sliding outwards of the drawer. She must have it wrong. Perhaps it needed two pins, but then she would be in danger of bringing her magnificent pin rolls tumbling to her shoulders. She would have to risk it. But as she reached up for the second pin, a noise outside stopped her. Paul, returned already.

Not Paul, but his father. Valentin Boucher strode into the office and looked astounded to see her. As well he might. She was still standing behind the desk but thanked heaven she had not been at the lock.

'Miss Verinder!' He almost barked her name.

'Monsieur Boucher.' She glided out from behind the desk with her best smile pinned to her face. 'How good to see you again.'

He looked at the hand she was offering but did not take it. 'Why are you here, Miss Verinder?'

'I am waiting for Paul. He has been so good. He escorted me to the Grand Bazaar today, and it was wonderful. I'm sure you know it well,' she gushed, 'but for me the experience was unparalleled.'

He cut across her flow of words. 'Where is he?' It was clear he had no intention of making small talk.

'He is looking for my shopping bag,' she said brightly.

'Shopping bag!' She thought he might explode. His colour, always high, had reddened considerably. A heart attack right now might be convenient, she thought brutally.

'You should not be here,' he ground out. 'This is private property.'

'Of course, Monsieur Boucher. I understand this is your office or your son's office, but I am doing no harm, simply waiting. I am sorry to have upset you.'

'I cannot understand why my son has left you here alone. And I cannot understand why you have dared make yourself at home behind his desk.'

'No, no,' she trilled. 'I would not take such a liberty. It was only that I wanted to study this...' She hoped she was remembering aright. Yes, there it was, just above her head. A terrifying face mask of an Islamic warrior. 'I have been intrigued ever since I first saw it and thought I would take a closer look.'

'You will not come here again.'

'If that is your wish, certainly.'

'It is not my wish, it is my command. You will do well to heed it.'

His threats were stoking anger in her, and she abandoned the girlish silliness that had failed to mollify him. 'Surely you are not threatening me, Monsieur Boucher? I may work at Topkapi, but I am also a guest of the palace.'

'As you wish,' he said indifferently. 'But you are a guest only if you are invited and you have not been invited to this office. You are not welcome here, Miss Verinder. Please leave.' She seethed inwardly, but there was no benefit to be had from tangling further with the man.

She had reached the door just as Paul arrived back. 'I can't for the life of me see where you may have—' He broke off. 'Papa, how good to see you.' His voice betrayed his nervousness.

Boucher did not acknowledge his son's greeting, but said, 'Miss Verinder is leaving us.'

She gave him what she hoped was her most disdainful look and walked out. But she did not go far, doubling back to stand beneath the open window. When she had met them both at the Sultan's gathering, she had thought their relationship awkward, but it seemed to her now that Paul was afraid of his father. Elise had seemed afraid, too, and Lydia wanted to know why. She had not long to find out.

'What do you mean by leaving that young woman alone in this office?' He spoke in French, and Lydia had to concentrate hard to understand.

'I was away for only a few minutes.'

'What have I told you?'

'Never to leave the office open.'

'Never to leave the office open,' the older Boucher thundered, 'and never to allow access to anyone other than Ibrahim.'

'It was only Miss Verinder. What harm can she do?'

That was brave of him, Lydia thought. She stood on tiptoe and peered through the window. Both men were too involved in the altercation to notice a pair of wide blue eyes staring at them. Valentin Boucher walked up to his son and, though the men were of similar height, he seemed to tower over him. He jabbed the younger man in the chest.

'Never. Do. That. Again.'

'No, Papa,' his son said miserably.

'If I ever find you have contravened my instructions, you will suffer for it. Your wife will suffer, too. You understand my meaning?'

'I understand.'

'You had better. Now check your desk to make sure nothing has been disturbed. I will lock the door myself – and keep the key if you cannot be trusted.'

'I can. I promise. You must know I keep them on my person always. I made a bad mistake today, but I won't make it again.'

'You won't have the chance. Be sure of that.'

Lydia had heard enough. It was clear Paul Boucher was under the control of his father. She acquitted him of knowing the full wickedness of the man, but any faint hope that she might get help from him was dead. He was his father's puppet. She could flatter and trick all she wanted, but she would not get back into that office. Paul was too scared to contravene Boucher's instructions again. She would have to find another way. She must get into that desk drawer and to do that, she needed keys. It required some thinking.

Chapter Twenty One

By the time she reached the harem, a new plan had formed in Lydia's mind. She was under no illusions that it would be difficult, requiring a bravery that, so far, she had not had to show. But the plan offered a way to get the keys into her hands, and she must think hard how best to achieve it. Naz was standing in the deep shade of the corridor as she neared her room. The slave seemed able to compress herself into the smallest space possible, then flatten what was left of her against whatever wall she stood by, almost disappearing into the decorative tile work. It was only Lydia's acute sense of the girl always being near that meant she was aware of her now. Naz was the perfect spy and Lydia wondered, not for the first time, just who was paying her.

She spent the evening with the other women, listening to their talk and nodding where she thought appropriate, though she still understood only a little Turkish. She had brought to the meeting room her sewing, and under Sevda's guidance managed to complete a small decorative flower. Embroidering the purse was proving a slow process – she was an awkward needlewoman – but she hoped this laboured-over gift would one day be ready for her friend.

Trays of sweetmeats were brought in halfway through the evening and when they had been passed around and the women had taken their selection, a young girl rose from one of the divans and walked slightly apart. An older woman clapped her hands and the talk dwindled. More poetry, Lydia thought, and hoped the recitation would not last long. The girl performed two ghazals, her female audience listening with rapt faces. Sevda, sitting beside her, tried to translate the lyrical verse. *Where are you now? Who lies beneath your spell tonight? Whom else from rapture's road will you expel tonight?* Lydia wished she wouldn't. She understood the drift of the poetry – the beauty of love and the pain of loss – and that was all that was needful. And though the language remained a mystery, she found herself responding to its rhythm and refrain. The entertainment was short and she was soon able to make her excuses and find her bed. Tomorrow she would put her plan into action, but tonight she must make sure she had its details firmly in her mind. It would be a day when she would triumph – or fail miserably.

-

It was early morning when she set off for the small local market that did a brisk trade outside the palace gates. She had to forage deep in her wardrobe to find the infamous shopping bag. Poor Paul. She hoped she would not meet him and have to explain its miraculous reappearance. Naz was in the corridor outside her room, as she knew she would be. She smiled benignly at her. 'No breakfast for me, Naz, thank you. I am off to buy fruit and maybe one or two souvenirs.'

As always, the girl's face was a blank and she merely bobbed her head and slid past into the empty room. Ostensibly she was there to clean. But what else? Lydia never left her bedroom now without locking away anything that might interest the palace authorities, if they were indeed the ones paying Naz to spy.

The market was in full swing when she arrived. She was unsure if this was a good or bad thing: it gave her cover certainly – she would have been a little too obvious if there had been fewer people – but there were also more pairs of eyes to observe her. Now, though, was not the time to be fearful; she squared her shoulders and walked boldly into the market. She went first to a fruit stall she had patronised before and bought two large containers of oranges. Tipped into the linen bag, they would provide the necessary disguise for what she had really come to buy. Her biggest problem was where she could run to ground this illicit purchase.

She walked down the main thoroughfare, taking note of the small passages running at right angles. Then she walked back again, beginning her search along these same dingy alleyways where fewer pedestrians trod. There were fruits stalls here, too, though of a decidedly lesser quality. Stalls selling battered pots, cracked china, second-hand clothes. Stalls piled high with raw meat, the flies feasting on it. The smell made her feel unwell and she turned away. Three or four of the alleys came to dead ends, several led to tumbledown houses and nothing more, and she was beginning to worry that her plan might falter at this early stage.

There was a tug at her elbow and she turned to see Latif's happy face. 'Mees Werinder. Hallo. Ismet wonder how you do?'

She had thought Ismet himself might by now have made an appearance in the garden, but there had been no sign of him. It was disappointing. She had looked forward to seeing his handsome face, his wide smile.

But the boy might just be her saviour. 'Latif,' she said, 'I need whisky.'

He blinked at her and she made a drinking movement with her hand. 'Whisky.' Then she wobbled her head as though she had already drunk a few drams. A passer-by looked at her in amazement, but Latif said, 'Ah, whisky. Sssh!'

'Yes, ssh. Can you show me?' She knew that somewhere in this market someone would be selling illegal alcohol.

He beckoned to her and she followed him full of hope. But when he stopped at the fruit stall where earlier she had bought the oranges, she thought he had not understood after all. She was about to try her mime again, when Latif spoke very quietly to the man behind the counter and he gestured to them to follow him. He led them to the back of the shop and parted a thick curtain of beads for them to pass through.

'What you want?' he said in English.

'Whisky?' she asked hopefully.

He nodded and climbed on a step ladder to reach a shelf high above them. He brought down a bottle which Lydia judged was smaller than usual, but plenty for her purpose. She thought the golden-brown liquid looked like whisky, though Scotland would never own to it, but she had no way of knowing. It seemed foolhardy in the extreme for the stallholder to be making illicit alcohol when the penalties were so fearsome. But she paid the money, and crossed her fingers; the bottle had cost her almost a month's salary. Then she hid it beneath the pile of oranges, and with smiles and bows they slipped back through the curtain and into the shop beyond.

'Thank you, Latif,' she said once they had walked a little way on. 'Tell Ismet, it is tonight.'

'It is tonight,' he repeated slowly.

'Yes, tonight. He will understand.'

Latif gave his customary grin and, before she realised, had disappeared back into a crowd that had grown considerably since she had first arrived. It was time for her to go – she must hide the contraband. And in a few minutes, she was hurrying past the bored gaze of the guards and making for her room.

She was lucky that Sevda arrived with a new batch of sherbet a few minutes after she had secreted the bottle amid a pile of clothes in the bottom of her wardrobe. After they had exchanged greetings and she'd related her visit to buy the oranges, she began on the speech she'd prepared on her walk back.

'You were right, Sevda. About the visits I've made with Monsieur Boucher.' Sevda looked concerned. 'There's nothing really wrong,' she was quick to say, 'but I think I have put him at odds with his father and I find that upsetting.'

'How have you done this?'

'I was in Paul's office.' She would say nothing of the missing bag and certainly nothing of the search she had made. 'I was waiting for him. He had to speak to someone outside, I'm not sure who.' She was now constructing the story as she went. 'And Monsieur Valentin Boucher came in and was very upset with his son. Apparently, I should not have been there.'

Sevda nodded wisely. 'It is as I said, Miss Lydia, you are better to stay far from the Bouchers.'

'You were absolutely right. You are a good friend. But I feel very bad about it. Paul has been so kind, showing me the sights of the city. Nothing has been too much trouble for him. I want to apologise, but I dare not seek him out in case I cause more trouble. If I wrote a note, do you think you could have it delivered to him personally?'

The girl looked doubtful, but Lydia pressed her point. 'It's the only way I can say sorry. And if you make sure the note is put into his hands alone, no one else will know.'

That seemed to make up Sevda's mind. 'I will help you. Have you the note?'

'I can write it in a moment. It's a simple apology, very short. Have an orange while you wait.'

Sevda declined the orange, but sat patiently while Lydia wrote:

Dear Paul

I am so very sorry that you found yourself in trouble because of my stupidity. Do please accept my apology. I would like to make it up to you in some way, but naturally I cannot now come to your office. Could you perhaps come to me? There is a small summerhouse in the garden behind my bedroom – you must know it. I will be there after supper this evening. I would love to sit with you a while.

My very best wishes
Lydia

She made sure to seal the note in an envelope she had to hand. She trusted Sevda, but an open letter was a temptation to even the most honest person. She knew the girl would find a dependable eunuch to deliver the message, as she had asked. Now all that worried her was whether Paul would come. And whether he would bring his keys with him.

Immediately after the evening meal, Lydia excused herself, saying she had a mild headache and would go to bed early. There were murmurs of sympathy and no one seemed to find it strange that a usually healthy young woman should be ready to sleep at eight o'clock in the evening. Once back in her room, she hauled a blanket from the cupboard, folding it carefully and tying it into a large square with one of her belts. She opened the window and threw it out into the garden, narrowly missing a hellebore just coming into bloom. She was lucky tonight. The weather had turned distinctly colder of late, but today the sun had shone for hours and the evening was balmy.

She delved back into the cupboard and rummaged in the pile of clothes for the precious bottle, then took it in one hand and two tea glasses in the other and threw them out of the window to land on the blanket. Thank goodness Charlie had taught her cricket. She was the only girl, he said, who could throw straight and true. In a second, she had climbed onto the chair, then on to the sill, teetering slightly as she found her balance, and dropped down on the other side with a soft thud.

The intense light of sunset had disappeared and the shadows lengthened, turning the brown earth into burnt umber. Dry leaves were everywhere underfoot and she heard the rustle of lizards as they scattered at her approach. An owl hooted in the near distance. Darkness had almost fallen, but rooms other than hers looked over this garden and she knew she must take care. With some difficulty, she picked up her treasure in both arms and made for a clump of boxwood. If she moved from tree to tree, she should be sheltered from prying eyes, but it was not easy and she was breathless by the time the summerhouse came into view. She felt her mouth grow dry. Would he be there?

Chapter Twenty Two

The blurred outline of a figure filled the pavilion doorway and she felt a surge of relief, her limbs slackening as the tension she'd hardly known she was carrying seeped away.

'Lydia! You came!'

She stumbled to a halt and took a deep breath before she spoke. 'Naturally I came. I sent you the note.'

'I know, but I wasn't sure you would be able to make it. It's wonderful to see you. Let me take that – whatever it is.' He reached out for the bundle she carried.

'It's a blanket. The seat is rough in parts. I've caught my dress on the wood before.'

'So how did you make your escape?'

'It was easy enough. I pretended a headache after supper and slipped away.'

He spread the blanket along the wide wooden seat and waited for her to sit down. It was then she produced the bottle and glasses from behind her back.

'What on earth! Alcohol?'

'I'm hoping so. I bought it in the market this morning. All very secret. But I've no idea if it's the real thing.'

'You took a risk by bringing it into the palace. Why did you do it?'

'You don't like whisky?' she teased.

'Who doesn't, but—'

'It's my way of saying sorry for the trouble I caused.'

He reached out and stroked her arm. 'It wasn't your fault. I should never have left you in the office. And you said you were sorry in your note. That was sufficient.'

'I felt wretched about the whole business, Paul. And I wanted to do something to cheer you up. To cheer me up.'

'Well, the whisky certainly should. Shall I pour?'

'Please. I don't think I've ever tasted it before.'

'You're in for a treat, if it's half as good as the real thing.'

He handed her a tea glass filled with the golden-brown liquid. At first, she sipped it gingerly, trying not to grimace.

Paul was not so hesitant and drank deep. 'It's good,' he said, sounding surprised. 'Illegal distilling has evidently become a fine art.'

She remembered to raise her glass then, and he followed suit. 'To a happier week,' she said. The toast was meaningless but safe. 'I'm so glad you could come. I was worried you would find it too difficult – at such short notice.'

'Unlike you, I couldn't plead a headache.'

'What did you plead?'

'Only that I had work to do and was returning to the palace to finish it.'

Her spirits lifted a little more. Another problem solved. If he had mentioned to his wife that he intended to work, she would expect him to take his keys. They would be on his person right now.

'And Elise did not mind?' It felt strange naming her in these circumstances.

'We… we live mostly separate lives,' he said awkwardly. 'But I imagine you must have guessed that.'

'I wasn't sure.' She took another sip and the liquid traced a fiery path to her stomach. A pool of warmth spread upwards and she sipped again. It no longer tasted quite as bad.

'Elise is accommodating. We are good friends and I am very fond of her,' he said. Then seeming to realise how odd this must sound, he continued, 'I've known her all my life and I feel great loyalty to her, but as a wife…' He left the sentiment unfinished. 'It's difficult to explain. But how about you – is there no one in *your* life?' The whisky was having its mellowing effect, their conversation more personal than ever before. 'No, I suppose not,' he answered himself. 'Sometimes I forget how young you are.'

'It's my family that's most important,' she said defensively. 'They are dear to me.'

'They must be. But do they not mind your being so many miles from home?'

She chose her words carefully. 'They were unhappy to see me leave, but circumstances made it necessary.'

He looked enquiringly at her and she decided that a little confession might ease things. 'I had to leave England. I was a criminal.' She gave a soft laugh.

'Surely not.'

'Oh yes. According to English law, I was guilty of a felony. I threw a brick through the window of a Member of Parliament.'

It was his turn to laugh then, but much louder, and she had to hush him. 'You must be one of those' – he struggled to find the English word – 'one of those suffragettes.'

'I *was* a suffragette. Now I am an English teacher.'

'That is some transformation. Is it that you have you lost your interest in politics?' A note of wariness had crept into his voice.

'I'm not one little bit interested now,' she lied. 'It was a passing phase. I suppose I got involved out of boredom more than anything else. Life in Pimlico can be unbelievably boring.

But I'm not sorry. It was fun while it lasted and I ended up at Topkapi because of it. I find Turkey far more interesting.'

'And you met me, which has made it even more interesting.' He was enjoying teasing her.

'And I met you.' She smiled at him over her glass. 'You have been a good friend, Paul.'

'I wish I could be more than a good friend.'

He held up the bottle, offering her another whisky, and she thought that perhaps she should refuse, but she could not leave him to drink alone and allowed him to fill her glass near to the brim.

'I know you wish to be more than a friend,' she said gently. 'And I am sorry that it cannot be.' She put her glass down and clasped his hand. 'I'm sorry, too, that your marriage is not what you hoped for. Did you believe yourself in love when you proposed?'

He looked surprised at the notion. 'Never. I knew I wasn't in love. I always liked Elise immensely, but in a brotherly way, if you understand.' She nodded and moved closer, feeling the hard outline of the keys he carried digging into her hip. 'It was my father's idea,' he went on. 'He has much family feeling, you know, and he saw a way of helping Elise's parents and of binding the family together.'

'It's good that your family is close. Elise seemed very fond of her parents when she spoke of them on the train.'

'She loves them dearly.' He took a large gulp of whisky. 'Even though they have caused her much trouble.'

'Really? Are you able to talk about it?'

He took another gulp. 'I suppose it would not hurt. Years ago, Elise's father made a grave mistake – a mistake that turned him into a criminal. He "borrowed" money from the company he worked for and then found he could not pay it back when the auditors announced they were calling. My father restored the money and saved him from going to gaol, but there was always some suspicion in his company and he was never promoted after that. It has meant that Elise's parents have stayed poor. They rely on my father's goodness to help them through.'

She stayed silent for a while, digesting what he had told her. It was clear now why Elise was so scared of Valentin Boucher. Her father-in-law had the whip hand over her parents. If she stepped out of line, he could report her father to the police – anonymously, no doubt – and the poor man would be thrown into gaol. If Boucher had ever to explain to the police his own role in the drama, he could say he was an innocent, a concerned friend who had lent money without asking questions. That was the meaning of the threat she had overheard in the office: *Your wife will suffer, too.* Marrying his son to Elise had been a master stroke. It meant Boucher controlled them both since Paul would not see his wife suffer. How did Paul live with that? He was weak, she knew, and would not challenge his father. But it went much further. To live daily with the knowledge of Valentin's true nature, he must have to pretend, construct a fantasy world for himself, see his father as a benefactor. What contortions of the mind and heart must that involve?

Lydia drank down the rest of the glass. She needed it. The nature of this dreadful man was plainer than ever. Ismet had told her he was a murderer, had said she would find proof of the crime, but even as she'd agreed to help, she had felt the claim far-fetched. Now she confronted the reality. Valentin Boucher had sacrificed his son's happiness, had sacrificed his niece's, and for years had kept her parents in terrified serfdom. At least the chain of misery would stop with Elise and Paul. That was the sole comfort.

She made sure she filled his glass again before saying, 'I imagine your father must be sad that you have no children.'

He didn't answer immediately but put his arm around her and gave her a small hug, and she allowed herself to nestle against his shoulder. 'Naturally, he is disappointed. Doesn't everyone want a grandchild? But it is not to be.'

'Are you sure?' she dared to ask. It was a painful subject.

'As sure as I can be. Elise has told me she is barren.'

It was a horrible word and she felt like defending Elise against the men who were using her for their own purposes. Even Paul was guilty of that. He was his father's puppet and too weak to protect his wife.

She felt his lips brush against her hair. 'Have you thought that it might be you?' she said provocatively.

A wry smile filled his face. 'It might, but I doubt it.' She wondered if he had fathered children that no one was aware of but thought not. He was a decent man – and a scared one.

'Another drink? You must be getting cold.' His arms tightened around her and she found that her head was swimming slightly.

'I don't think I should.'

'They are such small glasses,' he joked, but his voice came thickly.

She giggled. 'In that case...'

They drank again, and when their glasses were once more empty, he took both of them in his hands and with great ceremony placed them carefully down on the earthen floor.

'I am going to kiss you,' he announced. 'And this time you will let me.'

'I might,' she murmured. Distantly, she recognised there was danger here, but she was falling fast into the most delightful haze.

He took her face in his hands and kissed her lips very gently. She rather liked it and kissed him back. That roused him to kiss her again, this time not so gently. She reached up and put her arms around his neck and in return, he pulled at the pins in her hair, then stroked the curls as they came tumbling down.

'I feel giddy,' she stammered.

'Me, too. But I'm not surprised – we have emptied the bottle. We should lie down a while.'

It sounded a good idea. She needed him to lie down, didn't she? Lie down and sleep deeply so that she could tweak those keys from his pocket and glide through the dark to his office. She would be swift. There was only the one drawer left to search. The file would be there and she would hurry back with it to the garden and throw it through her open window. Then back to Paul and wake him. He would not even know the keys had left his pocket.

There was little room on the wooden bench for them both and he lay close beside her, cradling her in his arms. Then he turned his head and began to kiss her beneath one ear, small delicate kisses that travelled down her neck and on towards her breasts. She knew this was the moment she should leave, but he wasn't yet asleep, and the kisses felt good. A strange yearning deep inside made her kiss him back. He had slipped on top of her and was undoing the small pearl buttons on her dress. She thought that maybe she should help him. It was exciting and she enjoyed excitement, didn't she? He kissed her bare skin and she fumbled with the buttons of his shirt. She liked the feeling of nakedness. It was the first time in her life she had ever lain close to a naked man, and it was surprisingly pleasant.

But she had a plan to follow. What was it? Her confused mind struggled to remember. She needed him to sleep, that was it. But he was far from sleeping. The plan was not working and she should abandon it before it was too late. She tried to push him away but the push was curiously feeble and she sank deeper into his warmth, feeling the pleasure of his body against hers. She would let him kiss her a little more perhaps – did he not deserve some reward? – and then she would leave.

–

She woke cold and stiff. Paul was sitting beside her, stroking her hand, kissing her bare arms.

'Lydia, my darling Lydia,' he whispered.

She sat bolt upright. What had happened? The empty whisky bottle sat glowering on the brushed earth with two tea glasses tumbled on their side. There had been something about a reward, then letting him sleep. He had slept all right but so had she, and now her one chance of finding the file was gone. She could have wept with frustration.

He was kissing her again and she pushed him away. 'Don't, please don't. Whatever happened between us last night, it should not have.' She wasn't entirely sure what had happened, but she could take a humiliating guess. When she said, 'You have a wife,' he looked shamefaced.

'I know,' he muttered distractedly.

She looked through the entrance to the garden beyond. The pink of dawn was streaking the sky, painting the leaves of the trees with an unearthly glow.

'We cannot meet again.' Her voice was strong, determined.

'Lydia, I—'

'No, Paul.' She must be firm. She must leave him in no doubt, but abandon him as gently as she could. 'This is a love that cannot be.' She hoped that sounded right. She thought of the ghazals of yesterday evening and they gave her inspiration.

'We must be brave in our loss. Brave, and remember how wonderful tonight has been.'

'I will remember. How could I forget? But surely we can see each other?'

'That isn't possible. Elise must not suspect you have been unfaithful, and if we continue to see each other, she is certain to. And there is your father. Think what he would say.' She hoped the mention of Valentin would frighten him into agreement, and it did.

'You are right,' he said dolefully. 'But you cannot know what this has meant to me, darling Lydia.'

'And to me.' She was desperate now to get away. 'We must clear the summerhouse before we go. We cannot leave even a hint we have been here.'

He folded the blanket and tied it again with her belt. Then picked up the bottle and glasses. 'I will look after these.'

'Are you sure?'

'Don't worry. I'll make certain we leave not a trace.'

She reached up and planted a soft kiss on his cheek. 'It is for the best.'

And then she was gone, weaving her way through the boxwood until she reached the window of her room. She clambered over the sill, the blanket in her arms. Then threw it to the back of her cupboard and lay in a huddle on the divan. The full horror of what she had done fell like a mountain of rock, crushing her with its sheer awfulness. She had lost her virginity. She felt no shame – her body was hers to give where she wished. But she had given it for nothing. Not for love, not even for a cause that was dear to her. She had made a mull of it. More than a mull, a disaster. Now she must tell Ismet there was no chance of obtaining the file he was desperate to find. And once that was done, no chance, she suspected, of ever seeing him again. His lovely face, his beautiful voice, would go from her life for ever.

Chapter Twenty Three

Alice
Constantinople, March 1907

Alice finished reading the journal entry and tore the page into shreds, then crushed the shreds into a ball and pushed it under the divan. Her sister's voice was there in every word, but she would never read it again. She could not even look at it. It was Lydia, but a Lydia she barely recognised – a woman without heart. Her sister was impetuous, at times stupidly reckless, but she had never been heartless. She was the girl who brought tea to Alice's bedside if ever she was ill, who held their elderly neighbour's hand through the night after the sudden death of her husband, who played for hours with the children of a fellow guest while their mother took time for herself. That was the Lydia Alice knew, not this coldly driven person. It was not how she wanted to think of her.

For an hour or so, she sat by the window, her figure rigid, her mind trying to make sense of what she had read but finding she could not. Somewhere a clock struck the hour and she roused herself. What, in fact, was there to make sense of? She was convinced the Bouchers held the key to Lydia's disappearance, but learning of her sister's attempt to trap Paul Boucher was as near as she would get to the truth. No member of his family would tell her more, not even Elise, who had good reason to malign her sister. All Alice could do was hold tight to the woman's parting words, her insistence that Lydia would come back.

There was a soft knock and Sevda put her head around the door. 'I can come in, Miss Alice?' She had with her an armful of clothes. 'I have dresses for you.'

'Yes, do come in. And thank you. The laundry is just in time – I must start to pack shortly.'

Sevda laid the dresses lengthwise on the divan, but when she turned to speak to Alice again, she was frowning. 'Forgive me, Miss Alice, but are you well? You did not stay to eat with us.'

'I felt a little faint and decided to rest, that's all.' She excused herself the small lie. 'And I'm fine now. How did you like the catalogue Madame Boucher gave you – the one for the house of Paquet?'

'The clothes were most beautiful, but I would not wear them.'

'I think you might like to.' Alice was guessing.

The girl blushed a pretty pink. 'They would be too – daring.' She delved into the large pocket of her tunic. 'See, I have brought you something that will make you feel better.' She thrust a small velvet object into Alice's hand. 'It is the purse I spoke of. Miss Lydia has finished her sewing – and my name looks most splendid. It arrived yesterday at the palace gates, so you see your sister is safe and well or she would not have sent it. You need not worry.'

Alice turned the purse in her hands. If indeed it had come from Lydia then she must be safe as Sevda claimed. It validated Elise Boucher's words that Lydia would return. But why then was she staying away? Would she not have heard Alice was looking for her? Not, she supposed, if her sister were at a distance.

'Where did the package come from?' she asked.

Sevda looked blank. 'I do not know.'

'But did it come in the mail?'

The girl spread her hands. 'Everything is delivered to the guard house by the main gates, then passed around the palace.'

'Could you find out?'

'Perhaps I could.'

Sevda was looking forlorn. The wonderful surprise she'd thought would cheer was turning into another problem, and Alice felt bad for her. Why was she harassing people like this? Could she not accept that her sister, for whatever reason, had disappeared voluntarily and at this moment had no wish to reappear. Everywhere she had met with the same story and she must believe it. And yet – she looked down at the purse. It had been finished well, the sewing strong and even, only one small loop out of place. That would be Lydia's inexperience showing. Or a clever ploy by some unknown needlewoman – Alice could not stop herself from thinking – tasked with pretending she was a novice.

'Can I help you hang your frocks?' Sevda asked quietly.

'No, but thank you. I will do it later.' She must make an effort to free herself of these bad thoughts. 'The harem's launderess is excellent,' she remarked. 'She irons with such precision.'

'Your blouses are a puzzle to her.' Sevda was trying to lighten the atmosphere.

'How is that?'

'These.' And she pointed to the pin tucks.

'Ah yes.' Alice held the garment up and shook it out. 'I can see why. But blouses such as these are fashionable in England – if they have enough pin tucks! Now this one—' and she turned to pick up a heavy cotton dress with a tucked bodice, then stopped. 'There's a camisole here, but I don't think it's mine.'

A slip of silk lay between two of the dresses and she looked at it hard. Not hers – but her sister's. She had sewn it for Lydia herself. Her sister must have sent it for laundering the day she disappeared, but why it had taken so long to find its way back to the room was strange since each item was labelled with the owner's name. The garment must have circulated the wardrobes of every woman in the harem until the Verinder initials had brought it back with her own clothes. She stroked the lace trimmed garment, wanting to feel its softness, to feel the true Lydia. To blot out the harsh words she had just read. She had begun to raise it to her cheek when a small white cap fell from its folds to the floor.

Alice picked it up. 'It's a baby's lace bonnet.' She looked puzzled. 'It's very small. By the look of it, it would fit only a newborn. Whose is it and what is it doing in my laundry?'

She smiled across at Sevda and saw the girl had lost her colour; indeed, was staring in horrified fascination at the bonnet.

'Whatever is the matter?' Alice was seriously concerned for the young woman. She had never seen Sevda look so sickly.

'Nothing. It is nothing, Miss Alice.' She swooped on the bonnet, tucking it tightly into one hand. 'It is a mistake. Forgive.'

'There is nothing to forgive but…' She could not understand Sevda's violent agitation. Another mystery, it seemed. 'It's a very pretty cap, but where is the baby? I imagine there must be babies in the harem.'

'Yes, yes. They live elsewhere in the building,' Sevda answered in a voice that seemed not quite her own.

Babies in the harem were likely. After all, she had seen and heard plenty of children. They mixed freely with the adults and took part in many of their mothers' daily activities.

Esma and Rabia, Lydia's pupils, were among them and she had hoped to meet the girls, but a message from the Valide Sultan had decreed it would be too upsetting for her grandchildren. They were still lamenting the loss of their governess, the great woman had said, and meeting Lydia's sister would revive their unhappiness.

'I would love to see the babies,' Alice said on impulse. She was feeling desperately low and to spend time with the very young would be heartening. 'Would it be possible?'

'Not possible,' the girl responded firmly. 'I must go now, Miss Alice. There are things I must do.'

She began to back out of the room as swiftly as she could, but Alice was too quick and caught her by the hand. 'Stay a minute, Sevda. And let me look.' It was suddenly important to hold the bonnet in her hands.

Reluctantly, Sevda relinquished the child's cap and Alice stood staring at it, then thought that she must look quite mad and went to give it back. But as she did, she noticed ink marks on its tiny rolled hem. She brought the bonnet close to her eyes and could just make out two small initials, the kind the laundry used to link a garment to its owner. *LV*, she read.

'LV,' she said aloud, feeling her breath stutter. LV? Lydia Verinder?

'The bonnet belongs to a concubine of the Sultan.' Sevda's mouth adopted an uncompromising line.

'Does it? Or are you lying? Whose are these initials really?' She felt brutal and faced the girl furiously. 'From the moment I arrived here, you have pretended. Pretended you have no knowledge of my sister's whereabouts, evaded every one of my questions. But this one, Sevda, you will answer.'

All of a sudden, the girl's face crumbled. 'Oh, Miss Alice, do not ask me please.'

'I am not asking. I am demanding. You must tell me the truth.' She steered Sevda towards the divan and stood over her. 'Does LV stand for Lydia Verinder?'

The girl nodded dumbly.

'So why would she have a baby's bonnet in her laundry?' In her heart, Alice knew why. Every impulse was shrieking that here was the truth at last.

'It is a mistake. The bonnet must have gone missing. Now it is returned.'

'I can see a mistake has happened, but you haven't answered my question. Was my sister, was Lydia, looking after a baby?' She could not bring herself to say more.

Again, Sevda nodded.

'Hers?' Alice croaked.

'Yes.' It was barely a whisper.

She sunk back onto the divan next to Sevda, still holding the white cap in her hand. 'Tell me everything. Tell me now,' she said harshly.

'Your sister, she become with child,' the girl said simply. 'I know no more.'

But I do, Alice thought grimly. The diary page was beginning to have a deeper meaning. But why had her sister not written home, not confessed the trouble she was in? And how had she managed, where had she lived, when was the baby born? So many questions.

'Miss Lydia stay here when baby grows big,' Sevda offered, her English beginning to fracture under the strain. Her hands sketched the round shape of a stomach.

'How is that possible? Surely there was talk in the palace?'

'It was not so difficult. The clothes she wore...' For a moment, Sevda seemed lost for words.

'I think I understand. Loose clothes, you mean.'

'Everyone knew Miss Lydia loved Turkish dress. When she began to wear it every day, it did not seem strange.'

Alice's composure did not slip, but though some deeply buried instinct had known this from the moment she had caught hold of the baby's cap, she was struggling to grasp what she was being told. 'Her work,' she stammered. 'Her teaching?'

'There was no problem. To begin, she was unwell, but then she was fine and happy to teach. The princesses are very young. They are not curious.'

Alice hoped that had been the case. 'If the princesses did not know, others must have. You, for instance. You knew, and who else?'

'The women.'

'The women of the harem?'

Sevda nodded.

'All the women?'

The girl nodded again.

Things began slowly to slot into place, and the women's silence to make sense. 'Is that why they would not speak to me of Lydia?'

'They liked your sister very much and they felt for her trouble. When you came, they did not want you to know. It would hurt you and you would think bad things of Miss Lydia.'

Alice got to her feet and walked to the window and back. 'What you are saying is that they did not trust me. You did not trust me.'

'We did not know you, Miss Alice.'

'Is that why, when I arrived, you pretended your English was poor?'

Sevda jumped up and walked over to her. She took Alice's hand and stroked it gently. 'I thought it best. If you ask me, I say I do not understand.'

'But you soon spoke differently. What happened?'

The stroking continued. 'I decided you were a good person. You loved your sister and we loved her, too. You see, I did trust you. But I did not want you to be sad. I could not help you find Miss Lydia. None of us could, so it is best to say nothing.'

'I see.' And she did. The brick wall she had encountered in the harem had a very substantial foundation, one built of friendship and care for a vulnerable young woman. It prompted another question, though, and she wondered if she dared ask it. But this was a time for truth and she *must* ask.

'Did Sultan Rahîme know?'

'She was told. She had to be told.'

'And she allowed my sister to stay and continue teaching her grandchildren? From what I have seen of the lady, I find that extraordinary.'

'The Valide Sultan is a kind woman. Miss Lydia must be discreet, that was all. She must stay within the walls at all times and speak to no one outside. But when the baby comes, Miss Lydia must go as soon as she can travel.'

Sultan Rahîme had behaved with unusual generosity. Perhaps after all she was not the dangerous presence Alice had thought. The woman could not have tolerated an unmarried girl living in the harem with a baby whose father was unknown. Within days of arriving, she had seen the strict code of morality within the palace. It was a very different code from the one she knew, but every bit as severe.

'And you say Lydia's pupils did not realise that anything was amiss?'

'They are very young, you understand. Maybe they teased Miss Lydia with liking Turkish food too much, but this' – and she pointed to her loose overcoat – 'this covers much.'

'But the birth?' She could not imagine how that could have been kept quiet. There would be doctors, bustle, perhaps confusion. Lydia would have been unable to teach for days, and then would have a baby to suckle. The thought made Alice close her eyes in anguish.

'It was lucky – the princesses go to Dolmabahçe Palace for their summer holiday. It is by the sea and Miss Lydia told them she did not like the sea and preferred to stay here. The baby came while the children were away and when they returned, your sister had left. They never saw her again.'

Alice slumped down once more onto the divan. There was a part of her that saw clearly, but another part that was a jumble of pain and bewilderment. She felt unable to cope with anything more, but there was still one question that clamoured to be answered.

'Was the baby a girl?'

'It was a little boy.' Sevda's face broke into a smile. 'I took him in my arms when he came. He was beautiful.'

'Did he have a name?'

'Miss Lydia called him Charlie. That is how you say it?'

Alice could hardly speak for the tears that choked her. Then she rallied. She must know everything. 'When my sister left, how old was the baby?'

'A few weeks only.'

'A few weeks! But surely, then, you must know where she went. A woman still recovering from childbirth and carrying a tiny baby?'

Sevda shook her head. 'No, Miss Alice, no one knows. She asked me what she should do. To write to you and tell you what had happened and hope you would understand? Or go back to England and hide herself away? Or maybe hide herself in Turkey?'

'And what advice did you give her?'

'I could not advise. I do not know her life in England. Then one morning, I come here for her and she has gone. The baby has gone.'

'What did you think had happened? Did you not search for her?'

'We looked for her in the palace, but she had gone. I thought she had made her decision at last.'

'You didn't think it strange she said nothing to you of what she intended?'

'I wished that she had and was sad. I thought maybe she did not trust me after all. Or maybe she thought it best for everyone that she went with no word.'

Alice stayed sitting, her shoulders bent beneath the weight of this dreadful discovery. She felt Sevda looking anxiously at her and tried to pull herself together.

'I am sorry, Miss Alice, that you are so troubled. Maybe a little sweet tea? I can bring you some now.'

Sweet tea was not going to ease the heartache, but she was grateful for the girl's sympathy and guilty that she had suspected her of bad deeds. 'No, thank you,' she said quietly. 'It's not necessary. I need time to think, that's all.'

'I understand.' Sevda rose from the divan and went to the door. 'Do not think bad things of her, Miss Alice.'

Alice could hardly swallow for the force of emotion, but she managed to say, 'I promise. And thank you for being a true friend to her.'

Sevda gave a small bob and disappeared.

Chapter Twenty Four

Left alone, Alice remained sitting with the tiny bonnet in her lap. The story of Lydia and the baby would have seemed unbelievable if she had not read that page from her sister's journal. She could have dismissed it as cruel hearsay, but she had read the diary entry. She knew what Lydia had intended and now the sequel seemed all too credible. How on earth was she to tell her parents? Even Aunt Cissie, more open-minded than they, would be shocked. Everyone she knew, every acquaintance she had, would be shocked. And somehow she would have to find the words to tell them.

But not telling might be worse, and she wouldn't tell if she never found Lydia. How could she? For her parents, the anguish of a child conceived in such tawdry circumstances would be unbearable. She would have to hold the truth fast to herself and allow it to eat her slowly from within, the knowledge that her sister was alive somewhere in the world, that there was a nephew she would never see, a grandson of whom her parents knew nothing. Which was the worst outcome? It was hard to choose.

And what of Paul Boucher? Undoubtedly, he was the child's father. For a brief instant, Ismet had come to mind, but it seemed Lydia's friendship with him had been a disappointment – shallow and short-lasting. The night Alice had met him in that miserable room, his attitude to her sister had been detached, impassive. Lydia was the girl who had failed him and nothing more, that was the overwhelming feeling with which she had come away.

Whereas Paul Boucher had clearly been entranced, if the diary entry was to be believed. How had he reacted to the news of the baby? Or perhaps he did not know he had a child. Lydia had remained hidden within the palace, most of her time spent within the harem, and the wider world including Paul Boucher could have stayed unaware of her plight. Her sister's feelings towards the man, so clear in the journal, made it more than likely she would not have told him herself. But Elise – a sudden thought gripped Alice. Elise knew. She knew about the baby. It made sense of her conviction that Lydia would return, since she must also know of her husband's part in the disaster. It was why she was so sure that Lydia would come back. She believed the girl had run away – perhaps fearful of the scandal she had caused – but in the end would stop running and return, because the father of her child was here in Constantinople.

Alice could see now that the kidnap was a tale she had allowed herself to create, her frantic attempt to explain the inexplicable. It was true her sister had been forced to leave Topkapi, as she'd always maintained, but for a very different reason. Lydia had run away, too ashamed to tell her family the disgrace into which she had fallen. Run away and left behind a pendant and a baby's bonnet. Alice was distraught. The thought of Lydia, still recovering from the birth, with no settled home and living from hand to mouth in a strange country, was horrifying. Was the embroidered purse sent to Sevda in fact a cry for help? She could not condone her sister's conduct – Lydia had behaved very wrongly – but it was fear not moral scruples that triumphed. Fear for her sister wandering in the unknown, somewhere in Turkey maybe, or Greece, or in another country still. Somewhere of which Alice had no idea.

How could she ever find her? How could she rescue her? Her hands kneaded the small white cap, twisting and pulling at it until the seams began to unravel. *I am close to breaking down*, she thought in an oddly detached fashion, *but I cannot afford to. Not now. I must tell Harry*. Harry would be her anchor in this ocean of troubles. There was a lump in her throat that would not be dislodged, but now there was something she could do, some action she could take.

She tucked the baby's bonnet into her pocket and stepped into the corridor. For once, Naz was absent, and Alice was grateful for even such a small mercy. She made her way to the harem entrance meeting no one, another mercy, but as she was about to step into courtyard, she came to a halt. Outside one of the pavilions in the middle of the immense square, Harry was talking to a man she did not know. He was wearing a different suit, she noticed. It did not quite fit, the jacket a shade too long, the trousers bagging a little around the ankles. He must have bought it from the local market, or maybe the Grand Bazaar, to replace the clothes he had lost in the fire. As she watched him, she was swept by a feeling of tenderness. 'Lost in the fire' was a simple phrase, said in a moment, yet the man had been left bereft of everything he cherished – books, pictures, letters, the illuminations she had admired. He had lost them all, and had done so because of her. 'Sorry' was a poor reward.

His companion was thickset, an expensively tailored jacket struggling to contain him. As they talked, she noticed he had positioned himself very close to Harry, too close, as though he were about to step over him. But their conversation appeared friendly enough. When the older man clapped Harry on the shoulder and strode away, she walked swiftly across the courtyard. Harry had turned to go back to the library, but when he heard her footsteps on the gravel, he looked round.

'Alice! How good to see you. You are in time to admire my new clothes. I've been shopping.' And he pointed to his suit and shirt. 'What do you think?'

'They are very smart.' A small white lie would not hurt. 'Who was the man you were talking to?'

'That was my employer.'

'Valentin Boucher?'

'The very same.'

It would be, of course. The man's figure, the language his body spoke, chimed perfectly with the image Alice carried in her mind of the person she felt she knew but had yet to meet.

'Did you speak to him of the fire?'

'I mentioned it certainly, but he claims to have no direct knowledge. He congratulated me on my escape.'

'And you believed him? That he knows nothing?'

'No, but I hope I gave a good impression of doing so. I have no proof he was involved, not yet at least, and I would be foolish to voice any suspicions.'

'Is that all he wanted with you – to congratulate you on your escape?'

Harry looked annoyed. 'That was by the way. He stopped me to ask me – no, tell me – to close the library for the day. Tomorrow. It's a bad time, too – I have a stack of new books to catalogue.'

'Why does he want it closed?'

She gave herself an inner shake even as she asked. She had sought Harry to share with him the awful weight she carried, and instead here she was asking paltry questions. They were a distraction, she could see, a distraction from news that was tearing her apart.

'He said something about fitting the Sultan's reading corner with a new divan. An even more opulent design apparently. I wasn't consulted so I have little idea of what has been decided.'

'The old divan looked fine to me.' Again, the distraction. Anything to stop her thinking.

'Me, too, but it his library and I have little say.' They had walked together into the third courtyard and reached the library steps. 'I never asked you – were you coming to see me?'

Harry, the new suit, the closure of the library, all faded to pinpricks. Reality returned. 'I was.' She swallowed hard. 'I have to tell you something that is shocking.'

He paused on the top step, looking alarmed. And it was then that she began to shake violently, unable to control her juddering limbs. His arm went around her and he half carried her over the threshold and into his office, pushing her gently into a chair. He poured a glass of water and knelt down beside her. 'Here, drink this.'

She did as he asked, clutching the glass in a hand that still shook. 'I am so sorry,' she said, barely able to breathe.

'Don't speak. Just drink.'

When the glass was empty, he took it from her, then sat back in his chair. 'When you are ready, Alice, I am ready to listen.'

She could still feel her wayward legs twitching and trembling beneath her skirt, but she knew she had to begin. Very slowly and with many stops and starts, she managed to relate her conversation with Sevda. When she had finished, he sat immobile, looking as stunned as she.

'Did you have no idea of what might be happening?' she asked him. It was a foolish question.

'None. I hadn't a clue. Although… looking back, I suppose it was strange that I hardly saw her in the new year. But if I thought anything, it was that the princesses had tired of their library visits long before they left Topkapi for the summer.'

'If you *had* seen her, I doubt you would have suspected. She wore clothes that concealed, and never went beyond the palace. And the women of the harem protected her behind a wall of silence.'

'Alice,' he began, and then seemed to think better of it.

'What is it?'

He fixed her with a steady look. 'Forgive me for asking you this, but do you have any idea who might—'

'Who might be the father? Almost certainly, Paul Boucher. I can think of no one else – Lydia spent a great deal of time with him.'

He got up then, striding back and forth across the small office, his hands sunk deep in his trouser pockets. 'My God, what a mess! But where could she have gone with such a small baby?'

'I have no idea. And… Harry, I cannot bear it – she is out there somewhere, struggling, ill maybe, and I have no way of finding her.'

He came to a stop beside her and lifted her into his arms. 'There *is* no way of finding her, Alice. You must face that. But she is sure to come back.' It was an unconscious echo of Elise's words. 'If we think this through rationally, how far could she travel, so impeded? She cannot have gone any distance.'

'You think she may still be in the city?'

'It's more than likely.'

'Yes… you're right. Sevda has a purse that Lydia is supposed to have sent. And Elise seemed certain my sister would be back.'

'Elise – you have seen her?'

'I didn't go to her house,' she assured him. 'She was visiting the Valide Sultan and I stopped her before she left. I wanted to get from her everything she knows.'

'And what does she know?'

'Very little, or so she contends. She says only that Lydia will come back.'

'And so I think.'

'And if she does not?' Alice wailed.

'She will. You have to believe that.'

His arms tightened instinctively around her. She felt the lump in her throat expand and burst, and the tears that had so far refused to fall spill down her face. He bent his head and kissed her wet cheeks, then found her lips and kissed her gently on the mouth. She hardly noticed, but clung to him until he kissed her again, and then again.

'You kissed me,' she said, dazed. She was surprised to find herself lying against him, her head on his chest.

'And very good it was, too.'

'Despite the tears?'

'Despite the tears. But without them I think it might be even better.' And this time he made sure she knew she was being kissed.

Chapter Twenty Five

Lydia
Constantinople, December 1905

There were no Christmas celebrations at Topkapi. It was obvious there would not be, but Lydia still felt cheated. It was a time of the year she had always loved, until, that is, Charlie died. Every December when he returned from Winchester or from Oxford, they had decorated the Pimlico house from top to bottom, laughing and joshing together, teetering on tables and chairs, hanging off step ladders. A few days before Christmas, they would go to the market and buy the largest tree they could find, then climb up to the attic and rescue the odd assortment of decorations that survived year after year – baubles that had lost their paint, stars no longer quite as sparkling, the misshaped plaster of Paris figures they had made as young children. Christmas Eve brought a tantalising rustle of tissue and crackle of paper, and next morning the delicious aroma of an enormous Christmas lunch that even Cook could not ruin.

Last December had been different though. There had been no Charlie. And no tree or decorations, and the family's present giving had been confined to a single hastily wrapped gift each. The four of them had sat doggedly through a silent lunch, much of it remaining uneaten. There had been no joy, but it was Christmas and they would celebrate. Charlie would have wanted it. *Charlie would have wanted it* became a constant refrain over that holiday until Lydia felt she would scream if anyone so much as began the phrase. It had been summer when she had left for Turkey, months away from the winter festival, but she could remember thinking, *Thank goodness, I will miss Christmas this year.*

Now, though, her heart yearned for it. Or rather, yearned for her family. Her sister would manage some kind of celebration, she knew, even though they were only three. Alice could be controlling at times – she knew that to her cost. But this Christmas Day the silver would be newly polished, Dora and Cook would have their annual boxes, and lunch would be on the table at one o'clock. Lydia wanted to be there, sitting down with them to eat.

These days, though, she could hardly bear to think of her sister, but still she longed to see her, to confess her misdeeds, to receive some kind of absolution. Writing home had become a torture and put off for as long as possible – her letters were a few lines only, superficial and guarded, giving nothing away. She was adrift and unhappy, but could not allow Alice to know it.

She had no idea of the path she should follow. After that shameful night in the summerhouse she had vowed to leave Topkapi as soon as she was able, but here she still was. It was as though, along with her virginity, she had lost herself. She had become a different person, someone without purpose, without conviction, and without the energy to take charge of her life and make the decisions she must.

Her friendship with Ismet was dead. She had met him only once since that night and it had been a demeaning experience. She had been in the library with the princesses, and Ismet had come to collect a briefcase he had left behind. The librarian, Harry was his name, was looking gloomier than ever since

Ismet had been told he was no longer required and Harry would have to do without his colleague's help. When he had disappeared into his office to get the briefcase and her pupils were busy studying a sumptuous volume of Islamic art, she had managed to speak to Ismet alone for a few minutes. Her plan had failed, she told him. She kept from disclosing the true account of that night – she could not acknowledge how low she had fallen – but said merely that she had managed to gain access to Paul's office only once, and then had been interrupted by an angry Valentin Boucher.

'I am sorry to disappoint you,' she said, when she saw his face darken.

He looked past her shoulder, refusing to meet her eyes. 'It is not your fault. The task was too difficult.' He did not add 'for a woman', but the unvoiced phrase hung in the air.

'And I cannot try again,' she was quick to say. 'Valentin Boucher is already suspicious of me.'

'I would not ask you to.' The beautiful brown eyes held a look she had not seen before. 'I would be stupid to do so – it's more than likely you have alerted the Bouchers to what we seek.'

'I very much hope not.'

She felt a rising anger. Swayed by his beautiful face and smooth manners, she had scraped the depths for this man and his cause. Yet his response now was dismissive, almost hostile. She would have liked to beat him with her fists, but then hope-lessness took over. She had believed – what exactly? That the attraction between them might one day flourish into something wonderful? Instead, it withered as she stood here. How naïve she had been – and how stupid to be surprised now. Ismet was no different from any of the men at that meeting. From the moment they had seen a woman in their midst, their objection had been clear. She had been worth their notice only as a means to their ends.

'I hope not, too,' he said stiffly. 'But it has left us with a problem.' He ruffled his thick brown hair until it stood up in a sharp cockscomb.

She saw Harry Frome coming out of his office, briefcase in hand, and was quick to say her goodbyes. Ismet drew himself up and brought his heels together with a click, almost as though he were an officer dismissing a particularly hopeless recruit. 'Thank you for your help, Lydia,' he said, his tone even more formal. 'I know you will remain committed to our cause.'

That was something she didn't know. Not any more. It was all very well to talk grandly about freedom, but there was nothing grand about the tawdry encounter she had shared. These last few months her desire for justice had faded and she no longer knew herself. As long as she could remember, she had refused to accept the way the world was. She had challenged and fought, but now the urge to fight had gone. She was tired and listless, her enthusiasm for the palace, for Constantinople, even for teaching, was waning by the day.

Maybe this was the real Lydia and the mission for Ismet the dying embers of a woman she had pretended to be: the rebel, the plotter. Just a girl who needed to make waves. But for what? To say in some way who she was? Perhaps it was being a third child, the afterthought of the family, that had been the spur. Alice was the dependable daughter, Charlie the beloved son. She couldn't be a boy like Charlie, though she had often wished it, and she couldn't be a girl like Alice, loved for being good, though she had wished that, too. There had been no space for her, it seemed, unless she made one for herself. By being different. By being unconventional. And where had that led her? There was nothing more conventional, she thought bitterly, than being seduced by a man who said his wife did not love him.

'Miss Lydia?' It was Sevda, tripping through the door and looking excited. 'You are busy?' *Busy tormenting myself*, she thought, but found a smile for her friend.

'There will be a party for the Christmas,' Sevda announced.

'How is that?' She could not imagine there had been a mass conversion overnight.

'For you,' the girl insisted. 'For Christians to celebrate.'

'Oh, I see. Where?'

Her languid tone surprised Sevda. 'You do not want to go? But you must.'

'Where is it?' she asked again.

'Monsieur Valentin Boucher is giving a party. At his house on Friday, and I will find you beautiful Turkish clothes to wear.'

Lydia had no wish to dampen her companion's enthusiasm, but this was one party she would not be attending. 'I am afraid I will have to miss it. I have a fair amount of work to do – reading and marking and finding new books for the girls. I don't think I can spare the time.'

Sevda looked around the room. The evidence of work was meagre, but it had been the only excuse Lydia could immediately summon.

'Soon your school duties will lessen.' The girl was never anything but diplomatic. 'The princesses are not here and you need not prepare yet for their return. They remain at Yıldız for several weeks.'

She felt a fraud and tried to turn the conversation. 'I know. I had a message from Esma this morning. She seems fascinated by the renovations that are going on there.'

'They will see the palace come alive again. It will be good for them. And they have their brothers and sisters and their cousins to play with.'

'I am sure they will have a great deal of fun.'

'They will. And you will have fun, too – at the party.'

She was not going to escape. Sevda was looking expectant and she cast around for a way in which she could avoid the threatened event, since avoid it she must.

'I will think about it,' she prevaricated.

'And I will look for a special tunic.'

'You are such a kind girl, Sevda. I don't deserve you.'

Sevda beamed. 'Is anything I can get for you?'

'Nothing. I am a little tired that's all. I'd like to rest.'

Her companion made small noises of agreement and slipped quietly away. As soon as the door closed behind her, Lydia felt relief. All she wanted these days was to be left alone. She would have to give thought to an excuse for Friday, but first she must sleep.

By Friday, though, she had thought of nothing and when she woke that morning, her limbs felt almost too heavy to move. It was depression, she realised. Somehow she would have to get through this hateful evening, since if she absented herself without good reason, it could provoke the kind of talk she wished to avoid. She dragged herself from the bed and across the room to the chest of drawers. She had begun pouring water into the flower-covered basin when a sudden flush drenched her face and her forehead burst into beads of perspiration. There was a dreadful heaving deep in her stomach. She was going to be sick.

Afterwards, she tottered back to the divan and fell exhausted onto the counterpane, just as Naz came in. The girl's nose twitched censoriously.

'I am sorry, Naz. I must have eaten something that didn't agree with me last night.' What it had been, Lydia could not think. She had eaten hardly anything. The girl removed the bowl and returned with cold flannels which she placed on Lydia's forehead and the nape of her neck. She felt pathetically grateful.

'Naz,' she called to the girl as she left. 'I am feeling horribly weak. It would be better I don't attend the party tonight.'

The girl seemed not to understand. 'The party at Monsieur Boucher's?' Naz nodded at that. 'Do you think you could get a message to him that I am unwell?'

Naz bowed her head. Lydia was sure the slave had understood and would be quick to report to Valentin Boucher. And to the Valide Sultan, she imagined. The woman had stayed aloof and anonymous, a sinister presence at the centre of the web of intrigue that pervaded the palace. The girl could well spy for her, and certainly spied for Boucher. This time, though, it would work in Lydia's favour – at least now she had her excuse. When Sevda arrived an hour later with an armful of clothes, she faced her with a smile.

'That is so sad, Miss Lydia.' Sevda was genuinely upset. 'This is only celebration for Christmas. Such a pity you are sick.'

'I'm feeling a good deal better now,' she assured her, 'just too weak to spend all evening at a party.'

'But yes – you must stay in bed.'

Lydia snuggled down beneath the silk counterpane. There was nothing that appealed to her more than to stay in bed. Thank goodness the princesses were happily employed elsewhere and she had no responsibilities for at least two weeks.

'I think maybe it was the *kofta*,' Sevda said anxiously. 'It is very rich and perhaps last night the taste was not quite right.'

'Perhaps that was it,' she agreed, knowing full well that she had eaten none of the *kofta*.

–

A day in bed had her wake bright and early the next morning, feeling considerably better. But when she swung her legs from the bed, the same rush of nausea rose in her throat and almost choked her. She ran to the basin and retched uncontrollably. Naz must have heard her because, within seconds, the girl had slid into the room and silently taken the basin away. Whatever sickness she had contracted was not going to let go easily. The next morning she was ready for it and as soon as she woke, rushed from her room to the bathroom a few steps away.

Sevda arrived an hour later and brought with her a new dish of sherbet. When she saw that yesterday's remained untouched, she frowned.

'You no longer like my sherbet, Miss Lydia?'

'I like it very much. But my stomach is misbehaving at the moment. I will feel better soon and then you must bring me three dishes of sherbet a day.'

She was almost certain that would not happen. A dreadful suspicion had been growing in her. Surely, it could not be. *Please God, let it not be*, she prayed. But as the week progressed, so did the sickness. She began to feel nauseous throughout the day and stopped eating almost entirely. The occasional glass of pomegranate juice and a few slices of *pide* bread was all she could manage. She had never felt more miserable. The weather had turned cold and wet, and she slept and woke to the sound of rain beating at her window. Outside, the sky lowered to a uniform grey and the summer sheen of the bushes had been replaced by a dull ochre.

Sevda had continued to call each day and this morning she arrived looking determined. 'Miss Lydia, you must see doctor. You are a sick person.'

The time had come, she knew, when she must confess. 'I will see a doctor, but I don't need him to tell me why I am unwell.'

Sevda's innocent face nearly broke her heart. How could she say the words she must? She sat her friend down beside her, taking her hand but looking blankly across the room at the window opposite.

'I have something to say that will be painful for you to hear.' Then after a deep breath, her voice hardly audible, she said, 'I believe I am with child.'

Sevda gasped. She said something in Turkish, then tightened her grip on Lydia's hand. 'It is not possible.'

'I am afraid it is.'

'But—'

'I cannot speak of it, Sevda. All I can say is I have made a very bad mistake and now I must pay the price.'

'Oh, Miss Lydia, this is terrible.'

Lydia inclined her head. 'I am in a wilderness. I have no idea what I should do.'

The girl's response was immediate. 'We must tell the Valide Sultan. She will know what to do.'

Lydia pulled sharply away. 'That I cannot.' The thought of that imperious woman sitting in judgement on her was too much to bear.

'But you must. She has to know. This is *haremlik* and she is in command.'

They sat silently for some minutes and then Lydia said wearily, 'I suppose she will know soon enough.'

Sevda glanced down at Lydia's still flat stomach. 'It is best to tell her now. I will go.'

Without waiting for a response, the girl got up from the divan and whisked herself out of the room. Lydia remained where she was, stupefied and too weak even to get up and close the door. She had no need since in ten minutes Sevda was back, her face grave.

'Sultan Rahîme is most displeased.'

'I didn't think she would be dancing on the ceiling.' The old Lydia had surfaced momentarily.

As always, the irony was lost on Sevda. 'This is what she say: you may stay until baby is born, but then you must go.'

'Go where?'

Sevda lifted her hands helplessly. 'This I cannot tell you. Valide Sultan has said she wishes you to stay within the *haremlik* always and you must never leave the palace.'

'To hide myself away, in fact.'

'This is necessary. No one must know.'

'And what about the women in the harem?' Her friend looked uncomfortable. 'Do they know already?'

'They wonder. There is gossip.'

'And where will that gossip go? Will they spread the story?'

Sevda shook her head furiously. 'They talk only here. They are sorry, Miss Lydia. They know it is very bad for you and wish you well.'

Lydia felt tears pricking her eyes. The women could do nothing to help her, but their friendship was precious and she knew she would be cocooned in kindness for the next few months. After that, there was only darkness. But her pupils, what was to become of them?

'Esma and Rabia?' she asked unhappily. 'They return at the end of the week.'

'Sultan Rahîme say you may carry on teaching, but now you must put on Turkish dress. It covers much.'

'So, I can stay and teach her grandchildren, but only on her terms?' Her helplessness infuriated her, but she was in no position to refuse the woman's commands.

'The Valide Sultan is always right,' Sevda said simply.

Chapter Twenty Six

Constantinople, May 1906

'Not fair. *I* want to be Peter, Miss Lydia. Esma gets best parts.'

'Peter Pan isn't the only good part,' Lydia said pacifically. 'You can be Tinkerbell. She is a fairy. That's magical.'

'But Peter Pan magic, too. He flies.'

'And Tinkerbell dies,' Esma added unhelpfully.

Lydia sat down, an upsurge of weariness hitting her. The girls were generally well behaved but today they were tired from a late bedtime and the schoolroom was uncomfortably sticky. In the last few days, the weather had become a great deal hotter, and adjusting to the change was taking its toll on all of them.

'Tinkerbell does not die,' Lydia corrected. 'In the end, she recovers thanks to all the little children in the audience. Remember? And if you play Tinkerbell, Rabia, you can also play Captain Hook. He is a pirate and you would like that.'

At this, Rabia jumped up and danced around the room chanting in Turkish.

'What is she saying?'

'That she is a pirate,' Esma translated gloomily. 'But it's not fair. I want to be a pirate, too.'

Lydia sighed. She had heard enough. 'You are either Peter Pan or you are Tinkerbell and Captain Hook. You can go away and talk about it. Come back when you have chosen. We have done enough for today, but if you really want to put on the play for your mama and her friends, you will need to stop quarrelling. We have two weeks left – that's all.'

The girls looked ashamed and began packing their books way into their desks without speaking. At the door, they stopped only to say, 'Goodbye, Miss Lydia.'

'Goodbye, girls. I hope tomorrow we can make better progress.'

Two weeks, she thought, packing her own books into the old linen bag. Then her pupils would be off to Dolmabahçe Palace for their summer break. And not before time. She had been mercifully free of sickness for months now, but the tiredness never left her, and once the girls were gone, she could rest. At least for a while. They would be miles away when she gave birth and would know nothing of their teacher's predicament, and that was how it should be.

She did not want to think about the birth. This was a child foisted on her in the most wretched circumstances. A child conceived without loyalty and without love. An intruder in her life that for ever she must wear like a stone around her neck. The future was too bleak to think of; all she wanted was to rest. But when she reached her room, she found it unusually stuffy though Naz had thrown the windows wide. She would walk a while in the courtyard, she decided. It was a good time of the day to choose, since most inhabitants of the palace were eating and she could walk there unobserved. Not that her figure had changed that greatly, and in baggy trousers and loose overcoat, her growing bump remained undetectable.

Once in the courtyard, she found welcome shade beneath the palace walls and walked slowly up and down, trying to breathe deeply. The temperature had risen astonishingly fast and the air was cloying and heavy. The garden would have made a far more pleasant walk, but she had never returned there since

239

the morning she'd bid Paul Boucher farewell. Thinking of him now for the first time in weeks had seemingly brought him to life, since at that moment, she saw him cross the courtyard and make his way towards the arch that led to the buildings housing his office. His head was down, his eyes fixed on the gravel. Had he seen her? Most probably, but she had told him all those months ago they must have no further communication and he'd been obedient to her word. He could know nothing of the baby, and for that she was grateful. Naz must have reported the fact to his father; she had seen the slave eyeing her stomach when she thought herself unwatched. But Valentin Boucher would not tell his son. He would assume Paul's involvement – who else could it be when the two of them had spent so many hours together? – but he would not tell. The marriage he had arranged was already rocky and he would not want to add fuel to the fire.

No one else would know of her plight, except the inhabitants of the harem, and amazingly none of the women had spoken of it unless it was among themselves. They had fussed over her, brought her small presents, given her what she took to be titbits of advice. Many of them were mothers several times over, but none had forgotten their first experience of childbirth and thought her fearful of what was to come. In truth, she felt no fear. She had no idea if she would come through the ordeal and thought that on balance it would be better if she did not. For everyone. But if a miracle were to happen, and she and this child lived, how would they survive? It was this that made her fearful. Of one thing she was certain: she could not return to England with an illegitimate child. She could not pile such distress upon her family.

'It is possible you stay here in the city,' Sevda said one day, standing at the dressing table and twisting Lydia's hair into an elaborate plait.

'For that I need money. I have managed to save a little of my salary, but it will not go far.'

'There are very cheap rooms in Constantinople, and if you are in the city, maybe I see you.'

'It's an idea,' she agreed, though she could not imagine she would be allowed any kind of contact with the palace once the baby arrived. But she knew the girl was worried and did not want to see her upset. The suggestion of a room in the city appeared her only option, but it was only a temporary solution. The savings she had amassed would not be sufficient for a long stay in even the cheapest room, and what was she to do when they were exhausted? Find another job, she supposed, but where and how when she spoke so little Turkish? And if she were lucky enough to find some menial work cleaning or cooking, who would care for the baby?

'Maybe I should go to another city in Turkey,' she said. 'One that is cheaper. It might be better in the circumstances.'

Sevda nodded sadly. She had never asked the father's name, though she must have guessed. They had all guessed, she imagined, for who else could it be?

'It is best you go home, Miss Lydia. To England.' There was a decided note in the girl's voice.

'I cannot do that. It would bring disgrace on my family. Women who have babies and are not married are considered very bad in England. People turn away, you understand?'

'Here it is the same. But you can pretend – you had husband, but he died.'

'A widow?' Lydia forced a laugh. 'I doubt I'd be a very convincing one. I would never manage to keep up the pretence

– I'd be found out in no time and that would be even worse.
I'd be guilty then of deception as well as loose morals!'

–

The girls left for Dolmabahçe Palace on a hot, sunny day. She
envied them. From several of the corridors in the harem, she
could catch glimpses of the Bosphorus glinting in the gold of
the sun, and would stand and look and think how wonderful it
would be to spend days by the sea.

'Why do you not come with us?' Esma asked, as they waited
for the carriage to arrive.

'I would love to, but the sea does not agree with me,' she
lied.

They looked doubtful. 'It's the smell, you see,' she improvised. 'It is very bad for my chest. But you will have many
weeks there to enjoy yourselves.'

'When we come back, we do *Peter Pan* again,' Rabia said.

Their English had come on amazingly well over the last year
and the play had been a great success within the harem, even
though each of them, Lydia included, had been forced to act at
least three parts.

'Perhaps we could do a different play?' she suggested.

'What do we do?' Rabia was already jumping up and down.

'I will think about it while you're away.'

She felt desperately sad at having to lie to children she loved,
but it was necessary. On no account must she let them suspect
their governess would not be at Topkapi when they returned.
The Valide Sultan had been clear in her instructions, relayed
by Sevda and repeated several times. Lydia kissed them both,
one kiss for each cheek, and helped them into the carriage. It
was the last time she would see them and she had to fight back

the tears, pasting on a bright smile until the vehicle disappeared from sight.

Her world felt as though it had reached its end. The princesses would be by the seaside, but where would she be? Her future was still a large black hole. The days were ticking by and she must do something. The cloud that had menaced her from a distance would soon be a tempest, and she was in the middle of it. A cheap room in the city is what she must look for. She had heard only once from Ismet, a message delivered through her window by a furtive Latif. He had expressed the stilted hope that all was well with her, but nothing more. She had not replied but wondered now if she dared ask him for help – if she could find him. He would know of somewhere she could afford and he owed her that at least. But when she returned to her room, she found writing the note an impossible task. He had been cold and indifferent when they'd last met, so how would he react when he read of the baby? Shock, distaste, a desperation not to be involved in something so indecorous. She laboured for a long time on a carefully crafted message, but then tore it into small pieces. She could not do it – it was too humiliating.

A month to the day after the girls had left for their summer sojourn, the pains began. At first it was nothing worse than a cramp in her stomach and she rode it easily enough. But within the hour, the cramps had grown in intensity and the interlude between them become shorter. She had called out with that first sharp pain and three of the older women in the harem had bustled through her door. *They have been waiting for this*, she thought. Through the haze of pain, they helped her undress and laid her on a large sheet with which they had covered the divan. She was only vaguely aware of their preparations but saw bowls of water being brought and a stack of towels placed on the chest. She would have liked Sevda to hold her hand, but the young girl had been barred from the room. Instead, one of the women, a mother in the making herself, chafed Lydia's hands while another laid sweet-smelling cloths on her forehead.

She tried not to call out again, but it took all her fortitude. At intervals, a searing pain roared through her as though her body was made of glass and was breaking in two. Then she could breathe again – though not for long. As her muscles twisted and squeezed harder and harder, the pain became unbearable and she began to drown in it, caught in the undertow of a wave she could not control. She yelled out again, and the women smiled in response and nodded knowingly. 'Ssh,' one said, making a soft sweeping action with her hand. *They want me to relax*, she thought. *How stupid*.

But she tried to let go, not fight the pain, allow the wave to pass unhindered until release came again. Two hours, three hours, half a day, passed. She had no notion of time. She was trapped in an underworld of pain and smiling women. Then at last, a colossal, overwhelming desire to push, and the pain left her. She was whole again. She heard the murmurs of the women, felt them washing and tidying her, and then a shawled bundle was put into her arms. She was aware of the door opening and Sevda appearing at her bedside, pink with pleasure.

'Miss Lydia. You have son. He is beautiful.'

Chapter Twenty Seven

Constantinople, September 1906

Early that morning she had flung the windows wide, but the sudden return of high summer had made the room unbearably hot. Her son seemed not to mind. He lay, couched in her lap, while she waved a fan of peacock feathers to and fro, barely stirring the torpid air. He was a most obliging baby, Lydia thought, and stroked his cheek with her forefinger, any thought of his being an intruder abandoned since the moment she first held him in her arms. He opened one eye, looking for all the world like a buddha just awakened, and making his mother laugh.

'You are true to your namesake,' she murmured into his ear.

The baby's face puckered slightly. He was smiling at her, she was certain, and despite the heat she gathered him to her breast and hugged him tightly.

'He smiled!' she said to Sevda, who had come quietly into the room.

'Really?' The girl's face expressed polite scepticism. 'Babies do not smile for a month, maybe two?'

'Well, Charlie did,' Lydia said stoutly. 'He is a happy baby.'

'He is.' Sevda came across to the window where Lydia sat and lifted the baby from her lap. 'But maybe it is too hot to hold him.'

'I suppose.' Reluctantly, she let Charlie go, and her companion gently lowered his tiny form onto the cool sheet of the cradle. 'Sevda, is he not the most beautiful child you have ever seen?'

The girl smiled indulgently. 'You are in love with him, Miss Lydia.'

'Is that so bad?'

'Not bad. Not at all, but…'

The big 'but'. Lydia knew what Sevda wanted to say but could not. Charlie was two weeks old and the time was passing quickly. Esma and Rabia would return to Topkapi the next week and their erstwhile governess must be gone. The girls had written already – a few lines of their best English – to say how much they were looking forward to seeing her again, and would she find them a particular book a cousin had mentioned. She had gone to the library and asked Harry Frome, who had found it immediately and set it aside. It was the only time she'd ventured beyond the *haremlik* for months and she made sure to be at her liveliest with anyone she met, wanting to allay any suspicion she was in trouble.

But she was, since she still had no idea of what she should do, other than to find a room. Sevda had stopped urging her to buy a ticket for the London-bound train, realising her friend was adamant that she would not, could not, return home. At some point, Lydia knew she must find the courage to write to her family, to reassure them she was well. She would say she intended to stay and travel a while in Turkey now that her contract at Topkapi was ended. She doubted she would have the courage to tell Alice that she had a nephew.

'Today you must look for somewhere to live, Miss Lydia,' Sevda dared to say at last. 'Go into the city this evening when it is cooler and ask. I will come to the room and stay with the baby.'

'I will go. But tomorrow.' She wanted to push the future away, not think what it held for her, for Charlie. It would be a miserable room in the poorest part of a city she did not know; it was all her small pot of savings would buy. And for how long?

'The women have made more clothes for you,' her friend said brightly, trying to inject some hope into a hopeless situation.

'More clothes! I shall soon be able to open a shop.' A stack of beautifully embroidered gowns was already assembled on the chest top. 'And I cannot even finish a small purse. Shame on me.'

'You must take it with you when you leave.'

'I will, dear Sevda, and I will embroider your name bright and bold so no one can mistake whose purse it is!'

Sevda spread the new garments across the existing pile. 'I am sure you will need all of these. Baby will grow quickly.'

'I know and I am most grateful. I must thank all the women before I leave.'

She realised now how much she would miss the harem, or rather miss the comradeship the women offered. She was leaving for a world where she knew no one. When she walked through the palace gates, she would be completely alone. It was a terrifying prospect. For herself, she cared nothing, but for her baby, she was sick with worry.

Charlie's birth had changed everything. Had changed her. He had brought alive feelings that for a long time she had suppressed. When her brother died, she had turned away; she had been desperate to save herself from the pain that pervaded every corner of the Pimlico house. But loving this new Charlie had been a revelation. She saw how selfish she had been.

Unbearably selfish, cutting herself free at the expense of those who loved her. She hoped she was no longer that person. She had never meant to be.

All she had wanted was to live life on her own terms, to be free of the shackles that bound all too tightly. As long as she could remember, she had nursed a powerful sense of injustice, an anger that women were not respected for themselves, but lacked any power to change their lives. She had wanted to make an impression on the world, but the world had not valued her rightly – not for her looks or her person, nor for her ability to manipulate and charm, but for the woman she was. Yet looks and charm were exactly what she had found herself deploying – her sense of a true self had proved surprisingly fragile. Until Charlie. In loving her child, she had found that deeper, truer self and for the first time in her life she felt at peace. If she still challenged, it was not now to change the world but to protect this small creature for whom she cared more than life itself. If she were still bold, it was to confront a censorious world for his sake.

When Sevda left, she spent a long time watching her small son sleep before reaching for her book. The room had grown even hotter as the sun rose high and *Constantine the Great* did not make for easy reading. Small dribbles of sweat dotted her forehead and she began rubbing her eyes and twisting her hair clear of her neck. She got up and walked across to the cot where Charlie slept on, undisturbed by the stifling atmosphere. If she were quick, she could run to the bathroom before he woke and sluice herself in cold water.

She was gone minutes only, but when she returned she saw the door to her room was open and a figure was bending over the carved wood cradle.

'What are you doing?' she asked sharply.

Naz spun round. 'I look at baby. Beautiful.'

'Yes, he is beautiful. But I do not want him disturbed.' The protective armour she had grown strengthened even more.

'It is boy.'

Lydia frowned. 'Did you not know that?'

'Yes, I know.'

'Well, now that you've confirmed it for yourself, perhaps you should go.'

Naz, understanding the word 'go', left quickly. Lydia's serenity was momentarily punctured. She did not trust the girl and never would, yet Charlie slept peacefully still, unmolested. She dragged her chair across the room to sit by the cradle, and casting *Constantine* aside, gave herself up to contemplating her son's perfection.

—

The next day she was again sitting by the window, this time feeding the baby, who was drinking noisily from her breast, when the door opened and Sevda came in, looking anxious.

'What now?' Lydia asked wearily. 'You can tell the Valide Sultan I intend to leave on Monday.'

'No, not Valide Sultan. But there is a message for you.'

'Who on earth from?' She noticed Sevda was looking paler than usual and her pulse quickened. The baby, sensing her tension, stopped sucking.

'This note was delivered by Ibrahim.' She waved a small piece of white paper in the air. 'He works in the offices.'

'I know who he is.' Lydia moved the baby to the other breast and Charlie began feeding again. 'But what does he want with me?'

'It may be that Monsieur Paul has sent him,' Sevda suggested delicately. 'Ibrahim is his clerk.'

'I can't think it would be, but why don't we find out? Read the message.'

'You are sure?'

'Of course, I'm sure. There is nothing he has to say I would wish to keep from you.'

Sevda opened the folded note and scanned the page. 'He says – oh no, it is not from Monsieur Paul Boucher, but from Monsieur Valentin.'

Lydia felt a sickness settle in her stomach. The man's name was enough to make her hold Charlie more tightly.

'He say, "Please come to my son's office this evening at six o'clock. He will not be there but I will. Come alone. I have a proposition for you." It is signed Valentin Boucher. That is it. What can it mean?'

'I have no idea and I won't be going to find out.'

Sevda slumped onto the divan. 'Do you think he knows?' She nodded towards the now sleeping Charlie.

'Naturally, he knows. He is omnipotent.' She tried to joke, though she was feeling unnerved.

'Then think, Miss Lydia. Maybe he offers you money to help with the baby. You will need it.'

She considered this for a while. 'Do you really think that possible? If so, he would have to be a very different man from the one I met.'

'Maybe his son ask him.'

'Paul is controlled by his father. He would never dare suggest such a thing. And what about Paul's wife? Offering money would be tantamount to admitting paternity.'

The girl did not understand and Lydia shook her head. 'Don't worry, Sevda. I cannot imagine why he wants to see me, but your suggestion is a good one. Just in case there is money for Charlie, I will go. I need every lira I can lay my hands on.'

That evening she wore one of the outfits she had brought from England, hoping she looked serious and determined, a young woman who had come at Boucher's request but would ask nothing from him. Just before six, she wrapped Charlie in his shawl and took him to the meeting room. The women were about to eat and slaves had already brought the large round trays piled high with dishes and placed them on small, portable tables. But as soon as Lydia appeared in the doorway, food was forgotten and the women gathered excitedly around her, clucking over the baby, cooing and stroking him, and waving wooden rattles with enthusiasm. An older woman took him from her arms when she explained she would be gone a very short while and began singing what sounded like a lullaby. He would be in good hands.

The office door was ajar when she arrived, and for a second she paused on the threshold. The last time she had been here, it was to play the opening scene to her downfall. But she would not think in that way. She could not wish Charlie away. Ever.

Valentin Boucher looked up as she walked through the door. 'I am glad you came, Miss Verinder.'

'Why would I not? I cannot stay long though.' Her tone was brusque in an effort to control her nerves. The sight of this bear of a man had sent her stomach somersaulting.

'Please sit.'

'I prefer to stand.'

'As you wish,' he said indifferently.

They stood facing each other, their stony expressions a mirror image.

'I will be brief. You have recently given birth to a child, a boy. I have reason to believe the child is related to me. Am I correct?'

She did not answer him.

'I shall take your silence as assent. We need not discuss past history – I imagine it is painful to you – but then your future seems destined to be as painful.'

Sevda had been right. He had brought her here to offer her money. She did not want to take it, she wanted nothing to do with this man or his family, but she could not afford to reject a sum that might provide security for herself and her baby.

When she still made no response, he said, 'I cannot see how you will cope with a small child when you are without support. Without a husband. The slightest suspicion that a woman is not chaste ensures she is looked down upon by everyone. Yours is not, shall we say, a regular situation. I am prepared to help you.'

Here it comes, she thought. Would that help be enough to set her up in a small house of her own? The man was so rich he would hardly notice a dent in his stack of gold.

'This is my proposal. I will take the boy and raise him as my grandson. He will have everything that money can buy. He will have a father and a mother – Elise will be a good mother. She has been disappointed in that regard. We have all been disappointed. But in this way we can alleviate a sad situation. In fact, two sad situations. My son will let it be known that he is adopting the orphaned child of a distant relative. It will be seen as a benevolent act for the child's own good.'

Lydia grasped the back of a nearby chair. She thought she might faint for the first time in her life. She could hardly believe what she had heard. Boucher was not offering her money. He wanted Charlie – for Elise, for himself.

'And for you, it is a way out,' he continued smoothly. 'You will leave Constantinople a free woman and return to London and your family without the burden of shame you carry. You can be certain we will never speak of this again. Your passage home will be paid – a first-class berth on the Orient Express.'

The man was actually serious. The proposition he had made was astonishing, shocking. Her limbs felt like cloth, ready to give way at any moment. Somehow she must continue to stand there and face him. 'I—' she began.

He held up his hand. 'No, say nothing for the moment. In the circumstances, I consider it a generous proposal, but I see that it has taken you by surprise.' He was a master of understatement, she thought, and tried to form a sentence that would not come. 'You have a day in which to decide. Ibrahim will wait at the harem entrance after supper tomorrow and you will give him your decision. If you do not respond at that time, the offer will be withdrawn. But I cannot imagine you would be so foolish as to ignore a proposal so obviously beneficial to you. Once I have your decision, we will proceed.'

She stumbled to the door and, without any attempt to say goodbye, walked out into the courtyard and made her way blindly through the Gate of Felicity and across the gravel to the *haremlik*. Sevda was at the entrance waiting for her, and she collapsed into the girl's arms, wracked by violent sobbing. When she was at last calm, her friend took her hand and led her like a small child along the winding corridors. Only when she had helped Lydia into bed, did she speak.

'What did he say, Miss Lydia, that has made you so unwell?'

Slowly and with many hesitations, Lydia told her. Sevda gasped. 'I did not imagine.'

'How could you?' Lydia said brokenly. Then something clicked in her mind. 'I must find Charlie.' She sounded frantic.

'Hush. Do not upset yourself. The baby is well. I will bring him back, but you must rest.'

When Sevda returned with the small bundle, Lydia gazed down at him, a new pain in her heart. 'How could I ever do what that man wants?' Charlie was awake now and chirruping quietly to himself.

Her companion did not answer immediately, but then seemed to decide she would speak. 'It would be very sad, but…'

'There is no "but", Sevda. How can you suggest such a thing?'

The girl looked uncomfortable. 'Charlie would be with his father. The family is very rich and he would have a good life with them. And for you, you could go home and never tell.'

It was almost word for word what Valentin Boucher had said.

'He would have a good life,' her friend repeated. 'Better than a tiny room in a bad part of the city that is hard to pay for, even if you find work and someone to look after Charlie.'

Lydia's eyes filled with tears and the girl hugged her tight. 'It is very horrible, I know. But you must decide.'

Sleep would not come that night. When she was not feeding her son or settling him to rest, she lay awake, her eyes wide open looking into the darkness, tormenting herself over the right thing to do. She could not bear to let her baby go, yet Sevda, the kindest creature in the world, was right. What kind of life could she make for this little boy? If she gave him to the Bouchers, it would break her heart. More than that, she would not wish to live another day. Yet she must not think of herself. It was Charlie and only Charlie that mattered. Paul Boucher was his father and Elise would be a competent mother. The woman's delight at having her own child at last would surely overcome any grudge she might feel. No doubt they would hire a wet nurse until the baby was weaned. Charlie would grow up in a family that wanted him, one who would see him as an answer to their prayers, and he would lack for nothing. Could she deny him that, because of her own selfish love for him? Or did she have the courage, the real courage to let him go?

Chapter Twenty Eight

It was towards dawn before she finally drifted into a light doze, but she had slept for only an hour before she was woken. It was the slightest of noises. She scrambled upright and stared across at the cradle, but Charlie's small snorts reached her as a comforting rhythm. What had woken her then? She swung her legs from the bed and searched for slippers. There was the noise again, a scratching at the window she had made sure to close. It might be hot in the day but nights had become increasingly cold. In a daze, she staggered across the room and opened the shutters, then fell back in surprise at the figure that stood a few feet away. It was Elise Boucher. *The woman has come to take my son* was Lydia's first thought. She was about to slam and bar the shutters when she saw the expression on Elise's face. It was anguished and drawn.

The woman gestured to her that she wanted to talk, and she cautiously opened the window a fraction. 'Miss Verinder, Lydia. May I come in? I must speak to you.'

'But what are you doing here at this hour? And how did you come?' How was it the woman had evaded the palace guards, the harem eunuchs?

'There is a small gap in the palace wall where the stone has crumbled. It is at the other end of the garden.' Elise waved a hand leftwards, a direction in which Lydia had never walked. 'Some of the stones have been piled back and the crack is very overgrown, but if you bend and slide it is just big enough.' She drew in the air the shape of a low, narrow opening. 'It leads beyond the palace walls.'

'Do many people know of it?'

Elise shook her head. 'If they did, it would have been made safe. You have to know it is there to find it. Melek, my slave, told me. Last year she had a sweetheart in the palace and it was forbidden they meet. So...' She spread her hands in a Gallic gesture.

Lydia had never troubled herself with how Latif had managed to deliver Ismet's messages, but this must have been his way into the garden. Did he know Melek, she wondered? She would not be surprised; this was a very small world, she had come to realise.

'Who knows you are here?' she asked. Elise had arrived secretly, but she could have been sent by her father-in-law to pressure, to browbeat. It might be a trick.

'No one. You are safe – for the moment. That is why I have come at dawn. I am watched day and night, but even Yusuf has to sleep. I must be home before the household wakes.'

The mystery deepened. The only thing clear to Lydia was that in some way this woman's appearance was connected to the dreadful offer Valentin Boucher had made. She would take a chance, she decided, and threw the windows wide.

'You had better come in.' She did not relish conducting a conversation at a distance. There were too many ears in the palace always ready to listen. 'Are you able to climb over the sill?'

'Yes, I think I can – with help.'

Lydia supported the woman's thin figure until she landed safely on the floor. 'Please, lock your door. I must not be seen here.'

Elise's voice was barely above a whisper. Knowing that Naz would soon be lurking in the corridor outside, perhaps even now with her ear to the door, Lydia quietly turned the key. If later she had to explain the locked room, she could say she had slept badly and wanted not to be disturbed.

'Won't you sit down?' she said.

Elise sank gratefully into the chair by the window. 'I will be quick. You met my father-in-law last evening and I know of the proposal he made you. We are to adopt your baby. Pretend he was born in France and has been brought to Turkey by his nursemaid. We are to say he is the son of a relative who died in childbirth, and there is no one else in the family who can look after him.'

She had been ignorant of the details of the adoption Boucher proposed, but they had all the hallmarks of the ruthless man she had come to know. Neat, plausible and, crucially, details that could not easily be checked.

Her mouth puckered in distaste. 'If I agree, you will become the mother you have always wanted to be, Elise – and I will go back to England without a stain on my name.'

'You must not.'

'Not go back to England?'

'No, no. Go back to England, but take your baby with you.'

Lydia stared at her. 'You do not want him?'

Elise looked longingly towards the cradle. 'I want him more than I can say, but for his sake you must not agree to this proposal.'

Lydia shook her head in bewilderment. 'I have been thinking that for his sake, I should.'

'If you do, you will sentence this poor child to a life of unhappiness.'

'But you will be his mother. How can you say that?'

'I would do my best for him, how could I not, but I am no match for Valentin. I have no power within the family. Look at me, Lydia, what do you see? A figure of sorrow, *n'est ce pas*?'

Lydia looked and her heart filled with compassion for this lonely woman. And guilt, too, enormous guilt. She had made things a hundred times worse with her shallow flirtation. 'Do you know…?' She could not bring herself to finish the sentence.

Elise was unfazed. 'Do I know of your affair with my husband? I am fairly sure that Paul is your child's father, yes.'

Lydia wished she could shrink to inches high and crawl beneath the divan. 'I am so sorry,' she said, knowing how inadequate the words were. 'It was never supposed to happen. I was foolish – more than foolish. I have hurt people I never meant to.'

'My dear, do not distress yourself. Paul and I are friends, good friends. He has spoken to me of you and I know he feels most ashamed of his conduct. But *tant pis*, it is done and we must pick up the pieces, no?'

'You are very generous.'

'I am not a jealous woman. And you have been foolish, I agree, but you are very young and it is a hard lesson you have learned. But you must not make it worse. Paul is this child's father, but Valentin is his grandfather. That is what you should fear.'

'Surely he must welcome a grandson. What worries you so?'

'Look at what Paul has become,' she said simply. 'That is your child's fate. Yes, he will live in luxury – he will eat the best food, wear the best clothes, receive the best education money can buy – but he will be ruined. It is an heir that Valentin wants, not a grandson. A boy to carry on his wicked work, to continue the corruption and violence. As soon as he was sure the child was a boy, he made his proposal. If your baby had been a daughter, you would have heard nothing from him.'

Naz! That was why the slave had hung over the cradle. It was dreadfully plain now. She had been ordered to confirm that the baby born in the harem was indeed a boy.

Elise got up and went over to the cradle, looking down at the sleeping child with love in her eyes. 'What is he called?'

'Charlie. It was my brother's name.' Her throat tightened with incipient tears.

'Charlie,' Elise said in her French accent. 'It is a very English name. I like it.'

'I like it, too.'

When her companion was once more seated, Lydia said tentatively, 'Elise?'

'Yes.'

'I understand you fear your father-in-law, but you must have wanted a child for years. Why have you come to me? You are near to having your dream come true.'

'It would not be a dream, Lydia. It would be a nightmare. I have longed for a child – in my heart I always will – but not like this. I have grown glad I am barren. At least I have not the torment of seeing the child I brought into the world twisted to another's evil.'

She was struck dumb, for the first time waking to the terrible reality that Elise had painted. But her companion had not yet finished. 'Valentin will mould him, school him in whatever way it takes, until the child becomes an echo. If he is weak, as Paul is, he will buckle and become a mere shadow. If he is strong, and I think Charlie will be at least as determined as you, he will be whipped into shape until you would not recognise him as yours. That is his future.'

Lydia jumped to her feet and strode agitatedly towards her visitor. She was a jangle of pain and confusion. What this woman had said had turned her thoughts upside down. She ran her fingers through her hair, tugging at it wildly. 'I cannot bear to hear another word.'

'You will hear nothing more from me, except that you must leave the palace as soon as you can.'

'I am to leave in any case – I go on Monday.'

'That is good. And where will you go?'

Lydia shrugged. 'I have no idea. Wherever I can find a room.'

Elise stared at her. 'Here in Constantinople? You do not return to England?'

'How can I? If I did, I would bring disgrace on my family and I'll not do that. I have hurt them enough already.'

'I think you are wrong. Your family will be shocked, yes, but they will love you. And they will love the little one.'

Lydia shook her head and Elise sighed. 'If you are determined to stay, I will find rooms for you. Out of the city a little, somewhere Valentin Boucher is unlikely to find.'

'Can you do that?' A small pinpoint of light had emerged through the darkness and Lydia was eager to follow it.

'It will take a few days, but I will do it. When I have an address for you, I will come again.'

'I cannot thank you enough.' She felt a rush of love for the woman she had so thoughtlessly injured. 'I have been at my wits' end not knowing where to go and lacking anyone to advise me. Now all that concerns me is the meeting with Ibrahim.'

'Ibrahim? The man who is clerk to the library?'

'Yes, he is the bearer of messages from your father-in-law. He is coming this evening after supper. I must give him my decision then.'

Out of the blue, her companion lurched forward and grabbed Lydia's hand. 'This evening? You say he is coming this evening?'

'Yes, why?'

Elise jumped up, abruptly letting go of Lydia's hand and beginning to pace up and down the room. 'The minute you say no to Ibrahim and he takes the message back, you will be in danger. Valentin will be enraged. He sees the boy as his – he has already employed a wet nurse – and he cannot imagine you will not agree. He will make threats and you can be certain he will carry them out, or order others to do so.'

'But I must be safe here in the palace,' she protested.

'I would hope so, but I fear it is not certain. I must go immediately. I will find rooms for you today without fail.'

'But you are watched, you say – how will you manage?'

'I must lose Yusuf.' She thought for a few seconds. 'I will be unwell and take to my bed. Then he will be idle and go to the steward's room to play *okey* with him. Once he is involved in the game, I will slip through the rear door and through the garden. There will be carriages to hire in the road below.'

Elise had been speaking almost to herself, but now she turned to Lydia. 'Pack your belongings, but on no account allow anyone to know you are doing so. There are spies in the palace, too.'

She walked quickly towards the window and Lydia rushed to help her climb on to the sill. Once on the other side, she said, 'I have a few friends who will help. One will be your guide – he will have the new address. Tomorrow at dawn, climb through this window, and turn to the left. Some distance along the wall, you must look hard and find the small gap I spoke of. Crawl through the opening and wait on the other side. Your guide will be there to meet you.'

'Is it possible you can arrange everything so swiftly?'

'I must. The moment you speak to Ibrahim and refuse the offer, you are in danger.'

'And is Charlie in danger? Not Charlie, surely.'

'If Valentin cannot get the boy through barter, he will take him by force.'

Her heart beat so hard she could hear its thrum in her ears. 'But if I don't meet Ibrahim this evening? Your father-in-law was clear that if I refused his offer or made no decision, it would lapse.'

'The offer may lapse, my dear, but his determination to have the boy will not.'

Lydia's face looked ghostly in the dawn light. 'How can I protect my son?'

Elise stood quite still, silently looking at her. 'There is a way,' she said at last. 'But you will not like it and you may refuse if you wish. I can take the baby with me.'

'Now?'

'Yes, now. You can trust me, Lydia. I will keep him safe. Then tomorrow you have only yourself to get through the wall.'

'But what will happen to him? Where will you take him?'

'To my friends. There is a lady in the old city… I have helped her in the past and she will help me now. It is her husband who will come to guide you. If you agree, I will go straight to her with Charlie. Her daughter lives in the same house and has her own small baby which she still feeds. She will care for your son until you arrive tomorrow.'

The thought of losing Charlie from her sight for even a few hours tore Lydia apart. But what choice did she have? 'The baby's absence will not stay a secret. People will notice he is no longer here.' It was a prevarication.

'You can say he is a little unwell, and you wish to him to have quiet. Keep your door locked and ask for your food to be left outside.'

'I could, I suppose.'

'I must leave now or my absence will be discovered. I can take the baby with me and deliver him to a safe place, but it is your decision.' Elise's whisper had grown hoarse.

'This woman might refuse to take Charlie. What then?' Lydia was still prevaricating.

'She will not, I assure you. We are friends for many years. I must go now if I am to leave the baby with her and find rooms for you both. Is that what you wish?'

Lydia choked on tears that had been edging ever closer and lifted the sleeping child into her arms, wrapping him in several layers of blanket. She stroked the soft nape of his neck with her forefinger and kissed each of his cheeks several times. Then through a haze of misery, handed him through the open window. Elise took him and glided away like a ghost, melting into the September dew. For a moment Lydia wondered if she had imagined the whole thing; it seemed too fantastical. But she had only to look across the room – the empty cradle proved it all too real.

Chapter Twenty Nine

No day had ever gone more slowly. Lydia kept the key turned and when Naz scratched at the door, she made sure to open it a few inches only. Charlie had a few snuffles, she said, nothing serious, but she did not want him disturbed. The cleaning could wait. If she guessed right, the girl was in Valentin Boucher's pay and would almost certainly know of his proposition. No doubt she knew of the meeting with Ibrahim that evening, too. She would be expecting, along with her paymaster, that Lydia would hand over her baby without a murmur.

She had done just that – given Charlie to another. Somehow she had fought back the tears, and after an hour when she had stayed at the window, motionless and unseeing, had gone about the business of bundling the baby's clothes into the linen bag. But her mind was besieged. Had they really been in danger and could she trust Elise to deliver the baby to a safe house? Or was the woman so frightened by her father-in-law that she would have second thoughts and give him straight to Valentin? But she had to trust her. She had no other option. And surely Elise would not brave Valentin's reprisals unless she judged the situation so bad she could do nothing else?

At this very moment, the woman could be in danger. And Charlie, too. If Boucher's spies worked through the night, they would have seen her creep into the palace garden and leave carrying a bundle. And what could that bundle be, but a baby? A hellish vision filled Lydia's mind. Boucher's henchmen could follow Elise, snatch the baby before she reached the safety of the old city. His mother should be with Charlie; she should never have let him go. She should have left with Elise. Why hadn't she? She tried to calm herself. This way was better, she argued. Her visitor had been desperate to go before daylight and there had been no time to collect what was needed for their new life. And though one woman and a baby might escape scrutiny, two European women wandering the streets at dawn with a baby in their arms would almost certainly give rise to gossip and lead to discovery.

Elise had shown courage, and now she must do the same. She had little to pack for herself, which was as well since the trunk she had brought to Topkapi was stored elsewhere in the *haremlik* and she could hardly ask for it to be found. Her cloak bag would have to suffice. She would leave behind most of the cumbersome dresses she had brought with her; the dress she wore and one change of clothes was all she would take. It took a while to unearth the bag from the top of the vast wardrobe, but a few minutes only to push into its depths a dress and underclothes, together with Alice's letters and the several family photographs she cherished. Then she buried the bag into the furthest corner of the cupboard and sat down to wait.

Sevda came to the door at midday. She would have loved to talk to the girl who had become such a fast friend, but she knew she dared not. Instead she must lie to her and leave without saying a word of goodbye.

'I am sorry to hear Charlie is unwell,' the young woman said.

'There's no need for worry. He's not too poorly – just a little cold. It could be the rapid changes in temperature, but I want to keep him quiet. Do you mind if I don't ask you in?'

Sevda nodded wisely. 'No, the little one must sleep. But here, I have brought you food. You must eat.' She pushed a tray into Lydia's hand. The grilled aubergines and tabbouleh were normally favourites with her, but not today. Sevda was right, though. She must eat even if the food tasted of ashes. She must stay strong for her child.

'Thank you, my dear. You are a generous friend.'

She bent her head and gave the girl a kiss on the cheek. She wanted so much to confide in her, but she could not risk Charlie's disappearance becoming news and circulating the palace. A few whispered words would be enough to sound the alarm. Naz had ears that could hear all the way to Pimlico, she was convinced. Sevda looked surprised at the kiss, but then smiled and whisked herself back along the corridor.

One by one, the dreary hours passed. She counted them off on the wristwatch her father had given her as a farewell present. For a moment the image of Theo couched in his armchair, slippers on his feet, pince-nez at the end of his nose and a newspaper in his lap, almost destroyed her resolve. How had she come so far from what was right and ordinary and decent? But she had, and she must deal with the consequences. Just before six o'clock, she closed the window, pulled the shutters tight and barred them. She could not risk anyone climbing through the window or seeing the empty cradle standing forlorn to one side. Then she slipped out into the corridor and relocked the door from outside.

She hurried down the familiar blue and green corridors, but this time followed a path to the entrance of the harem that avoided passing through the women's meeting chamber. The prayer before sunset was over and most of the women would be gathered there. She had discovered the new route one fortunate day just before the girls left for Dolmabahçe Palace. In fact, it was Esma who had shown her. It brought a smile to her face for the first time that day, remembering the young girl's pride as she had shown Lydia what she called her secret way to the schoolroom. And from the schoolroom to the harem entrance took Lydia a mere minute.

Ibrahim was already there, kicking at the loose gravel with a frayed shoe. He brightened when he saw her. It meant his day was coming to an end. He waited for her to speak and she tensed herself to deliver her message. But she had nothing to fear from the servant, she told herself, only from the man who sent him.

'Good evening, Ibrahim,' she said formally. 'I have a message for your master.'

He nodded impatiently, evidently wanting to deliver the message and find his way home.

'You must tell him that my answer is no.'

'No?' he queried, as though he had not heard her correctly.

'I decline Monsieur Boucher's proposal. I do not wish my son to be adopted. He will stay with me.' She could not have said it plainer and it was clear that Ibrahim had now digested her words – his eyebrows had risen sky high.

He gave an indifferent shrug. 'Very well, Mees Werinder. I tell.'

When she once more stood outside her bedroom door and tried to fit the key into the lock, she realised her hand was shaking. Delivering defiance had taken its toll, but she would soon be out of Boucher's reach. Elise would find her rooms on the outskirts of the city where she would be safe – where Charlie would be safe – and at dawn tomorrow she would be on her way. Night had fallen quickly and a sliver of the moon's silver was creeping through a crack of the shutters. She was exhausted from last night's wakefulness but doubted she would sleep. More hours of waiting, and then, freedom. For an hour she tried to read – really, she must find something more interesting than this history book – but when its black and white characters began dancing in front of her eyes, she put the book aside and lay down on the divan. Within seconds, she was asleep.

It was a brief respite since once again she was woken by a noise coming from the window. Elise? Elise had come back, but why? Something must have gone wrong. She was struggling to her feet, trying to see through the gloom, when a hand came out of the dark and grabbed her, pinning both her arms behind her back. Something rough was being tied around her wrists. She went to cry out and a second hand, large and sweating, clamped her mouth shut. She fought furiously, but there were two men and she was no match for them. No, there were three, she realised, hearing the baby's cradle overturned.

'Where baby?' one of her captors demanded, very slightly releasing the hand he held over her mouth, but ready to silence her again if she called out.

'I don't know,' she gasped. She had been thoroughly winded by his companion's assault.

'Where baby?'

It was the turn of the man holding her from behind, and as he spoke he twisted her arm until she cried out again. The clamp was back on her mouth and she bit at it, sinking her teeth into hot flesh. He let go of her with a smothered howl and cursed at her in Turkish. He raised his hand and she knew he would strike her if she dared fight back again.

'Baby,' he snarled.

'As you can see, he has gone.'

The men muttered among themselves. Then, 'You say where.'

'I have told you, I don't know.'

The man who had overturned the cradle had been standing to one side, but now moved close to her. 'You tell,' he barked, and swung his hand, landing a blow against her cheek that sent her reeling. It was only his comrade's imprisoning hold that kept her upright.

'Bad things for you. You tell,' he threatened.

So, this was Valentin Boucher's reprisal and it had come far sooner than Elise had predicted. She should have left with her and taken the chance they would reach safety together. She could see that now, but it was too late. She had no notion of where Charlie was, but she would not have said if she had. *They will have to torture me*, she thought. *And they probably will.*

'Who take baby?'

This was another tack. And it was something else she would not say. Elise had put herself in danger to help and she would do nothing that would make the woman's plight worse. And Elise had Charlie. If she should die… but she wasn't going to. She would fight these thugs. With a stupendous effort, she kicked out, catching the man who stood closest to her on the shins. He gave a soft yelp of pain. At the same time, she dug her elbows backwards into the other man's ribs and for an instant he loosened his grip. She tore herself free and ran for the window. The men had broken through the shutters and they hung limply to one side. She reached up and hooked her fingers into one of the wooden slats, pulling herself upwards in a vain attempt to climb to the sill. The shutter swung fully back, moonlight flooding the room, and its brightness momentarily blinded the men. Then two of them cannoned across the floor towards her and grabbed her by the waist, flinging her to one side. Her head caught the sharp edge of the shutter as she went down. Her last thought before blackness overcame her was of Alice. Charlie would need her.

Chapter Thirty

Alice
Constantinople, March 1907

Alice had decided against breakfast and walked through the palace gates before her watch showed eight. It was two days since she had spoken to Elise Boucher, two days since Harry had kissed her. In the hours since, she'd had plenty of time to feel pain and feel joy, too. Pain that she might never see her sister again or even discover how she fared, and joy that the man she had come to love loved her in return. Or so she hoped. She had not visited the library again, worried that her presence might harm Harry further, but had hoped for a message. When it hadn't come, she thought he must be busy but would be sure to contact her soon.

The sentries on the gate took little notice of her, and she set out towards the market with a bounce in her step. As always when she escaped the palace, she felt a heavy curtain being rolled back and the fresh air of normality return. She walked to the market entrance, where several carriages stood in line at the side of the road, the lead horse kicking at the dusty ground, impatient to be gone.

'Telegram,' she said simply to his driver. He nodded and helped her climb the steps into the carriage.

It was a short drive to the post office, but a slow one. The streets were already bustling with people and animals, and the carriage was forced to negotiate a path along several winding roads before they came out onto the broad highway that led to the Sublime Porte. The driver dropped her at the large arch that fronted the government buildings and she paid him off before mounting the steps of the post office, her mind concentrated on the message she was to send. Somehow she had to combine reassurance and apology with the confirmation that she was coming home. The telegram took a long time to compose this time and a large number of forms ended as crumpled balls, stuffed out of sight in her handbag. In the end, she decided brevity would be her friend.

> *Am well and catching train tomorrow. Will be home in*
> *four days. So sorry for worrying you.*
>   *Love Alice*

It was the best she could do and she felt a good deal better having done it. Home in four days. It was difficult to envisage, surrounded as she was by a very different world. And once she was home, she would have to adjust fast to life in London. There would be little sympathy for her experiences at Topkapi and she deserved little. She had deceived her family badly, allowing them to believe she was safe in Venice. Even worse, she had conspired for months to keep Lydia's disappearance secret, and despite the worry she had lately caused, was no nearer telling them where their beloved younger daughter might be.

She decided to make her way back to the palace on foot; for a short time at least it would keep her mind occupied. She walked briskly – the sun might shine from a cloudless sky but there was still a nip in the air – and had nearly reached the palace gates when, to her surprise, she saw Harry.

He came towards her, his expression strangely subdued. 'You are up and out very early,' he said. She had the impression he was not happy about it but dismissed the thought as soon as it arrived. This was the man who only hours ago had kissed her passionately.

'I had to visit the post office. A telegram home to say I'm on my way. But should you not be at work?'

'You have forgotten. The library is closed today.'

'Ah, yes, the Sultan's new divan.'

'The very same. But the weather is too good to be indoors and I thought to take a walk.'

'What a good idea – I haven't a great deal to pack, so may I join you?'

'Yes… yes, do.'

There had been a definite pause before he replied, and her fleeting sense of unease returned. 'Where were you thinking of going?'

'There's a walk by the Bosphorus that makes for a pleasant stroll.'

'Then lead the way!' she said with a brightness she did not feel.

The beautiful stretch of water she had only previously seen from a distance was a good twenty minutes' walk away. Harry guided them expertly down small side streets and crowded alleyways until they reached the water's edge, where a broad walkway followed the shoreline for miles. He had hardly spoken on the journey and she was unsure whether to feel angry or sad at his attitude. She thought of those kisses in the library, decided she was angry and resolved to confront him before their walk was over.

'This path stretches so far!' she exclaimed. 'And look how many lamps there are!' They had begun to stroll along the walkway, a line of illuminations dwindling far into the distance.

'There must be a thousand lights dotted along the shore. I imagine the sea must look wonderful at night.'

'It does. The gardens, too. Look to your right and you'll see how they reach right down to the water – every one of them will be brightly lit.'

She turned to look. A large house, surrounded by enormous grounds, sat atop a gentle slope. She walked over to the iron railings marking its boundary and pressed her face against them. 'They have a magnificent garden.'

'All the gardens are magnificent and there are houses like this right along the shore. They are called *uyalis* – waterside residences.'

'You must have to be very rich to own one.'

His smile was wry. 'Valentin Boucher owns one, naturally, and Paul Boucher another.'

The name prompted her to say suddenly, 'I have to believe Elise. That she doesn't know where my sister is. That she is sure Lydia will come back.'

'It sounds as though you might not believe her,' he said lightly.

'I want to. She sounded sincere. It's the not knowing that's so difficult, but that's something I must learn to live with.'

Her voice had trailed off unhappily, and for the first time that morning it was the Harry she had come to know who looked directly into her face. 'It's painful for you, I can see, and not likely to get easier. But if I hear even a whisper of where Lydia may be, I will tell you immediately.'

'You will write?'

'I will, I promise.'

'Thank you. I know you'll do all you can to discover her whereabouts.'

They walked on for several minutes, while Alice struggled to find courage enough to speak her mind. But then she turned her face to the sea and took a deep breath. 'Since I came to Turkey, my life has been turned upside down – in all kinds of ways. I never imagined for one moment I could meet a friend like you.'

He looked away at that, but she had found a new determination. 'You *are* my friend, aren't you?'

'Of course.' There was that indifferent tone again. But then suddenly his voice changed and she heard the old sincerity. 'Alice, I need to apologise. I have not behaved well. I should never have kissed you in the way I did.'

So that was it. He was regretting the passionate embrace and now he was trying to let her down as gently as possible. Could dreams crash? If they could, hers had just done so. But she would go down fighting. 'I'm glad you did,' she said defiantly. 'Even if we are not to be friends.'

He groaned and she looked across at him in surprise. 'If only you knew.'

'I want to know – can't you see that?' And she took his hand in hers and squeezed it tight.

He stayed holding her hand and said with difficulty, 'I want to be more than a friend. Isn't that obvious? I've wanted it for days, but it just can't be.'

'Why do you say that?'

'Because… I had planned to take annual leave at Easter and come to England. I wanted to meet your parents. I wanted them to approve of me.'

'How could they not?'

'Quite easily. I had an important question for your father but the more I thought of it, the more I could see it was impossible.'

Her eyes widened. 'An important question? Are you talking of marriage?'

'You shouldn't be surprised. You must know how I feel, but since we kissed I've come to realise how unfair I've been in loving you.'

Alice came to a halt, her expression bewildered.

'It's simple,' he tried to explain. 'I'm not good enough for you. You know my family's situation – it's enough to make any father run. And my own position is little better. I'm a librarian with only a modest future in front of me.'

'Is that what this is about? The apology for kissing me? The coldness when we met?'

'I'm sorry for that, too. It was all I could think of to keep you at a distance. I'd decided I mustn't see you again, but then you were at the gates this morning – that was an accident.'

'A fortunate one.' She reached up and kissed him on the cheek. 'You are talking utter nonsense, you know. It's that failing of yours.'

It was his turn to look puzzled.

'You know, the one that says your family being poor matters. It doesn't. Even if my father were as wealthy as he once was – and he's fallen on hard times, too – he has always been able to recognise a good man. He will be delighted I've found you.'

'Is that really the truth?'

'It is, though he'll be surprised by my news. It's so unexpected. I believed my chance of finding love was over – and my family believed it, too.'

'How wrong can you be.' He wrapped his arm around her waist and hugged her close.

'So, does that mean you will come to London?'

Another hug, closer still, and they walked on. 'I will if you say yes to marrying me. And you should – I don't go around kissing every woman I see!'

Dreams did not crash after all, it seemed, and she was filled with such joy she wanted to sing her happiness aloud or shout it across the sea they walked beside. 'You need not ask. What else would I say but yes? And it's not so long to Easter.' She sounded wistful.

'I'll be sure to write to you every day. Or nearly every day,' he corrected. 'The mail can't always be trusted.'

'And once I'm in England, you'll be under less suspicion. I'm afraid I have brought you ill fortune.'

'That's nonsense, and you know it.'

'I don't. I'm certain you will sleep more safely once I'm gone. I am sure every minute of my day is watched over. At this very moment, someone will be ready to report my disgraceful walk with you.'

He laughed and stopped walking again. 'Shall we make it really disgraceful?' And before she realised what he intended to do, he had scooped her in his arms and kissed her deeply. A passing sherbet seller stared at them in amazement, his tray of little brown clay basins swinging dangerously to one side.

'Sometimes, Harry Frome, I hardly know you,' she said, when she had regained her breath. But she was smiling as she said it.

He was intrigued. 'In what way?'

'When I first met you, you were so stiff, so punctilious. Unbending, I would describe you.'

'And you were not?'

She considered this for a moment. 'You are right, I was just as much a prig. I am not quite sure what has happened to me. It's as though by travelling I have come back to the world, back to life. I have felt so much pain here and yet the flowers are brighter, the sun warmer. It sounds odd to say, but I feel I can smile from the heart now, as well as cry. I've become almost a different person.'

'Or perhaps it's the one you used to be – the one you should be?'

Harry was wise. The years of being the dependable daughter, of running a household, of managing a budget, of fetching and carrying and organising for others, had taken their toll. The girl who wore the fancy lace petticoat had been smothered beneath the weight of responsibility. But the responsibilities were still there. How had she forgotten?

Her face was downcast when she said, 'I may have said yes too quickly. I want to marry you, Harry, more than anything. I cannot imagine a happier future, but how would it work? Your life is in Turkey and I cannot leave my parents. And even if I could… I've become fearful of Topkapi, though I know it sounds stupid.'

'Not stupid at all. You have good reason. But I'm not asking you to make your life here. I intend to return to England myself. A new opportunity is what I need. Perhaps by the time we see each other again, I'll have found one.'

'You will leave Turkey – for me?' He nodded. 'But you love your work in the library.'

'I love you more. If you did not expect to fall in love, neither did I. I had determined my life would be one of work. Getting on in the world was the only way I could repay my parents. That's how I thought. I believed I could somehow make up for the disaster of my father's life. But I've come to see how mistaken I was. If you have become a different person, so have I. I was foolish to think my parents' happiness depended on my worldly success. It doesn't. My loving you, being happy with you, will bring them far greater joy.'

'And joy to my family, too. Seeing my happiness won't bring Lydia back, but it might make her absence more bearable.'

He tucked her arm in his. 'We could walk for miles, but I think we should turn back now. We have come almost as far as the Dolmabahçe Palace. It's where the princesses spend their holidays. Look.' He pointed ahead and she glimpsed grey stone walls rising, it seemed, from the water itself. 'It's a pity you cannot see it at night. The façade actually glitters. There are other smaller palaces lining the Bosphorus, some of them no longer used, but every one is illuminated and together they form a ribbon of light which is quite stunning.'

'It's the sea I love most. I've caught glimpses of it from the harem, but only glimpses. I can see now how wide it flows, from bay to bay, from Europe to Asia – it's magnificent.'

Her eyes delighted in the shining waters that seemed to stretch for ever. A shallow-bottomed boat skimmed past them, two men at the oars and a veiled woman reclining in the stern. The woman had raised a sunshade, though the sun was not yet hot. Other boats were crossing the strait, too, their owners enjoying a day of good business in ferrying passengers from one side to the other.

'So much activity,' she said, 'and we are playing truant!'

'One day's truancy hardly matters. And to be honest, I am relieved to be out of the library. I'm finding it difficult these days.'

'Difficult? I thought it would be hard for you to leave the place.'

'I have loved working there, but I won't be sorry to go. I suppose I've become disenchanted with Topkapi. This business with your sister has depressed me a good deal. I know no more than you what has happened to her, and I'm prepared to believe that others are similarly ignorant. But it's the wall of secrecy you've encountered I find so upsetting. And then there is Ismet's part in whatever has happened to Lydia. I knew what kind of man he was, but I didn't intervene.'

'He has not behaved well,' she agreed. 'But what could you have done?'

They were almost back to their starting point when she said, 'I don't suppose you have seen him again?'

'No, but I haven't expected to. He is a hunted man. Ibrahim tells me there are posters everywhere in the old city offering a reward for his capture. I cannot think it will end well for him.'

'If you do see him, tell him I am no longer angry. To be truthful, whatever trouble there's been, it must be Lydia's fault as much as his.'

'I'll pass on your message if ever I meet him again.'

They made their way slowly back along the small pathways they had walked earlier and reached the street that led to the market. 'Would you like to take a carriage from here? I can see one just ahead.'

'It might be a good idea. I still have packing to do and I suppose I'll have to find a way of thanking the Valide Sultan for her hospitality, though the words will stick in my throat. I can't stop feeling she is this dark presence – that we are puppets whose strings she pulls at will.'

He grinned. 'Be brave. Only a few more hours before you are on your way home. What time do you leave this evening?'

'A carriage has been ordered for nine o'clock, plenty of time to get to Sirkeci. The train doesn't leave until way past ten.'

'I'll come to the station with you. The driver can wait and bring me back to the palace. That way, there will be no problem with the guards. At that time in the evening they challenge anyone who attempts to pass through the gates.'

'Are you sure? It will mean a late return for you.'

'I doubt I'll sleep much anyway.'

'Nor me,' she agreed, realising anew how very much she would miss him.

–

She had barely reached her room when Naz appeared on the threshold, a suitcase in her hands. The girl's eyes still refused to meet hers and she was glad when the slave left her alone. Very soon she would never have to see Naz again. She dragged her dresses from the carved wood cupboard and threw them onto the divan, folding them as tidily as she could to a shape that would fit the case, then with some difficulty arranged their long skirts, one on top of another. She was careful to smooth each length of fabric, hoping her frocks would survive the long journey without a crease. It was a journey she was not looking forward to. Three long days alone, without Lydia and missing Harry.

But she was returning to her family, she must remember. Cissie was sure to be at Victoria station; Cissie, who had held things together all this time, not knowing what predicament her niece might be facing. There would be questions, explanations, apologies. She must confess her pretence over Lydia's letters and explain how anxiety had led her into further pretence, journeying not to Venice but to Constantinople. She had not wanted to worry them, she would say, had wanted to bring them news of Lydia, even bring their daughter back with her. But she had failed – and this would be the most pitiable moment of her confession. She would have to admit that despite the distress she had caused, she was no further forward in tracing her sister. All any of them could do now, she would tell them, was to wait and hope. Hope that Lydia would give up her wandering soon and return home. It would be a bitter message to accept.

She looked across the room to where her sister's book lay on the desk. She had so little of Lydia to take back with her, she would pack that, too, despite its weight. The baby's cap was already secreted away. She doubted she would ever tell her parents the full truth – that would have to wait until Lydia herself returned home. The bonnet would remain her secret, and she would keep it close until her sister was once more with her. She walked over to the desk to gather up this last possession and the Turkish slippers she wore, bought in the market a few days earlier, caught the edge of the rug and nearly tumbled her to the ground. She would be best to leave them behind; they would be too dangerous once she was home again and every day up and down the Pimlico stairs.

She bent to flick the upturned rug back into place and stared. There was a mark staining the otherwise pristine floor. It was a curious shape and she got down on her knees to look more closely. The stain was large and irregular, a cluster of mushroomed clouds, for the most part a dirty pink, but in the very centre a deep red, edged with brown. The stain was old and must have lain here for months but the rug had hidden it from her view, from everyone's view.

There was a familiarity about the shape of the image and she tried to think where she had seen something similar. Then it came to her – *Beeton's Book of Household Management*. Dora's bible. The maidservant was a devotee of Mrs Beeton and had gone straight to the book the morning the postman had caught his hand in the letter box and dripped blood over the polished wood of the hall. *Beeton* had given sage advice, but it was a nasty stain that had taken Dora many hours of labour to remove. A blood stain. This was blood!

Chapter Thirty One

But whose? Her mind had leapt to an inevitable conclusion, but she tried to suppress the thought. The blood could belong to anyone. Yet deep within she knew it was Lydia's. A stain this large meant a considerable injury, certainly something that needed medical attention, but there had been no mention of Lydia seeking a doctor or going to a hospital for help. Which meant that she had been right all along – her sister had not made the decision to leave as everyone assumed; she had been abducted. The blood had been spilled and Lydia forcibly taken. But how could it have happened without anyone knowing or seeing? If it were just one assailant… another thought skittered through her mind. Perhaps this wasn't her sister's blood, but her attacker's? Lydia could be a hellcat in a fight, she knew that well. She had beaten even Charlie in their childhood battles, and she would have put up the most tremendous struggle defending herself and her baby. But Alice had only to think of the physical power of a man like Yusuf to know that Lydia would have stood little chance against such an enemy.

She looked down at her hands, her knuckles bloodless from clutching the desk in a fierce attempt to stay upright. But she was allowing her imagination to rule, she chided herself, relaxing her hands as best she could. There could be other explanations. The stain was old and it was possible the room had housed others before Lydia, and it was a former resident who had met with serious injury. That was probably the answer and she must forget the instinct telling her otherwise. She steadied herself and walked over to the carpet, flicking it back into place. She would say nothing of what she had found.

A knock on the door and Sevda glided into the room. 'How are you, Miss Alice?' Her cheerfulness forced Alice to a welcoming smile. 'I am here to help you pack. Ah, no.' She had caught sight of the suitcase lying open on the bed. 'You are nearly ready.'

'I think so, but thank you for your offer. In truth, I've hardly anything to pack. I brought little with me and I've only a few souvenirs to add.'

'I have brought you another, but it is small. I hope you will like it. It is a farewell gift from Sultan Rahîme.'

She could not prevent her surprise showing. 'This is most kind.' She took the parcel from Sevda, turning it in her hands. 'And you are right, it is small enough to fit easily into my suitcase.'

Its size belied its value. She gave a small intake of breath when she opened the package. A beautiful filigree bracelet set with emeralds, flawless and shining, lay couched in velvet cloth. 'I cannot take this. It is far too expensive a gift.'

Sevda spread her hands. 'Rahîme Perestû is a generous woman and she wishes you to take good memories with you.'

'I will go to her immediately. I must thank her – and I can say my goodbyes at the same time.'

'That is not necessary,' Sevda was quick to say. 'The Valide Sultan is a busy woman and she is happy for me to wish you goodbye on her behalf.'

The distant farewell was unsurprising. The woman had remained shrouded from sight for the entirety of Alice's stay, but why this expensive present? Her suspicions broke out anew. Was the bracelet a memento of good memories, or a way of ensuring her silence if she were ever tempted to throw doubt on the palace?

'Who has lived in this room?' she asked suddenly. 'Apart from myself and Lydia?'

Sevda blinked at the question. 'No one, Miss Alice.'

'I'm not talking only of the recent past, but for years back.'

'No, no one. The room has never been used, not since I am in the palace and that is fifteen years. The women do not like to be so close to the garden, but your sister loved it for that reason. She could have had many rooms, but she chose this one. Why do you ask?'

For a moment she could not reply. Fifteen years and the room never used until Lydia had chosen it. It had to be her sister's blood. There was a ringing in Alice's ears she could not dislodge, even when she shook her head violently. Her suitcase swam across her vision and she felt the empty cloak bag at her feet. She could not leave. Not now. When she had thought her sister had gone freely, it had hurt to be abandoning her, but now she was certain Lydia had been hurt, kidnapped as she had suspected almost from the start, she could not go. She had to find her. She had to see Harry.

'Miss Alice, are you feeling well?' Sevda had moved towards her, and there was a deep furrow on her beautiful forehead.

Alice forced herself to regain control. 'Well? Yes, I am very well. But I have had a thought. I need to say goodbye to Mr Frome,' she improvised. 'I should have done it earlier, but I thought I might walk over to the library this afternoon. Then one of the ladies mentioned the building is closed today. Where would I find him, do you think?'

'If he is in the palace, he will be in his room. His new room in the men's quarters. They are the buildings beyond the library.'

'Can I go there and look for him?'

Sevda looked slightly shocked. 'It is not advisable.'

'I suppose *you* could not find him for me?'

The girl was now looking scandalised. 'No, not at all. Perhaps you write a note?'

'And you can deliver it?' she said eagerly.

'I will ask a slave to take it. Male slave.'

Alice was thinking quickly. A note would take time and she had none. 'Perhaps, after all, writing would be discourteous. I should speak to him directly. Could the messenger ask Mr Frome to meet me at the harem entrance?'

The girl nodded, though it must have seemed an odd request, but she was plainly relieved that Alice no longer intended to storm the men's accommodation. 'I will go now and see to it.'

Fifteen minutes later, Alice saw him come into view. He was hurrying from the far courtyard through the Gate of Felicity, a worried expression on his face.

'What on earth has happened? I thought we were to meet tonight, but the slave who came to my room insisted we say goodbye now.'

'It was a lie, a ploy. Harry – I have something terrible to tell you.' She swayed a little and he caught her by the forearm and steadied her.

'Let us walk a while. We will not be so noticeable.' He tucked her hand in his arm and the solid warmth of his body made her feel stronger. They had walked into the first courtyard before he spoke again. 'Now tell me.'

'There is blood in my room, a stain on the floor hidden beneath the rug.' He did not seem overly surprised, but in itself she thought the fact was not alarming. 'It is an old stain,' she went on, 'and a very large one. Someone has suffered serious injury in that room.'

He looked at her enquiringly. 'Forgive me, Alice, but at the moment I cannot see why this should have thrown you into such distress.'

'The only people who have slept in the room are myself and Lydia. And I have suffered no injury.'

She saw the dawning comprehension on his face. 'You think Lydia… Lydia was hurt?'

'What else can I think? It has to be her blood. She has suffered a very bad injury, but no one knows of it. Why would she willingly go away in such a terrible state? The answer is she would not unless she had been forced. She has been abducted, Harry. I have always known it.'

He passed a hand through his hair, disordering its trim style. 'Is there no other explanation?'

'Can you think of another?

'Not immediately, but someone in the palace must know how that stain came to be there.'

'Someone does, I am convinced. I have always been convinced of it. But she does not live in the palace.'

'You mean Elise Boucher?' He shook his head. 'I have never agreed with you over Elise and I still do not.'

'I know I am right,' she said simply. 'But I will not drag you further into this morass. All I need from you is an address.'

They were at the palace gates now and he stopped walking and looked hard at her. 'We will both go,' he decided. 'We will find a carriage and go. Whether she is at home and will see us is another matter.'

The carriage swept around the circular driveway, crunching the gravel beneath its wheels, and coming to a halt before one of the beautiful houses they had seen that morning. Its façade was as imposing as its magnificent garden, the one she had glimpsed through the iron railings, and for an instant her resolve faltered.

These people had wealth beyond her understanding and with wealth came power. Power that had hurt Lydia, she was sure, and was likely to hurt her, too. But she had to go on. She walked towards the front entrance while Harry was paying the driver. The door was large, forest green in colour, and cast in wrought iron set in a fluted arch of stone. A heavy, ponderous door, but its lace-like decoration was intricate and fragile. She wondered if Elise had chosen its pattern.

She was about to raise the iron knocker when a woman emerged from the side of the house, holding an enormous bunch of flowers. It was Elise. And right behind her was Yusuf, her constant shadow.

'Miss Verinder – and Harry?' She sounded flustered.

'Good afternoon, Elise.' Harry's unfailing courtesy made Alice smile despite the dangers of their situation. His smooth tones managed to suggest they were welcome visitors, their call nothing out of the ordinary. 'We were in the district,' he went on, 'and Miss Verinder said how much she would like to say a personal goodbye. She leaves this evening.' He placed particular emphasis on 'this evening' – for Yusuf's benefit, Alice thought. She looked at Harry admiringly. The unassuming man he showed the world hid a talent for diplomacy and quick thinking.

Elise's eyes roved anxiously between them, clearly trying to resolve just why they had come. 'Yusuf, take these please.' She thrust the flowers into the man's hands. 'Take them to the kitchen and get Pembe to put them in water. And ask her to make lemonade for my friends. I would like to show them the garden before Miss Alice leaves for England.'

He was reluctant to go, but after a tense few seconds, turned and walked back into the house.

'Come quickly,' she said. 'I have a small hideaway in the garden. Yusuf has not yet found it.'

She led them to the far side of the house and to a path that skirted the walls and travelled deep into acres of greenery. The house was set at the top of a gentle hill and the quiet waters of the Bosphorus stretched below them. Was it only this morning they had walked by the shore, unaware of this new, deadly twist to Lydia's story?

The hideaway proved to be no more than a rough wooden bench in a small glade, but a refuge invisible from the rest of the garden. Harry sat himself down cross-legged on the grass while the two women perched side by side on the bench.

'What is it you have come for?' Elise's voice trembled. 'You need to speak quickly. Yusuf will be looking for me.'

Poor woman, Alice thought, the man was her gaoler. Aloud she said, 'We will be brief, Madame Boucher. Last time we met, you convinced me that Lydia would come back.' Elise sighed. The old subject had raised its head yet again. 'I have come to say that I believe you mistaken. I ask you again to tell me all that occurred between you and my sister.'

'Why do you question me in this way?'

Alice looked at Harry, seeking confirmation. He nodded and she plunged in. 'There is a bloodstain in my room. In Lydia's room. It is a very large stain and could only have been made by a terrible accident or a brutal attack, and there is no mention in the palace of an accident. My sister has not gone away of her own free will. She has been kidnapped and badly hurt. Where is she, Elise? And where is her baby? I think you know the answer to both of those questions.'

Elise's face crumpled like a sheet of ancient parchment. 'I can answer only one.'

'Which one?'

'The baby. I know where he is.' Alice had to lean so far across to hear the words that she was bent nearly double.

'Where? How?'

'He is with an old friend in the city – with her daughter, in fact – waiting for Lydia to return. I took him there for his safety.'

'Why did you not tell me of him?'

'He was your sister's secret, not mine to reveal. And I have been hoping every day that Lydia would come back.'

'And Lydia…?'

Elise hung her head, fixing her eyes on the hands she could not stop from a violent twisting. It took several minutes before she could speak. 'What you have said is new to me – this bloodstain. I do not know what to think.'

'What did my sister do when you took her baby?' Alice pursued, ruthless in her determination to extract this last secret.

'I sent a guide,' Elise mumbled. 'She was supposed to meet him outside the palace walls at dawn. He would take her to the baby and then to new lodgings I had found just outside the city. But she never came. The man waited an hour and then left.'

'And when she did not come, you did not think to look for her?'

'You can see how I am situated.' Her shoulders drooped helplessly. 'There was no possibility I could search for her. I thought that maybe she had become scared and decided to leave the palace before the time we agreed.'

'So, if she left the palace early, why did she not meet the guide?'

'All I could think was that she had hidden away, and then something had prevented her from getting to the meeting place on time. Maybe she got there too late and the guide had left.

Without him, she had no way of knowing where to go. No way of knowing where her baby was.'

'She could have come here,' Alice objected.

'I thought she would, eventually, try to get a message to me – my address is well known. But it is almost impossible to send a message here without being discovered and that would have worried her. I hoped that when time passed, things would calm. My father-in-law would forget about the baby and no longer search for him. Then Lydia would make contact with me. But then you arrived, Miss Verinder, and there was more trouble. This is why I begged you to stop asking questions.'

Alice was stung. She wanted to demand what Elise would have done if she had lost a sister, but instead she pressed on.

'Why is your father-in-law so interested in my sister's baby?'

'He is my husband's baby, too,' Elise reminded her gently. 'There will be no children for us, and for Valentin Boucher this is an insult and a tragedy. He considered the baby his to take.'

Alice could feel her body tense. Her feelings for the child had been uncertain, his birth a cause of shame and humiliation. But how could Boucher possibly think he had the right to take a child that was not his. And just what had he intended by this little boy? But now was not the time to ask. For the moment, Charlie was safe – it was Lydia she must find. She turned to Elise again.

'Do you still believe that… that Lydia is out there some-where, waiting for your father-in-law to grow tired of his search?'

Je suis tellement désolée.' The woman hung her head. 'You have brought me dreadful news today.' For a long while she continued to stare at her feet, but then burst out, 'It makes sense of something I did not understand.'

'What is that, Elise?' Harry prompted her gently.

'There was trouble – the day after Lydia disappeared. Paul's father came here and there was a fight. I could not hear what they said, but Paul has never fought his father, never in all the years I have known him. It had to be something bad, very bad, to make Paul so angry.'

Alice braced herself for the question she must ask. 'Do you think now that Valentin Boucher came here to say that Lydia was... dead?'

'I think it is possible.'

Alice could not speak. Her throat had closed and she was finding it difficult even to breathe.

'If so, where would she have been laid to rest?'

Dear Harry, trying to make terrible things sound a little less terrible. Alice slipped from the bench and knelt beside him. His arms enfolded her and cradled her tight.

She looked up and saw Elise's face, her eyes full of unwept tears. 'If she has been... if she is dead,' the woman stumbled, 'it will be because Valentin's men got to her before she could escape. My father-in-law wanted the baby for himself and he is a man who gets what he wants. He is wicked, he has many crimes to his name, but none that can be proved. And many victims – a young man whose land he took is one. His sister tried to speak to me, but I could do nothing for her. She said she had found her brother's grave at the edge of the Eyoub Cemetery, though it was unmarked. The graves Valentin fills are all unmarked.'

'Does the Court know of these graves?' Harry said. *He means the Sultan and his mother*, Alice thought, remembering her suspicions that the emerald bracelet had been a gift to silence her.

'I think not, but perhaps it suits the Sultan to look away.'

'We must go to this cemetery. I have to know.' She had suddenly to be moving. She jumped to her feet and pulled Harry up beside her. Elise rose quickly, too. 'You travel tonight?'

'I was supposed to, but now I am unsure.'

'You must go. Go tonight and take the child with you.' Elise walked over to her, standing so close she could feel the woman's breath on her cheek. 'Take the child,' she repeated. 'Keep him safe for ever.'

'But how do we find him?' Harry asked.

'I will bring him to you after dark.'

'You are watched – Yusuf…'

'I will ask Pembe to cook Yusuf a large meal and Melek to serve it. She is his favourite slave and she loves me. She will keep him busy long enough for me to fetch the child from the family who cares for him and bring him to you. As soon as it is dark, you must leave the palace.'

Alice's hands went to the sapphire pendant at her neck and fingered it anxiously. 'I am watched. How am I to meet you without anyone knowing?' She thought for a moment. 'Can I escape the way Lydia intended?'

'Not any more. The crack in the wall has gone. I have driven past in the hope that Lydia might be near – *tellement stupide*, but what else could I do? – and I saw weeds have been cleared and the wall mended.'

'So, what do we do?'

'We go for a walk,' Harry put in.

Elise nodded agreement. 'You must take a stroll and then disappear,' she said.

'I can distract the guard while Alice slips through the gates.' Harry was warming to his theme. 'I will say I need to stretch my legs before bedtime. They will let me do that as long as they expect me back, and expect *you*, Alice, to be in the carriage that leaves at nine o'clock.'

'But my suitcase?'

'You must leave it,' Elise said. 'Walk out with nothing. It is the only way. When you are through the gates, follow the wall to the right and when you reach the point at which it turns, look across at the street opposite. There is a small mosque on the corner, behind a tall tree. It is not remarkable, but it has a shelter in front of the entrance and I will wait there.'

'I suppose it will be no great sorrow to leave my dresses behind.' Then as she thought of the evening to come, she stopped speaking. A lightness was in her chest, a flutter in her stomach. The unwanted child had suddenly come alive to her. 'Will I really see my nephew tonight?'

Elise managed a half smile. 'You will, and so shall I. I have not seen him since the day I took him to my friend's house. He was two weeks old, and beautiful.'

'I am so sorry we have brought this trouble upon you.' Alice bent to kiss the woman's pale cheek. 'I pray you will be safe.'

'What happens to me does not matter. It is the little one who is important.'

There was a rustle in the grass nearby, then the sound of footsteps coming closer. The three of them froze as though figures in a tableau. Elise whispered, 'Go quickly. Keep to the wall on your right. It is far enough from the main path that Yusuf will not to see you.'

'And you,' Alice asked in a troubled voice, 'what will happen when he finds you here and us gone?'

'We will play cat and mouse again, Yusuf and I.'

Chapter Thirty Two

Harry held her hand all the way to the cemetery, though they hardly spoke. Her mind was splintered – fragments – words, sounds, images, rising and falling, circling in a dance of madness – too much with which to grapple. It was not Lydia's political engagement that had decided her fate after all, but a very personal one. Boucher had brushed aside her sister's paltry attempts to incriminate him; it had been her child he had wanted. A child he considered his own. Elise had done her best to save the baby, but why Valentin Boucher wanted him so badly was a puzzle. She thought she could make a good guess. Elise was childless and would remain so, her father-in-law was enormously wealthy and, according to Ismet and now Elise, ran an empire of criminal activity. He would want an heir beyond the son he already had, a son that from Lydia's musings in her journal must be a disappointment to a ruthless man.

She was still groping her way towards some kind of understanding when she realised they had reached the Eyoub cemetery. Now she must face the moment when the true extent of Boucher's savagery could be revealed. The carriage dropped them at the entrance and, hand in hand, they began the walk along a pathway that was almost a small road. It meandered a route up the hillside, cypress trees shading the way, while far below the waters of the Golden Horn curled back on themselves to meld with those of the Bosphorus and the Sea of Marmara. They were walking among gravestones, legions of them on either side. Most were very old, some leaning drunk-enly towards each other, some mingling with fallen masonry that had been abandoned to the long grass. Carved on each stone were lines of Arabic or Turkish and at their pinnacle, sculpted headwear – a turban or fez or tarboosh.

'What a strange sight,' Alice said quietly, as more and more gravestones rose into view. 'Each stone has some kind of head covering.'

'They distinguish who the person was in life. What their profession was or their social standing.'

Alice hardly heard him. She was looking ahead at the hundreds of gravestones they had yet to pass. 'The cemetery seems to stretch for miles.' Her voice had begun to shake a little. 'Now that we're here, I doubt we'll find anything.'

'Elise said the men her father-in-law killed or had killed are buried at the very edge of the cemetery. We should take a narrower path and head towards the boundary wall.'

Harry's words steadied her and she allowed him to tighten his hold on her arm and guide her from the main walk onto a smaller track, and from there to an even smaller one. The forest of gravestones began to thin until finally they petered out and she was left looking at a wasteland.

'Come,' he urged. 'We must walk a little further.' In the distance, a low stone wall marked the extent of the graveyard and they walked towards it.

They had gone some way when he stopped and pointed. The earth here had been disturbed, not heaped as was usual for burial, but chafed and disordered. It was plain that someone had been digging. They drew closer, staring at the clumps of earth scattered roughly across the ground's surface, neither of them knowing what to do or what to say. There was a shout behind them and a figure erupted from between a group of trees. The man waved excitedly at them. *One of Boucher's henchmen come to make sure we go no further*, was Alice's first thought. But when the man drew nearer, she saw he wore workman's clothes and carried a shovel, and on his fez was a badge that looked official. He spoke in Turkish.

'He wants us to follow him.'

She did not argue and, still holding tight to Harry, followed after the man. The custodian – as she imagined him to be – jabbered a few more words at Harry and waved his hand.

'There. He says the grave we seek is there.'

'How does he know what we seek?' It was a cruel confidence trick, she was sure. It would be nothing more than a way of extorting money from them.

'This is how he knows,' Harry said gently. And led her to a patch of earth marked only by a wooden cross, one made from twigs and bound with twine.

She stood and looked down at it, unable to say the words. Then a whisper was jerked out of her, 'Do you think…?'

'Almost certainly, Alice. Look around you. How many crosses do you see?'

The man was talking again and Harry nodded and translated but held her even more tightly. 'He says it was a young woman, a girl. It was night time and he had been working late. He hid when the men came, but he saw everything. He watched them bury her and felt sad. He realised she was a foreigner and far from home. He thought she must be Christian, so he made her the cross.'

The howl when it came was not from Alice, but from a tormented creature plunged headlong into darkness without end. The sound echoed through the tombstones, over the bushes, in and out of trees, and across the stretch of calm water flowing below. She threw herself onto the ground, her arms outstretched as though she would cradle her lost sister in her arms. Harry allowed her time to sob, then raised her gently to her feet and wrapped his arms around her, rocking her to and fro as a parent would a small child. It was minutes before she recovered any semblance of calm, but eventually took the square of white linen that Harry offered and dabbed her face.

'Tell him thank you from my heart,' she said in a voice that was not hers.

'I will.'

He pulled his wallet from an inside pocket and spoke to the custodian in rapid Turkish. The man nodded and his hand closed over the notes. Harry took her arm once more and in sad procession they made their way back to the main entrance.

'We may have to walk a little, Alice, before we find a carriage. Can you do that?' She nodded dumbly. 'And I think it wise if we walk singly here – there is no pavement to speak of.'

They had gone only a few paces, Harry in the lead, when they heard carriage wheels. He turned ready to hail it, but it was driving fast, much too fast. As it drew alongside, the driver deliberately swerved inwards, the horse rearing as it saw the stone wall of the cemetery rise before it. Then its hooves came crashing down, the nearest catching Harry on the shoulder and throwing him to the ground. Alice was tumbled to one side by the force of the carriage as it passed.

She was the first on her feet and rushed to Harry's side. He groaned, then rolled himself into a sitting position and struggled to his knees. She saw him clutch his arm. 'How badly are you hurt?'

'Bruised, pretty badly bruised, but I think I'm in one piece.' She helped him to his feet and he flexed his right arm back and forth. 'I am guessing that means nothing is broken. How are you?'

'Winded and very dirty, but unhurt.' She looked down at her filthy skirt and buckled shoes.

'We must give thanks for that at least. It was the cemetery wall that saved us. The horse was frightened and veered away. It could have been a lot worse.'

'It was meant to be worse, wasn't it?'

'I reckon so. Monsieur Boucher is back at work, it seems. We evidently worry him.' Harry brushed his trousers free of dust.

'That will be Yusuf. He will have reported we called on Elise and disappeared with her into the garden.'

'The man would have had to send a message to Boucher after we left. Mind you, his house is only doors away. It would be easy enough for him to order one of his minions to commandeer a carriage and follow us. Whoever was driving must have known why we were here, and he would know we'd find what Boucher wants hidden. Once we had left the cemetery, he had the perfect opportunity to run us down.'

'He only half succeeded.'

'And will be in trouble for it, I would guess. But we need to get to the palace in case he tries again. We should make for the streets where there are people – and pavements – before our friend has time to confess his failure and receive new orders.'

They were soon in the thick of a jostling crowd. It was Saturday, the day after the Moslem holy day, and a favourite time to shop. Now their immediate danger was over, Alice slowly drowned, lost in a sea of sorrow. Lydia was dead and she was consumed with guilt. That she had not come to Turkey sooner, that she had not done more to save her sister. That so many times she had felt angry and resentful of Lydia's easy passage through life when hers had seemed so burdensome. How could she have felt so meanly? She could see her now, her darling sister, sparkling eyes and shining curls, laughing at life, loving its every moment. And loving them, too: her mother, her father, her brother. And Alice. The girl's generous spirit rebuked her. All gone. All vestige of that spirit gone.

'I am so sorry.' Harry spoke into her ear as they navigated a path through the crowded streets towards the palace.

'I know,' she whispered back. There seemed nothing more to say.

But as they walked towards the palace gates, she realised there *was* something more – the life of the man she loved. 'I am not safe here, Harry, but neither are you. That carriage, the horse. Boucher wants to be rid of us both.'

'It would seem so.'

'I suppose it could change when I have gone,' she said hopefully. She had said something similar before, but this time was finding it harder to believe.

'Wishful thinking. I know as much as you and that makes me an enemy. And today we learned what Boucher does to his enemies. I intended to leave very soon in any case, but it will be a little earlier now than expected. I'll leave tonight.'

She opened her eyes wide. 'You are coming with me?'

'I had already decided I would travel with you – before we were mown down. I knew I would come as soon as Elise told us of the child and urged you to take him with you. I couldn't leave you to cope alone. But I'd thought to return once you were safely back in London. Not any more though.'

His words were balm to her sore heart. If she had Harry beside her, she could manage anything. But how was it to be done? 'I have a ticket, but you—'

'We cannot fret over a small piece of paper. I have the money to buy a ticket and enough in my pocket to soften the chief steward's heart. He knows me well and I'm sure a little *douceur* will help him find me a spare compartment. At the worst, I can sleep propped up in the drawing room.'

'You will do no such thing. If necessary, you can share with myself and Charlie. Charlie! I cannot believe I will see Lydia's baby in a few hours.' She could feel the treacherous tears begin to well.

'We should plan, Alice – before we go through those gates. We must stay put for a few hours; we should still be safe within the palace grounds. I doubt Boucher would jeopardise his position by attacking us there, at least not during daylight hours. It was in the middle of the night that my room was set on fire, remember.'

'So, what is the plan?'

'I must go to the library first. Hopefully the new divan will be installed and the workmen gone. I want to leave the place in good order, and I've papers of my own to collect. I've been working on something for *The Studio* – you won't know it, but it's a prestigious art magazine. My article explores *taswir*, Ottoman miniature painting.' He brightened for a moment, but then remembering the present danger, hurried on. 'Other than that, I have nothing to bring with me. I'll eat early and be by the palace gates soon after dark.'

'I will do the same – after the meal I can pretend I need a short walk. That will be the easy bit. Do you really think we can make it through the gates? Boucher might have primed the guards to stop us.'

'Somehow we'll make it. And we'll make it to Sirkeci, and Charlie with us. There will be an hour or so before the train leaves so we'll need to find a place to stay out of sight. Even if

Boucher doesn't tamper with the palace guards, his spy system is too efficient and I'm afraid there are pitfalls to Elise's idea. Her bodyguard may be entranced by the beautiful Melek, but a man other than Yusuf could have been ordered to watch her as well.'

'I find it terrifying.'

'Terrifying,' he agreed. But then he smiled and hugged her. 'We will make it. Together. All three of us.'

Chapter Thirty Three

It was still early when she joined the women in their meeting room, but a line of slaves carrying huge silver trays was already queuing at the door. Sevda jumped up to greet her.

'This meal in your honour, Miss Alice,' she said, 'to say goodbye.' She pointed to the enormous spread being laid out on every available table, and then patted a large cushion on the raised divan.

Alice sank gratefully down. Her legs felt as flimsy as cotton and her head a confusion of sorrow. She could see and feel nothing but Lydia: Lydia as a five-year-old on the beach at Southwold, dancing joyously in the waves; on her sixteenth birthday when for the first time she had worn a low-cut gown and Alice had put up her hair; and the morning her sister had left for Constantinople, her farewells a little sad but her face behind the hansom window vivid with expectation. A jumble of images to cling to. But she must put them aside for the moment, she knew; the next few hours would be crucial, and she forced herself back to the present and to the girl sitting patiently beside her.

'You are very kind, Sevda. All of you. When I am in London again, I shall remember everyone with happiness.' *Well, almost everyone*, she thought silently, but the women had been kind. Discovering their silence had been out of love for Lydia and not hostility had made all the difference. She had felt them allies in the battle she fought.

Sevda translated her words and the women nodded and smiled. One after another they came forward to pile her plate with a spoonful of this, a spoonful of that. She hoped they would not be offended if she ate only half of what they had served her – *dolmas, köfte, manti,* fried eggplant and *tzatziki.* There were lots of smiles, some laughter, then caresses to her arms, her hands, her hair. But when she noticed long shadows appearing in the gardens that ran along one side of the chamber, she knew it was time to go.

'I think I will take a walk,' she announced. Sevda looked startled at this eccentricity. 'The carriage comes at nine o'clock, Miss Alice,' she reminded her.

'Don't worry, I will be ready. I should have said a stroll, not a walk. I will be in the courtyard looking at the stars. I'll not be long.'

She made her way back to her room, to Lydia's room, her stomach so tight she could hardly breathe. She took her sister's letters, the book, the baby's bonnet, and a very few undergarments from her suitcase and stuffed them into her large handbag. The sturdy leather strap slashed by Boucher's ruffian had been mended by a palace servant and the bag was now as good as new. Her case was left on the divan, open for anyone to take what they wished. Naz would take most of it, she was sure. Over her shoulders she flung the dark cloak she had found bundled at the top of the cupboard. It had been a good find. The cloak was woollen and she would be glad of its warmth – glad, too, that it hid her handbag from view. She walked through the door and into the corridor without a backwards glance. Now she knew what had happened in that room, it had lost any appeal.

Passing by the meeting room a few minutes later, she gave a small wave of her hand to the women still gathered there.

A few had already left for their night prayers, but most had stayed to talk. It would be the last time she would see them and she felt genuinely sad. She pulled the cloak tightly around her and slid from the harem entrance into the dark shadow of the wall, gliding along its length until she reached the archway that led into the first courtyard. For a few seconds she would have to forsake the shade and pass through the arch in full view of the moon's bright stare. She took a deep breath and scurried through. Not a sound or sight of anyone, and she could let her breath go. She was back in the shadows again, creeping along the side of yet more buildings, this time with a line of trees to provide cover. It was growing darker with every minute, but as she drew near to the gates, she made out the shape of a figure standing to one side. Harry, with a battered briefcase in his hand.

'You had better give me that,' she whispered. 'I can hide it beneath the cloak.'

'What a useful garment!' he whispered back and kissed her on the cheek. 'I'll try to get the soldier talking, the one on our right. The other guard patrols the wall on his side. When he is halfway along the wall and I've distracted his companion, slip through if you can.'

'If I can.' Her voice sounded hollow.

'We'll do it.' He gripped her hand for a moment. 'Good luck.'

Then he was through the gates and talking, making sure his form blocked the soldier's side vision.

She tiptoed forward and looked to the left. The soldier on that side had reached the midpoint of the wall. She needed to go before he turned. Clutching handbag and briefcase beneath the cloak, she walked through the gates as quietly as she could, making sure she kept as far away as possible from Harry and his reluctant conversationalist. And she kept on walking, expecting all the time to hear a shout behind her, but there was nothing but the low murmur of Harry's voice – the soldier himself seemed disinclined to talk. A road ran beside the palace and she made for one of the houses fronting it, one that had a roof overhanging almost to street level. It would provide good shelter.

Through the gloom she saw the first soldier return to his post while the other abandoned Harry and began a march along his side of the wall. In a moment, Harry had joined her. 'I must be losing my charm,' he said softly. 'My new friend had little to say and was obviously wishing me away. I told him I would be back in a matter of minutes and he was happy to agree.'

'You did it. I did it,' she said excitedly.

'We still have to reach the meeting place without being seen,' he warned.

'But soldiers don't guard the far wall, do they?'

'There are no gates there, so hopefully not. I've never noticed soldiers patrolling. If we keep close to the houses, we should be out of sight for most of the time.'

Once Harry's sentry began his march back to the gates, he was facing them, and they were forced to move very slowly from house to house. It took an unnervingly long while to arrive opposite the point where the great stone wall made a right angle. But then the soldier was back in his niche, and they could cross to the far wall of the palace and find the mosque Elise had spoken of.

She was already there, silvered by moonlight, and holding tight to a bundle. Alice rushed towards her and very gently peeled back the blankets Elise held, to see a small, perfect face. A baby's face. Charlie's face. She reached out for him and took him in her arms. Holding him for the first time, feeling him nestle against her, something close to a miracle happened. The knot that had twisted itself taut within loosened and uncurled. The rawness of Lydia's death was eviscerating – when would it not be? But alongside the rawness, there was another emotion. One of hope, one of new love for this tiny creature her sister had cared for more than life itself. Lydia had always been courageous; she had died protecting her child. Now it was Alice's turn. She would fight for the baby that was all she had left of her sister. She would love him as fiercely as ever Lydia had.

'He has her eyes,' she whispered. 'And he is quite beautiful – as beautiful as she.'

Oblivious to the world around her – the dark, lonely street, the companions who waited – she tightened her grip on the small bundle, speaking softly to the baby and rocking him gently. A rat scuttled past them and ran up the stone wall of the mosque. She hardly noticed but Elise jumped at the movement.

'You must leave now,' she said. 'Immediately. I have ordered a carriage for you.'

Alice blinked, coming out of her rapture. There was the sound of hooves, loud in the stillness of the evening, and coming closer. Elise walked into the road and waved down the approaching carriage. 'He will take you to the station. Now I must leave. I must be at my piano when Yusuf comes from the kitchen.'

'Can we not take you home?' Alice asked. 'There is plenty of time before the train leaves.'

'That is not a good idea. You must drive straight to Sirkeci and when you get there, stay hidden. For me, it is better I walk. The rear gate is locked at night, but I have stolen a key and will get to the house through the garden.'

She gave Alice a swift embrace and there was a handshake for Harry. 'Stay safe,' were her parting words and then she was gone, into the shadow of the overhanging trees.

'We should go,' Harry said. 'Climb in.'

Reluctantly, she allowed him to take the baby from her while she mounted the carriage steps. Once she was settled, he placed the small bundle gently into her lap. Charlie opened his eyes and blinked at the strange face looking down at him. He seemed about to cry, but Alice stroked his cheek with a forefinger and the cry was stopped at birth. Perhaps it was the memory of another finger that had once stroked his cheek, but instead of the cry a smile quivered on his lips.

'He is smiling,' Alice whispered.

–

The clocks high on the towers either side of the station fore-court showed ten minutes past eight. They walked swiftly past arches and railings towards the heavy, carved entrance. The door stood wide open to welcome early passengers, but when they passed through into the booking hall, they found it almost deserted. A solitary man sat reading a newspaper on one of the hard wood benches but did not raise his head. Alice gazed around her. She'd had no time when she first arrived to admire the station's glory, but now its patterned windows of orange diamonds and the huge circular spread of glass set high above drew a murmur of appreciation.

'Look at that window, Harry. It's shaped like a flower with its very own petals.' She pointed upwards.

She was talking to herself, she realised. Harry was abstracted and when he spoke, his tone was urgent. 'We cannot stay here. We need to find shelter.'

That brought her back to earth. For an instant, she had forgotten the dangers they were facing, forgotten that a safe return to London was still far off. If only things could have been different. She had seen so little of Turkey, but it was a beautiful country, and a country that held her sweet sister close to its heart. She could not forget that for an instant.

Once through the booking hall, they saw platforms stretching into the distance, their glass roofs faded and yellow. Six platforms, but only one train. The Orient Express stood quietly alongside the furthest, its windows darkened.

'Do you think we can board?'

He shook his head. 'The train doors will be locked, unfortunately – it would have helped to have squirrelled ourselves away.'

She sensed his growing agitation and tried to sound reassuring. 'The staff must be resting – the train could only have arrived this afternoon – but they will be back on duty very soon. In the meantime, I'm sure we can find somewhere off the main concourse to wait.'

'Stay here and I'll take a look around.'

Uneasiness took hold as soon as he disappeared from sight. She felt vulnerable, alone and carrying a small child, but he was gone only a few minutes, arriving back at her side breathless.

'Beyond the platform on our left there's an area used for stacking baggage. It's the point at which the platform runs into grass. I think it will do. There's no one there and not likely to be. The Orient Express is the only train for some hours.'

It was a short walk to the place Harry had found. 'What do you think? he asked anxiously.

'You're right. We should be well out of sight here.'

He pointed to a baggage trolley, then fished another handkerchief from his pocket and dusted it down. 'Look, there's even a seat for you.'

Except for a few small boxes, the trolley was empty, and she stood looking at it for a while. 'I wonder if we could fashion a nest for Charlie. I think he would sleep more soundly if I could lay him down. At the moment, he is in and out of slumber and I'm worried he might start crying.'

'What do you say to those sacks? The ones in that pile. They look reasonably clean and Charlie is swaddled in several blankets.'

'That's an excellent idea!'

Once they had constructed a nest from the sacks, and Charlie and his blankets snuggled into its warmth, they sat down by his side. Harry looked at his watch. 'Eight thirty. They should allow us to board in an hour.'

'You must know. You will have caught this train a dozen times.'

She hoped he might talk of the journeys he had made, anything to take her mind off their situation. She should not be feeling so fearful: they were free of the palace and no one had seen them leave.

'Did you manage to get into the library?' she asked, still hoping for conversation. She could feel that Harry was as tense as she.

'I did.' He gave her a curious look and she was about to ask what it meant, when a noise sounded behind them and she jumped to her feet, ready to snatch Charlie from his bed.

'Don't worry, Miss Alice. All is well. It is only me.'

'Ismet?' she gasped. 'What on earth are you doing here?'

'I have come for something important – and to say farewell, naturally.'

He took her hand and kissed it. She had thought her anger had dissipated but seeing him so cheerful and untroubled, she had to bite back bitter words. It was true politics had not been the key to her sister's downfall, but if this man had not asked her for help, Lydia would never have become entangled with the Bouchers. She would still be alive today.

Ismet seemed unaware of her hostility. He clapped Harry on the back. 'My friend, how can I thank you enough?'

She watched bewildered as Harry took from his bag a thin manila file. 'I hope it will be worth it,' he said, his tone barbed.

Ismet, oblivious to his meaning, flicked through the file, peering down at it in the station's dim light and scanning the few sheets of paper intently.

'Yes!' It was almost a shout and Harry hushed him. 'This is wonderful. This is – dynamite! All these transactions, the contracts Boucher signed to build the school on land that was not his. Land he had been refused. And signed before the owner was dead. I already have his letter that threatens the man's grandson. Together they will be sufficient to demand an audience with Abdülhamid. I can do this even though I may be thrown into prison after the event. I will give the Sultan this evidence and wait for justice to be done.'

'Justice will be far from certain.' Harry was deliberately downbeat.

'It is an uphill struggle, I know, but when is something worthwhile not? And it may become easier than we think. Once it is known there is proof of Boucher's wrongdoing, his old comrades will turn on him. People who have benefited from his crimes will try to wash themselves clean. They will not want anything to do with him. It is the beginning of the end for Valentin Boucher. And for the Sultan. Abdülhamid will be

313

weakened by his adherence to this man. He will have to accede to our demands.'

Alice had tried to follow, but became lost somewhere in the middle of his speech. He saw her perplexed expression. 'I am sorry, Miss Alice. I become too excited. But I will go. I need to deliver this to a safe place. You know I am a wanted man? In some ways it is flattering, but it is not at all a comfortable life. I wish you all' – he looked at the sleeping child with a slight shake of his head – 'a very safe journey.' In an instant he had disappeared the same way he had arrived.

Alice was not sorry to see him go; she could not think well of him, but she was curious. 'How did Ismet find us? And what was he talking about?'

'When I paid the driver who brought us here, I gave him a message to deliver. I sent him to the address where we met Ismet, though I wasn't sure he would be there. It was a gamble but I needed to pass on that file. It contains the information he asked Lydia to find. I thought you would want me to do it.'

'But how did it come into your possession?'

'By chance. I went to the library after I left you this afternoon.'

'I know, to pick up papers. But not those papers surely?'

He smiled. 'No, indeed. But while I was there, I thought to check the cupboard in my office, to make sure there was nothing I should take with me. The box at the bottom of the cupboard had been disturbed. There was a copy of *Peter Pan* lying half in and half out. It's a box of children's books – your sister used it to teach the princesses. I went to tuck the book back and close the lid, but then another book fell out. I thought I should tidy that away, too, and lifted the entire box on to my desk. I saw then that the boards at the bottom of the cupboard had been levered up to provide a hiding place.'

'But why would the Bouchers hide such incriminating papers there?'

'I couldn't believe what I had unearthed. Not at first. It seemed an utterly foolish place to hide such a file. But when I thought it through, it wasn't so strange. The file must originally have been in Paul's office. I know there was a locked drawer – the one Ismet told us Lydia had not managed to search. If Boucher senior became suspicious of her, he would wonder how safe the file was there. And the cupboard was a good alternative. The box had been returned from the schoolroom and no one would go to it again searching for books. No one used the cupboard, except me. Boucher invented the excuse of replacing the Sultan's divan as a way of getting me out of the way and moving the papers from the drawer.'

'But why move them now? Lydia is no longer a threat.' She tried hard not to think what those words meant.

'Because of you, I think. He must have come to believe you were as interested as Lydia in finding proof of his corruption. He wouldn't understand your interest has only ever been in finding your sister. To him people are expendable. It is beyond his comprehension that anyone would travel as far as Turkey to search for someone they had lost, and put themselves in peril by doing so.'

'I still don't understand why he chose the cupboard in your office. There must be a hundred other places far more suitable. Or he could just have got rid of the file.'

'He wouldn't destroy it. It contains material he could use to blackmail his partners if it ever became necessary. And he cannot hide it in his house or his son's house, that would be too dangerous. So why not the library – a monument to his benevolence? Don't forget, I'm the one who manages the place and I am such an upstanding character that no one would suspect me of concealing – what did Ismet call it – dynamite? I don't know how far Paul is implicated, but both he and his father knew the cupboard was hardly used. It is a good hiding place and clever of Boucher to invent the Sultan's divan as an excuse for getting me out of the way.'

'They could have done it at night when you had finished work.'

'I often work in the evening,' he confessed. 'There is little else to do. And they couldn't be sure I'd not be there.'

There was a long silence before she said, 'So Ismet has his file after all.'

He knew what she was thinking and hugged her close. 'Lydia would be pleased, would she not?' Alice thought of her headstrong sister, her passion for justice, her desire for freedom, and thought that yes, Lydia would be pleased.

'The lights are on in the train, I think.' Harry stood up and shielded his eyes to look across the station to the far platform. 'Yes, definitely on. We'll give it a few minutes and then get on board. They may be a trifle surprised to see us so early, but it will be good to be safe.'

'Not so safe.' She gripped his hand. 'Look.'

Chapter Thirty Four

Two men had walked out of the booking office and now stood shoulder to shoulder, an immovable column, scanning the forecourt. Then one set off to the right and the other to the left. Harry shot up and grabbed hold of the trolley handle, manoeuvring it further into the shadows.

'Cover your dress with a sack – it's too noticeable. And shrink as small as you can.'

She curled herself into a ball and waited, her heart racing, her limbs suddenly weak. The man who had turned left was walking towards them and she shrunk down even further. Harry bent over her, his dark suit extra camouflage in the gloom. From their crouched position, they could no longer see the man, but they could hear his footsteps. Closer and closer. If Charlie chose now to wake… The footsteps stopped. For what seemed an age, the man stood still. *He must be peering into the darkness, looking for us*, she thought. Then there was the sound of shoes scuffing the stone platform and the footsteps moved away.

'Thank God,' Harry breathed.

'Don't be too thankful. Boucher knows I am supposed to travel tonight. It's common knowledge in the palace even if Naz has not sent him word. And she will have. I think he believed I would try to stay – that's why we were attacked today. But now my room is empty except for an abandoned case, and when a search of the *haremlik* fails to find me, Boucher will deduce I have left secretly and draw his own conclusions. Why would I need to leave secretly, unless I had something to hide? That's why those men have come and they will stay until they see the train leave. They know I have Charlie and they want him.'

He nodded slowly and she grasped hold of his hand. 'Harry, how on earth are we to get on that train?'

'Can you climb? That skirt looks a trifle tight.'

'It depends on how high I am supposed to climb. What are you suggesting?'

'Boucher's villains have searched the station and found nothing, so they'll think you've not yet arrived. Their next move will be to watch for you. They'll be waiting on the far side of the train – that's where passengers for the Express will board.'

'So how does that help?'

'People may be boarding on the far side, but the doors facing us will be open, too. While the men wait for you to appear on the platform, the way will be clear for us to get on the train from this side.'

'But there is no platform this side.'

'You said you could climb.'

'I didn't, in fact, and the idea is completely mad. Have you seen how high the doors are from the railway track? Plus, we have Charlie and bags. Elise handed me a bag full of baby things before she left.'

'It is a mad idea,' he agreed, 'but do you have a better one?'

'We could board like normal passengers and hope the train staff stop the men from attacking us.'

'You saw those men – is it likely that stewards and cooks would be up to a fight with them, even if they were minded? By the time the police were called, you would have lost Charlie.'

She thought of the rock-like column the two ruffians had formed and knew he was right. But it was still a crazy idea. 'It will be hard enough for me to clamber down onto the tracks, let alone climb up to a train door.'

'I know, Alice, but it's our only hope. Or we will stay here as fugitives watching the Express pull out of the station without us.'

It was a fearful image. 'I will try,' she said, and received a warm kiss on her lips.

It proved every bit as hard to climb down from the platform as she had thought, but somehow she made it, and with Charlie in her arms and Harry carrying the several bags, they stole across the lines of track to the waiting train.

'So far, so good,' he whispered.

She was far from agreeing with him. She looked up to the door she was supposed to reach. It was yards above her head – it would be like climbing a mountain in slippers. Charlie had once attempted Ben Nevis with ice on the ground and without the help of crampons, and he'd confessed to her how dangerously he had failed. It looked likely she would follow suit.

But Harry was undeterred. He reached up and caught hold of the ledge of iron grating that sat some way below the door. His shoulder was still badly bruised, but slowly and painfully he heaved himself up until he was within reach of the door's handle. He stretched out one hand, supporting his whole weight with the other, and grabbed. The door flew open. He rested for a moment and then again, slowly and with huge effort, stretched his arm forward until this time he managed to grip the floor of the train. Straining every muscle, he pulled himself upwards, inch by inch, until both knees were planted securely on the floor of the corridor.

It took a few seconds for him to regain his breath, then he whispered down to her, 'Hand me the bags.'

She passed him her handbag, the briefcase and the bag Elise had given her, but when he said, 'Now, Charlie,' she baulked.

'You must, Alice. He will be safe with me.' From his kneeling position on the train floor, he reached out. By balancing on a rail and standing on tiptoe, she managed to hand him enough of Charlie to be safe.

'Your turn now.'

She tried to emulate what he had done, jumping with outstretched hands to reach the iron grating, but each time falling back. Harry, with the baby in one arm, was bent nearly double trying to reach her. She was terrified he would topple over with Charlie in his arms.

'Try again.'

She tried, but once more fell short. 'I can't make it,' she said. 'You must take my ticket – it's in my handbag. Take Charlie home.'

'And leave you on the railway tracks?'

'Someone will find me.'

'And we know who that would be. This is crazy. You can make it. You must – Charlie needs you.'

'But how?' She found she was crying with exhaustion and fear.

'Wait!' he said, and disappeared. When he reappeared, he was without Charlie.

'Where is the baby?' she asked, horrified.

'He is fine. There is a bathroom down the corridor and I've laid him in the bath.'

She did not know whether to laugh or cry and started to do both until Harry said sharply, 'Stop, Alice. I need you with me.'

Once again, he knelt down on the corridor floor, but this time leant out with both arms so far he was in danger of falling onto the tracks himself. 'Now try for the ledge,' he commanded. 'If you can get yourself there, the rest will be easier.'

She used all her strength to jump one last time and catch at his fingers. He had her, just, in one hand, her feet swinging wildly and looking likely to pull him down on top of her.

'Move your feet up the train side,' he gasped, 'and try to find the grating.'

She did as he said, scrabbling her feet against the smooth blue and gold livery until she felt one shoe connect with the iron ledge. He had her by the arm and had hauled a little further up the side of the door. 'Now reach up with your other hand and take mine.'

Very slowly she reached up. Both his hands were holding her now, but her arms were almost pulled from their sockets. She wanted to scream with the pain, and bit down on her lips to keep herself silent. It seemed a lifetime before her second foot found the ledge, and Harry was able to pull her the last few yards up and into safety.

They collapsed together on the floor of the train, their hearts pounding, their breathing erratic. She looked across at him – his suit was crumpled and smeared with dirt – then down at her beautiful wool dress, covered from head to toe in dust. She pushed a loose hair back from her face and left a smear across her cheek. Tenderly, he rubbed it clean.

'We must rescue Charlie,' she said, suddenly panicked, and scrambled to her feet.

Charlie lay sleeping in the bath, as peacefully as if he were in a Mayfair nursery. Anxiously, she bent over him. 'He seems fine.'

'Of course he's fine. He is a brave chap like his mother. And his aunt.'

'I wasn't very brave just then. I'm sorry I broke down.'

'Darling Alice, you misjudge yourself all the time. And that has to change. You *were* brave, you *are* brave, believe me! I must go for the bags now before anyone sees them.'

When he returned, she delved into her handbag and found her ticket. 'I am in carriage H, compartment ten. Fingers crossed there's no one sharing with me. What carriage is this, do you think?'

'I'm not sure, but it might be wise to wait before we look. The men will be searching the platform and might see us. We're certainly not inconspicuous.' He pointed to the baby.

'So we stay here?'

'Until the whistle goes. I'll lock the door.'

'We could have a worse hideout, I suppose – a bathroom that's a work of art.' She gazed at the tiled walls and floor. 'At least this is more cheerful than the one on my outward journey.' She moved her feet slightly and studied the floor. 'A mosaic of Perseus, I think. It was Medusa last time – she gave me a scare in the middle of the night.'

They fell silent, listening as the bustle from the corridor gradually increased with more and more passengers arriving. There was a bumping of luggage, the polite tones of the steward, exclamations from husbands as they fought a path through the crowded corridor with cloak bags and hat boxes.

'Just look at this wood,' a woman said on the other side of the door. 'The inlay is magnificent.'

A squeal came from the compartment next to them. 'Oh, Dicky, how absolutely adorable! There's a washbasin behind this cupboard. Fancy that!'

The huffing and puffing seemed to continue a very long time, every minute feeling like an hour. The bathroom was windowless and there was no possibility of being seen from the platform, but Alice was in dread that a passenger might need the room and they would be discovered, or worse, that the two ruffians would board the train in desperation and make straight for the only locked door.

At last, the moment they had been waiting for. A whistle. They felt the jolt of the engine as it began its slow pull, heard the rattle of carriages as they followed suit.

'Time to go,' Harry said.

Alice scooped Charlie into her arms and they crept from the bathroom, hurrying along the corridor and looking for a sign that would take them to carriage H. There was a shout from outside and Alice stopped in her tracks. Out of the window she saw one of the men running along the platform. He was trying to grab at a door handle. She held her breath and Harry froze beside her. But the train was gathering speed and gradually the man fell further and further back until the Express broke free of the station canopy and his figure disappeared from sight.

A steward came around the corner and looked at them, slightly askance. 'I am sorry,' Harry said in the smooth tone he summoned at moments of crisis. 'We seem to have taken a wrong turning.'

'You have a ticket?' The steward was definitely suspicious.

'Yes, of course. Darling, can you find our ticket?'

She thrust the paper into the steward's hand and his attitude changed immediately. 'Please, madame, monsieur, come this way.'

Her fingers were still crossed that the compartment would be empty.

Chapter Thirty Five

They smiled at each other in relief when they opened the door. 'We needed some luck.' Harry stored their bags beneath the small let-down table. 'I'll leave you to settle in while I search for my friendly chief steward. I shouldn't be long.'

'Make sure you come back with a ticket.' She wasn't certain he would, and it worried her.

He said nothing but gave a small wave and was gone. What if the man refused his money? she thought. Even worse, if he insisted Harry leave the train? But she must not waste energy in this way, she needed to be practical. Charlie had woken a short while ago, and had been gazing at his new surroundings with interest. Now, though, he was growing restive and she thought it time to bathe and change him into the night clothes Elise had packed. The small basin that lay behind the polished wood cupboard proved a challenge, and the bathing took far longer than she expected. She was worried her fumbling might upset a baby used to more practised hands, but he seemed not to mind and when she dipped his toes in and out of the water, he gurgled with pleasure.

Flushed by her success, she burrowed into the bag that Elise had given her and found food. There were several small containers of minced vegetables and she peeled open one and began to spoon its contents into a happy Charlie. Thank goodness he was old enough to eat solid food. There was a glass bottle in the bag, too, but Alice was sure she had heard stories about babies' bottles. She remembered some dire tale that Dora had told her about a friend of a friend whose baby had caught some dreadful infection and died. The doctor had suggested an unclean bottle might be the culprit. She must be sure to ask the room steward to scald the bottle clean each time she used it. And what was she to do for milk? Evaporated milk, that must be the answer, and the Orient Express was bound to keep it on board. There was something, too, buzzing in her mind about sugared water, but she could not recall exactly what. Caring for a small baby was a journey in itself and she knew she would make mistakes. But she would do her very best to ensure Charlie thrived.

A knock at the compartment door and their steward put his head into the room as she was wiping the baby's mouth clean.

'Would you care to eat, madame? I can bring a tray to your compartment.' She realised then how hungry she was. She had barely touched her supper in the palace, and the terrors of the past few hours had driven any thought of hunger from her mind.

'I could eat a small meal,' she said.

He handed her the supper menu. 'I will be back to take your order. And you can tell me then what the baby will require.'

'Thank you,' she said gratefully. But as he was shutting the door, she called after him. 'Before you go, can you tell me where we are?' She could not lose the dread that while they were still in Turkey, Boucher's reach might extend even to the train.

'We have just crossed the Bulgarian border,' the steward said.

'Thank you, thank you so much.'

He seemed surprised at her pleasure, but smiled and went away. The relief was huge. Now they were over the border, they must be safe. She would tell Harry as soon as he arrived back.

When he came through the door, though, he had news of his own. 'All well,' he said, when he saw her expectant face, and waved a slip of white paper. 'My acquaintance was a tad hesitant. Buying a ticket on board is extremely unconventional, but he took the money nevertheless, and here we are.'

'Thank goodness. I was beginning to have visions they would leave you behind at Bucharest!'

He sat down beside her. 'There is one thing you might not like as much. The train is full to capacity and I will have to share this compartment with you both. Charlie isn't going to complain but—'

'And neither am I. We are in Bulgaria, Harry! We are all three of us safe! I daresay I won't sleep anyway. Charlie is bound to wake through the night.'

'Three days is a long time not to sleep. I suggest we alternate the spare bunk between us.'

'Nonsense. You can take the top bunk and I will have Charlie with me down below. He takes up very little room.' She looked lovingly down at the child beside her. 'He is such a good boy. I haven't been exactly skilful, but he hasn't once complained. By the time we get to London, I may even have mastered how to pin a napkin.'

He smiled broadly. 'If not, your mother can teach you.'

When she looked startled, he said, 'She had three children and unless she had a separate nursemaid for each of you, I imagine she learned how to change the odd napkin.'

His words made Alice realise how rarely she thought of her mother as a young woman. Somehow the frail invalid had become her abiding image of Edith, as though her mother had lived no life before these last few unhappy years. The notion that she might help to care for the baby felt strange, but when Alice allowed her mind the freedom to wander, new possibilities began to emerge. A new way, perhaps, in which her family might live.

'I'm not sure she would be well enough to do much,' she said at length, 'but do you think she would want to help?'

'My guess would be that once she sees Charlie, you will have to stop her from taking over.'

'Oh, Harry, I have to tell them.' She was struck by sudden grief. 'And it is worse than I ever imagined. I thought I would be saying that Lydia was missing, but now I must utter the most terrible words. That she is dead and that this is her baby.'

He took both her hands in his. 'You will do it, Alice. No one could do it better and I will be with you when you do.'

'But how will they react? I am so frightened this news will affect their health for the worse. Don't forget, my father has had a massive heart attack and my mother's nerves are shot to pieces.'

'You'll find a way,' he comforted. 'A way to tell them the full truth, but perhaps only gradually. For the time being, we can think of a story that will explain Charlie's presence. Maybe his parents died in an accident together, but the palace knew them very well and wanted to help.' He thought for a moment. 'The Valide Sultan asked you to take the baby back to England with you, that's it, and look after him until his relatives arrive.' The furrows on Harry's brow deepened. 'I think the relatives would have to be living at some distance – that would explain the delay.'

Alice could not help laughing. 'How did you think that up? Far-fetched is not the word!'

'Of course it's far-fetched, but it will give your parents time to know Charlie and time for them to accept that Lydia is not coming back. When you feel it's right, you can tell them he is

Lydia's child. Gaining a grandson will seem a gift they could not have expected.'

'I'm still not sure about your story, but I agree it's wise not to confess everything at once.'

'So we have a plan – and we will soon be home. I hope that makes you feel a little happier.'

'I do try hard.' There was a suppressed sob in her voice. 'But I cannot lose the thought that I am going home and leaving Lydia behind. It breaks my heart. And she has only a rough wooden cross to mark her grave.'

He jumped up then and began to walk up and down the small space, his hands in his pockets. He seemed suddenly nervous, and she wondered why.

'I don't know if I have done the right thing.' He cleared his throat. 'I hope you will think so. Before we left the cemetery, I paid the man – I believe he is guardian of the place. I paid him sufficient money to order a headstone. A Christian headstone. I thought that when you felt able, you could decide on the carving you wanted. Then I will send him details and I know he'll make sure it's done.'

She was the one to jump up now, wrapping her arms around him and hugging him close. 'Thank you, Harry. It is the right thing to do. I have been harbouring the wild idea of bringing Lydia's body home to England – if only for my parents' sake – but realistically I know it's not possible.'

'I doubt it is. And not realistic, I'm afraid, for your parents to visit her grave. But *we* could go back – when the dust settles – which it will, given time.'

'Quite some time, I think. And will you still know me by then?' She was only half teasing. The advent of Charlie had changed everything.

'There is something else I have to tell you.' He had hardly noticed her remark.

'No more news. I can't cope with more. I am exhausted.'

'Dear girl, don't you think I know that? But this is something I have to say, and I am hoping you won't find it upsetting. I had to tell Gustave, my friendly chief steward, that we married in St George's a few days ago. The Orient Express seems keen on policing morals – or maybe it's just Gustave – but it was the only way he was going to sell me a ticket.'

'Oh, is that all.' She yawned. 'Luckily, I bought my jewellery with me. I don't have much but I know there's a ring. I'll make sure I find it before I meet Gustave.'

'And then we can play the old married couple.' He laughed and gathered her up in his arms.

'Careful,' she warned, 'or we'll topple over onto Charlie.'

'And how is the little chap – after your ministrations?'

'I wasn't that clumsy,' she objected. 'And he is doing well. Look at him, Harry, isn't he the most beautiful child you have ever seen?'

'What I see is that you're an adoring mother – already.'

'That's not so,' she protested. 'I am his aunt, not his mother.'

'His future mother then. Of that, I'm sure. Your sister would want it so, wouldn't she?'

'Yes, but…'

'But what?'

She moved away from him slightly. 'I am immensely tired and I did not want to have this conversation now, but perhaps we need to. You are right to say that I will look after Charlie, whether as an aunt or a mother. But I am also committed to caring for my parents. If it were just they who were depending on me… but now I have the baby, things have changed. It means, my dear, I am no longer able to marry you.'

'What! How can you think that?'

'It's simple. When you asked me to marry, you could not know you would be taking on a child as well as ailing relatives. It would be unfair on you and I absolve you of your promise.'

'I don't recognise those words. I will not be "taking on a child". I will be marrying you and together we will build a family. Charlie will be our firstborn.'

'But you cannot wish to burden yourself in that way. It is too much. And think of your own mother and father. Your life will be so far from what they expect for you.'

'Look at him.' He pointed to Charlie, asleep now on the lower bunk, long eyelashes resting against a peachy skin. 'Are you seriously suggesting that my parents would not love him?'

She felt utter confusion. She wanted to do the right thing, but her mind was so encumbered she could no longer think sensibly. He took her by the hand and walked her to the small oval mirror that hung above the wash basin. Standing behind her, his arms wrapped around her slim figure, he said, 'And look at you. This is the girl my parents will learn to love. How could they not rejoice in my marriage?'

Confusion was still there, and a pain she knew would stay with her always, but looking at their two reflections, her spirits lifted.

'You are a beautiful woman,' Harry said. 'In all senses of the word. How could they want more for a daughter? And how could I want more for a wife?'

She nestled back against him and a small smile touched her lips. 'I think you mean it.'

'I couldn't mean it more. Now,' he said with decision, turning her to face him, 'It's time I stopped adoring you and—'

'And what?'

'And ordered supper for us both.'

The October rain has washed itself away and fingers of pink-tinged cloud drift through a sky of blue and mauve and deep violet. The sun is rising, breaking through the dark horizon, spooling the surface of the Bosphorus with gold. Its waters are satin, washing gently against fishing boats already out to sea. In the Eyoub Cemetery beside the city walls, a headstone of shining pink marble stands proud. From its surface, a carved bird takes flight, soaring free above a carpet of wild cyclamen, over the bay and out to the wide sea beyond. Within the city walls, the spires of Hagia Sophia thrust upwards amid the crumbling beauty of narrow streets and winding alleys. A city at peace. Then the muezzin's call to the faithful, echoed in a thousand mosques. The miracle of another dawn. Another day.

Historical Note

Rahîme Perestû was born in 1826 and was given the title and position of Empress Mother when Abdülhamid II ascended the throne in 1876. She died at her villa in Maçka, Constantinople, on 11 December 1904, but as she was the last Valide Sultan of the Ottoman Empire, I have had her live for a few years longer.

Topkapi Palace was the first home and administrative centre of the Ottoman Sultans and was used until the middle of the 19th century when it was abandoned in favour of the newly constructed Dolmabahçe Palace. However, the Treasury, the Library and the Mint always remained at Topkapi. In the late 19th century, Sultan Abdülhamid II left Dolmabahçe for a new home, Yıldız Palace meaning 'Star Palace', built in 1880, because he feared a seaside attack. Dolmabahçe Palace is located on the shore of the Bosphorus strait. The refurbishment of Yıldız, mentioned several times in the novel, is purely imaginary and allows the action of the book to centre on Topkapi.

Haremlik refers to the private portion of an Ottoman house rather than its public rooms. It was where the men and women of the immediate family lived and socialised, although the women of the household were traditionally secluded there. *Harem* implies a female-only enclave or a seraglio. I have used the terms almost interchangeably, since the *harem* was a considerable part of the *haremlik* at Topkapi Palace.

About the Author

Merryn Allingham was born into an army family and spent her childhood moving around the UK and abroad. Unsurprisingly it gave her itchy feet and in her twenties she escaped from an unloved secretarial career to work as cabin crew and see the world.

Merryn still loves to travel and visit new places, especially those with an interesting history, but the arrival of marriage, children and cats meant a more settled life in the south of England, where she has lived ever since. It also gave her the opportunity to go back to 'school' and eventually teach at university.

She has written seven historical novels, all mysteries with a helping of suspense and a dash of romance – sometimes set in exotic locations and often against a background of stirring world events.

For the latest news of Merryn's writing, visit her website at www.merrynallingham.com or join her on Facebook or Twitter @MerrynWrites.